Still..g .... Thunder

Teresa L. Arrowood

This book is dedicated to those who are survivors of abuse and to those who serve. This book is a salute to those who have given of themselves to aid those who are in pain and distress, helping to make a better life for us all.

Acknowledgments

Thank you to my husband and friend for life. I love you. Thanks for putting up with me and the crazy ideas that I come up with and the time I spend in front of a computer. You are truly the love of my life.

Thanks to my children and the support they have given while their mother has gone off on this wild tangent of becoming an author. I am blessed many times over.

Thank you to my parents and family members who have loved and supported me and still believe I can move mountains.

Thank you to my photographer, Wesley Smith, who was gracious enough to help with my author's portrait. I wish him all the best in his business.

Thanks to Ms. Lori for supporting an unknown author and opening up her business for me to have my first book signing. Salute to the wonderful lady that gives of herself unselfishly.

But most of all, thanks to my God, for the inspiration behind *Standing in the Eye of the Storm* and *Stilling the Thunder*.

4/17 ; donations

PROLOGUE

Alonzo Moretti Davis was looking sharp in his black tux as he stood waiting for his wife to kiss the children goodbye. They had waited for this night out for the last few years. Miriam didn't seem to trust any one person with the children, and it had made it difficult for them to go out alone. Tonight was different. Alonzo had the perfect venue picked for their anniversary. He had looked forward to it and had planned it down to the second of each activity he wanted to share with her. If it had been up to him, they would have taken at least the night to spend together. They hadn't been alone since before the birth of their son. He missed the time he had been able to be alone with her, but he loved that she embraced motherhood. He loved his children, and Miriam would have given her last breath for them.

He watched her with a grin as he listened to the instructions she ticked off to Mrs. Rosen. Each instruction was laid out in order of importance. Alonzo had to laugh as he listened to his overly protective wife. "Miriam, if we don't leave, we aren't going to be on time. Besides, Mrs. Rosen knows what she's doing." His wife had smiled, and her brown eyes danced as she admired him. Assisting her with her coat, she shrugged it on. His son had looked up in wonderment of him as he assisted his mother. He had always tried to teach his son to treat the women in his life like a delicate flower. From the time he was able to

1

understand, he had told him that women were strong, but they needed attention and love. It was their job to see that they were protected and well taken care of. He winked at his boy and knew that he had gotten the message when he had given him a sheepish grin and saluted his father as they walked out the door.

As they drove toward the Riverfront Restaurant, Alonzo talked with Miriam, and they both had smiled and laughed as they remembered how they had met. The ice on the windshield had reminded him of the day she had walked into the cafe where he was sitting after a class. She had walked in the little café, preparing for her shift at Whitecaps Java. She had just rounded the counter when he had noticed her. He had known her shift by then like the back of his hand and had made a point to be there. He had never gotten up enough courage to ask her out, but he was determined that was going to change. He had watched her all through their freshman year of college, just waiting his turn between boyfriends, and this was his chance. He had thought many times over that she hadn't noticed that he was around, acting mostly like the young men didn't matter, but they were attracted to her like bees to honey.

Walking over to the table next to him, she had slid on a patch of water. The iced coffee she carried had spilled on the floor at her feet. Before she had hit the floor, he had reached out to catch her, and she had fallen back into his arms and against his chest. I guess you could say that the opportunity had inadvertently fallen into his lap. She gasped as she had seen him looking down on her. Her doe-brown eyes were large and hypnotizing, leaving him

2

unable to speak a word for a moment. "I am so sorry," she had said and had tried to push up from where she had landed. He wanted to assist her up, but he couldn't let go of her. She hadn't offered to get up again, and he had bent down and kissed her. The tray that was now empty skidded to the floor among the coffee and ice. Her kiss had left him breathless. She had him from the moment she looked at him. Her eyes remained wide as she remained silent and had caressed his cheek. "I guess I have to marry you now and make an honest woman of you." Miriam wasn't sure how to react. She was stunned from his remark and continued to hold on to him as the patrons of the shop looked at them. The stares hadn't made much difference as she was cradled in his arms. All had become right with the world from that moment.

Picking up her hand, he placed it to his lips and pressed a soft kiss against it. "I love you, Miriam. I would have never thought that you would have gone for a guy like me."

"And what was wrong with a guy like you?" Miriam had prompted him.

"You know I didn't have much at the time and I was so backward."

"Yes, but that was part of what made you so charming. The material things didn't matter to me. I would have gone out with you anytime."

"You hadn't noticed me before that day in the cafe." He laughed. "You were too busy with Bob, Bill, whatever his name was."

"Brandon, and yes, I was. You just hadn't ever gotten around to asking me out."

3

"Well, I'm glad I did. I can't imagine my life without you."

"Or I you." Miriam squeezed his hand as he studied the road in the darkness of that winter night.

"What do you think of Elijah? Isn't he becoming the charmer?"

"He's a carbon copy of you, Alonzo. Even at his tender age, I am surprised that the little girls aren't falling all over him. You have taught him well."

"Yeah, the lady killer." Alonzo had laughed, and he could see the smile on his wife's face from the corner of his eye. "I just hope when he grows up, he knows how to love and appreciate a young lady."

"I'm sure that you will teach him well. You haven't done so bad yourself. You are the charmer, Mr. Davis."

"Well, it wasn't because my father was there to teach me."

"You can't blame him, Alonzo. He was just a boy when you were born."

"My mother was a young girl without any support, but she managed without him. My father doesn't even know where I am or my name. I am not sure that he's alive. All he ever did from the time I remember was drink."

"Give him a benefit of a doubt. It wasn't easy to raise a child at his age."

"Momma was fifteen, Miriam. My father had a responsibility, and he walked out on us. I'm surprised that I turned out as well as I have."

Alonzo reached over his chest and adjusted the sidearm he had strapped against him and continued driving through the snow and slush of the semi dark night.

The lights approached him at a rapid speed, and as he tried to adjust his thinking of what was happening, he placed an arm over his wife as if she was a child. Miriam had not noticed, as she was placing lipstick over her pale lips. "Move." Alonzo gritted his teeth as he had seen there was nowhere to go but off the road. The driver of the car was headed straight for them, the high beams of the lights reflected on him as it illuminated the interior of the car like daytime. "Hold on, Miriam," Alonzo had said in a cool voice. Her scream had filled the car as it skidded. Alonzo had tried to veer it out of the path of the oncoming vehicle, but it had been in vain. The car hit a patch of ice, and it had thrown them directly in the other car's path sideways, being hit on the passenger-side door. The impact had thrown Miriam over into Alonzo's lap, snapping her seatbelt in two pieces. Alonzo had tried to protect his wife as he held to her, trying to steer the car out of the path of the driver. He had died instantly. The car had been pushed once it was hit into a ditch. The impact had broken his neck. Miriam had survived but for only minutes after the crew arrived to retrieve her from the twisted vehicle. The last thing that she had said prior to her death was Elijah's name.

CHAPTER ONE

The day was cold, not to mention the fine mist of rain that fell. Sitting there among family, I felt numb. The pain that dwelled in my heart was beyond anything that I had ever felt. I was oblivious to everything that surrounded me, except for the flag-draped casket that lay before me. The piercing sound of the gun salute was the only thing that had caused a reaction. Grayson sat with his arm around me, as did my own father, but I had little thought of anyone supporting me. I felt desperately alone and troubled without any chance of anything being normal again.

Molly sat on my lap, unmoving, with her blanket wrapped around her. Her long, dark hair flowed down her back in rings of curls. With her thumb in her mouth, she clung to me, and I to her. The child I carried and Molly were my only solace. They were the only part of him I had left. I hadn't even cried. I couldn't. I had promised him that I would take care of the lives entrusted to me. They were precious to him, and if I didn't care for them, who would?

I had watched as they removed his body from the horse-drawn carriage he had been encased. Landon led the crew of eight officers, their lines straight as arrows as they carried him to his rest. Beth sat unmoving, holding their son, awaiting her future husband to join her.

I was angry that she had someone to comfort her when Carter was gone. I would never feel him hold me ever again. The guilt consumed me of the very idea; she

6

had lost a brother and Molly her father. I wasn't the only one suffering, even though it's how I felt. Landon had taken his seat beside her, dressed in his dress blues; he looked stately and sat as straight and tall as an oak. His emotions lacked, but I knew he was deeply saddened by the loss of his friend, partner, and brother-in-law.

The buzz from the overhead PA system had awakened me from the thoughts racing through my head. An unfamiliar voice called out as we sat there still as stone. This had been part of this arrangement from the department. They did this for all their officers. The lone voice was haunting as it came across the dispatch system.

"All units, stand by for broadcast." The line popped and cracked, then fell silent. The silence had a lost and eerie feel to it. The few minutes that had passed felt like hours.

The voice broke the airwaves once more as they began to speak. "Last call for Carter Blake 6, 2, 9. 6, 2, 9. Officer Blake badge 629, end of watch March 2, 2013. Officer Blake, you've completed your mission here. A good friend to all, a loving husband and father, we will remember your warm smile and compassion. You fought the good fight and finished the course. Now is the time to rest. All units break for a moment of silence." Again, the silence ensued, breaking me into tiny pieces. "Carter Elijah Blake, may you rest in peace knowing your strength and passion lives on in your children, that your love lives on in your wife, and that your honor will live on in us all. Officer Blake, thank you for your service and ultimate sacrifice. You are clear to secure and remain with the Lord your God in peace. Officer Blake, this is your final call."

That was it, all I could take. The silent tears ran down my face, uncaring of what others saw. My husband, the love of my life, was gone; and there was no bringing him back. I would have given anything, just for him to tell me everything was going to be okay. His words came back to me as Pastor Conley concluded the service.

"Carter had come to me before he married his beautiful wife and spoke to me of some things that he hadn't been able to understand. But he also told me that in what he had experienced in his life, he had tried to accept what God had done or was doing in his life without question. We don't know why God chose to take such a loving man from his family, but, like him, we must accept it and learn not to question. God knows what is best, even though it doesn't seem so at the time. The hope we have is that we will see him again and never be separated. God bless you, my friend, until we are reunited in God's house."

The guard folded the flag that rested on the casket and brought it to me. I caught a strange sensation as the officer placed it in my hands, and the familiar scent of Carter's cologne rose from the unsettling scene. The ID on the officer's uniform read Davis. It must be my imagination. He can't be here. It's impossible. *Isabella, your mind is playing tricks on you*. Once he had presented the flag, he saluted the family and the casket and took his place at the end of it. The family and friends had begun to file out, and I walked up to say goodbye once more. Molly had left with Beth, and I was glad to have the time alone

8

with him. Gently, I ran my fingers along the edge, wishing for one last touch, one last kiss, and one last goodbye.

Paying no attention to the guard at the end, I stood there trying to collect what thoughts I had of him before returning to the family. I needed this. "What am I going to do without you?" I whispered softly. "Molly misses you already, and I know that I will carry you with me all of my life. Why didn't you say no? Why did you leave me? I can't do this without you." I dropped to my knees beside the casket.

After two days of showing little emotion, the dam broke. Relieved that I was alone except for the lone guard and Peirce, who had been gracious enough to keep his distance, I just sat there broken. The chill in the air felt so cold. It was if it went to the bone. In the state I was in, it had become hard to take a breath. My chest heaved as I poured out all the pain that had been trapped.

My hand lay on the casket, and I shook in pain as if someone had stabbed me through the heart. They hadn't allowed me to see him, to say goodbye. Landon had explained that he was so badly disfigured that I didn't want to see that. It was better for me and Molly to have a closed casket.

"I love you so much," I had managed to speak through the tears, and the knot in my throat never seemed to go away. My hair fell forward against my face like a veil. Laying my hand on my stomach, I ran it across the black lace dress I wore where our son or daughter was growing inside of me.

"What will I tell our baby, Carter? How will he ever know his father and how much you loved him?"

9

A gloved hand assisted me to my feet and into the waiting arms of my brother-in-law. The touch of the stranger's hand had brought back the memory of Carter extending his hand to me when we had first met. The kind gesture did not go unnoticed. As I turned to thank the guard, his head bowed. He stood silently at the end of the casket with his hands clasped in front of him.

"Thank you." My voice shook as I spoke. His head remained bowed, never saying a word. He shook his head in acknowledgment as we walked away.

Landon stood strong, having to almost carry me at times. I was lost without him, totally lost. Landon assisted me into the family car, beside Beth. He had arranged for the family to ride in limos so they could be together. All I wanted was to be alone.

"Bella, I have to take care of something. I'll be back." After assuring that Beth, the children, and I were settled, he returned to the grave site. All I could think of was going home.

"You're lucky she didn't recognize you," Landon huffed.

"I made sure to cover my tracks."

"Carter, you could jeopardize the whole mission."

"I can't leave my wife. Can't you see how fragile she is?"

"If you're not careful, the next one will be for real." Landon looked at Carter with great distress. "You could potentially risk her life, your babies', and your own."

Carter never uttered a word, nor did he move an inch. "You've never been careless before."

"It's never involved my wife and children before." His voice was low and harsh, his tone agitated. "Look at her, Landon. She hasn't slept or eaten the last few days."

"I promise you I will take care of her. The quicker we get Arnell Andrews behind bars, the better off we will all be. Until then, you're going to follow orders."

"How's Beth?"

"She hasn't spoken since she was told." Without further prompting, Landon continued, "Your mother is a mess. Your father hasn't had a chance to fall apart. Molly cries herself to sleep. She doesn't understand, and Isabella, I can't do anything with. She sits in the bedroom with your picture and a shirt."

Carter grinned as it had brought back some good memories. "The shirt has a little history to it."

"Well, Grayson and her parents are trying, but nothing seems to help her."

Carter took a deep breath. "I knew this would never work. My wife runs the risk after all she has been through losing our baby. She doesn't need the added stress. It isn't worth putting my family through this."

"You stay put. I have enough with them and JC, without having to worry about you following orders."

"JC?"

"He's a basket case. He thinks it's his fault. He has threatened to leave the force."

"You promise me this." Carter's jaw clenched. "If Bella has problems with the baby, I want you to pull the plug on this."

"You know I don't have the authority to do that."

"I don't care if Brooks likes it or not. Get me out. I won't let her go through it alone."

"Fine, I'll take care of it. In the meantime, take care of yourself. Bella wouldn't be happy if she knew you hadn't. I'll keep in touch."

"Just dismiss me. They're watching."

Landon stood stiffly and saluted, dismissing him.

～～～～～～～～～～～～～～～～～～～～～～～～～～～

Upon reaching home, I retreated to the bedroom as the mourners gathered. I wanted nothing to do with company of any kind. Being tired and emotionally spent wasn't all that affected me. My soul ached for him. I lay quietly running my hand over the space where he would have lain. His cologne still remained on the pillow and on the shirt he had offered to me months before. I gripped them to my chest and cried, but there were barely any tears left to cry. My eyes were red and sore, and my body ached from lack of sleep. I felt limp and lifeless.

I could remember flashes of him: his smile and his laugh. *Isabella, you certainly know how to unravel a man*, I had heard his voice echo in the room. My grief consumed me as I lay thinking of him.

I could still feel his hands on my body and the warmth of his embrace. This was unreal. It just couldn't be possible. We were celebrating the future arrival of our child. In the short time he knew, he had planned the nursery down to the last nail. Now he wouldn't be here to see his child. How cruel was that for a child to never know its father?

Curling into a tight ball, I grabbed my knees. My mind and heart ravaged with pain as I began to pray. My words barely formed. "Pl-please, it hurts. Please make it st-stop. Pl-please help me," my voice whispered.

"Isabella, can I come in?" the baritone voice of Grayson was unmistakable. I lay still, not answering. He continued in and turned on the desk lamp where Carter had written reports and bills at times. His personal belongings remained in a bag that was never opened. His wallet, watch, firearm, and shoes were untouched from the time they had been brought home.

Listening to his footsteps against the wood floor, the distance closed between us. My back remained turned to him as he sat on the edge of the bed.

"I know you're awake. Do you want to talk?"

I shook my head, and he continued to sit there.

"I know you miss him and that you're hurting. Nothing can compare to what you must be feeling. I wanted to thank you for the joy you gave him. He waited a long time for you. He had told me once after Andrea had passed that when God wanted him to have someone new in his life, he would present them to him. He called me the night of your first date. I couldn't believe how thrilled my grown son was about going out with you. He told me about how he planned to have a horse-drawn carriage to take you both for a drive along the coast. You would have thought it was Christmas morning and he was five years old." He laughed. "He even called and told me when he was going to propose. He wanted us there, all of us. In October, he came home and had his mother go ring shopping with him. Iris came home crying and laughing at the same time, telling me, 'He loves her, Grayson. He loves her.' I really thought her reaction had topped it all until Carter called and told us about the baby. My boy was on cloud nine. He wanted so much to have a child with you. I don't think I had ever heard him so happy."

My bottom lip quivered as the tears gently fell against my cheeks. Turning, I sat up in the bed and looked at Grayson. He was trying to hide the pain, but it had shown all over his face.

"I loved him, Pop."

"I know you did, honey."

Reaching for me, I clung to him, sobbing. In the length of time I had known Carter's dad, I had for the first time saw the love and compassion he had for his son. Gently, he patted my back in an attempt to comfort me. "He loved you and these babies."

My heart burned and ached, my throat was sore, and I wondered if I was going to take my next breath. Grayson had taught his son such loving gestures. He sat and cradled me like I were a child, allowing me to cry. His cheek rested against my face, wet from his own tears. "We'll make it, honey. Together we're going to make it."

Later that evening after everyone had left, my parents and Carter's remained. I had left the bedroom only briefly to check on Molly and found her curled up in my father's lap, holding on to a book. She lay in a restless sleep as my father rocked her. "If it were as easy with you." He sighed. "I'm here for you too, you know." I squeezed his shoulder and bent to kiss him on the cheek. My parents and

Grayson sat in the living room, trying to make sense of it all. Iris went to bed. The doctor had given Grayson tranquilizers for her, which now she needed to survive this nightmare. I myself was now living in a bottle. I rarely had taken anything over the past month, but now I needed something. I wasn't sure if it were safe to take what I had since I had found out that I was pregnant. I was going to have to tough it out. I couldn't take a chance on something happening to his child.

The night was long as I lay there next to the empty spot where he had once lain beside me. Our room felt cold, along with our bed. After lying there for three hours, unable to sleep, I walked into the bath and turned on the water to the garden tub. Pouring lavender oil into the bath, I was hoping it would relax me enough so that I would finally be able to sleep. Stepping into the bath, I sunk into the water, closing my eyes, taking in the aroma of the oils mixed with steam and water. I thought of the time I went to the station to tell him that I was pregnant. He had gone into a spiel about going to see the precinct's physician, the physician running tests, and finding nothing. He looked at me, and I had wondered if he were angry with me. I knew then that he knew about the baby. Sitting petrified, he had asked me, "Is there anything you want to tell me?"

It had brought a laugh and a crying jag as I had remembered his grin when he found he was a father again.

We had talked about the nursery and what we were going to do with it, where it would be, and when he would buy the crib. We had decided not to buy a crib until a month before the birth. Not because we didn't want to be ready, but because he knew that it was possible that there could be problems, and he didn't want me to have to look at it if something happened.

He had teased me about some baby names, and some were really out there. I knew one thing for sure: if it were a boy, he would bear his father's name in any form. Carter or Elijah, one of them would be his name. A daughter was another story. I had no idea. It was early, and it wasn't good to name a child until you knew if you were going to be able to carry it. I was going to do all that I could to ensure that this child would be born healthy. I couldn't stand the thought of losing someone else I loved.

I had sat in the water so long that my hands and fingers had puckered. Taking the towel from the rack, I stood before the mirror and looked at my body. It didn't appear to be any different than before, but there was a child in there, Carter's child. After drying off, I took his shirt and put it on, leaving the last few buttons unfastened enough to view my belly. Rubbing it slowly, I spoke to my unborn child.

"Well, look at you. Your daddy would have been so happy if he had been here. He loves you. Do you know that? He wanted so much to hold you and to kiss your little face. When I told him about you, he was so happy. He started planning your room and talked about how he was going to take you to ball games and fishing. It didn't matter if you were a boy or a girl. He would have done the same." Tears fell, and I pushed them back with the back of my hand. "I love you too. Mommy loves you so much. You hang in there, okay? Things are going to get better for us, I promise. You have Pop, Nan, Granpa, and Mim to love you. Uncle Landon and Beth will be there for you too. We'll be fine." Trying to reassure myself wasn't helping much, but I had to try to get myself together. I had children to think of.

Weeks had passed, and I was no better off than I had been from the time he had been killed. The only difference was that the days and nights had both gotten longer and more unbearable. Grayson and Iris had wanted me to shut the house up and move in with them until at least the birth of the baby, but I couldn't stand the thought of leaving when this was where we had lived. This is where Carter was for me. The only other place that had existed was the cabin in Tennessee, where we had spent a weekend together. My mind would not let go of the fact that he was gone. I had reminders of him everywhere. Pictures of us together while we were in Tennessee, our wedding day, and others of just Carter and Molly together were scattered about our home. I had been in the desk recently and found pictures of Andrea and Carter together. He had them wrapped in a stack of old cards and letters that had been carefully preserved. The last thing I had found was an envelope addressed to Molly. I had assumed it was from her mother. It remained sealed, and I never bothered to open it.

I had started back to work. Most days I walked around in a stupor, more of a robot than a person. The only saving grace to it was it did keep my mind occupied while I was there. It had been a month since Carter had died, and no one mentioned a word about it, well, except for Marilyn, who always seemed to draw her fingers down the

17

chalkboard. I had thought of a couple of things in the time period that had passed. My life needed a change; I needed to do something to make his death so meaningless.

I had spoken with Gus a couple of times, and he had talked over a couple of things with me. He had advised me not to make a snap decision based on what had happened, and I took it to heart. I had still frequented the academy for self-defense and the firing range. It had made perfectly good sense to me, but then I needed a little more time to think a few things through.

After one of the first full days I had put in, I walked into the house followed by Peirce. Quentin had become a fixture. He followed me everywhere. He was my age, or thereabouts anyway, with a slim build, and was fairly good looking. You would think he would have some kind of social life outside of this job. He was average height and solid as a rock with a no-nonsense personality. He wore his copper-colored hair in a military cut and had dark brown eyes. He had kept his distance with me, which was fine; it's the way I had wanted it.

When he had seen Landon there with Molly and Beth, he turned to say goodbye and saw himself out. He was a man of few words, and I liked that; the more time to be alone, the better. It gave the time I needed to reflect on things. Beth had shortly made her leave, and it left me with both sets of parents and Landon. For some reason, they felt they needed to stay with me. Each night, I would read to Molly and tuck her in as usual, kissing her good night. Tonight had been no different.

I was so tired, and I needed to get to bed. I had said good night to both sets of parents as they made their way to the other bedrooms. Landon had gone on to lie down on the couch as I walked into the bedroom. It had reminded me of the first night I had stayed with Carter, bringing back those raw emotions of loss once more. All I had were memories, and I had to get used to it.

Lying down, I reached across the bed to where Carter had once been and turned off the light. It wasn't going to take long to go to sleep. Regardless of the emotional roller coaster I was on, my body was not going to allow me to be awake for long. This would be one of the few times I wouldn't be crying myself to sleep.

"Get him out of the way before he gets us killed," the voice shouted. Carter stood in the doorjamb, hunkered down almost to the floor with rapid fire around him. "Radio for some help, or we're all going to die." Running feet scurried away, and a voice called over the radio for assistance at a makeshift warehouse in the downtown area. A shot was fired, and Carter had jumped back against the frame. Reloading, he hadn't stood a chance from the shooter. As he had kicked the magazine, the shot pierced his chest and a second to the side of his face. "Isabella, run!" he had screamed.

"Carter!" I screamed, sitting straight up in bed, panting like I had been in a race. I could still see his face and the blood running down his body even after I had awakened. I clutched his pillow to my chest, trying to regain some control of my breathing, which had become erratic and strained. My hair was wet, and my clothes felt damp.

19

Landon burst through the door, followed by both sets of parents.

Landon ran to me, pulling his cell from his pocket. I couldn't understand what was going on until I looked down at myself and the bed. "I need an ambulance at Blue Ridge Avenue. I have a woman approximately twelve weeks pregnant. I don't know. Just get someone here now!" Looking down, I sat in a pool of blood. There was excruciating pain; I was in shock at what I was seeing. What was happening to me?

"Isabella, look at me," Landon coaxed. "Hey, Bella." He patted my face until he had my attention. "You need to lie down, okay? Let me help you." The rest of the family had left except Grayson. Landon had insisted on Grayson staying to help, having him get extra pillows and a blanket. "Isabella, I need you to take some deep breaths and let me deal with this. Don't get upset, okay? I need to prop your feet up. It may not be comfortable, but we need to do this." Taking my feet, he held them with one hand and placed a stack of pillows under them.

"Landon, please help me. Please don't let me lose this baby."

"Don't worry. I'm not going to let that happen. Close your eyes and relax for me. Grayson, go see if the squad is here and let them in."

"Carter, help me. Where are you? I need you," I cried and couldn't stop.

The ambulance crew rumbled their way through the room and over to me. I couldn't remember much more other than Landon picking me up and placing me on the cot. "I'm going with her."

20

"Are you the father?"

"For now, I am."

As far out as I was, I thought that a little strange. He followed close by me holding my hand. He pulled his cell from his pocket and quickly dialed. "Get Brooks. Now!" I'd heard him shout. The ride was bumpy, but I was in and out of whatever they had given me. "Donavan, pull the plug. I don't have time to explain. I'm on my way to the hospital with Isabella. Bad enough. Look, you promised me. We're a brotherhood here. Pull it, or I will. I don't care if you are. This affects more than one life." He clapped the cell shut and run his hand across his face. "Hang in there, Bella. We're almost there."

"Carter," my voice was barely above a whisper as I drifted in and out.

Landon patted my hand and kissed the top of it. "Hang in there, Bella."

It was morning before I realized what was going on. I awoke to find myself on the maternity ward with Landon sitting in the chair next to me. His head rested against his propped arm, and his other held my hand. I felt weak. My hand that rested in Landon's was white as the sheet that it lay against.

"Landon?"

He stirred and looked down at me. "Bella."

"The baby, what happened?"

"It's all right. The baby's okay. Just rest. They're coming to do another ultrasound in a few minutes."

I drifted off into darkness once more, not awakening until I found myself in a dark room with Landon and a technician. I could hear the clatter of movements behind

21

me. There was another doctor there other than my own. He was shrouded in darkness and never spoke as Dr. Carley explained to Landon what he was looking at.

"Isabella, just in time. Look at this, honey," Landon gushed at me.

Dr. Carley pointed to the space in the storm of white-and-gray waves. "See that? That is your baby. There's its little heart. See it beating?" She moved the wand around a little as Landon and I watched the screen. The second doctor also watched intently. Standing almost to the head of the exam table, he didn't move. "Isabella, I hope you don't mind. I asked Dr. Jeffers to stand in. He is in his internship here."

"No, I don't mind," I managed.

"Would you like to know the sex? We might be able to find out today if you want."

"I don't know."

"Come on, Isabella." Landon smiled over at me. "It'll be good for you to know."

"Landon, I don't want you to think I'm coldhearted, but I don't think I want to know yet. I'm not sure if I'm going to be able to carry this baby."

"Sure, I understand." His expression darkened.

"I can record it for a later date if you like, if you decide later you want to know I can tell you." Dr. Carley smiled down at me. "Would you like for me to print out a picture?"

"Yes, I would like that. Thank you."

The second doctor cleared his throat and walked from the room. Landon remained watching the screen, then looked over to me. "It's going to be all right," he reassured. "I need to make a couple of calls. I need to let the parents know what's happening and call the office. I'll meet you in the room." Bending down, he kissed me on the forehead and left, leaving me with Dr. Carley.

"He seems to be a happy daddy."

"That's my brother-in-law. My husband died a couple of weeks ago. He was killed in the line of duty."

"Oh, I'm sorry."

"It's okay. I'm trying to get used to the fact he isn't here. Landon has been good to me. I don't know what I would do without him."

"Sure you don't want to know what you're having?"

I thought for a moment then decided there was no harm in knowing. Carter would have been happy either way. She finished examining me, and I was soon ready to return to my room.

"I thought I told you to stay put until I could get this resolved."

"Landon, that is my wife and child in there. I deserve to be here with them."

"I'm doing my best with Brooks, but you're going to have to lie low, like it or not. It's dangerous."

Carter ran his hand through his hair after removing the surgical cap. He was dressed in scrubs, had grown a beard, and was wearing glasses. "You're lucky no one has recognized you. You have to leave before someone sees you, especially your wife."

"How's she doing, really?"

"She's okay for now. She gave me a pretty bad scare last night. I thought for sure she had miscarried. The doctor has put her on bed rest and has given her some mild sedatives to help her sleep."

"This has got to end." Carter clenched his fists at his sides. "There has to be a way out of this."

"Right now the only way out is to catch Arnell and put him away for good."

Carter, frustrated, turned his back when he saw another intern walk to the area. He ran his hands through his hair now cut more in a military style. "I need to be with my family. I could have lost my wife and child last night. Nothing is more important to me than them."

"I'll try to work something out, but for now you need to go back into hiding until he tries to come after Bella. You don't have to worry. Peirce is still guarding her, and what time he isn't there, I am. She's safe. Grayson has his own security team on her just because of your death. He's fearful for them and has been there with her himself. He knows how to handle a firearm, believe me."

"Just make sure you take care of them. I can't lose them."

"I took care of your sister. Entrust me with them. I promise they will be taken care of. You better take off while you can. I'll talk to you later."

The tech wheeled me out of the ultrasound with my picture in hand. As I left the ultrasound, I saw Landon standing outside the door with the intern standing beside him, with his back to me. I could smell Carter's cologne and studied the man that stood with his back to me carefully. His hair was dark and short, his shoulders broad. Looking at him, he stood with his hand propped against the wall. The other bore the gleam of a gold band he wore on his left hand. He carefully placed his hand into the pocket of his scrubs and had looked down. It couldn't be. At the funeral and now here, I had to get over this. He was gone.

"Landon." I reached for him, and the intern walked away.

"I called the parents. They will be in to see you later. I'll bring Beth over later if you're feeling up to it." He held my hand, trying to comfort me, and smiled.

"Wait, wait. Landon, something isn't right."

"What do you mean? Are you having pain?"

"No, I mean there is something that doesn't fit. It's Carter. I feel like he is here. I felt it at the funeral, and I feel it here."

His smile fell as he continued to hold my hand as we continued down the hall to my room. "Isabella, you and I both know that he isn't here. It isn't possible."

"I smell his cologne, Landon."

"It's just cologne, Isabella. Dozens of men wear it."

"Not this one. I bought it for him for Christmas. It was made for him from a perfumery in Paris. It's unique."

"Isabella."

He's at a loss of words and shook his head. I knew I had knocked him off his axis, but he kept his cool persona. I'm not sure if it was me. Maybe it's my imagination. I was there when they brought him in, but then again, I was kept from seeing him. Landon had explained that, and he had given me no cause to doubt what he had told me.

"Never mind." I waved my hand as to dismiss what I've said and what I was thinking. It wasn't possible. He was right.

"Why don't you try to rest before the parents come in to see you? I'll sit with you for a while until they get here. The baby's fine. That's what's important. And you need to start eating and sleeping. Molly needs you home. She misses her mother. Close your eyes."

"Landon."

"UT . . . Close them. That's an order, Mrs. Blake."

"OK, Sergeant Mason," I grumbled as I closed my eyes, and he chuckled.

"Behave yourself and follow orders."

I lay there quietly, but I couldn't go to sleep. My eyes remained closed, and I listened to Landon's breaths as he sat beside the bed. I knew he was watching. I could feel his eyes on me as I rested. At least I had him to watch over me, but he should have been home with Beth. Not that the alternative was better. Peirce would have been here sitting; over the last few weeks, he had become my shadow. He took me everywhere: to the store, to work, and to doctor appointments. It was getting to be a common thing. You would have thought we were married. He stayed close at all times unless Landon was there, then he would take time off. It wasn't that I didn't like Peirce.

He had to be excellent at what he did, or Carter wouldn't have assigned him to security detail for his family. I wasn't sure why he still hung around, but Landon had insisted that he remain. I never knew where he stayed when he wasn't in the house with me. He always knew my every move and was ready when I was going out the door for anything. I felt like I was being stalked. I lay there remembering the last thing Carter said to me that night, and it broke my heart all over again. *I want you to promise me something. I want you to promise me no matter what happens that you take care of yourself and the two children. It's very important that you do that for me.* I could still see him as he had spoken those words to me. I was so angry with him. He left me that night, and I was still angry with him. I was never able to tell him that I was sorry. His voice echoed in my head. *This is it, angel. I'll keep in contact somehow. Don't worry. Everything will be all right, I promise you. I love you.* I could still hear his feet clicking on the tile floor as he had walked away.

The creak of the rocking chair beside me slowly soothed me to sleep as I lay remembering his dark-blue eyes and unruly dark hair. I could imagine him wrapped around me and his breath against me, with his fingers laced through mine. Seeing him in my dreams, just being able to see him, to touch him and talk to him, just for a moment, brought so much happiness for me. In that short amount of time, I was there with him. I heard his laugh and felt his hand in mine.

Landon's voice was muted as I tried to awaken. He spoke low, attempting not to awaken me. I seemed to be so tired as I struggled to get awake. I could hear his shoes click off the tile as he paced the floor and talk to whoever happened to be on the other end of the line.

"I know, but you can't . . . Okay . . . Doing fine for now. I'm staying here until the parents come. Quentin will be here somewhere on duty after I leave. He doesn't normally. She doesn't mind. She knows things are delicate. No. I know, but it can't happen now."

Turning over in the bed, I saw him pacing, holding a cup of coffee in one hand and the cell in the other. When he turned, he saw I was waking and cut his conversation short. "I have to go. Yeah . . . Later."

He closed the cell and placed it in his jacket pocket. As he does, I notice he's wearing his holster. "Hey, Izzy, you're awake." He took his seat by the bed and sat down, taking my hand as I tried to awaken. It wasn't easy.

"Did they give me something?" I asked him in a gravelly voice.

"No, you were just tired. You haven't slept much. It's catching up with you. Everything is fine."

CHAPTER TWO

Carter tossed and turned as he lay there in the darkness from a restless sleep. He missed his wife; there was no doubt in that. He lay with his hands folded behind his head, remembering past events that he had left far behind him. Sitting up in bed, he ran his hand through his hair as he did when he was frustrated. He hadn't had a good night's sleep since the last night he had been with her. His thoughts had taken him back to the darkest part of his life.

His parents had been gone for more years than seemed possible. They had gone out to celebrate their wedding anniversary when they were hit by a drunk driver that had killed them both. He was just four years old, and Beth hadn't celebrated her third birthday yet. She had a difficult time when the court had pulled them from the home they had shared with their parents.

Neither side of the family was able to take them in. The others in the family just didn't want the responsibility of having two small children. The only one willing was a grandmother; they had been with her for a short time in which she was found to be terminally ill. She had tried to care for them, but with the progressiveness of her illness, she was unable to care for them.

The system, however, had managed to keep the children together; both children had been shifted from foster home to foster home for at least a year. At that time, they remained for at least nine months before the

Blakes had adopted them at the one foster home they landed in. The foster home belonged to a businessman and his wife Eldora. They were bitter and angry people, but more often than not, they knew how to put on a good show when they were being watched. Strangely, this couple was Mr. And Mrs. Arnell Andrews. When Isabella had mentioned she had remembered the men's names, she had mentioned Arnell. Not thinking that it could possibly be the same man, he did some investigating on Arnell Andrews.

He had found they had been denied further foster children once he and his sister had been adopted. They had been suspected of abuse and child molestation. He had also found that he had two children from a previous marriage but had not been able to access the records.

He remembered the man's large hands were hard and cold as steel when he would discipline them, which had been often. "Spare the rod and spoil the child," he would say in a low, menacing voice as he would literally beat them with a belt or performed some sexual act with them. It wasn't because they had done something wrong for being whipped with a belt but because he derived pleasure from it.

It wasn't until he was six years old that he had walked in on him doing unspeakable things to his sister that he didn't understand that he stood in for her, taking what he would have done to Beth. He heard his sister scream and cry as he held her down. Jumping on the man, he attempted to pull him off her.

His steely green eyes had burned through him. He had backhanded him, causing him to bounce off the wall.

Shaking his head, trying to regain his senses, he continued to hear Beth scream as if she were being burned, piercing and lingering.

He had yelled at the man to stop and instantly had offered himself as his sister lay in a ball, crying uncontrollably.

"You wanna take her place, boy? I can see that it happens. As long as I get what I want, it doesn't make a difference to me."

The things this man had done to him before he was adopted out of that home had haunted him for years. He had carried the scars with him. His parents were aware of some of the hell he had endured, but only pieces. Beth had been spared most of the nightmare, but both had undergone counseling for years.

The incident had led him as a teen to drink, but he had also experimented with drugs. Luckily, he had never gotten into anything that he couldn't get out of. He was a fighter. He had started fighting when there was no need, and it had gotten him expelled more than once. Grayson and Iris, the people he had grown to love and trust, had tried to help him; but when he had threatened suicide at the age of twenty-two, they had him placed in a lock-down rehab center for counseling, and he had hated them for it.

The only light during that time was the time he spent going to see a young lady down the hall. She had been in a similar situation, being admitted by her physician. During group sessions, she would sit in the hardback chair with her knees drawn to her chest, never speaking or looking at anyone. She rarely spoke to him, but he had continued to see her each day until he had been released. Most days he read to her a classic book, but she seemed a little more reachable after he started reading *Cinderella*. He never knew her name. He just called her Cindy, and she knew him as Eli.

In the days before he had left, he would walk down to her room and eventually had gained her trust enough to get her out of her bed and had taken her to the recreation hall. He held her hand as he had walked with her. Her hand had fit perfectly in his.

With no one around that evening, he had picked a piece of music he knew she would like. He extended his hand to her and glided her around the room, holding her as if she were glass. She looked to be fifteen or sixteen at the time, way too young to have been suffering from the trauma she had endured. He had been taken by her from the moment he had set eyes on her. She was angelic. She wore her dark hair in a braid down her back to her waist.

That evening was the first time he had heard her giggle, and it had thrilled him to hear it. He had helped her in some part, and she had helped him. He had never forgotten his dance with Cinderella. He had released her hair from the braid and let it fall over her shoulders, hating that he would be leaving her. He constantly reminded himself that she was much too young to get involved with. She could be nothing more than a friend. It was too bad, really; he had felt an instant connection to her. She brought him to life, something he had been missing.

After he had been released, he made a point to see her at least once a month. He had left for the academy and was home Saturday afternoon to Sunday evening when he returned home. She was the first one he would see on his return trip. After his third trip, he had found she had been sent home to her family; the time before, he had brought her a gift, a necklace that resembled Cinderella's slipper. She had accepted it, and he had placed it around her neck. The first time she had shown any emotion was then as she had stood on tiptoes and kissed him on the cheek. It had never occurred to him that in his research for Arnell Andrews he would find out who this young woman was.

He was sure she had never guessed because it had never been mentioned. He smiled as he thought of how God worked, and his plan had made it possible for their lives to cross. He had seen the same reaction and had the same feelings but only once. His Cindy, his beautiful young woman he had met years ago, was his own wife.

He had danced with Isabella and had made a connection with her then. She had held on to him then, and she would now. It was sad to think that had he been really gone. She may never recover from what he had seen, but it had also assured him of her love. She had been there two months with little to no involvement in anything until he started visiting her. His decision to join the police force was there. He never wanted to see that kind of pain ever again. It hadn't been the only time he had seen her. Unfortunately, he had been part of a plot to get her out of the mess she was in. The first time he had seen her, she was talking with a young man who was arguing with her about leaving. Her back had been to him, and he hadn't gotten a good look at her. She had retreated to a dark room in which she was dressed in clothes that were way too sexual for her age.

The young man had explained that he needed a way to get her out before the man that ran the place killed her. He feared for her life and was willing to do whatever it took to get her out. She wasn't willing to play her captor's game, and the result was him starving her. His punishment was to withhold food or take it out in sexual favors when she didn't respond properly to the clients. He had explained that neither of them had been there by choice. The only plan he knew that may actually release her was to impregnate her. The young man was in trouble up to his neck himself, and she had refused to leave because it had ensured his safety.

She had called him Lee, but he now knew this young man to be his brother-in-law, Cooper. How would he ever tell her that he was the one, that Jenna more than likely had been his daughter?

Cooper had drugged his sister that evening. Carter, being high himself, hadn't thought through the consequences. His intention was to get her out safely. He had prescription painkillers in him, enough to put down a horse, and had been drinking heavily. He had no intent of adding to her pain. He remembered enough that he knew there was no protection used. The one stipulation to every client that had entered, he really hadn't wanted to be any part of it, but Cooper had been his supply line.

The next time he saw her, she was bruised, bloody, beaten, and tied to a chair so that she couldn't move. She went into preterm labor, and he had just happened to be there. Cooper had begged him to get her out of the building anyway he could, to meet up with a ride he had called for her.

Cooper had kept them distracted until he was able to get her to safety. When he had seen the little sports car coming, he sat her down at the tree near the bus stop and watched from behind a nearby building to see a young man pick her up and hurriedly carry her off. He couldn't be seen with her. It would have gotten back to his parents what he was doing and where his supply was coming from.

As he remembered how she had looked when he had seen her there, his eyes welled with tears. The absolute torment she must have endured. He had been in the same warehouse where she had been. This had been one of the few times that he had not been under the influence of drugs or alcohol.

Landon, by this time, could possibly know about his stay at the South Shore Rehabilitation and the connection to Isabella. He had never spoken of it to anyone. He hadn't shared anything that had happened to him with his family, not even his sister. She didn't need to know. He could handle it easier than she could, even though he had spent three months locked in a rehab center. He, on rare occasions, had seen Dr. Mike Gilding. He had been his psychiatrist there. Not for treatment, however; they had become friends. He was the only one that actually knew everything about him.

He wasn't sure which was harder to watch: his wife before he knew her at the rehabilitation center or at his staged funeral. He had wanted to be there for her; it had been his decision. It hurt so badly to see her in so much pain and he could do nothing. Landon would have been furious if he had known what he had planned; as it had been, it had been bad enough. When he had shown up for her ultrasound, Landon had cooled somewhat and had understood, but the edge had remained in his voice. He knew what it meant if he were found out. He had left Isabella in capable hands, but in this instance, nothing would have taken the place of him for her.

He had listened to her at the funeral, asking why he left her and how much she loved him, and his heart had broken watching her. It had been nights like this that he missed her most. Her side of the bed was lonely, and he had longed to hold her body next to his. The cabin held good memories for him, but they had become bittersweet. Lying there, searching the room in the darkness, his mind found him thinking of their first night here. It was truly the first time she had given herself to him without fear or reservation; she had loved him. She had been nervous, and he had understood that, and so had he been.

The firelight had cascaded over her; she had looked like an angel as the light beamed from around her. A glow radiated from her that night, so much so that his heart had leapt from his chest. That night, she had allowed her feelings for him to rule her, and she had taken him with her. She didn't have to try; from the time they had stepped into the bedroom, she had him. Wanting to make the timing and the room just right to what he felt would be inviting to her, he had it planned by a local service to have candles placed around the room and flower petals placed on the linens. It had been perfect, and he had been rewarded by her smile.

The day had dragged on as I lay there in the hospital. The pale white walls and curtains left the area depressing. I didn't need anything more to decrease my mood. I felt like a robot now. It hadn't helped much either that it was raining; the sun had taken its leave for the past few days. Landon had taken a moment to step outside, but I was sure that I wasn't alone. Just because I didn't see anyone didn't mean a thing—Peirce was always around when Landon wasn't.

I had nothing to do but sit there and think; I would have been better off knocked out the way I felt. If I had more than five minutes of time on my hands, I sat and thought of how desperately lonely I was without him. I couldn't do this. I had a family to consider, and letting myself get to the point where I was unable to function was out. I knew what I was going to do now. When the doctor gave the okay, I would return to work, and if the academy would take me I was joining the force. It was the only lawful way to bring this man down. Carter had been killed going after him, and I wasn't going to let him die in vain.

I hated the man for what he had done to me, but I hated him more for taking the only man I knew in my life that had truly loved me and accepted me for who I was. Carter was the only one that had been able to break down the barriers. Seeing this man's handiwork for what he had done to me and the teens that had lost their lives along with my own husband, I was determined that he wouldn't live long if I found him. He would pay for what he had done, and I would do it legally. All I needed was to get with Gus. I knew starting now I couldn't do the physical requirements, but I could work on my criminal justice

37

degree. He would know what to do. He himself had made the statement that I would have made a good officer.

There was only one thing holding me back, and that was our children. What if I met with the same demise their father had? They would be left without either parent and would be worse off than they were now. I couldn't let that happen. I would be unable to discuss any of this with Landon because it would be an automatic no. I'm sure my parents would back him, and I didn't really want to talk about it. I had my own reasons. I had intended on doing what I felt was right.

First things first: I had to get well enough to go home, then I would concentrate on what I needed to do. I couldn't let Landon know what I was doing until it had already been done. I could train physically mildly for a while, but it wouldn't be long before I would not be able to. There was too much of a chance on falling while running, I knew that was part of it. There would be no physical classes until January, so that would help; at least I could train some with Gus before the endurance part of the training was expected. He was the only one that had any idea of what I had in mind, and he still had no idea of the entire scope of things. All Gus had thought, I'm sure, was that there was interest in what Carter had done all his life. He knew that I had thought of joining the force, but not in the capacity in which I had in mind.

It was getting late in the day, and the night started to fall early, or so it appeared. With the darkness of the sky filled with rain, it hadn't taken much to take what light that had been left in it. I hated it here and wanted to go home. I was here enough on a regular basis without being a patient. This hospital was where he had taken his last breath, which was enough for me to hate what I was doing. I couldn't take the bed any longer. I had to get up and start moving even if it were to just walk around the room. My feet set on the floor weakly as I held to my IV stand and stood cautiously. What a relief; just to be able to stand was an accomplishment.

Walking over to the small vanity, I looked into the mirror. The reflection looked like a shell of me. I didn't appear to be there anymore. Oh, it looked like me and talked like me, but it was nothing more than a shell standing there. The brush on the counter had reminded me of the rage I felt on the morning after our wedding. I had been angry with what I had found out about myself and who had inflicted all that pain on me. I hadn't had the chance to talk with my mother. I had anticipated on doing it soon. I needed to know what the story was and why it had been kept from me.

I stood, brushing my hair and watching each stroke in the mirror, suddenly seeing a figure standing behind me. A memory of a man's smile, someone I loved, reflected back. I could see him picking the ends of my hair up and pulling it to his face, smelling it. I could feel his touch as he ran his long, deft fingers through it. His beautiful blue eyes danced as he watched me through the mirror. "I've missed you," I whispered softly. "Don't ever leave me again. Come home with us. I miss having you with me so much." His smile had left, and a frown replaced it, with him never saying a word; he shook his head. Looking away, he slowly faded out of sight. "Carter, please don't leave." I turned to see Landon standing behind me, looking a little mystified

39

at what he had witnessed. Feeling weak, Landon had taken hold of my shoulders.

"Isabella, who are you talking to?"

My mouth went dry, and the tears had started all over again. I saw him; I wanted him with me so badly that I had seen him standing there.

"Bella, you're scaring me. Who did you see?"

"If I tell you, he'll never be back." My voice was frail. And I didn't want to say it because if I shared what I had seen, Carter would never be back. Besides, he would never believe me anyway.

"Isabella, you have to tell me who you saw."

I shook under his grip, and he walked me back to the bed. "You shouldn't be out of bed anyway." Walking me part of the way to my bed, my legs started to give out from under me. He picked me up in his arms as a nurse came through the door and assisted him. Laying me down on the bed, he covered me. My eyes closed as I lay there, hearing them running around me and the quick breaths of Landon standing over me. "Is she okay?"

"Mr. Mason, she's fine, just tired. She shouldn't have been up, but I'm sure you know as well as I do that you aren't going to keep a nurse down for long. Don't worry. Everything seems to be all right. Just watch her. Make sure she doesn't get up on her own anymore."

The nurse's footsteps left the room as I felt Landon sit down on the bed beside me. He never said a word. He just sat there. Taking my hand in his, he rubbed it gently with the other, then smoothed my hair away from my face.

I was so tired. Why had it hit me so fast? Carter, he was here, and I wanted him back. I wanted him back so

40

desperately. I know he's alive. I can feel him. "Carter," I whispered his name softly, and my heart ached for him.

"Isabella, what am I going to do with you?" Landon breathed sharply.

I hadn't gone to sleep. I just lay there with my eyes closed, feeling like the wind had been knocked out of me. I lay motionless, still seeing his face. Flashes of a puzzle came as I had seen a younger version of him in a different setting. He looked the same, except his hair had been cut short, a man that had sat by my bedside and had begged me to talk to him. A cold environment of multiple people that I wanted nothing to do with, I sat tight in a ball. "You need to talk to someone. It might as well be me," he had said. Pieces of that time hit me, but none had fit. I could see a young man dancing around a room to a not-so-familiar tune but one that was simple and sweet. The face was never evident, but I heard his laugh. That laugh had belonged to my husband.

It made no sense to me. Where was this? Had my mind invented it? I hadn't met Carter before his accident, I was certain. The pictures soon left my mind as I heard my parents and Grayson enter the room.

"Has she been awake?" I had heard my mother speak as she addressed Landon.

"Yes, and of course, as stubborn as she is, she decided to get up and found herself too weak to return. She was standing in front of the mirror, brushing her hair, talking to someone that wasn't here. I had Peirce check the room while I sat with her, but he hasn't found anyone, and no one could have possibly gotten in. We had both been in the hallway down just a couple of steps at the coffee

41

dispenser. She never goes unguarded at any time." He breathed a sigh of relief. "There wasn't anyone here other than us."

Grayson's heavy footsteps had come closer as I felt his eyes on me. "No one could have gotten in from the fire escape. My detail has been watching the entrances to the hospital along with the fire escape next to her room."

They had no idea that the person they were trying to keep out was not in a physical form. A cell phone rang, and I attempted to open my eyes. "I need to take this," Landon had voiced. My eyes fluttered as he was walking from the room. "Landon, come back," I had pleaded with him as I reached out for him. He turned to see me looking at him.

"I'll be right back, Izzy. I need to take this call."

Another figure walked over and sat by the bed. My vision was clearing. I found my father by my side. "Hey, little girl, you okay?"

"Daddy, I'm so glad to see you."

"I heard you had a pretty rough time for a while. Everything okay?"

"Yes, I'm fine. How's Molly? I know she's probably scared to death."

"She's fine. Iris has her in the hallway. They wanted to make sure you were up to seeing her before she came in. She hasn't stopped asking to see you since they brought you."

"She's scared, Daddy. She thinks I'm going to leave her like Andrea and Carter has. I'm all she has as a parent now."

"Carter couldn't have left her to anyone better to raise her, and you know we're all here if you need help."

"I know, Daddy."

"Are you going to tell me what's bothering you?"

"What do you mean?"

"Isabella, you're talking to your father. I know when something is bothering you."

I had to smile. He always knew when something was off, and I hadn't ever been able to hide a thing from him. "Nothing, Daddy. I'm not sure it's anything."

"Okay, try me. I dare you." He grinned in that crooked smile he had. "I've always been able to help you before. Try me."

"I don't think so this time. I'm not sure if what I saw or heard was real. It could have been the effect of medications I know they must be giving me. You aren't a nurse as long as I have been and not know that you are being given something."

He smiled. "Never could keep anything from you."

"Daddy, I saw myself in a different place, somewhere. I'm not sure where. I don't remember much, just flashes of pictures. I didn't want to be there. I sat there saying nothing, doing nothing, until this young man had come to see me. It's strange, but he reminded me of Carter at a younger age. His hair was cut shorter, like a patrolman's cut or a military cut. I remember him dancing in this large room and to music that wasn't familiar to me. It was an instrumental piece of some kind. I'm sure if I heard it, I would recognize it."

My father smiled at me. "You'll remember. When you're ready, honey, it will come."

"Daddy, do you know what I'm talking about?"

"I want you to remember only the good things. I would rather you remember on your own."

"I only remember bits and pieces."

"In time, it will come back. I can tell you this. That one memory is a good one for you. It helped you to survive everything else. It'll surprise you when you do remember."

~~~~~~

Carter softly played the piano, and the sounds of a sweet melody filled the air as he thought of her. Unable to shake the feeling that she was in trouble, he got up and paced the floor. Before he knew it, he had pulled out the cell phone and called Landon. Knowing he couldn't contact her, Landon would be the next best thing. At least he would know that she was protected and if there was any danger to her or to the baby.

"Mason," his voice echoed.

"It's Carter. How's my girl?" Carter's voice had become tight, but he tried to control his emotions. He liked to be in control, and this was not his normal to just sit back and do nothing.

"She's had a few issues, but she seems fine."

"Landon, I can't take this much longer. Have you heard any more on your end about Andrews?"

"Not yet. Have you?"

"Last I knew, Cooper was in San Diego. I can't find a thing on Arnell. I've been through every agency and police department I can find, trying to find some kind of trace of him and come up with nothing. He's slick. It wouldn't surprise me if he hasn't changed his name."

"Look, bro, we're going to do this. I'm going to see you back with your wife as soon as possible. She's trying to be strong about this, but I'm worried about her."

"Why? What's going on that you aren't telling me?"

"I'm not sure how to explain it, but I think she thinks you're here. I caught her talking to someone earlier like she was talking to you. She called you by name."

"It sounds insane, I know, seeing that I'm not really dead, but have you thought of setting her up with the grief counselor at the station? She has to have an outlet of some kind."

"I'm sure Roxie would be glad to see her, but the only thing that's going to help her at all is for you to be part of her life again."

"It's not my choice. I didn't make it. If it were my choice, I would be back there in that hospital room with her."

"I know you want to be here, but don't take a chance. Arnell could be closer than what we think, and we don't want to spook him."

"I want him. If I get the chance, he's going down."

"Where are you now? Are you still in Tennessee?"

"Yes, but I'll be leaving soon."

"Why?"

"I'm just checking on a few things between here and home."

"Carter, don't come. If someone catches you, we're done."

"Don't panic. I'm where I'm supposed to be. I'm following a lead. I just want to make sure it isn't him before I contact anyone for assistance."

45

"Well, don't try to be Superman. The man's dangerous. He wouldn't think twice about killing you."

"I promise, Sergeant Mason, I'll do what I'm told."

"Gee, that's the second time I've been called that of late."

Carter laughed at the statement. "Let me guess, are you ordering my wife around?"

"Yeah, she isn't real happy about it."

"She can be stubborn. Forgot to fill you in on that little detail."

"Thanks. First, your sister. Now your wife. I'm living in an estrogen ocean here. You better turn up something soon."

"Don't worry. I intend on getting this over quickly. Take care of my girls. I'm counting on you."

"Isn't that what a mean sergeant-type brother-in-law's supposed to do?"

"I'll contact you soon. Let me know about Bella and Molly."

"Sure. Later."

Carter had taken the cell and laid it on the table. Isabella would eventually figure this out if she thought he was still alive. She was smart. When she found certain items missing, eventually, she would put it together: one, his keys; two, his driver's license; three, his cell phone; and a few odds and ends that maybe she wouldn't have noticed. No one had thought to make sure he had a second cell and a spare driver's license and keys. The whole setup had been so fast, there hadn't been time for provisions. He was sure they would have come up with some explanation if questions were asked. He almost wished she had contacted him by accident sometime, just so he could hear her voice. He was missing one of the most precious moments in life because of what was going on, not to mention he was worried about the added stress she was under. All he could do for now was to pray for her and for this nightmare to be over for the both of them.

He had to accept that in his heart God knew what he was doing, even though being separated from his family was killing him. His little girl must wonder why he hadn't come home. She couldn't understand death. She knew he wasn't there anymore, just as she understood that Andrea wasn't there. The pain on Isabella's face was a constant reminder to him what this particular assignment had caused in his family. He was concerned about his mother, father, and sister and how they were doing. His mother had to be medicated from what he had understood from what few times he had talked to Landon. He had been his only contact with them. He hadn't been able to talk to any of them, even though he had shown up at a couple of things. The department didn't allow for it, and he was sure Landon had kept it to himself. If he hadn't, it would have meant probation and possible dismissal from the force. At this point, he didn't care. He just wanted this over.

Most nights here were spent by playing the piano or looking at some old photographs that Landon had managed to copy for him and brought to the cabin. The one he kept the closest was one of him and Isabella on their wedding day. He had traced that picture hundreds of times in the time that he had been here. The hurt was still the same, never knowing when this might end and knowing that she was living her life without him. He turned the ring on his finger and looked at the detailing in it. It had been special to her from the moment she had given it to him. He would never forget the night it was placed on his ring finger. She had promised to be his and, even in the hardest of times, had kept her word. It had held the promise of love and protection, both for her and his Creator that had brought her to him. Their wedding night had not been ideal, but they had grown together since then, and the feelings of fear and shame on Isabella's part were starting to give way. He himself had held issues because of Andrews; Andrea had unfortunately seen a lot of the pain and anger from that situation. He still carried some of the pain and shame of that time in his life. Even after all the counseling he had and the time he had spent with Pastor Conley, the fact remained that his youth had been stolen from him along with its innocence. He had been part of a nightmare that he didn't think he would ever recover from.

It came back to God, Andrea, and her understanding—loving him even when she was dying. Each time he had touched her, he saw the monster that had forced him into his sexual desires. He had been just a child, but it had left a lifetime of scars behind. He knew exactly what Isabella had gone through because he was sure that if it had been the same man, he knew the mind games he could play. He also knew the physical and emotional pain he was able to inflict. He himself had been a character in his fantasy of sexual distortion. It had been no wonder he had threatened to end it, to end his life. It had been by the grace of God that it hadn't happened and by Andrea's insistence of going to church and getting things right before God. She had told him that God was the only help he needed. He had been to multiple therapists and medical doctors, but none of them had been able to take the pain away that he had carried around in his heart. God had taken it away when he became his. It hadn't been instant, but he knew that everything that had happened before had been automatically erased and he was to live a new life in him.

Finding Arnell had nothing to do with revenge. It was about justice, justice for the teens that he had killed and the ones that still lived in bondage under him. It was also for the protection of his family. Bella may then feel safe once he was behind bars.

"Mrs. Blake, are you ready to go home?" Dr. Carley's voice had brought me back from a daze, blankly looking out of my hospital room window.

"Yes, anytime."

"There doesn't seem to be any further threat to the baby, so I'm letting you go home. I do suggest that you take some time off for a while, perhaps FMLA. You have been through a lot since the announcement of your pregnancy, and the baby doesn't need the added stress."

"So what do you suggest?"

Landon strode into the room as Dr. Carley made her suggestion and sat down in the hardback chair at the foot of my bed.

"I suggest that you take some time and get away from your job and from the area that is a reminder of all the

49

pain from the last few weeks. Mind that it's only a suggestion, but you do need to take it easy for a while."

Landon spoke up with sternness, enough that I knew he meant it. "She'll do it, and I'll see she does."

Looking at him like a rebellious teen, it was done, and I knew it.

"Well, it seems things will be taken care of. I do suggest, if you go somewhere other than home, that you make sure you have a caregiver setup. With your history and the threat of this past couple of days, I wouldn't take it lightly. Isabella, I'll see you in a week, sooner if needed. Make sure you get your rest and that you are eating. I know it can be difficult when your stomach is upset, so eat something small about every two to three hours if you have to. You can take Tylenol and Motrin if you have to, and make sure you take your prenatal vitamins. I'll give the nurse a list of dos and don'ts for you, and you can always call the prenatal nurse. Take care of yourself."

She stood to leave and shook my hand, then Landon's. "Mr. Mason, see to it she does these things and she will have a happy, healthy baby. Take care." She smiled and left us.

Landon clapped his hands and rubbed his hands together. "Well, Izzy, let's go home."

"Wait a minute. How do you get to dictate what I can and cannot do?"

He looked at me solemnly. "Because Carter can't, and I promised him I would see that you were taken care of. I intend on honoring that request. Now I suggest you do as I ask and honor your husband's wishes."

He knew that was all it would take, and it wasn't fair. Carter was all I thought of, and if that was one of his last requests, I had to listen to him. The nurse walked in the room in an unhurried manner and went over each detail before she would allow me to leave. She removed the IV and insisted that I ride down to the truck, even though I was perfectly fine with walking. I felt like an invalid. No matter what, when Landon's back was turned, I would do what I needed to do to take care of my family. I loved Landon for who he was and his good intentions, but I couldn't live under a microscope for the next six months.

On the way home, I kept thinking that had Carter been here and this had happened, it wouldn't have been any different. It had already gotten to the point that he didn't want me to lift a finger. Of course, I had. I had still been working and doing the normal cooking and cleaning. It was more of a pleasure than it was now; it had been more for him. Anything that I did was for my love for him.

Easter was coming within a week, and I hated to see it come and go without the presence of my husband. Each special day and holiday just served more of a reminder that he wasn't there. Walking into the house, the silence was deafening. There was nothing. The only sound was the slight click of the wall clock, and it made a hum so low, it sounded haunting. Walking around my home, it felt cold and empty. Walking back to the bedroom we shared was painful as it had been the day I was told he was gone. I still hadn't touched his belongings that he had on him that night, still wrapped in a bag after all this time. I guess I should have checked the firearm he had on him. It could have been loaded. I shuddered at the very thought that Molly could have gotten hold of it.

Picking it up from the bag, I checked that the chamber was empty. It had been unloaded. Thank God for that. Picking up the remaining pieces, I sat down on the edge of our bed and took each item out. I placed his shoes on the bed beside me and stared at the remaining items, then shook the bag. His keys were missing. That was odd. He wouldn't have been able to drive without them. Looking through what remained, his cell phone wasn't among his belongings. It was something he never went without, and he had been fanatical about carrying it since he found I was pregnant.

"Izzy, I think I have everything."

I never said a word. I just studied what lay there on the bed beside me.

"Izzy?"

I could hear his footsteps approaching the door as I looked at the few things I had left from that night.

CHAPTER THREE

The day dawned as Carter sat at the cabin, looking out on to the mountains. It was a warm spring day as he sat in the wooden rocker sipping on his coffee, still steaming. The morning was bright as the sun rose slow like a ball of fire. It had been weeks since he had seen Isabella, but he had made progress on tracking Arnell. He seemed to be in the same area he had been. At least the activity was still there. If the activity was still present, more than likely, so was he. It hadn't taken long for Carter to put things together, although he wasn't sure how Isabella fit into the picture, unless, well, that just didn't make sense.

Last night, he had been up late going through files and was sure of one thing. Arnell was Cooper's father, and if Isabella was his sister, it wouldn't be a good situation. No wonder there had been issues. He couldn't be certain, without the written documents of Cooper and Isabella's birth. He would contact Landon later in the day when he knew he would be able to talk to him freely. He couldn't take a chance on someone overhearing their conversation.

If what he was putting together was true, it could be potentially devastating to Isabella. He was sure she knew, and that was part of what was being blocked from her memory. To think Arnell was her own father and he had forced Cooper to have sexual relations with her. Arnell having done this to his daughter was disturbing enough without adding in the fact he forced his son into it. It happened; he knew. If Arnell Andrews was the same man that had taken him and Beth, he was a cruel, evil man, and destruction followed him. He had to be part of all of this. It made sense more now than it ever had.

The idea of telling Isabella the truth, especially now, was dangerous. She had intended to talk to her mother about past events and about Cooper Lee. She obviously had not seen Cooper in years and hadn't put it together that Beth had been married to her brother. He had been the one who had beaten her in a drunken rage. Carter had hated what he had done to Beth, but at least he understood a little more of where the anger came from.

Cooper was on a path of destruction with no way out. The storm was coming in large waves, but he had to find a way to still the thundering in her heart as well as his own. If what he had thought was true, Cooper was as much a victim as Bella had been. No wonder his life was so screwed up and had become derailed. He knew the feeling of that, the feeling of being lost and not knowing how to stop feeling like he was on a runaway locomotive.

Rubbing his hand across his unshaven face, he felt the harsh stubble of at least two days' growth. It haunted him each time he thought of Cooper and Isabella being forced by Arnell. That was bad enough, but if it was her own father abusing her, it was worse. There were so many ifs and scenarios in this, it was unbelievable. He kind of knew what had happened now. Where was he, and how would he stop him?

His thoughts drifted to one other person connected to this disaster, Ryan Bentley. He had been part of Isabella's life then and was one of those who had engineered a way out for her. Granted, what Cooper had done to get her out was bad enough, but Carter himself had inflicted the most pain on her. Searching information on Ryan Bentley, he found he was a professor at the University of Knoxville. Maybe it was time to pay Mr. Bentley a visit. He would never know who he was, but then if Andrews found out he was part of the plan to get Bella away from him, he was in just as much danger as she had been. Standing and pacing the porch, Carter began to think about the current situation. The more he thought about it, the more he knew he was going to need protection for him too, if nothing else, for Isabella's sake. He had been her friend, and she would never forgive him if he knew he was in danger and stood by doing nothing. When she heard the whole story, she may leave him anyway. It was a long time ago, and poor choices on his part were made to aid his fix. If being abused wasn't enough to haunt him, the fallout was going to catch up with him too.

Silently, he prayed for God's forgiveness and for Isabella's. As much as he loved her, he understood if she ended up despising him. As long as God would allow it, he would fight for his wife. He had a daughter and an unborn son or daughter to think about. Eventually, the truth would have to be told. There were two ways of going about trying to find the paternity of Jenna, and that was exhuming her or hunting the medical records. DNA was reliable, but it would take Isabella's signature to have it done. Medical records could, however, show some markers of both parents' history. It wasn't accurate, but it did help. It was heartbreaking to him that he and Isabella could have conceived a child approximately six years prior and that she was now gone. He hadn't got to touch her or see her little face. He didn't get to hold her. Back then, he was concerned with one thing, and that was him. His main concern back then was making the pain go away with any drug he could get his hands on. OxyContin and oxycodone were his choice, but he had taken hydrocodone, Valium, and alcohol, mostly mixed drinks and straight whiskey from the bottle. It hadn't been anything to finish off a bottle in a couple of hours. It numbed him to every feeling and detail of his life, and he liked it that way. Most of the time, he didn't know how he had gotten home. After he and Andrea had married, he still used for some time. He was grateful that his abuse hadn't affected Molly.

He hadn't touched a pill for at least two years and was now working on three. He no longer had the craving for them. Thank God for that. The night he had broken down to a man he had not recognized was the first time he had anything harder than champagne, and that was rare since he had been in rehab. He wasn't sure why he had resorted to it that night other than feeling the loss of control, and he hated the feeling. He had that as a child and didn't like the idea that he had no control over a situation. He dealt with it the best way he knew at the time. It had been the wrong choice, and he knew it when he took the first drink from the glass. He had been weak that night and had hated himself for it. He knew better than to try and stand on his own.

The cell buzzed in his shirt pocket, and he picked up quickly. "Yeah, Blake," he answered sternly.

"Carter, we have a problem," Landon's voice was at unease.

"What's going on?" Carter's jaw clenched, waiting for an answer.

"You're not going to believe this one. Isabella is on to us. After all the time she let your things sit in that belongings bag, she went through them last night. She discovered that your keys and cell phone are gone."

Carter couldn't help but smile at her discovery. He knew it meant trouble, but his wife was some woman, and he knew she wouldn't stop if she thought there was any chance. "What did you tell her?"

"I made an excuse that maybe those pieces were still at the hospital or at the department, at least your cell phone, but she hasn't bought it. I swear that woman has a nose on her like a bloodhound."

He wanted to laugh, but all it would do was rattle Landon's cage further. "Calm down. I'll have duplicates made of my keys and buy a new cell phone. I'll express them to you. Both items will be at the office in the morning."

"What about your license? She hasn't discovered it's gone yet, but she will."

"You can get a duplicate out of my desk. It's for the company car, but she won't be able to tell the difference. It doesn't look any different."

"Blake, your wife is a piece of work. I can't keep up with her. I don't know how in the world Peirce does it! At least he has cameras in the house. He can stay a step ahead of her most of the time. I'm surprised she hasn't found them yet or the tracking in her cell phone."

He couldn't stand it any longer. He had to laugh. "Yeah, she's a smart woman. I have to give her credit. I can't believe she isn't out looking for Andrews herself. If she knew his last name, she probably would." He chuckled at the thought.

"Carter, this is serious. Isabella is not like anyone I have ever met."

"Calm down. Calm down. She's only going to go so far, then it will stop, I promise you. My wife has too much on her plate right now, and you need to keep her calm and quiet."

"There's where you're wrong. Isabella was put off on FMLA for a while by her doctor. It's hard to tell what she will get into."

"Landon, you're worse than some woman. Let it go. I'll take care of it."

"If you saw the determination in her eyes, you wouldn't wonder why I'm so off balance."

"I know you can handle it. I wish I was there, but I can't. I would love to be there for her. That's the whole thing. She's grabbing at straws. Get her into therapy before she does something terribly wrong. Take her to Roxie, Dr. Bentley, or the pastor. She needs to be distracted and needs time to deal with what's going on. She's had a loss. Granted, it isn't real, but until she knows that, it has to be dealt with. Isabella has been through a lot, and this was not the time for Brooks to send me on assignment.

"Before I go, I want you to check into some things. I'll do what I can from this end, but you need to get a man on Ryan Bentley. He helped get Bella out of the hell she was in, and if Andrews knows that, he'll come after him. I'm making arrangements to talk to him myself."

"Carter, you're on dangerous ground. If he figures out who you are, your cover is blown."

"Don't worry about it. I have a plan. I still have my dress blues and a different ID. He'll never know who it is. I need to find out what he knows and get him under protection. If that means putting him in protective custody, I'll have it done. He's a witness we can't afford to lose. Where is Bella?"

Landon took in a deep breath and let it escape slowly. "Peirce took her out for a while, or I wouldn't be able to talk to you freely. They're due back soon. She goes to the academy for self-defense and firearm practice."

"You mean she still goes to see Gus? I thought she quit going."

"Surprise! She hasn't. I told her not to be doing any throws, Gus knows she's pregnant. He's smart enough not to let her get into something that would hurt her. At least it keeps her busy, and while she's there, I can breathe a little."

"That's good, I guess. Just don't let her do something to jeopardize herself or the baby. I know she's headstrong, and it's difficult to get her to do something when she gets her mind set on it."

"Dear god, you're telling me. I didn't think I was going to get to put your things away before she found something else wasn't there."

"I appreciate that you're taking care of her. I know she can be a handful. It takes a lot of time away from Beth and Gavin. I'm sure that's hard on Beth."

"She's okay. She understands. Besides, she knows it's not going to be forever. There are times I think I'm more married to Isabella than I am to your sister. Believe me, it's been a rough ride, bro. You need to wrap this up and get home."

Carter ran his fingers through his hair and tried to keep his composure. He wanted to go home to Bella. It certainly hadn't been easy. "I hope to be home soon. Do me a favor and try again with Brooks. I really miss my wife."

"I can't believe it. You have it so bad for her. She consumes you, doesn't she?"

"You could say that."

"I'm glad you found someone. Andrea would have been happy for you."

"Yeah," was all he could say.

The door rattled behind Landon, and he quickly wrapped his conversation. "I better go. Someone's coming. I'll call you later with the information."

"Sure.

Walking into the living room, I laid my jacket and purse down on the chair. Landon had slid his cell phone into the inside pocket of his jacket. He had just finished a call more than likely from the office. "You finished? I could go in the other room for a while."

"No," he answered. Appearing more nervous than usual, he was normally pretty collected. "I'm finished, just a few calls to the office, nothing major."

"Where's Molly?"

"She's with Mrs. Freeman. She had called and asked if Molly wanted to make cookies with her, and of course, Molly wanted to." He grinned. It was the first normal reaction I had seen from him since I came in.

"Mrs. Blake, I'll be going," Peirce had graciously backed off when he had seen Landon there. "If you need anything further, please call. I'll be close."

"Of course." Peirce turned and walked from the room, closing the door behind him.

"Are you sure everything's okay? You seem a little on edge today."

"I'm fine. I told you, just simple things to deal with today. Did you, uh, get your workout in with Gus?"

"Yes, but he took it way too easy on me, thanks to you."

"Izzy, you're pregnant. You could have lost that little guy. My job is to protect you. Like it or not, that is exactly what I'm going to do. We're family, and I can be as stubborn as you are."

I had to smile at him, but I could feel a little anger rise in me. I felt more like a child than a widow with two children. "You have no idea. I'm a single mother now, and I'm going to do what it takes to bring my children up to the standard I feel Carter would have wanted. I'm completely capable of taking care of myself.'

"Whoa, woman, don't get testy. I'm doing a friend a favor in taking care of you. I didn't once say that you weren't capable of caring for yourself. At least accept the extra help you have graciously. No matter what you think of me and the situation, you're still my sister-in-law, and I love you." He walked over, taking me by the shoulders, and looked me directly in the eyes. "I know you have been in a lot of pain, and there is a lot of anger. I understand that totally, but you need to let the family help you, at least for now. You have Molly and another little one to think of. We aren't trying to step on your toes. Izzy, your family loves you. Don't turn them away. They're hurting too."

I fell into his arms and sobbed as he stroked my hair. His arms felt reassuring to me, but I missed my husband's arms wrapped around me. There would never be anyone else for me. My heart belonged to him.

"We love you, Izzy, all of us. Don't shut us out. You've been trying so hard, but I know you're not doing as well as you have let on. Don't you think I see you when you think no one is watching? I see you when you think I'm not looking, tracing his picture with your finger, holding on to that shirt of his like it's a life preserver. The pain will end soon, I promise you that. When it does, accept it for what it is. Carter loves you, loved you, for the strong, independent person you have become."

My body shook in his arms. "I love him and I miss him. With every breath in my body, I miss him. I want him back so much. He's never coming back to me. He's never going to be here to put Molly to bed or kiss our baby's precious little face. He'll never talk to me or touch me again. I hurt, Landon. Every fiber in my body hurts." My body trembled. I tried hard to control it. I didn't have Carter to calm me any longer. I had to deal with it myself, and it was crushing me. "I feel like I'm dead, like an empty shell walking around. There is nothing real about me anymore. I remember bits of a past that may or may not exist. Did you know I remember pieces of a place that I don't remember or could begin to place where or what it is? My husband was there, I'm sure of it. I can't see his face, but I remember the laugh. The laugh the man had that led me into a large room where I watched him dance had my husband's laugh. I never met him until the night of the car crash, so tell me how he could have been in this place, wherever it is. My family won't help me in what I have discovered. Do you have any idea how frustrating and painful that is? To hear Molly cry every night because her father isn't there to tuck her in and kiss her good night? Going into work is worse because every time I go, I know that's where he took his last breath. That's the last place I got to see him, and I didn't tell him goodbye because I was angry with him."

I felt Landon's body tense as he continued to hold me next to him. "I don't know what to tell you, Izzy. All we can do is to live one day at a time. If it means one hour at a time or minute at a time, we don't have a choice."

Wiping my face, I pushed my hair behind my ears and backed off from Landon. "I've made a decision. I think you should know. I didn't tell you before because I knew you would try to talk me out of it. Monday morning at 7:00 a.m., I will start classes for my criminal justice degree. I'm going after him, and when I find him, he's good as dead." My jaws clenched, and my hands drew into a fist. "He's taken enough away from me, and I'm going after him."

Landon stood back in shock at what I had just delivered and shook his head. "Bella, are you out of your mind? You can't do the physical training now with a baby in tow. Besides, you have to think of them. What happens to them if you go out and get yourself killed?"

"I have no intention of letting him have the upper hand." In staccato, I made it clear. "I will win." With clenched fist at my side, I looked him in the eye, not backing down. "He will pay for everything he has done to me and my family. The physical part of the program doesn't start until January. I'll have plenty of time to qualify."

Landon pulled back and rubbed the back of his neck and started toward the living room window. Standing, looking out onto the yard, he dropped his hands to his waist, with his back remaining toward me and shaking his head. "Izzy, I can't tell you what to do, but this bitterness you're harboring isn't going to make things better. It's just going to tear you apart." His voice was soft and despondent, his tone equal. "I can only tell you that you need to think of your family first. Molly needs you and so does that little baby you're carrying. You need to think long and hard about what you're getting into. It isn't easy."

"I've never had it easy, Landon. I can't remember ever having it easy." I sounded robotic. My voice was monotone and determined. I had made my choice. Giving up was not a choice I had. One way or another, Arnell was going to be brought in, and I would see justice served on him. Everything I was and had ever been was wrapped up in his sorry excuse for a life. "I want this. I know it isn't easy, but it's what I need to close this chapter in my life. I need it for me, I need it for my children, but most of all, I need it for my husband, who can longer speak for himself. I hope that someday you will be able to understand that."

Landon shook his head and threw his head back and took a sharp exaggerated breath. Frustration was evident, even though his back remained to me. He turned and faced me, looking at me like he was heartsick with my decision. "Isabella, I understand what you're feeling, but don't give up on your nursing career. Do me a favor, and think about this. You have until Monday. Even then, you don't have to continue to pursue it. You're good at what you do. People need you. You're their angel when they're in trouble. They trust you to help them. You brought Carter back from the grave. He could have died, but you were there for him. You took care of him and showed him what a compassionate, loving soul you have through your nursing. You stayed with him and took care of him when you didn't have to. I watched you with him, or have you forgotten? He fell in love with you there. Don't look at it as if that is where he died. Look at it as it's where he lived."

Walking closer to me, he leaned his head to the side, and his expression was that of true pain. "If you decide to do this, I will do what I can to help. I just don't want you to make a mistake. Look up all that being an officer is and what it entails. Look at what you could physically and mentally go through and choose wisely." Leaning in, he kissed my cheek. "I need to see about Molly. She should be about ready to come home." I nodded my head, and he walked out the door. Letting out a sigh, I walked to the bedroom, picking up Carter's picture on the way. Sitting down on the edge of the bed, I looked at it, hoping that he could talk to me. What would he do if he were me? Would he do this in hopes of setting things right, to make this man pay for the pain he has inflicted on our family? Well, that was a no-brainer. He would do whatever he had to do to bring Arnell in. I didn't have to think twice about it. He would take whatever steps he had to bring him down. He had been killed by the man he was hunting because of what he had done to me and the teens that had suffered at his hand.

My favorite picture of him had him in a black dinner jacket and black dress pants with his white linen shirt. He had been to a formal dinner of some sort and had been sitting there as a passing photographer had asked to take his picture. He had a rough beard of a few days' growth. It had been taken a few months after Andrea's death, and he had gone only because it had been business related. His beautiful eyes had shown the most magnificent shade of blue and his dark hair askew as if he had been running his hands through it.

I traced my finger along the edge of his image. If only I could touch him again. All I could do was close my eyes and imagine he was there. "I wish you were here. I miss you so much. You can't imagine how lost I have been without you. I promise you I will find Arnell, and when I do, he's going to pay for everything that has happened to us. I'll never let go. I'll never let you go."

Holding the picture to my chest, I closed my eyes and tried to imagine him in front of me. His smile and his piercing blue eyes, feeling his touch, I longed for it. At times I could swear he was still with me, feeling his arms wrap around me at night when I lay down in our bed. Looking over to where he slept, I had slowly opened my

66

eyes, only being disappointed to find he wasn't there. All I had was our children and our home. If it meant working day and night to protect them, I would. I heard a voice rush through me, a voice that was familiar and sweet. "Pray, Bella. Pray for the answer. It will come." Carter's voice came to me crystal clear. God knew what I was going through, and he would lead me. The answer lay with him. It was getting increasingly difficult to get on my knees, but if I could just make the attempt. Slowly, I found my way to my knees beside our bed and tried to pray, but the words weren't coming. The tears found their way down my cheeks and fell onto the quilt. "God, I'm so unsettled without him. My heart breaks every day. I'm not sure what I am to do, but I don't want to make the wrong decision for my family. I don't want to make a choice that is going to be against what you want for me and my family. I don't want the pain of losing him to rule my thinking because if it did, I would be out for revenge. That isn't what I want. The man needs to be brought to justice, and it isn't my right to end his life, even though that's what I want in my heart. Forgive me for wanting that.

"My heart is so shattered, I can't begin to pick up the pieces, but I know that you can. Carter told me that you helped him when he felt he had no chance at a life again after Andrea. Thank you for the time you gave us. I know I'm not supposed to question why things happen or why he's gone, but I wish I knew. I'm trying to understand and to go on. Please help me to take care of the family that he loved so much, and help me to keep him safe in my heart. I never want to forget what he has done for me and that he loved me. I never want to forget his face, his laugh, his touch, or his heart that he had for you. I want to honor you through my life. Please show me how." My body shook as I remained on my knees and folded my arms on the bed and lay my head on them and cried. I promised myself that this was the last time that I would cry. Carter would have hated that I was so unhappy.

I wasn't exactly comfortable where I was, but God was calming my heart. The warmth covered me from the top of my head to the bottom of my feet. He allowed me to see Carter and me together during the short time we had been together, happy wonderful times: being in the park, the first time he kissed me, and during our wedding as I walked down the aisle to him.

I heard a small rustle beside me that brought me from my thoughts. Looking to my side, I see the small figure of Molly, now on her knees beside me with her hands folded, her eyes closed. She was silent as she sat there beside me. He would have been so proud of his daughter. She was smart, gentle, and had a heart for God. There was no question that she understood that she had a direct line to heaven. She talked to God like he was standing in front of her and like she was talking to a friend.

Looking through the doorway, Landon stood watching. I had rarely seen a tear escape the man, but a tear slid down his face, which was expressionless. I held a finger to my lips for him not to disturb her. He bowed his head and prayed silently.

The sun rose as it did every day, and I felt as hurt and helpless as before. I hated the feeling and was determined in my mind that I would survive any way I could. It was Easter Sunday, and I had spent the last couple of hours preparing for church and supper afterward. We had planned for the kids to have an egg hunt. Even if it was a bit one-sided, they would have their candy. It was an attempt at trying to make the day as normal as possible. It wouldn't be easy, but normal was what was needed. Our lives needed to have some stability.

Molly came from her room, dragging her blanket with her, and planted herself on the couch. Placing her thumb in her mouth, she took the hand she held her blanket in and twirled her hair around her finger. She had been very quiet, and it was a little concerning for a three-year-old not to be bouncing around. It had been almost two months since Carter had passed away, and Molly still hadn't been herself. On occasion, you could see a glimpse of normal, but it had become rare. I sat down beside her and ran my fingers through her long hair.

"What's wrong, Tink?" She buried her head into my arm. "Don't you feel good?"

"Me okay." She wiggled a little closer.

Picking her up, I sat her on my lap, and she leaned into me. It wouldn't be long before I didn't have much lap for her to get in. "You miss Daddy?" She shook her head but never said a word. "We shouldn't be sad for Daddy, Tink. He's happy where he is. He's with your Mommy Andrea, my baby Jenna, and Jesus. He's singing with the angels and playing in the river, and he gets to see Jesus and talk to him face to face."

69

"Me know."

"Then what's wrong, honey?"

"Me not want you to cry, Mommy. It makes me sad. Daddy not with Mommy Andrea. Me see her. She plays with me sometimes. He not with her, but her say him okay."

"You saw your Mommy Andrea? When did you see her, baby?"

"Wast night. Her come play with me. Her tell me Daddy okay."

"Oh, okay." I rocked her for a short time then helped her get dressed for church. She looked so pretty in her little mint-green dress. I had taken her shopping for a dress, and she spun around, allowing the skirt to fly around her. Her white ruffled socks hung over the edge of her patent leather shoes, and her ribbons bounced as she skipped around the room. I had dressed for the service and was waiting for Quentin when the telephone rang. I started to answer it, but by the time I had gotten to it, the line went dead. At that moment, the doorbell rang, and I walked quickly across the floor to answer it. It was our ride, but I was surprised to find Landon instead of my watchdog. His smile was a blessing to me. I didn't need to be chauffeured around, but for weeks, I was under constant watch of Landon or Quentin. If I had to have a guard, I guess I would rather opt for my brother-in-law.

He stood in the doorway, dressed smartly in his navy-blue dress slacks, pink polo, and a navy-blue jacket. He pulled his sunglasses from his face and placed them on his head. "You ready to go, Izzy?"

70

"Let me get Molly and we'll go." Turning, I see Molly bouncing into the room, running at Landon.

"Wandon," she squealed with glee at the sight of him. He bent down to catch her up in his arms. He raised her above his head and wiggled her back and forth. She laughed more than I had seen her do in weeks.

"Tink, you look beautiful." She laughed and looked at Landon and grabbed his face with her hands, making him pucker. She kissed him with a loud smack of her lips. Bobbing her head up and down, looking at him, she smiled brightly. "You buteful too." She laughed. Landon couldn't help but laugh out loud at her.

"Thank you, Tink. I always knew you had good taste."

Just then, the telephone rang again. Stepping over, I took the phone from the cradle it rested on. "Hello." The line cracked and popped without a voice. "Hello. Is someone there?" I heard a harsh breath rise before anyone answered me. "Is someone there?" The cracking and popping stopped, and a familiar voice came through the line.

"Isabella, my favorite boy toy. Too bad your husband got in the way. He had been such a good customer too."

"Look, I don't know who you are, but you're a sick bastard." Landon jumped to me, and I retained the telephone as he stood there. My hands shook as this man laughed cruelly on the other end.

"Don't get so testy. I just wanted to catch up and let you know my time with you isn't over. Now that at least one of your protectors is gone, it makes it a little easier."

71

My jaw clenched, and my throat tightened with anger. "You make one step toward me or my family, and I assure you that it will be the last step you ever take."

"Come on, honey. I'm just having a little fun. Geez, you're spunkier than you used to be. I like it. You actually grew a pair, didn't you?"

"Make no mistake. I will hunt you down, and when I do, you're good as dead." My hands gripped the phone tightly, and I slammed it down on the cradle, making the table rock as I did. Landon looked at me in shock, like he had never seen me before. Never missing a beat, I looked at him. Feeling the heat rise from my face, I turned to walk out of the room. Without looking back, I walked into the bedroom and picked up my handgun and loaded it, placing it in my purse. He wasn't coming near me or my daughter. I would kill him first. This just lit a fire under me, and I knew my temper was going to give way to rage if I didn't take hold of it. Taking a couple of breaths, I stood collecting myself and walked back into the living room where I found Landon standing with Molly in front of him. Looking at him, I smiled as if nothing had happened. "Shall we go?"

"Izzy, you're not serious."

"About what, going to church? Of course, I'm going. It's Easter, and I'm looking forward to the service and spending the day with my family."

"That's not what I meant, and you know it."

I fidgeted with my purse and gloves and continued to grin at him like a Cheshire cat. "I know what you meant. Let's not talk about it. I want to go out and enjoy this spring day with the most important people in my life."

"He threatened you, didn't he?"

"I took care of it, and I intend on taking care of it further, so can we please go?"

He didn't say another word. As he turned to go out the door, I saw the holster peek from under his jacket. He was prepared, so he knew something was going down. I rarely had seen him pack his gun when he was off duty. One thing was for certain: I wasn't afraid of this man any longer. I was armed, I had protection from the police force, and I had God. Either way, it looked like I was a winner. I was no longer helpless to the point I had to do whatever this man pleased. My police career starts now whether I'm in training or not. Picking up Molly, she looked over his shoulder with a smile on her face. He carried her to the car and placed her into the waiting car seat. Opening the door, I slid in beside her, and she was jumping up and down, singing "Jesus Loves Me."

Church was going to be totally different for her. We hadn't been back since Carter had passed away, and she was used to having him hold her or being able to stand between us. She had also turned to an age where she could go to Sunday school with the other children. I wasn't sure if she would go. She hadn't been separated from me for long since she had lost her father. She had spent some time with Mrs. Freeman and her grandparents but had never been totally out of my sight since before Carter's death.

The trip took all of a half hour, and we were pouring out of the SUV as Landon unhooked Gavin and placed him in Beth's arms and turned to unbuckle Molly. He lifted her into the air and wiggled her. She laughed loudly and stuck her arms out like she was flying. After kissing her, he placed her on her feet. Running over to me, she took my hand and walked into the church as Landon had held the door open for his family. Beth carried a sleeping Gavin in her arms as I followed with Molly close by my side. Landon shook hands with the members as we walked into the sanctuary. As we walked in, others were talking, but as soon as they had seen us, they were deathly quiet. You could have heard a pin drop in the room. Picking up Molly, she wrapped her arms around my neck, and we were soon greeted by Pastor Conley. Landon stood behind us like a pillar supporting all of us.

"Isabella, how wonderful to see you. And, Ms. Molly, glad to have you back to church with us." He spoke with Beth and Landon as Molly and I made are way to our normal seat. Landon soon followed, sitting between Beth and me. All eyes were on us. I guess it did look a little strange that he was here with two women with two different children. Sitting between the two of us was odd, I guess, but I knew what he was doing, and I didn't mind the stares.

"Don't mind the stares, Izzy. They have no idea what all has happened. Besides"—he grinned from ear to ear—"I have two lovely ladies to escort, and it's my honor."

Molly piped up, "Free, Uncle Wandon."

He chuckled a little and pulled her in for a quick hug. "Yeah, that's right, three."

CHAPTER FOUR

The service seemed to have worn on for some time. Molly had gone on to Sunday school with the other children. I was glad that she had made the attempt. I could tell she wasn't exactly thrilled, but when I told her that I would be there when church was over, she seemed more content to go with them.

I had wanted to take more of a part at church, but things had not been easy, especially when I had walked in with Beth and Landon. Everyone had stopped to look at each of us. Some of them had known what had happened because they had been to Carter's funeral, but others I'm sure had no idea as to why Carter was not with us. I had asked Pastor Conley to address the congregation, but I wasn't sure as to what I would say. God had blessed us with what we had. Even though Carter was no longer a living part of us, he was still part of our lives.

As Pastor Conley finished his sermon, I sat there unmoving, feeling that all-too-familiar chill run through me. It was like a cold blast of air that hit me from time to time, and it left shivers running down my spine. It was as if someone were watching me, and I would turn to find no one there. He was here, though. I could feel his presence, the presence of the monster I had talked to earlier, and I would eventually have the justice I had demanded.

Pastor Conley closed his sermon and finished introducing me. "Most of you know Carter Blake is not with us today and hasn't been part of the congregation for some time. What some of you don't know is that he was killed in the line of duty. His wife Isabella is here today with their daughter and wanted to speak to the congregation today in the remaining few minutes we have." He looked across the congregation as it remained deathly quiet. Each face scanned the room, and some had automatically fallen onto us. "Isabella, if you're ready."

As I stood, my heart quickened, and Landon stood with me. He leaned over and took me by the shoulder and whispered to me, "You sure you want to do this, Izzy?" He had no idea that I was going to do this or what I was going to say. Holding on to him, I shook my head. "Do you want me to go with you?" Nodding my head yes, he started to guide me from the pew and down the long aisle. It seemed extraordinarily long, and we were more than middle ways down it. He had taken my elbow and walked along behind me. As we reached the podium, Pastor Conley stepped aside, giving me a small grin, covering the mic briefly.

"Isabella, are you okay to do this? You don't have to, you know. It doesn't have to be you. Landon or I can do this."

"No, thanks, Pastor. I really want to do this for him. A lot of his church family had no idea what had happened, and I think it should come from me."

Shaking his head, his small smile remained. "Of course, if that's what you want. Landon and I will support you however you like. Just let us know if it gets to be too much. You've been through a lot lately."

"It's okay, Pastor. I'll be fine."

Stepping back behind Landon, he handed the mic over to me. I wasn't sure what I wanted to say. I felt every emotion that could possibly be mentioned, but it wasn't going to be easy to speak of him even after the amount of time that elapsed. The pain was still raw and cut me like a knife. Looking down to the floor, I took in a breath as Landon supported me with his hand at the small of my back, the other holding on to my hand. Looking up at a sea of people looking at me then at each other, clearing my throat, I started to speak.

"In the light of the Easter season and what it means to each of us, I wanted to speak to you about my husband and what it would have meant for him to have been here today." Standing there fighting with each breath, I managed to keep my tears at bay. I wasn't going to cry. Crying was done, and it was time to move on. "Easter is a time of new beginning and of renewed life. Jesus rose from the grave so that, as sinners, we would be free. He paved a road for us to God the Father through his death, burial, and resurrection. My husband for some time had a difficult time teaching a stubborn, hardheaded woman to remember that no matter what happened to us, there was one person that would never abandon us, no matter what we had done or what had happened in our life. He gave me a gift, one of love and devotion. He also gave me the gift of God. On a regular basis, he shared with me his love for God. It was what his life was based on, and I'll never forget that. He died doing what he loved and protecting his family. He taught me how to love without fear, and I'll always be appreciative of that.

"Knowing that God knew me so well, he put a very determined but softhearted, loving man in my path. He knew what it would take for me, a very bitter and self-defeating person, to come to him and what type of man I needed to bring me there. I thank him daily for Carter and what he gave to me. He was a very caring and loving man, and sometimes I feel like I never appreciated him for who he was.

"Today, as we leave this sanctuary, I want you to stop and think about your god and your mentor, whoever that may be, whether it's a husband, wife, child, parent, or friend. Tell them what you think of them because there's no guarantee that you'll get another chance. If you walk away today without God, remember this: you have so many chances in this life, and the end comes. I found it happens quickly and without warning.

"Carter and I were expecting to spend the rest of our lives together raising our family. Just before he died, we found that we were expecting our first child. He looked forward to the birth and had planned every inch of the nursery down to each and every nail. In a few short hours, he was gone. Our child will never know him on this side of heaven, but the good Lord willing, he will know him someday. Either by our eternal life from death or on his return, we will see him.

"We have one life to live for God. Carter told me once that I had to make a choice, and it had to solely be my own, that he could never make that decision for me. He told me that when we die and enter into the next life, we will end up in one of two places: heaven or hell. I'll never forget him telling me that when that time came, he wanted to be able to walk the streets of gold with me. I have never forgotten that. So the choice is simple really—accept him or reject him. It's your choice. My choice is

God. He has become my comforter and friend since the passing of my husband. My message is simple: don't wait. Don't wait till it's too late. Someone is waiting for you. Who better to go to than God?"

Stepping back from the podium, I turned to Landon to see the tears stream down his face. "Come on, Izzy. Let's go home," he whispered. Taking me by the hand, he led me from the sanctuary followed by Beth and their son. Sunday school was just letting out as we reached the door, and Molly came bounding out straight to me. She looked at her uncle and back at me. I know she was questioning the tears on his face. She had never seen him cry. Picking her up, Landon took her into his arms and gave her a kiss. She placed her hands on both sides of his face and ran them down his cheeks, wiping them dry, and hugged him.

Carter ran the hill next to the cabin in Tennessee, attempting to take out some of the aggression that he had stored within himself. It had taken longer than he had thought it would in trying to track down and catch Arnell at his own game. The longer it took, the more he uncovered. The more he uncovered, the worse he felt.

He was unsure of too many things others had been dead on. He needed to meet with Bentley before something else happened. Ryan had taught at the University of Knoxville for the last three years, and that was three years too sedentary for Arnell put things together. He guessed that he had put things together, but it hadn't come down to the part to where Isabella was going to pose a threat of uncovering what had happened to her.

He had run so much that morning that his muscles had grown tired and ached under his weight. It had been nothing under normal circumstances for him to run to keep in shape, but he had been doing it more often lately, mostly to think and for the main fact there had been little to do but go through multiple files. Running was his release, and it felt good. Returning to the cabin at midday, he bent down over his body, placing his hands on his knees and stretching out over them. Catching his breath, he stood and took his shirt off and wiped his face as he walked back into the cabin.

It had hit him that it was Easter, and his girls would be getting ready to sit down to dinner with the family. It had been difficult for him to imagine the day they would spend without him. He himself had a hard time. He hated that he wasn't with them. Isabella was close to her fourth month of pregnancy, and he had missed all of it. Well, not exactly. He knew about every time she was sick because he ended up sick himself. The doctor said he could experience a lot of the same symptoms she had since it started from the beginning. For the most part, it had been fatigue, but he wasn't sure if it were from that or just mental stress that sent him to bed more than at night.

He had read to the point that he knew about what Isabella would have been experiencing at this point of her pregnancy. It wouldn't be long before she started to feel the baby move, and he wanted to be there when she actually experienced it. She would have been starting to

80

feel better by now, with less of the fatigue and morning sickness, being able to enjoy her pregnancy.

Shaking his head, he plopped down on the couch and ran his hands through his hair. What was he missing? Why hadn't he found Arnell, and why wasn't he making an attempt on Bella? Had they fooled him at all at coming out of hiding? There had to be a way to light a fire under this guy, and when he did, he would be waiting on him.

Standing up, he made his way to the shower and turned the water on just enough to warm it. It had been hot for this time of the year, and he needed to cool off. Looking into the mirror, his face was red and flushed from the strenuous workout he had put himself through. He had really pushed, but it hadn't put his family out of his mind.

The steam rose in the room, and he stepped in, letting the water refresh him. It did little good as far as washing away the aggravation of the time he had spent alone, but it was an attempt at relaxation.

He had done little of it since he had left her behind. He knew that Landon was more than capable of taking care of her, and Quentin was number 1 at what he does. He was retired from the military early because of a health condition, but he was well experienced in police work. He couldn't have entrusted his family to anyone more capable than his brother-in-law and Quentin.

Quentin was stern and quiet, but he knew exactly what to do in a crisis. He had worked with hostage situations in the military and was more than willing to take someone out if it meant saving someone else's life. He was a calm, cool, collected character, taking little nonsense, acting much more mature than his age. He had been handpicked for this job, and there was no doubt that he could perform his duties well.

Standing under the shower, he remembered times of him being at home and Bella standing with her arms wrapped around him. It brought a smile to his face when he remembered being here and her having him sit down so that she could shave him. He had enjoyed every bit of that. She had been standing over him, giving him a clear view of her attributes. She was purely all woman. The warmth of her body had covered him as she stood there. He thought of her standing against him as he ran his hands up and down her legs. That was one for the books. That had never happened before; he didn't mind the thought that she had pampered him. He felt more like a child and she was taking care of him, and it had made for pleasant memories.

Stepping from the shower, he wrapped the towel around his waist and looked back into the mirror, at the beard that had appeared. There were several days' growth, and he wasn't sure whether to shave or to leave it alone. It did add to his undercover work. He had also been fitted with glasses temporarily for that purpose. His shorter hair, beard, and glasses had changed his appearance somewhat, at least enough that maybe he wouldn't be recognized.

He ran his hand across his face and assessed it then decided only to trim it for now, feeling it may be for the best to keep his full beard. Izzy wouldn't recognize him if she had seen him. He had been buff before, but with the running he had been doing, he was more lean and muscular than before, his body more defined. With the shorter hair and glasses, he doubted that, if she ran into him on the street, she would have recognized him.

He quickly dressed and returned to the kitchen when his cell phone rang. Picking it up from the counter, he answered. Without a single word from Carter, Landon spoke quickly. "Carter, we need to talk."

Landon's voice remained steady, but he could tell there was something amiss from him as he addressed him.

"Landon, what is it? Is there something wrong with Bella?"

"Bella's fine. At least physically, she is. We need to figure out how to bring this character in, and in a hurry."

"You can't believe how much I want to do that. I've been going over files for days, hoping to find something to flush him out. So far, I've found nothing."

"Well, I think I've found your way out. He called Bella today. I'm sure it was him. Carter, you should have heard her."

"Do you think he's coming after her?" Carter sighed.

"He threatened her, I'm sure of it."

"Well, maybe this is going to come to an end quicker than we thought."

"Hang on, bro. That's not all."

"What do you mean that's not all? You're there, and Quentin is there to protect Bella."

"I mean Bella threatened him. She threatened him. She told him if he came anywhere near her or Molly, she would kill him. That was point blank from her. I think she really means it."

"Bella would never do it. She's a preserver of life."

"Carter, hold on. She's changed. She isn't the delicate flower you left behind a few months ago. Believe me, she's empowered herself."

"You can't be serious. Isabella would never hurt a fly." His voice reflected disbelief of how his wife had changed in such a short time.

"Losing you was enough to make her take notice."

"I can't believe my wife." He groaned as he ran his hand through his thick, unruly hair.

"There's more. So if you aren't sitting down, I think you better."

Carter sat down on the couch, taking his brother-in-law's advice. He took in a sharp breath and ran his fingers through his hair and laid his head back. "What has she done now?"

"Your dear, sweet, innocent wife has decided to give up her nursing career."

"Give it up for what?"

"Your preserver of life has opted for dress blues."

Answering in surprise, Carter couldn't believe what he was hearing. "What? You have to be kidding me."

"She starts Monday unless she changes her mind, which I doubt."

"She can't handle that, at least not now. She's four months pregnant. She can't tolerate the physical part of the training right now."

"No, she can't, but she can do the classes. She starts her first class at 7:00 a.m. on Monday morning."

"I can't believe her. Who has she become since I left?"

"She's pretty self-sufficient. She doesn't want anyone to help her do anything, and she wants to take Arnell out because of what he has done to her and you. I can't keep her from doing it. All I can do is to slow her down."

"Landon, she can't handle going to school and working full time. It's going to be too hard on her. Why does she have to be so hardheaded?"

Landon chuckled. "I told you she's a piece of work. Besides, that's what you liked about her in the first place. I know you well. You enjoy a challenge, and believe me, she is."

"If it gets out of hand, you know what to do, and I don't care what Brooks likes or doesn't. Let him fire me if he wants. I'm not going to let her push herself into the ground. She and my family are way more important to me than any job. Let someone else go after him."

"I hope you know what you're doing."

Carter covered his eyes briefly and then ran his hand down over his face, wondering what happened to his wife. A few months ago, she was stricken almost helpless by a man that had done all but destroy her. Now she was going after him. "I do. This has to end."

"Look, I'll do what I can. If I have to, I will make arrangements to get her away from it all together."

"Landon?" Her voice rang in the background as Carter listened, and it caused his heart to sink.

Carter could hear her voice in the background, and it warmed him instantly. "Take care of her. She means everything to me."

"Don't worry."

The ocean air blew through my hair as I sat on the beach watching as Molly made a castle next to the shore. It was relaxing sitting there, listening to the gulls as they flew over. The rumble of the sea as it crashed into the shore only added to the peace I felt. The warm spring sun beamed down on me, giving me a renewed life. I felt better now than I had felt in months. Well, at least I felt better physically. On the mental aspect, it was a whole different ball game. Who was I kidding? I wasn't any better without him than I had been on day 1. I still sat hoping that I would wake up from this nightmare.

"Izzy, you okay?"

Landon sat down beside me and watched Molly as she played. Crossing his arms over his knees, he stared out into the ocean.

"Yeah, just remembering it isn't always pleasant. I don't know that I will ever get over him." It had come out of my mouth emotionlessly. Anything that seemed to come from me was without color or emotion these days. The things that should have been happy moments weren't any more than the ordinary days. I had tried to make a better show in front of Molly for her sake, but when I was out of view, my mood sank lower each day. The raging hormones from pregnancy hadn't helped. I had my family, Landon, and Lilly, but it wasn't Carter. I didn't really have anyone to support me, to give me what I needed. I needed my husband, and he was no longer there. Landon was the closest that I had to him. Taking so much of his time, it wasn't good for him or Beth. Beth and Gavin needed him more than Molly and I. I had thought of getting away for a couple of days before I started back into my life. Maybe I needed to get away long enough to think about my next move. I wanted to get started on Monday, but I wanted to make sure I was making the right decision.

"You know you can talk to me anytime, Izzy, if you need to. I'm always here for you."

"I know, but you have a family and you need to spend time with them. Most of the last month you have spent with me, I'm okay. Eventually, I need to go on and learn to stand on my own. Grief has had its moment. I just need to figure out what I need to do and what's best for my family."

"I thought you had made that decision."

"For the most part, I think I have, but I've thought of taking a few days on my own to sort things out. I want to go back to the cabin for a few days. Maybe that's what I need." Landon grinned sheepishly.

"What? Is there something wrong with that?" I asked, wondering why he had grinned at the thought of me going to stay in the cabin.

"There is nothing wrong with you going. I just hadn't thought that you might want to go there alone."

"It's calming, and I have some good memories there. Maybe after a few days, I'll have the answers I'm looking for."

"I don't know, Izzy. In a cabin out in the middle of nowhere doesn't sound like the best decision you've ever made. You know if you do go, someone needs to be with you. Having a high-risk pregnancy, you won't be alone. You're going to have someone with you."

"What do you mean? I can take care of myself."

"Izzy, I know you're capable of taking care of yourself, but I also know that this pregnancy hasn't been easy for you, and the loss of Carter hasn't helped the situation. Before you make that decision, and it's perfectly okay to do so, you need to know that Quentin or I will be with you. You can't go out there alone. It's dangerous."

"Quentin! Quentin can't go with me. That would mean I'm alone in the middle of nowhere with a man I hardly know. What would people think of that, especially this close to the death of my husband? I can't have him with me."

"Then, my sweet Izzy, you're stuck with me." He turned and smiled at me brightly. "Just remember you can't be out of my sight."

This is unreal. "Why do you have to go? Can't you just take me and let me stay for a few days in the cabin to think? I need this time, Landon. I need this time to heal and make decisions that is going to affect the rest of my life."

"Sorry, sweetheart. But if you go, one of us goes with you. So who will it be?"

I bit my lip and tried to hold back the frustration that I felt. Taking in some deep breaths, I found my voice. "Landon, I love you. You're my brother-in-law, and I appreciate what you have done for me, but don't you think that you're being a little over the top with this? I'm very capable of taking care of myself."

"Humor me, Izzy. When exactly do you want to go on this road trip?"

I sat running my toes through the sand, letting it mound on my foot. "I don't know. I need to make arrangements for an OB-GYN there. Maybe I can get Dr. Carley to recommend someone or set me up with someone. Then I have to find someone to take Molly. I would take her, but I really need this time alone."

"I'll take you whenever you like. As for Molly, Beth and Carter's parents would be glad to take her for a couple of days. I'm sure they would be glad to have her come visit or even your parents. We'll work out something. In the meantime, I want you to take it easy. No strenuous activity, no lifting, no pulling, or no getting emotionally upset. Doctor's orders, you know. Don't take chances. I know you want to be independent, but don't push yourself so hard. No one says you have to do everything overnight."

Landon sat watching me as I stared out at the ocean crashing in where Molly was contented making her castle. His eyes were fully on me, and I knew he was sizing everything up. "It's been a rough road, Landon. I've been doing all I can to keep myself from drowning, and it hasn't been a pretty picture. I need to stand on my own two feet."

"I'm worried about you." Landon ruffled his hair and turned his head, looking over at me. "I know you should be grieving and I can understand your mood, but it isn't good for you to stay like you are. You haven't smiled or laughed in months. I haven't seen you cry for weeks, and I know the emotion is there. Maybe you should see Roxie. She's a grief counselor at the station. She deals with spouses and children of fallen officers. She understands. She herself has lost a family member in the line of duty."

"I've been to counselors before, Landon. It doesn't help. Believe me, it doesn't help. I've seen Dr. Bentley since . . . since." Hesitating, he knew what I was getting at. "Carter helped me more than he did."

"Izzy, no one is going to be able to fill that void for you, but you need to talk to someone, at least start healing from this."

"There are a lot of things that I need to do, but I haven't managed to do it. It will come in time. I would like for it to be over much faster, but it isn't."

"Do me a favor, and see her at least once before you go on this road of exploration." He looked at me, more focused now.

"Okay, fine. You make the appointment, and no one needs to escort me. I'm a big girl. Last time I checked, I was wearing my big girl panties."

Landon busted out laughing, and it wasn't long before I was laughing along with him. "Isabella, I admire your wit. Too bad it isn't there all the time. I prefer you much more like this."

"I'll see what I can do." I sucked in a breath. I hadn't laughed that hard for a very long time.

Landon stood by my side as I looked out onto the ocean. "You about ready to head back home?" His voice was soft and assuring.

"No, I want to sit here a while longer. Besides, Molly is enjoying her time here. She hasn't had many happy times since her father died."

"Okay, just let me know when you're ready." Shaking my head, he walked away back toward the family and allowed me to sit quietly. *I wish I knew what to do, God.*

Lead me to where you want me to be. Show me what you want me to do. My family is all I have. My children are all I have left of the one man that I have ever loved. Sometimes I wish it had been me instead of him or I could have gone with him. I know that it sounds selfish. It's been so hard for me to give him up. I need to hear your voice. I need you, and you're the only one that can help me. Please give me something, anything that will help me. Point me in the right direction. My silent prayer continued as I watched my daughter. She was so young, and I could only imagine how this had affected her.

Standing, I cupped my hands around my mouth to enable Molly to hear me from where she was playing. "Molly, time to get ready to leave, baby." I motioned for her to come up the beach to prepare to go home and lost my balance, being caught promptly by Quentin. I fell directly into his arms, facing him. He was truly handsome; he looked at me with concern and wiped it away quickly. It was hard to tell how he was reacting. He wore dark aviator sunglasses, not allowing me to see his reaction, but his hands were strong and capable, helping to steady me.

"Mrs. Blake, are you okay?"

"Quentin, as long as you have been watching over Molly and I, don't you think you can address me as Isabella? Mrs. Blake makes me feel old, and yes, I'm fine. Thank you." I was reacting more harshly than I had intended.

He sat me solidly on my feet, with his hands remaining at my shoulders. "Of course, Isabella. Are you sure you're okay?"

He dropped one hand down, with the other remaining on my shoulder. I looked at him and started to make a step back and stumbled again, feeling dizzy.

"Isabella, we need to get you out of the sun." He never gave warning. He never said another word. Leaning down, he picked me up in his arms and started to carry me up the beach.

"Peirce! Just what are you doing?"

He opened his mouth, and very sternly he answered as his jaw clenched, "I'm taking care of you. It's my job." With me in his arms, he looked over his shoulder and called to Molly. "Ms. Molly, let's go. We need to get your mother in." Well, that was impressive. She got up from where she was and ran up to him without another word. She called back quickly, her little legs barely keeping up with her.

"Tummin', Ten," she answered and was soon by his side. The first time I ever saw the man smile, he looked down at her and told her to take hold of his belt loop on his jeans. One of the few times he had been dressed down. Quentin's copper-colored hair blew lightly in the wind as he walked up the beach with me. The ocean air had lifted his cologne and carried it around us. Landon had stopped what he was doing and started down the beach toward us.

Suddenly, I felt extremely tired and leaned against him and closed my eyes. I hadn't realized how tired I felt, and being held in his arms had left me thinking about Carter. God, I miss him. I missed him and found myself in my weak state, imagining I was in his arms. I knew in my heart it wasn't, but to be able to feel the security of his arms around me soothed me. I had wrapped my arms around his neck and relaxed against his chest. I could feel his body tense at my touch, and his muscles flexed against me as he walked.

"Peirce?" Landon was anxious, I could tell by his reaction. His voice became louder the closer he got to us. "What happened?"

"The heat, I think. She stumbled, and I caught her before she fell. She feels warm. I think it's best we get her in somewhere or at least under some shade." It was the last I heard.

Waking on my couch, I opened my eyes, still dazed from the earlier events. Quentin sat in a chair beside me, and I soon heard feet briskly walking toward me. I tried to focus; my eyes hadn't cleared exactly from whatever had happened. I looked up to see the ceiling fan rotating, and it buzzed and hummed in a slow steady rhythm. Looking beside me, I captured the eyes of Quentin. His face was filled with concern, his sunglasses perched atop his head as he looked at me, assessing me closely. "She's starting to wake up." Landon walked up behind him and handed him a cold rag, and he began to wipe my face. "Landon, why don't you get her a glass of water?" Landon left the room quickly. Quentin continued to wipe my face with the cool rag. "Mrs. Blake, can you hear me?"

"Yes, Quentin, I can hear you." I dragged out a little slower than usual. "Isabella, please."

"Yes, Isabella." He cleared his throat. "Feeling better?"

One thing about it, he was direct and to the point. "I think so." My thoughts started to collect slowly. "Molly? Where is she?"

"Ms. Blake is in her room playing. She's completely fine. Mrs. Blake and Mrs. Cameron are with her."

"My parents are here?" I swallowed, but my mouth felt like cotton.

"Yes. They came in later today."

Looking around the room, I assessed that it was darker than normal, looking more like evening. "What time is it?"

"It's five in the evening. You've been asleep for about four hours."

I closed my eyes and drew in a deep breath. "What happened?"

"You fainted. I think you had a little too much sun. Your body was pretty warm when I picked you up, but you seem fine now."

Landon walked quickly toward me. "Izzy, I have some water for you." He handed it to Quentin.

"Do you think you can take a drink?" Quentin had questioned.

"I think so." He helped me to sit up just a little and assisted me to drink from the glass. The water was salty, and even though the water glass felt cold, the water in my mouth felt warm. "Oh, that's hot."

"No, it isn't. It's you, Isabella. The water is ice-cold from the fridge, and there's ice in the glass. Go ahead and drink it. You need to get some fluids in. Just drink it slowly," Quentin coaxed as he watched me take sips. Landon's look was of worry, and he sat watching as Quentin made an attempt at nursing me back to health. I could tell his mood was uneasy with what was taking place. I just wasn't sure what the problem was: if it were the fact I had fainted or if it was because Quentin was actually taking care of me.

Taking the glass from me, Quentin eased me back down on the couch and laid the cool cloth on my forehead. The stern stone face had lifted, and I saw a grin break his lips. "I think you'll live, Isabella." His brown eyes gleamed and patted my hand as he stood up. "I'm going to check on Ms. Blake and take a little break. I won't be long. Landon's here with you. I'm sure he can see to you for the moment."

I held my hand out to him, and he took it. "Thank you, Quentin, for your assistance. Thank you for taking care of us."

That small smile parted his lips once again. "It's my job, Isabella. Get some rest." He walked slowly away from me and disappeared. Landon took his place beside me in the chair.

"Izzy, you scared me to death." The normal cool character of Landon had dipped considerably in front of me. "I thought we were going to lose you."

Reaching down, he took my hand and raised it to his face. "I'm fine. I just had a little too much sun. I'm pregnant, you know. Things like that are going to happen from time to time. It hit me before I knew it."

"That's my point. If something like this would have happened to you while you were alone, you wouldn't have been able to call for help."

Squeezing his hand, I gave him a little smile. "It's all right, Landon. I get the picture. When I decide to go away, I'll take you with me, but it looks like it's going to be a while. I need to get some things accomplished before that happens. Just make sure it's okay with Beth before you do it. If not, I'll take Quentin. I know it doesn't look good, but at least I'll have police protection and someone to look after me while I'm there."

Landon instantly looked relieved that he wasn't going to have a fight on his hands. My mind raced as I wondered what I had gotten myself into. If it weren't for the fact I had to have a bodyguard, Lily could have gone with me. I would have preferred to be alone, but if I had to have someone with me because of my condition, I would have taken her. I could see that my choices weren't what I had wanted, but it was going to be this way. One or the other of these two men was going with me. I hadn't really felt it appropriate for either of them to be alone with me, but if I had to pick between them, my brother-in-law had to be the more likely choice.

"I'm glad to hear that you aren't going to put up a fuss on this."

"Landon, you know it wouldn't be me if I didn't voice my opinion. It's not so much of someone going with me. It's taking you away from Beth, and taking Quentin with me doesn't exactly look right, especially in the fact that I've recently become widowed with one small child. Quentin is a young, good-looking single man roaming around with a pregnant woman and her little daughter. Now tell me, does that look good to others? I know there's nothing going on, and so do you, but it doesn't look good to others who happen to be looking and watching my every move."

"Izzy, you can't always live your life on what others think. Both Quentin and I are here for you and Molly's protection." Bending down a little closer, he looks around as to see if anyone else is looking. "Look, Izzy, you aren't the only one that has protection enlisted on them, so does Beth. She doesn't know it, and I don't want her to. I don't know what this guy is capable of. If he puts the connection together, he may go after any of us just to prove his point. I don't want you to worry about anything else but bringing my niece or nephew into this world. I'll get this guy, and when I do, he is going to get what is coming to him, I promise you."

"So you think this guy could go after any of us?"

"I wouldn't put it past him. The main thing is to protect you and see that he can't get near you. I want you to listen to me and allow Quentin and me to take care of you, whether you feel it's rational or not. If something would happen to you or to anyone in this family because of me, I could never live with myself if I could have stopped it. I know you want to be independent and that it's important for you to move on, but do this for me. If there is any doubt even if it's something simple, call one of us. That's what we're here for." My brother-in-law, the protector, always watching out for my best interest, but oh my, what a pain he can be. I couldn't help but love him. He had done a lot for me since Carter had passed away. I couldn't say no. He was the closest I had to a brother, and I was glad he was here whether I wanted to admit it to him or not.

"I promise," I said, motioning a "cross my heart" over my chest. He chuckled as he was watching a pact made between two kids. "You'll be the first to know, I promise you."

"Isabella, you are a piece of work, and I'm so happy you were chosen by that stubborn brother-in-law of mine. He's a lucky man to have you for a wife."

I reflected on what he had said and then grinned. "You can't get over he's gone either, can you?"

"What?" He jumped back, surprised.

"You addressed him in the present tense, like he was still alive."

"Did I? Well, old habits are hard to break, I guess. Nonetheless, you are a good woman, Izzy."

~~~~~~

Carter had a difficult time falling asleep and had finally drifted off when the phone rang, sending him sitting straight up in the bed with a jolt. His heart felt like it was going to jump from his chest from the noise that had rung from the stillness of the cabin. It wasn't like him to jump like he had been shot from a cannon, but he had a difficult time over the last few hours with a feeling of unease, a sense that something wasn't just right. Reaching over in the darkness, he flipped the light on and picked up his cell.

"Hello," he had answered in a voice that was barely audible.

"I know I shouldn't have called you this late, but I haven't been able to get away from the family long enough to call."

"Landon, what are you doing? It's three in the morning."

"I know, but I haven't been able to get away."

"Gavin wake you?"

98

"Well, no, not exactly." Landon's voice trailed off.

"What do you mean not exactly?" Carter ran his hands through his hair and leaned against the headboard of his bed.

"There was a small problem today, but it's resolved. She scared me to death, but things are better now. I wanted you to know that Izzy is planning on coming to the cabin sometime soon. I just don't know when. She has to set up a doctor there first before she comes."

"Why is she coming here?" Carter's voice raised in panic.

"Hang on. It may not be as bad as we think."

"Landon, if she comes here, she's going to know I'm alive."

"That's right." Landon laughed slightly. "That may not be all bad. You do want to see her, don't you?"

"Now that's a stupid question. Of course, I want to see her."

"We are supposed to do whatever we can to keep from raising suspicion on her part or anyone else. Now I can't tell Izzy she can't go because you're there, and she isn't going to take no for an answer. Believe me, I've tried. I even threatened to send Quentin with her, hoping that it would slow her down, but no dice. She refused to go with him where he would be staying in the same cabin with her. She can't go alone because she's in a high-risk pregnancy, not to mention she has to have a bodyguard.

"She is determined to come, so that leaves me. She wants to come to sort some things out, and it looks like I'm going to be tagging along with her. Of course, once she sees you, I will depart to another cabin at least for a couple of days. I can't go back home without her, or Beth will be questioning me."

Carter started to grin slightly. "You are one slick dude, you know that? No rules broken, of course. What can they say when it was her idea? Besides, they don't know where I am. They just know I'm in hiding."

"I'm sure it won't be long. I can't hold her off for long." Landon chuckled as he listened to Carter laugh on the other end.

"My sweet innocent wife, she is an enigma, always coming up with something totally unexpected."

CHAPTER FIVE

The morning started in a rush with me taking Molly to day care. It wasn't one of my easier mornings, what with waking up with an upset stomach and then having a few aches and pains that I hadn't planned on. As I had put my shoes on this morning, I had noticed that they felt a little tighter than normal. I was tired like I hadn't gone to bed, but I had to get ready for my first class in my degree. I wasn't sure how much I would be able to get by with; having had a husband that had been on the force wasn't exactly a blessing. I knew there would be some that would welcome me, and then there would be others that would think I got in on his coattail.

Walking into the class, I was followed closely by Peirce, who made his seat at the back of the room. I'm sure this was going to be a treat for him, having to listen to schooling. He had participated in already and had a degree. He sat behind me, dressed to kill in his jeans, a tight white T-shirt that made his ripped body more prominent, and his shoulder holster with his firearm close to his body covered with his jean jacket. A Bluetooth headset was perched in his ear, blinking blue, which more than likely connected directly with Landon. He was definitely the picture of the bad boy.

There were fewer women than men in the class, which I had expected. It wasn't exactly a woman's world when it came to police work. I have seen them in some places I hadn't thought of; forensics seemed to be one of the biggest interests. It wasn't exactly what I had my interest in, but it was a science and could be interesting. This was going to be a trip to say the very least. I watched as the students filed in when a man walked in that literally took my breath away. He sauntered in with purpose and confidence. His short dark hair is cut into a perfect line with each one in place as if it were numbered and fit perfectly with his full beard. He wore wire-framed glasses that looked expensive. He was tall with a lean, well-defined physique of an athlete. Dressed well in dark slacks and a dark-blue linen shirt, he looked understated but breathtaking, enough so that it made me uncomfortable. The vibe he gave off was unsettling, and he hadn't even looked my direction.

There was something about him that gave me the feeling of dread, but for some reason, I welcomed it. I was drawn to him, but I had no idea why it made me feel so incredibly guilty. My mouth went dry, and my hands shook as I looked down at my wedding band. What was it? It wasn't as if I knew the man; but his character, the way he walked and moved, was familiar. The professor had walked in the room and had started class without me noticing. Sitting there, I watched as the stranger pulled a notebook from his messenger bag and drew his pen from his pocket. Oh, this wasn't good. I was distracted, and it wasn't going away anytime soon.

The professor introduced himself and cleared his throat as I drew my gaze back slowly to the front of the class. *Come on, Bella, you have work to do. You don't have time to figure out why this stranger has you in knots.*

Taking in a deep breath, I try to center myself and concentrate on what's being said, and it wasn't easy.

"Welcome to my dreaded English class. I know some of you hate taking this course—let's be real—but it is a requirement." The older man stood in front of the board and picked up a dry marker and scrawled his name. "My name is Professor Daryl Thorn, and you will be in this class for the next nine weeks. For most of you, this will not be a difficult class, but I do ask that you make every attempt to be here and that you at least turn in classwork that has been assigned. There is no test per se, but you will be asked to participate accordingly. There are a couple of papers that I expect to be completed. You have until the end of this session to finish, and it will count as over half of this course grade. I suggest that you take the time to research the projects and do them well. You will notice since you are all vying for cadet status, it is in some sort of police detail. Each of you has a paper that was laid down on your desk, and you will be asked to write on that topic. You will also be expected to complete simple ones that will be assigned that there will be no letter grade given, but they will count as a complete or incomplete for the course. The first assignment to be completed for all of you is an introduction. I would like to get to know all of you better. It doesn't have to be extremely detailed. I just want to know who you are and what led you to decide to become an officer."

Professor Thorn pushed his gray hair back from his forehead and adjusted his glasses. The black frames looked fairly dated, but otherwise, he was dressed well. My guess was that he was in his midsixties and apparently

103

no pushover. His voice was stern and harsh at times. I sat wondering what I had gotten myself into when I felt eyes on me. Turning, I saw the gentleman that had raised such havoc with me earlier now watching me like he was assessing me. When he was caught, he turned his head back to the front of the class and back down at his notebook. His cool persona had become nervous as he twirled his pen in his fingers, reminding me of a nervous trait of Carter's. He did that when he was under stress, clicking the pen multiple times to relieve it.

The class continued, but before it was half over, I had to leave for the bathroom with Quentin on my heels. After leaving the room, I explained to him that I was fine. "I'm just going to the ladies' room." And he sat down on the bench outside. I can't believe this; it's getting worse instead of better. There was nothing worse knowing that you were being waited on like a child. Being four months pregnant still seemed to keep me in the bathroom often, but not as much as at the beginning. And let's face it, the nausea had eased somewhat, but I still suffered from morning sickness. I had managed not to lose my breakfast, what I had eaten of it for a change. I stood before the mirror and pushed a long piece of my hair behind my ear that had fallen away from the barrette. I looked tired; my eyes were red and had dark circles under them that no amount of makeup could hide. Turning to the side, I looked into the mirror, assessing my clothing when I noticed that I was beginning to show. Standing sideways, it was easily seen, the smallest of a bulge of our child. Running my hand down over my stomach, my heart lurched, thinking of Carter and how much he would have enjoyed this time. He was happy and was like a magpie after he found out, telling everyone that his girl had made him the happiest fellow that ever walked. He was going to be a daddy and was thrilled beyond words. Picking me up, he had twirled me around at the station after I had visited him that day. Of course, he already knew. He had been waiting for me to confirm the fact. His laugh rang in my ears as I remembered him hugging me close to him.

There was no reason to think of this. There was no changing it. What a wonderful thing it would have been if he could have been here. I know he would have been just as bad about protecting me as the other two had, doting on me constantly. I couldn't imagine Quentin letting his guard down on anything, but it was evident to me yesterday when he had taken the lead and took care of me like we had known each other for years. I had come to expect it from my brother-in-law, but not my protector. I had gone from a single woman with no prospects to one that seemed to be overrun with men. It wasn't comfortable at all. I was still in love with my husband, and one of those men happened to be his sister's husband. Then there was Quentin, the one I loved to hate. He seemed to be there all the time, whether it was welcomed or not. He followed me constantly, and it was starting to wear on me. Walking out of the ladies' room, I adjusted my sweater over my T-shirt, allowing it to hide the obvious. If they had known I was pregnant, it may hurt my chances of entering into school. Some schools frowned on that sort of thing when spaces were limited, and I was making sure until it came to the point they couldn't keep me out. Getting hold of myself, I met up with Quentin, and he escorted me back to class.

~~~~~~

Carter had sat in the class, trying to keep his distance from her. It had alarmed him when she turned and looked at him. At that point, he thought he had been found out. She had followed him from the time he had walked into the room. Even though he hadn't looked directly at her, he felt her gaze. He had second-guessed himself about coming, but he wanted to be there. He wanted to see her, and it had taken a lot to actually enroll himself into the class as an unknown. To everyone else, he was dead, and he had to get in on a fake name and school along with a fake birthday and address. Putting all of it together on short notice hadn't been easy. Now he was wondering if it had been a mistake.

He had watched as Quentin seemed to dote on her more than he would have liked. Keeping in mind that Quentin had no idea he even existed, he couldn't blame the man. She was beautiful and loving. He had picked him to protect his family, and he was doing his job, but he could see the affection he had for her. He knew because he had recognized the same behavior in himself when they had first met. To make matters worse, when Isabella had walked out of class followed by Peirce, Carter had risen to follow her. He was on edge and had feared she was ill. From the look on her face, she hadn't slept and was very pale. Professor Thorn had called him out on it and had asked him where the fire was. He had looked back at the

106

professor with a clenched jaw and kept his cool. Thorn wasn't the easiest man to get along with the first time around; he would either make you or break you.

Carter had bitten the inside of his jaw until it was raw to keep from saying something that would disrupt why he was here. It was worth a little inconvenience just to get to be in the same room with her, even though she had no idea. He had noticed that she had left her purse and notebook behind. Perhaps it was nothing, and she or Quentin would return soon.

The cop in him had started to question several things as to why she would even consider taking on this endeavor. Oh, he knew enough that it was partly him, but there was more to it than that. She had a settled career and had been working at it for some time. Why would she want to take this on? It would take at least three years to get classes in and another for just the training as a rookie to remotely get an idea of what to do to protect yourself and your partner. That time limit was pushing it. Had she really meant it when she told her attacker she would kill him?

He had watched her from the corner of his eye and noticed the difference in his wife's attitude and her carriage. She was more confident and didn't seem too willing to take much off anyone. She did however seem to allow Quentin a little more power than in the beginning. She was so dead set against him being there, and now it was if she had accepted it.

The door had slowly creaked open, and he watched her enter the room, trying not to be too obvious. Quentin followed close behind with his hand guiding her at the small of her back, supporting her. She found her chair and sat down with her usual grace, and he had sat back down a desk behind.

He watched his second as if he could choke him. He had his hands on his wife. Carter had to shake it off. After all, he was doing what he hired him for, and he and Bella had thought he was dead. Bella didn't seem to reciprocate it, which was good. His intention was to return to his family, and now it seemed it was going to be in a hurry. He couldn't stand the thought of another man with his hands on her. She belonged to him; his hands shook as he tried to control the anger that rested on him. He hated Brooks for putting him in this position. He ran his hand through his hair and tried to control his rising frustration. Soon, very soon, he was going to see his wife. He would tell her everything, whether Brooks liked it or not. He wasn't going to stand by and let another man step into his life and into the spot that was his.

Professor Thorn lay the marker down and was explaining to the class and had handed out more instructions, a syllabus for the class along with a paperback book that they were to read over the next nine weeks. How many times had he read *Crime and Punishment* through school? He could do a book report on it in his sleep. Every English course he had been in had encouraged them to read it. He had done at least four different papers on the book, including the one for this course. Looking over the syllabus, Thorn hadn't changed since he went through training. The grading system was even the same.

Thorn's voice broke through his thoughts, and he placed his pen back into his pocket. "Remember to go over the syllabus. It's how I do my grading and what you are expected to be able to do over the next few weeks, so be familiar with it. You're dismissed."

Carter picked up his notebook and slid it down into the messenger bag, not that he needed it, but he had to look the part. Sliding it onto his shoulder, he stood briefly looking back at Bella. Quentin had assisted her and now had her books, carrying them. He was talking to her about something, and she had acknowledged him. He started out of the room and heard her voice behind him. He held the door, not making a sound. "Thank you," she had said. Her arm had brushed against him, filling his body with unbelievable need for her. She had looked back when her arm had grazed him like she was trying to figure out what was going on, but Quentin had sidetracked her, encouraging her on to the next class. He stood there stone still, unmoving as he watched her walk down the hall from him. How much more was he going to be able to take?

That strange feeling had come over me once again as I had walked past the man that had caught me off guard this morning. There is something about him, something I was missing. I was close enough to touch him and had accidently brushed against him. I was so close that I felt the heat rise off his body and the tension from him. His cologne, the cologne, was identical to what I had bought for my husband. I was able to smell it, as it lingered softly on my sweater. The shiver ran down my spine like it had the first time Carter had ever touched me. It was impossible, but the beautiful blue eyes I caught made me think otherwise. No, it can't be. Impossible! You can't come back from the dead.

At each class, except for one, the stranger, along with my shadow, followed me. He kept to himself, but I couldn't shake the feeling of unease, from calm to fear. Something was totally off, and I couldn't seem to fit it together. If it had been something to the point of harm, Peirce would have picked up on it. Maybe it's my hormones that have left me overly sensitive, the call from my abuser, or the loss of the love of my life; nonetheless, it was there, and it was shaking me to the point I felt I had no control. That was going to stop; if I had to, I would investigate on my own. I wasn't going to mention anything to Landon or Quentin. If I did, it would make me that much more vulnerable, and I didn't need to make myself weak. I had the tools to do some digging and had the power to protect myself if I had to. I knew self-defense all too well from Gus. He had taught me Krav Maga basics with some advanced techniques. Knowing them well, I had landed a 210-pound six-foot man on his rear, not bad for a five foot three, 130-pound woman. Gus had coached me from the first time I had been taken to the academy by Carter, and he had never stopped. I didn't have the fear I once did, only for my family. I was more than capable of taking care of myself.

Lunchtime came, and I sat at a corner café with Peirce. He had gotten us each something to eat and had just sat down when his cell apparently rang. He answered and put up his finger, telling me that he would be right back. He stayed within earshot but was far enough away that I was unable to hear what was being said to his caller. Standing off to the side, he continued to watch me with one hand perched on the waistband of his jeans and the other adjusting the Bluetooth headset that remained in his ear. His movements revealed the shoulder holster that still clung to his body.

I started to stir the dressing into the salad. Looking up, I met the gaze of the stranger from school. He sat at the table alone in front of me. He grinned at me and then picked up his paper and started to scan it. That smile, that smile. It couldn't be. Now I knew I was losing it. Carter? I started to take a bite of my salad in which I wasn't hungry for. Taking a bite immediately made me sick, and I ran to the bathroom. In the midst, I noticed the stranger has taken off toward the men's room. I ran into him, almost knocking him down running to the ladies' room. I was so sick; and it didn't take long for everything, which was little, that I had eaten to come back up. I needed to sit down, but I couldn't, not here. The public bathroom, even though it looked clean, I'm sure was not the cleanest place to sit down on the floor. My body shook from the violence it possessed of emptying my stomach, leaving me feeling weak.

When I came out of the ladies' room, Quentin was waiting off to the side, but I also met the stranger who was now bent down over his body, holding on to his knees. I stopped long enough to ask him if he was okay, and he waved me off and answered me in what sounded like French.

111

He kept his head down, and I sat down on the concrete bench beside him. "Are you sure you're okay? Can I get you a drink or something?" This time, he answered in English, but the accent was made thick. He never raised his head; he just continued to wave his hand. "I'm fine. Don't give it another thought, really."

Quentin came to where I sat and held out his hand. "Isabella, you need to try to eat something if you can. Let's go. It will soon be time for your afternoon class." Taking his hand, I stood and placed my hand on the shoulder of the man who stood beside me.

"Are you sure you're okay?" I asked the gentleman once more, and again, he waved me off. The electricity flew from my body from the hand that lay against him. I jerked it away as if he had burnt me. As we walked away, I turned and looked over my shoulder at the stranger as he rose up and rubbed his face, adjusting his glasses back into place.

The day had to end soon; I was in serious need of a nap. I wasn't sure if I was going to be able to handle another class. I kept telling myself it was just forty-five minutes, and Peirce would be driving. One class at a time, and I would go after the man that had destroyed my life.

Carter walked into his hotel room just fifteen minutes away from her. By the time he threw down his messenger bag, his cell started ringing. Falling back onto the couch, he looked at the ID, knowing full well already it was Landon. There was no doubt in his mind that his brother-in-law had

112

been keeping tabs on him. He let out a sharp breath and picked it up, answering it suavely.

"Yep, it was me," he gloated. "And I'd do it again to see her. One other thing, I know I hired Peirce to take care of my family, but make sure that he doesn't *take care of my family*." Carter huffed. He laid his head back on the couch, resting it and crossing his legs, placing them on the ottoman.

"Wow, wasn't expecting that." Landon was taken aback at what he had said. Carter had sounded angry, and what was he talking about? "Just what are you talking about?"

Carter grinned at himself. He had given himself away. Landon had no idea that he had been there today. "Well, since I've given myself away to you, I guess it's time to fess up. I was there today when Bella was on campus. I'll tell you one thing. I'm too old to be going back to college for something I already have a degree in." He leaned down and untied his dress shoes and kicked them off to the side of the ottoman and rested back again.

"I'm sorry, I don't follow. Are you telling me that you are here in Portland and you . . . you went to class today?"

"Bingo! You win the prize! Congratulations!" The sarcasm was evident.

Landon laughed out loud, and Carter was shocked when he heard it. "I can't believe you. You went to Thorn's class again, after all the grief he put you through the first time around. That man hated you. He did everything but kick you out the first time."

"Well, I haven't exactly grown on him this time either."

"Man, you're a glutton for punishment, aren't you? Peirce told me how dull it was."

"Did he tell you that Bella was sick?"

Landon became quiet for a moment and then cleared his throat. "No, he didn't. He did say Bella had done well in her classes and that he had taken her home. He said she was tired and had fallen asleep on the way there."

"I wouldn't have known it, but it seems when she's sick, so am I. Funny how that works. I can be next to her or hours away, and I know when she's sick. Today she wasn't able to eat lunch and must have woken up this morning sick because for some reason, I was sick. I couldn't eat. Could it be that she's under stress from all of this?" Carter's voice raised in anger. "If she can't eat, she can't be healthy. If she isn't healthy, neither is our baby."

"I'm working on it. Give me a couple of days." Landon tried to soothe the beast in Carter, but he wasn't finding what he was saying to him of much use.

"I wasn't exactly happy either that Peirce seemed more than just a bodyguard for her. He has feelings for my wife. I can see them. When I can see them, I know it's evident to my wife, and seeing that she thinks I'm dead, I don't know, that makes her on the market!"

"Carter, believe me, she has no interest in anyone. She loves you, and I don't think that is going to leave her anytime soon." Landon continued as his demeanor took a nose dive. "She gave a speech Sunday at church about you, what you had done for her, and that she loved you. She talked about your love of God and what a wonderful, loving man he had put in her path. No woman that is ready to move on says those kinds of things. You would have been proud of her. She's a strong lady."

"I am proud of her. I just don't want her hurt any more than what she already has been."

There was a pause, and the two men took a brief silence before Landon continued. "Where are you staying? Maybe I can get her to you for a few moments."

"No, don't do it yet. I need to go back to Tennessee and see Bentley. I need to make sure he is protected and talk to him before anything else happens." As bad as he wanted to see her now, he knew it was a risk if someone found out.

"Okay, how about this Saturday? If I can get something set up, I'll bring her to the cabin."

"Just don't tell her until we know she's safe with me. I don't want to take chances." Carter rubbed the back of his neck.

"Do me a favor and turn on your computer when we hang up. I have a surprise for you." Landon soon hung up the phone, leaving Carter with that endless lonely feeling he couldn't seem to get rid of. He threw the phone over on the cushion next to him. Running both of his hands through his hair, he closed his eyes, taking in a deep breath, trying to relax.

He would go turn the computer on as Landon had instructed before he hung up. Going through the camera system set up on his computer, the screen sprung to life. When the picture cleared, he saw her. His beautiful Bella was there. He could almost touch her. The camera followed her around the house, and it wasn't long before Molly bounded through on screen. His daughter had grown so much since he had been gone. Adjusting the volume, he could hear them. It brought tears to his eyes when he heard his little girl sing as she ran over and sat down with Bella.

It took a lot for him to cry, and this was one he would remember. Molly crawled into Bella's lap and dragged a book with her. "Wow, look at that," he said as he sat watching them. He could hear Isabella as she read to her. Molly giggled and laughed as she did. He had missed them before, but nothing like he did right now. They were fifteen minutes from him, and this for the moment was all he had. At least he had this. Before, he was lucky to be in the same state with her. Just being able to see her, being as close as he had been today, but not being able to touch her killed him. He was glad that he had been able to keep up with the charade today; it wasn't easy because he figured if she had heard his voice, it was a dead giveaway. It was good that he knew more than one language. He studied four languages and was fluent in them. Through college, he learned Italian, Spanish, French, and Latin. Each one was difficult for him, but he had practiced them endlessly. They had come in handy several times during his police work. He had come across a few people that spoke no English whatsoever. He was their go-to man at the station when other officers came up against them.

He sat and watched as Bella read to his daughter, and they soon finished. She had sent Molly to her room and was headed to the kitchen when the doorbell rang. When the door opened, Lily had stepped in, hugging her. Stepping back slightly, she placed her hands on Isabella's stomach, rubbing it gently. JC walked in behind Lily, looking like he had been through the war. He was no way near the man Carter had seen the night they had set this up. He looked tired, and his face appeared to be lined tightly. Lily was trying to reassure him, and Isabella had taken his hand and asked him to come in. He instantly took Isabella in his arms and sobbed. Carter could hear him. He was telling her he was so sorry, saying it was his fault that Carter wasn't there. Bella had tried to assure him and had told him that she hadn't blamed him. Carter didn't think he was ever going to let her go. The weight on JC was heavy but was slowly lifting as Isabella talked to him and patted him gently, asking him to sit down. Lily sat down next to him and had looped her arm through his, hoping to calm him. From where he sat, Carter was able to see him extremely well. It was if he were sitting in the room with him. He felt bad for his friend and wasn't sure how he could fix it. Somehow it had to stop; it was affecting JC's mental health. It was hard to see the changes in Bella, but they had all changed. Bella kicked her shoes off and was talking with them when Carter's parents and Bella's came through the door. He had gotten to see his mother. His mother bore no emotion whatsoever. It was if she walked around in a haze. Bella immediately went to her and wrapped her in her arms, pulling her into her. His mother's long hair was pulled to the side and had little style to it. She had no makeup on nor was she dressed in her normal clothes. His mother had always been extremely picky about how she looked, and it had appeared that she had spent little time preparing herself. His father practically had carried her to the couch as they sat down.

Isabella's parents followed close behind and had hugged her close to them. Molly came running from her bedroom, changed into her footed pajamas. She leaped toward his parents but stopped short and looked at her grandmother and got down on her knees. She patted her gently on the knee, and his mother finally acknowledged her. His father reached down and picked Molly up and placed her on her grandmother's lap. Iris had taken her quickly and hugged her tightly to her chest. She rocked her gently and sang to her a song that was familiar to Carter. His mother had sung to him many times. Her sweet voice rose to the point Carter could hear each word. "You are my sunshine," she sang as she rocked Molly.

As much as he wanted to be able to see them all and tell them it was a hoax, he couldn't yet. Seeing his mother like that was difficult to watch. Bella and his father seemed to be the best of them, but then he hadn't seen her when everyone was gone. It hurt to see his mother and JC in the shape they were in and not being able to do anything to ease their pain.

~~~~~~

I finished tucking Molly into bed and shut the lights out as I left the room. Stepping into the bedroom, I remembered the first night we had spent together. I could feel his arms around me once I stood in the doorway. Would I ever be able to get over him? He was the only one that had been able to break through that hard exterior shell of fear. No one, as far as I was concerned, would ever be able to have that place again.

From the moment I met him, he held my heart. I hadn't recognized it at first, but when I did, it flooded me with emotions that had been buried for years. Sitting at the end of the bed, I took his picture from the table and looked at it as if he could talk to me. Tracing his features with my fingertips, I could almost feel the warmth of his face beneath them, the fine stubble of his six o'clock shadow burning against me.

Drawing in a breath, I brushed one lone tear briskly away from my cheek with my index finger and sighed. "I miss you." It seemed senseless to talk to his picture, but it was all I had. "There'll never be anyone but you. You were the love of my life. I still can't believe you're gone." Shifting on the bed, I reached to his side of the bed, picking up the shirt that remained on his pillow and took it to my face. His cologne had faded from his pillow. Taking in a breath, I tried to smell it, but it left me little comfort. "You know, I ran into someone today. He reminded me of you. I watched him for some time when he walked into the classroom. He probably thought I was stalking him. His character, the way he moved, I don't know how to explain it. If I hadn't known better, I would have thought you had come back to me." I smiled and let out a little laugh. "He even had your nervous gestures.

"His cologne—I was so close to him once that I smelled your cologne." The smile quickly faded. *Cologne, Carter's cologne?* I twirled my finger around my hair as I thought. Walking over to the desk, I took his things from the drawer. His wallet was still like he left it, his last pay stub, some cash, a copy of our wedding picture, one of Molly, his gym pass, a couple of credit cards, and his license, all there. His keys were lying next to his cell phone untouched since Landon had brought them from the office.

Getting up, I walked to the bathroom and opened the medicine chest, scanning the items there. I hadn't cleared anything of his, nothing. It had been left exactly as he had left it. His cologne bottle was there. Lifting the lid, I could smell it, so much for speculation. Replacing the lid, I looked the bottle over, seeing nothing out of character, until I noticed the order number was missing. The name, number, and code for that bottle were gone. The company coded it so that it was easily remade. Replacing it in the chest, I walked out. Making my way quickly to his closet, I felt the fine hairs raise on the back of my neck. Looking through the closet, I found nothing missing, but that feeling that something didn't fit wouldn't leave. Shutting the door, I went back into the bathroom to change my clothes, taking his shirt with me. Changing into it, I noticed it was starting to get tight around my belly. I wasn't going to be able to wear it much longer, maybe another couple of weeks, and that would be it.

Shutting off the light in the bathroom, I went over to the bed. For the first time since he had been gone, I got in on his side. Lying there, I thought of the man that I had seen today. Maybe he looked and acted so much like him because I wanted to see it. I wanted him to be here. I wanted to see him. Everywhere I went, I saw him. There had been more than one occasion that had brought the memory of him back to me.

Carter sat and watched her every move. He watched her taking his things from the drawer and looking at them, then going to the closet and looking through it as if she had lost something. The most incredible thing he had seen her do was talk to him. He heard her voice as he was changing for bed, and it had stopped him in his tracks. The picture she held had a micro camera attached, and he could see and hear her like she was standing in front of him. He watched as she traced her finger along the screen, assuming she was tracing his picture in the frame. His heart broke as she pushed a tear from her cheek, telling him no one would have the place he held in her heart.

What was he going to do? He couldn't let this continue much longer. The stress eventually would harm her. She meant more to him than anything he could remember other than their children. He prayed for her every day, sometimes all day long. It gave him great strength to know there was more than his security team to watch over her. Sometimes God allowed him to feel her presence. He had made it possible at other times to be with her even if she hadn't recognized him.

He had traced her cheek on the screen as if she were there. It would have been so easy to go to her. The longer he was away, the harder it was becoming. He was going to have a lot of ground to cover when they were reunited.

She walked from the bathroom dressed in his blue button-down. He had to smile as he slowly ran his finger over his bottom lip, remembering the first time he had seen her in it. Looking at her now, her hair lay in large waves down her shoulder and across her chest. Even at

121

four months pregnant, she was still the most beautiful woman he had ever seen.

As she turned to get in bed, he watched as she clambered in on his side of the bed. But that wasn't all that had caught his eye. As she turned, for the first time, he saw the small bump at her belly. He hadn't noticed it today. She had been well dressed, keeping it hidden from everyone.

His smirk slowly built to a smile that stretched from ear to ear. It had filled him with an overwhelming amount of joy. His baby, their baby, was growing, and from the reports he had gotten from Landon, it was healthy. From where he stood, he sank to his knees in awe as she lay there and talked to the baby. At times he could barely tell what she was saying, then he realized she wasn't talking. She was singing. The night-vision equipment allowed for him to see her as she rubbed her belly gently. She sang sweetly to their unborn child, "Saving Grace." His wife had grown closer to God more than he thought. She ended her little session with "Jesus Loves Me," then told their child how much she and Daddy loved him. He listened to her prayers and watched her as she drifted off to sleep.

When he was satisfied she was asleep and safe, he lay down, leaving the computer on, allowing him to see her. "Good night, angel." He cleared his throat and watched her until he could no longer keep his eyes open.

At the first hit from his hand, she had hit the floor. The sting still radiated from her cheek. Her eye felt like it was going to bulge out. Picking her up by the hair, he hit her again and threw her onto the bed, pinning her underneath him.

He uttered some obscenities she knew, but she couldn't understand them from the ringing in her ears. She felt sick at her stomach and could taste the blood in her mouth. She fought him with less power now as he had forced himself against her. His large hands had ripped what clothes she did have on her away, leaving the cold air to hit her skin. Pulling his belt from his waist, he wrapped it around her wrists behind her back to the point that she was unable to move. He got up from the rickety four-poster bed, which squeaked under his weight, shifting as if it were going to tip over.

The loud banging on the door brought me back briefly from a beaten stupor. "Isabella," Lee screamed from outside the door in terror that literally shook the room. The monster in the room with me screamed back at him in a deep devilish voice, shaking me to the core.

"Shut up, Lee. She's going to get what's coming to her," he answered him, gritting his teeth.

Walking back toward me, his green eyes blazed with hate. His voice was menacing as he growled and spoke a few obscenities as he made his way to me. "I'm going to do what I should have done a long time ago." Half clothed, he headed toward me. He gripped a metal coat hanger in his hand until his knuckles turned white. An evil smile crossed his face the closer he got to me. Trying to roll to my side, he jerked me back by the hair and straddled me, pinning me under him. His touch was harsh and painful, not allowing me an inch to move. "Be nice and I'll let you live," he sneered. He was close to my lips as he could get without touching them. I could smell the liquor on his breath and reeking of smoke, making me sick at my stomach. He ran his rough, unforgiving hands over my body. Lee continued to scream from outside the door as I tried to fight him off and being unable to.

"Flip the switch, Bella," I heard him scream, and his voice cracked.

Becoming willing to what he was doing, he hated it. When I became seductive, he detested it and would dump me like I was diseased. I had no longer posed a challenge. He had always walked away before, but this time, it had infuriated him. He had tried to induce an abortion on his own, leaving me feeling like my own life was slipping away.

"We can't have this anymore. That brat is costing me precious time and money." Grabbing me by the jaw, he looked down at me like he could have killed me. "I will have what I want."

I awoke screaming in terror, trying to get my breath, praying as I went. "God, help me. Please help me." Turning on the light in the room helped, but it was far from giving me comfort. Clutching my stomach, I tried to slow my breathing down. "Oh god, Carter, where are you?"

CHAPTER SIX

He heard her scream from a dead sleep and quickly threw on his jeans. Looking at the screen, she had drawn up her knees and was rubbing her stomach. *The baby!* Chills fell over his body as he started to slip his T-shirt over his head. Grabbing his cell phone, he started for the door and looked back again at the screen, seeing her attempting to recapture her breath. Then he saw something that disturbed him greatly. Turning on the light, she had illuminated the figure of a man that in great haste entered her room.

Flipping his cell phone open, he watched the screen intently as he dialed. When his party answered, he growled in agitation. He'd had enough of this. One way or the other, he was getting to his wife.

"Landon, get me out now!"

My heart raced as I continued to take back control of the situation. Before I knew it, a familiar and welcome voice called out to me. Quentin's voice broke the silence and brought relief to me.

"Isabella?"

I could hear his feet as they made a squeak against the hardwood floor. He appeared in the door and stood before me. Dressed in a black T-shirt and sweatpants, I hadn't expected him to come in. It must be late.

Looking down at me, he kneeled down and placed his hand on my shoulder. I jumped as his hand made contact with me. Taking in a few deep breaths, I tried to control my breathing. I was surprised to see him there, but grateful for his presence.

"Isabella, are you all right?"

Without thinking, I had thrown my arms around his neck. His body felt warm and strong against mine as he had slowly placed his arms around me. The panic ran through me, even though I knew it wasn't happening now. Pushing back, he looked at me and held my shoulders.

"Isabella, I want you to concentrate on breathing. Slow your breathing down, take in a deep breath through your nose, and let it out through your mouth."

While I was making an attempt, it wasn't working well. I sat there and shook like a leaf while he tried to console me. He tilted my face up so that I was looking directly at him. "Isabella, watch me. Take in a deep breath and blow it out." He continued to encourage me as he pulled his cell phone out of his pocket. Punching a speed dial button, he kept his eyes on me.

"Landon, can you come to Isabella's? Yes, now. So far . . . maybe ten minutes. Fine . . . I'll check it out while I'm here." He returned his cell phone to his pocket as my breathing had started to slow down. I closed my eyes and soon heard little feet hitting the floor. Molly climbed into the bed and snuggled up beside me with her thumb in her mouth. Never saying a word, she laid her head down in my lap and patted my leg gently.

Keeping his cool, Quentin assessed me and asked me if he could get me anything. Shaking my head, I pushed my

126

hair back away from my face. Molly moved and lay down on my pillow. Her quizzical eyes looked around the room as she rubbed the sleep from them.

"What time is it?"

Quentin stood from his kneeling position and laid his keys on the table beside me. "It's early yet. There aren't any classes for another two hours."

It occurred to me that he was here in a hurry, without anyone calling him. How did he know there was a problem? "How did you know?" I hesitated, thinking why he would be here. "How did you know there was a problem?" I watched him carefully, looking for a clue.

Answering me very matter-of-factly, he looked at me seriously. "I don't live far and was out jogging before the time to pick you up. I do it every day. It's normal routine for me to be out at 6:00 a.m. I was running when I heard a scream. I took it to be from this direction. I have a key. I hope that isn't a problem."

He had been running. His shirt clung to his sculpted body and was damp from his morning run. He hadn't just happened to be here. "No, it's fine. I'm glad you're here." He looked down at Molly, who was now drawing circles or something in the air.

"She seems fine." He pointed down at her and grinned.

"I tend to wake her up a lot, but I think she's okay."

Picking up his keys, he started to walk out the door. "Landon's on his way. I'll just wait for him in the living room after I check things out, unless you need something."

"It's all right. I'll just get dressed." I hesitated briefly. "There's no one here. I had a nightmare. I'm fine."

He nodded and walked off.

~~~~~~

"What do you expect me to think when I see another man in my room with his arms around my wife?" Carter paced the floor and ran his hands through his hair. Landon sat calmly in the chair in the corner, watching his brother-in-law, who was having a meltdown.

"Carter, I'm telling you, it isn't what you think. She was scared, and he happened to be there. Be grateful he was. Isabella could have gone into preterm labor, and he calmed her quickly. I was there within ten minutes. Nothing happened."

Carter continued to pace the hotel room like a caged animal. "That's beside the point. He should have never had his arms around her."

Landon tried to understand what he was going through, but he knew the truth when it came to Isabella, and he should have never doubted her. Quentin, on the other hand, he had seen a change in him. He had seen how he looked at her. He hid it well, but he recognized it. Quentin had some interest in her, but it was one-sided. Isabella had no interest in anyone but Carter.

"I know it looks bad, but you have to trust your wife. She loves you. She always has."

Carter turned and looked at him like he was totally lost. "I trust my wife. It has nothing to do with that. The one thing I can't get past is that she thinks I'm dead and so

128

does he. You can't tell me that if you were in the same situation that you wouldn't be upset. Would you want someone with Beth, hugging her?"

Landon looked at him, questioning himself, and Carter studied his reaction. "Yeah, I didn't think so."

"Look, I'll try to get her to you sometime this week, but you need to take care of Bentley before something else happens. We need him for a witness when we bring Arnell in."

Carter sat down on the couch and run a hand down his face then bent over his knees. "I can't let something happen to her. It's my responsibility to keep my family safe, and I can't be there. I knew when this was brought up, it was a bad idea."

"None of us thought it would take this long to bring him down."

"It would help if we knew exactly where he was."

Landon shifted in his seat, watching him. "We know where the operation is if we could just catch him at it."

"Well, that is a mighty big if."

Landon rose to his feet, and Carter leaned back. Fidgeting with his sunglasses, Landon took the mirrored frames from the neck of his T-shirt and put them on. "I better go. I have to check on Bella before I get down to business."

Carter looked frustrated and hit the table in front of him with his fist. "Keep your cool, bro. I'll take care of it."

"I don't like the loss of control, Landon. I had it when I was a kid, and I like it even less now."

The day had been long, especially when I had lost sleep from this morning's nightmare. Molly had gone to bed early, which was unusual for her, but like me, she had been up early. Finishing what work I needed to do for school, I started doing a little digging into records. There had to be something in my medical records that had shown what exactly happened to me. Everything I thumbed through, I found nothing.

I went through the desk drawer again and found nothing to explain anything about what I was almost sure didn't fit. Turning over the health care records of Molly and Carter, I found an envelope with my name carefully scrawled on it. I had never seen it here when I looked before. I knew before I opened it that Carter had written it. I would know his handwriting anywhere. My hands shook as I looked down at the carefully penned letter.

February 28, 2013
Angel,
If you have this letter, I'm no longer with you. I want you to know that no one has given me the color in my life like you have. I can't imagine what my life would have been if you had not been in it. From the day I met you, I knew that we were going to be together.

God gave you to me as a gift. It isn't every day that a person is blessed with a great love. I hate that I can't be there, but know that where I am now, I'll be waiting. I'll be watching you and loving you until the day we all can be together again.

Kiss Molly and tell her that Daddy will be with her during each important time of her life: her first day of school, the first time she rides a two-wheeler, her first dance recital. I know she will be wonderful. I'll be there for her first date, her prom, her first love, and her wedding. Encourage her to look for the man that God wants in her life and not to settle for less. She's such a precious young lady. Tell her I love her so very much and I never wanted to leave her.

Then there is our baby. Nothing could have thrilled me any more than hearing you were carrying our child. I wish I could be there to see you through this pregnancy, but know that I love you and this baby more than you will ever know. Kiss him and tell him about his daddy and how much I wanted to be there. Whichever it is, a boy or girl, teach them a love of God and encourage them in love and patience.

When you miss me, close your eyes and I'll meet you in your dreams. Don't fret. I'll always be close by. Know that I always felt you were innocent. You are a beautiful woman, and I cherished you. I'll take your love with me.

Landon will be there for you. Go to him. He'll take care of you. He's my best friend and promised me he would look over you, and my parents will always be there. Know that I will always love you.

Love you, angel,
Carter.

My fingers traced the writing on the paper before me. Looking at the date, it was just before he was killed. He knew? He couldn't have. If that were true, it meant he knew that the assignment he went on was almost certain death. How could he have left me? My heart clenched in my chest as I thought of him. It was if I had lost him all over again.

The words rose from the page as I read them and left a crater through my heart. One way or another, the man who had done this was going to pay for the life he took from me. Not being able to get through school fast enough, it would most certainly be delayed. If I found out for sure who this monster was, I would never say a word. He would be mine; I would be the one to bring him down. If it were done with the last breath in me, I would see it come to pass.

I needed to get away. I wasn't sure how I was going to manage it, but I was going to leave and go to the cabin alone. When the opportunity presented itself, I would take it, leaving Molly with the Blakes. The chance would come, and I would be ready for it. Maybe the cabin wasn't the best place to go. If I just disappeared, they would know where to find me. The cabin would be the first place they would look.

Pictures. There had to be more around here, and if so, there would be pictures of places that he had been before, places he had never had the opportunity to mention. Starting with the desk, I opened it and found the stack of pictures that Carter had wrapped a rubber band around and started looking through them. There had to be somewhere that was special, somewhere where I could get away without someone finding me.

~~~~~~

The day was warm, and the sun beamed down on Carter as he walked the green lawn of Knoxville University. The majestic brick building stood stately, with the clock tower ready to strike the hour. It had been some time since he had walked these grounds, but it had seemed like he had just set foot on it yesterday.

Today he was here to meet Ryan Bentley. He was sure where he would find him. It was something he had to do before he could get anywhere near home and back to Bella. Ryan taught one of the social sciences. He also coached for the university football team. It was ten in the morning; and if he had remembered right, they ran laps and calisthenics in the morning, preparing the new year of recruits. If the schedule was the same, he would find Bentley on the football field. Carter had no trouble getting past campus security, being dressed in his dress blues. There was no question as to his justification of being there, and that was what he was hoping for. He would talk to Bentley and get him under protection as soon as possible.

When he reached the field, he found a team of young men doing push-ups and a group of four coaches talking together. From the picture he had, Bentley was relatively easy to pick out from them, being the youngest of the group. The picture had once been Isabella's, the old black-and-white had them together and appeared to be a

133

picture of them from college. He had stood with his arm around her shoulder, looking down at her adoringly, but she looked haunted. Looking at Bentley's expression, there had been no doubt that he had loved her at one time. Walking up to the group of gentlemen, Carter addressed them and introduced himself, asking if he could speak with Ryan in private. Ryan had agreed and left the field, followed close behind by Carter. Making their way down the corridors, he found himself in the classroom where Bentley taught. The class was vacant, and Ryan sat down at his desk as Carter removed his hat and sat at the desk in front of him.

"Officer Davis, what can I do for you? When you met me outside, it seemed urgent that you speak with me."

Carter took the picture from his jacket, only to confirm that this indeed was the same Ryan Bentley and handed him the picture. "Do you recognize the young woman in this picture?" Ryan took the picture and studied it, but it didn't take long for him to answer with the positive ID that Carter already knew he would most certainly get.

"Yes, I recognize her. She was my college sweetheart. That was a few years ago. Is she in some kind of trouble?" He handed the picture back to Carter and waited for an explanation.

"The police force in Portland seems to think that her life may be in danger. Her family told the department that she had gone missing and that you were the one to find her. The man that had taken her is a threat to her and some others. At this time, we are concerned with anyone that had any connection to her. If you were the one that got her away from him, your life may be in danger as well.

The department is close to making a move on a man named Arnell Andrews. The man has been known to be armed and dangerous. My job is to see that you are protected."

"This happened six years ago. Why would he come after me or her now?"

"There has been some evidence that has come to light in some recent happening with a local teenage group that had been affected by some of his dealings. Three of them were killed. The young men were part of the Panthers football team, and the girls were two of the senior high cheerleading squad. Isabella Cameron was also a cheerleader, and we found that you were the center for the team when she was found."

"Oh, I see. Do they think this is the same man?"

"More than likely, it is the same operation. The man who runs a business of teenage slavery is wanted for kidnapping, assault, battery, trafficking, and premeditated first-degree murder. This guy is not small change. We need you as a witness when we bring him in since you were with Mrs. Blake that night. It is of the utmost importance that you are under protection."

"You have to be kidding. After all this time, why would he want anything to do with me?"

"I'm not sure he will come after you, but you were there to help get Mrs. Blake out of the operation. If he knows that, he will come after anyone that is connected to her to bring her back where he wants her."

"Wait, did you say Mrs. Blake? Izzy got married?"

"Yes." Carter hesitated and continued to explain that he needed to get him under protection as soon as

135

possible, then Bentley brought up something he hadn't expected.

"I'm all for trying to help her, but there's a problem. I have a girlfriend and a daughter I need to think of. I can't leave my daughter unprotected. She means everything to me."

Carter swallowed hard. He wasn't expecting this at all. "I wasn't told you had a family."

"Yes, my daughter is a student at one of the local elementary schools."

Carter's mind started reeling at the thought. If she were old enough to be in school that meant his daughter could have been the same age as Bella's. If that was so, the daughter he was claiming could be his own child.

"I hope that doesn't present a problem. If I'm in danger, I need her protected. I'm all she has. Her mother wasn't able to care for her so I took her and have raised her myself. I'm all she knows as a parent from her birth."

"I see. Is there a way I can meet your family? I would like to see that they are put under guard. It's important that they are under watch and know to stay with their assigned officer. If it gets out of hand, then we may have to put you in a protection program. I don't want to do that unless it's a last resort."

"Sure, I understand. Why don't you come by the house tonight? I'll give you the address and my cell number. It shouldn't be a problem. I'll get in contact with Gail and let her know you're coming so she isn't totally thrown at an officer arriving at our doorstep. I have class till three. I should be home by four thirty, and we can talk then."

Standing, Ryan met Carter in front of the desk and shook

his hand. "I hope Izzy's okay. She had it pretty hard for a while. I haven't seen her in over a year. We took a shot at a relationship, but it just didn't work out. I'm glad she's happy."

Walking in the door to his hotel suite, Carter felt the weight of the day lie upon him. Dropping his keys on the table, he removed his jacket and loosened his tie. Plopping down on the couch, he kicked off his shoes, hitting the floor with a thud. Leaning back, his attempt at relaxing was futile. It had been a difficult day. He had questions he wasn't sure he wanted answers to.

Running his hand through his hair, he sighed, trying to get a grip on what he had seen. The resemblance was uncanny. Ryan had invited him into his home and he had met Gail, but nothing had prepared him for what he encountered, nor was he expecting what Ryan had told him about his daughter.

He met the little girl as she bounded into the living room with a drawing she had made of who she said was her parents. The stick people sported yellow hair for her father and brown rings for her mother. Ryan's daughter had jet-black hair like his sister Beth and his own, her eyes were aquamarine blue, and her laugh was contagious. She had taken to him, immediately showing him her creation.

When he had asked her who the people were in the picture, she quickly reported, "That's my daddy, and that's my mommy." She pointed to each one then handed him the picture. "You can have it. I draw all the time." She had also drawn a picture of two other men, one with red shaggy hair and the other one with black hair, both with large smiles. She announced they too were her daddy. She knew them from a picture her father had. He had taken the pictures and folded them, placing them into his pocket, assuring her that he would find a special place for them.

She had told him in her innocence after Ryan had left the room that her name was Jenna and had asked him his. He had wanted to tell her, but he had replied with his given name Eli. She was about to tell him her mother's name when Ryan returned.

Jenna looked so much like Molly that they could have been twins. She was a beautiful little girl with the spirit of her mother. There was no doubt that this was not only Bella's daughter but also his. It presented a problem not only for him but also for Isabella and this little girl. Ryan was the only parent she knew. How did Bentley end up with her, and why was Isabella led to believe that she had died?

Taking the cell phone from his pocket, he dialed Landon. Any way he went about this, it was going to hurt someone. The cell phone rang for the fourth time, and Landon answered in an exhausted rush.

"Yeah, Mason."

"Landon, we have problems, major ones."

"Bentley under protection?"

"I assigned him three different officers."

"Three?"

"One for him, one for his girlfriend, and one for his daughter."

"He has a daughter?"

Carter rubbed his forehead and sighed. "It seems Mr. Bentley has a six-year-old daughter."

"What's wrong with that?"

"Landon, put it together. Six years ago would have put him in high school. It also puts Bella in high school."

"I'm sorry, I'm not following."

"If you saw this little girl, there would be no question. Her name happens to be Jenna."

"Oh!" Landon let out a hiss like he had been burned. "Isabella's Jenna?"

"Well, that's what I'm guessing."

"I can do a little digging, see what I can find out. Of course, adoption records are sometimes hard to crack. If it were a closed adoption, I may not be able to get into it."

"I'm not sure what you're going to find, so you need to know this." Carter took a deep breath. "Jenna could be mine."

Landon never said a word, leaving Carter wondering if he were still there.

"Landon, are you still there?"

Landon's voice reflected shock as he answered slowly, "Yes, I'm here." He paused for a moment, taking it in. "What makes you think that Jenna is yours?"

"It's a long story. I'll explain it later. I really don't want to go into it now. It was a long time ago, and I'm not proud of it. Just see what you can find out about Ryan, Jenna and her adoption, and her paternity if you can."

A cry came from him as a child. "Don't do that again, you little brat. You want us all to be locked up?" Carter stood on trembling legs as tears streamed down his dirty face. Pointing ahead of him, he had instructed him to go to his room. As soon as he had reached it, he had sat down on the floor on his knees, resting back on his heels. His hands lay on his knees shaking, and his head bowed as he cried. He knew what was coming from his foster father's behavior. This was his sacrifice to protect his sister.

Carter heard Arnell's belt clear the loops of his pants from behind him, and he cringed.

He knew nothing of what this man did to him other than it hurt. Once he entered the room, he closed and locked the door behind him. The pop of the latch sent terror through him. He never got over the fear, even though he knew what his foster father was going to do.

Taking him by the arm, he growled in a low menacing voice, "Get up." He knew the routine well. Standing, he took his shirt off and placed his hands on the wall in front of him, bracing himself for the inevitable. The sting of the belt burned across his back. Arnell would hit him so hard at times that it would cause his skin to bleed. The torment had caused him to act older than his years.

"Since you don't want this for your sister," he spoke gruffly against his ear, "then you will take it for her." He squeezed Carter's shoulder, causing him to wince, but he held in the pain. Carter could hear the dull sound of a zipper being pulled, wishing his parents were still alive. The bed creaked as Arnell had sat down.

"Undress, boy. Don't hesitate." Carter started and began to turn around when Arnell yelled at him. Carter had felt cold, guilty, and scared standing there. He soon felt the searing pain of his abuser. He was just a little boy and had no idea of what Arnell was doing. All he knew was that he didn't want to ever hear his sister cry out in pain again. He had seen what he had done to her once as he had forced him to watch. The acts of abuse Arnell forced upon him left guilt and shame on him not knowing what do with the feelings he had. He often had thrown up afterward at the thought of what this man was capable of doing. Carter awoke from his tormented sleep, breathing heavily. His hands shook as he ran them through his damp hair.

He had overcome night terrors and nightmares of that time years before. Looking at the clock, it was four in the morning. Sitting up, he found his way to the edge and leaned his arms on his knees with his head in his hands. Trying to take control, he rose from his bed and turned on his laptop. The light illuminated the room in a blue haze as he rubbed his eyes. Running his camera, he saw that Isabella was sleeping soundly with Molly snuggled into her arm. At least she was peaceful.

Leaving his laptop on with a view of their bedroom, he walked on into the bath, turning on the shower. Shaking his hand off from testing the water, he undressed. His clothes were drenched from a cold sweat the nightmares always seemed to leave behind.

Stepping in, the water washed over him. Standing in the shower, he supported himself by placing his hand on the tiled wall of the oversized enclosure. He ran his hand through his wet hair while he tried to let the shower wash away the anxiety. He hadn't had a nightmare of this proportion since his early twenties. As a matter of fact, one of the last ones he remembered was during his hospital stay.

Closing his eyes, he could still see Arnell making his demands. His helplessness came from not being able to be there for his family. After all the time that he had been treated for nightmares and night terrors, he knew what brought them on. Seeing Isabella go through them had broken his heart because he knew what they did to you. Night terrors she wouldn't remember just left you drained, but the nightmares were something else. They were vivid and just as real as the day they happened.

When he returned to the bedroom to dress, he watched her. She was up and pacing the room aimlessly. He wasn't sure if she were awake. She was talking and appeared to be awake, but there was no one in the room with her other than Molly, and she was asleep. The light remained off in the room, and she started toward the desk. Sitting down on the edge of the bed, his waist wrapped with a towel, he continued to watch her. She sifted through the mail that lay on the desk, the box of Jenna's things, and his bag of belongings from the hospital. She picked up his cell phone and dialed. Without a light in the room, she paced and would stop to listen and talk to no one.

He continued to watch her as his own cell phone rang. Picking it up, he continued to watch the screen in front of him. Not looking to see who was calling him, he hit talk and heard her singing on the other end. Her voice shaking slightly, he knew she was still asleep. She sang as if she was singing to a baby, then she talked to him. "Carter, honey, where are you? Don't you want to see the baby?" She rocked one of her arms back and forth like she was rocking a precious bundle. She held to the phone and continued to carry on a conversation without him making a sound. He sat and continued to sit and listen to her. "Honey, why don't you stop and get some milk on the way home. You will be home soon, won't you?"

Knowing she would never remember, he answered. "Yes, honey, I'll be home soon."

She smiled and giggled at his response.

"I love you, *amore*. We miss you." Her smile went to a distressing cry. "Please come home. Don't let him take her away. She's all I have. He took everything."

Carter choked as he tried to calm his wife. "Isabella, it's all right. Put her to bed, angel. I'll be home soon. Why don't you go back to bed? I know you're tired."

"But he will be back. He took my Jenna and you." She continued to cry as she rocked her imaginary baby.

"Isabella, let's go back to bed. I won't let him hurt you anymore. Put the baby in the crib and go back to bed." Walking back to the desk, she leaned in like she was laying the baby in the crib. She kissed her hand and lay it down on the paper before her as if she were kissing a child. "Good girl. Now let's go back to bed. We're both tired, and the baby is safe."

She walked back over to the bed and with the cell phone in her hand. She sat down on the bed and looked around the room. "What's wrong, Bella?"

She never said a word. She just looked around the room, studying it. "Honey, it's time to go to bed. Turn off the cell phone and lie down. Go back to sleep. You're safe."

"Okay."

As bad as he hated for her to hang up, he knew she had to. "Sweet dreams, angel."

"I love you."

She hung up and lay back down on his side of the bed next to a very contented Molly. He couldn't believe she had picked up his cell and had somehow connected to him. In her sleep, she had dialed his cell. Unthinking, he had answered and heard her sweet voice. He needed to go home and be with her. She needed him. Sitting on the bed, he continued to watch her, and after ten minutes, he was persuaded that she was now asleep.

Waking, I found Molly lying in a ball beside me. She must have had a nightmare. They were getting more frequent, and I found her in my bed as much as I did her own. Lying there, I stretched and looked around the room, noting that the desk was messy with papers spilled on it and Jenna's blanket knocked to the floor. Carter's cell phone was lying on the table beside me.

Running my hand down over my stomach, I talked to our baby and sang to him. I was scheduled for a doctor's appointment within the next few days and was hoping for a confirmation of what I was having. The last time Dr. Carley had tried, it was not exact. The baby had decided to cross his legs, not allowing me to know. In the length of time I would wait for my appointment, it would be close to five and a half months. I would have an ultrasound and some other testing to ensure that the baby was healthy. Lord knew I needed some good news.

Sitting up, I looked around once more at the disarray of the room. What in the world had happened? I didn't remember doing all of this. The cell phone lying on the table got my attention once more. Why would it be lying there? Getting up, I walked to the desk and picked up Jenna's blanket and folded it, laying it back into the box. Carter's wallet and keys lay on the desk as if he had come in and emptied his pockets. Picking up his keys, I examined them carefully and stood there still listening for footsteps, anything that would indicate someone was in the house. Walking to the door, I looked into the living room and dining room and heard nothing. As I started to walk into the room, I heard the kitchen cabinet rattle and started to walk toward the sound. The first thing to enter my mind was that I was dreaming, and it couldn't be what I had thought. I grew excited at the thought that he was home.

Picking up the pace of my feet, I walked a little faster to the kitchen and squealed with glee. "Carter!" But as I reached the kitchen, I found Quentin at the sink getting a drink of water. My heart sank as I stood there, stunned.

Quentin stood at the sink, holding a glass of water. He had just taken a drink when I walked in. He was dressed in khakis and a black T-shirt. His hair was gelled, and his sunglasses hung from the V neck of his shirt.

"Isabella?"

"Oh, Quentin, I'm sorry. I didn't hear you come in."

"It's okay. I should have called before I came, but I thought you would be up and ready."

145

"Ready?"

He lifted the glass once more and took another drink and lay it down in the sink. "You have an appointment with Roxie today, and you said you wanted to visit Grayson and Iris."

"I'm sorry I forgot. I must have missed the alarm. I didn't sleep the best last night. Just give me a few minutes."

"Take your time. We have about an hour before your appointment."

Turning, I walked away and I could hear his footsteps behind me as he walked into the living room.

"Isabella, I need to make a few calls, if you don't mind."

Without turning, I continued into the bedroom. "It's fine, Quentin. Do what you have to."

Sitting down on the bed, I took a breath and shook the remaining thoughts of Carter from me. I knew better. Why had I jumped to the conclusion that he was still alive? It hadn't taken long to dress, and it was the first time that I had worn a maternity outfit. It was official. I was truly pregnant. Molly was dressed and ready to go but remained lying on the bed. She was tired and hadn't awoken completely. Picking her up, I carried her into the living room where Quentin sat talking on his cell phone.

"You could say it was a little off . . . understandable . . . today . . . Maybe an hour . . . We'll be home tomorrow evening around eight. I'm taking her to see Grayson and Iris. That's right. It's fine, Landon. I'll take care of it. Sure. I'll call when I get back. Do you think Mrs. Mason would like to go with us? I see . . . No . . . Don't worry. You bloodhound . . . she's safe."

Quentin hung up the phone, putting it into his pocket, and secured his shoulder holster to his body. Taking Molly, he escorted us to his SUV, and we were soon on our way.

CHAPTER SEVEN

"Mrs. Blake, it's nice to meet you. Please come in." Reaching to shake my hand, Mrs. Summers was the presence of a well-educated woman. She carried herself well. Her light-brown skin was flawless. Her dark hair was in a sleek bob; her dark brown eyes set off her high cheekbones.

"Mr. Blake and my husband were good friends. I'm happy to meet you. I wish it had been under better circumstances." She showed me to the chair in her office as she sat down at her desk, pulling out a large yellow legal pad. "I hope you don't mind. I like to make notes. It helps me to keep my thoughts organized."

Shaking my head, she continued. I didn't really feel like talking, but then again, my loving brother-in-law had insisted on it. It had been close to six months, and I hadn't spoken much about Carter's death and really didn't want to. If I did, it made it real, and I wanted to keep him with me as long as I could.

Roxie sat there speaking to me, but I barely acknowledged her. "Mrs. Blake, I can understand you not wanting to talk about it. It's a devastating event, losing a husband. Jerry and I had been married for fifteen years, and we had two boys at home under the age of eight. It took a while to adjust, and I still can hear him calling me. You never get completely over the loss, but you learn to live with it."

She paused, waiting for me to speak. I could feel the tears welling behind my eyes. I didn't want to cry, not again. I knew if I uttered one word that was exactly what was going to happen. After this morning, I wanted so badly to see him again. I had to talk though. If I didn't, I would never get out of here.

"You don't have to talk if you don't want to, Mrs. Blake, but having someone to talk to is going to help you heal sooner. My Jerry would not have wanted me to mourn his death any longer than need be, and I know Carter would not have wanted you to suffer as you have." Looking up at her, she smiled softly. "I know, believe me, I know. Your brother-in-law is worried about you, and I can understand that. He and Carter had been friends for years, and they had always looked out for each other's families."

Taking a tissue from the desk, I managed to talk with Roxie. I told her of the events in which I felt his presence with me, especially this morning. She understood. I guess I wasn't crazy after all. She assured me that people mourn differently, and this was my way. She spoke to me of my abusive situation, and I told her about how Carter had helped me heal. I still had nightmares, but he had been my comfort. We spoke a while longer, and she then escorted me back to Quentin. She shook Quentin's hand as she met him in the lobby. He stood holding Molly in his arms. Molly patted him on the chest, leaning her head against him, sucking her thumb.

"Quentin, it's good to see you. How are you doing?"

"Aside from a few scattered battles, I'm fine," he offered, and I was dumbstruck.

149

"Well, at least you're doing better than before. I'll see you next week, Mrs. Blake, and do call me if you need anything. I would love to talk to you." She held her hand out to me and shook my hand.

The trip seemed long to Greenwich. Quentin had stopped at least three times before we got there, insisting that I get out and stretch. I couldn't help but think that he had other reasons for stopping than just his concern for my health. Each time, I found him on his cell phone talking as he returned to the car. I guess it was good though, since Molly did get restless on long trips. Giving her something to watch on a portable DVD player helped her pass the time.

Quentin took Molly from me and placed her in the car seat then assisted me. "Isabella, are you comfortable?"

Finding his comment strange, I questioned him. "Yes, I'm fine. Why wouldn't I be?"

"You look a little pale. I thought maybe the car ride was making you ill."

"I'm totally fine. It's just a little stuffy." Picking up a travel brochure, I fanned myself lightly.

Reaching over the console, he checked the vents on my side of the car and then adjusted the air conditioning. "That should help." Resting back into his seat, he pulled his seat belt across him and looked at me again with concern.

"Quentin, is there something wrong?"

"No, no, there isn't." He was completely out of character; his rough exterior shell had been broken somehow. The hard exterior that he normally carried was lacking, and I felt it a little strange. Picking up his sunglasses and placing them on, his eyes that had told a different story now were covered from the guessing game. The remainder of the ride was silent, and I stared out the passenger-side window. I hadn't been to the Blakes once since Carter and I had been married, but then we hadn't been married long before his death. I wasn't sure what to expect when we arrived.

Pulling up to a large gated area, I was shocked at what I saw. We hadn't seen a home yet on this drive being more than five minutes from the black wrought-iron-and-brick gate we entered. The drive was cobblestone, and the grounds were well manicured. The drive was lined with large oaks with the ground covered in pink hydrangea, purple butterfly bushes, and yellow rhododendrons growing against a brick wall. I was wondering if Quentin had taken a wrong turn when we met another gate where he stopped and placed in a code. The gate slowly opened, and the area beyond the gate opened up to a large colonial-style home with white pillars. The home was brick and looked like it had come from another time. It was more than I could have imagined. There was no way that Carter could have lived here. It had to be a mistake.

Driving up the oversized cobblestone entrance, Quentin stopped in front of the house. Looking over at me, he hid a smile. "We're here." Opening the door to the SUV, he unclipped Molly, and I slowly got out and looked around in complete and utter shock. My heart was in my

151

throat as I stood there in amazement. I knew his family was wealthy, but I had no idea.

"Isabella, how wonderful to see you." Grayson had hugged me before I realized he was there.

"Why don't you come in? Iris will be so glad to see you."

"Mr. Blake, if you want to take Molly, I will bring in Mrs. Blake's luggage."

"Nonsense. Marshall can do that." Grayson gestured for Quentin to follow us in, extending his hand before him. "Come in and rest and have some lemonade. Clarice has made fresh pastries, and dinner will be ready soon." Grayson walked me into the large living room that had wall-to-wall hardwood cherry floors. There was a large open area. At the center was a fireplace of the likes I had ever seen. The mantels appeared to be made of white marble and were finely sculpted. There were three brown overstuffed leather couches in the room with a cherry wood table covered with a glass top. Fine art hung on the walls, making it look like a museum of sorts. It gave me chills as to what I had walked into. I had no idea when Carter had told me that he could afford a large wedding for us that he was speaking of this type of means. Molly remained in Quentin's arms as Grayson continued on into the enormous home.

"I'll show you to your rooms, and you can rest if you like. Iris and I will see you at dinnertime. One thing before I do, though, I want to let you know she isn't well and hasn't been since Carter's death, but maybe with you here, it will help her.

Grayson had shown us around and had left me after the grand tour of Carter's childhood bedroom. It had been left as if he were to return home and take over his teenage years. The white walls were accented by a black musical-note chair-rail border. In the middle of the wall across from his bed was a brushed metal letter C set off by a recessed light. Under it was a black-finished desk strewn with car and guitar magazines of every type. Instead of pictures, there were jerseys on the wall in oversized picture frames with the number 26 on them. Under the prized jerseys was a shelf of trophies and metals that had been carefully placed. In between them stood a picture of two boys uniformed, their arms wrapped around each other's shoulders. The young teens in the picture could have been anyone, but there was no mistaking them. It was obvious the two boys were Landon and my husband.

He was just as handsome then at what appeared to be at the age of sixteen. An earlier picture of him appeared with Iris and Beth sitting on his nightstand. Carter looked to be around five or six when it had been taken. There was no expression noticed in either picture, and Beth was no different. Carter had grown up here, and the guitars and bass in which he played remained in a place of prestige.

The one true picture that had shown any emotion was that of him and Molly at the park. Carter was sitting in a swing, holding her around the waist close to him. Molly looked up at him with a near-toothless grin as he looked down at his daughter. It was eerie being here. I could

153

almost feel him. Then as I thought about it, the idea of this being his room brought comfort.

~~~~~~

"She's okay," Landon had answered him hurriedly. "Quentin took her to see Roxie then to see your parents."

Carter held tightly to the cell phone as he rubbed his forehead between his forefinger and thumb. "You should have told me. I was worried about her."

"If there was something wrong, I would have made sure to call you. Besides, you are supposed to be tying up loose ends so I can get Izzy to you."

"I hope how soon I can finish and get home to my family. The longer I'm away, the harder it's going to be when I get home."

"The only problem you have is a wife that loves you and is bent on getting her hands on your supposed killer."

"I have to hand it to her. She's consistent."

"Izzy should be at your parents by now. Quentin has called several times, keeping me updated. Everything seems to be fine."

Carter thought for a moment then smiled to himself. "I'm sure she has gotten a culture shock." Landon could hear the amusement in his voice as he spoke of his wife. "She knew that my parents were well-to-do. She just didn't know how well. I'm sure about now she's sitting down wondering what has happened."

"I am sure she is if you hadn't told her." Landon snickered on the other end as Carter listened.

"Landon, why did she decide to go see my parents?"

"I guess they invited her. It isn't unusual to visit your in-laws."

Taking a deep breath as he sat down, he leaned against the back of the couch with relief. "No, I guess not. Have you seen or heard from my parents lately?"

"The last time I saw them was the night I set up your cameras, but I heard from your father a couple of days ago. He told me that your mother has her good days and her bad ones. You know your father doesn't elaborate on anything."

Walking into Iris's bedroom, I found her dressed in a yellow bed jacket with her hair down on her shoulders. She looked as if she had aged twenty years. Grayson had walked me to the door. He explained that she had been coming downstairs little since Carter's death, and her depression was steadily getting worse. He had hoped when she found Molly and I were there, she would improve.

Trying to enter softly, I barely moved across the floor. The room was massive, as was the king-size four-poster bed she rested in. The hardwood cherry floor creaked beneath my feet as I made my way to the edge of the Oriental rug at the end of her bed.

Without opening her eyes, she smiled and lifted her hands into the air. Grayson supported me as I held to the Cherry wood frame.

"Eli," she whispered, "is that you, son?" She opened her eyes and looked around, searching. I looked over my shoulder at Grayson, who wore a pained expression. He squeezed my shoulder gently and gestured for me to sit down by her.

Taking her hand, I sat down. It never occurred to me who she was talking about. "Iris?" She looked up at me stunned, then a smile lit her face once more. Her face was thin, her body fragile. "It's Isabella. How are you doing?"

"I'm fine, honey, just tired." She patted my hand and continued to search the room. "Is Eli with you?" She smiled in anticipation.

"Who's Eli, Iris?"

"Call me Mom, Isabella."

Molly came in the room and stood by my knee. "Hi, Nan," Molly greeted her readily.

"Molly," Iris cooed. "Come sit by Nan." She rubbed the bed beside her, and I lifted Molly up on the bed. She found a secure place in the crook of her grandmother's arm and hugged her.

Iris slowly leaned over and kissed the top of her head. "You look so much like your daddy. He liked for me to read to him when he was about your age. He loved the story of Max and the beast and animals that lived on a mysterious island. He liked for me to sing to him, and I would rock him sometimes until he went to sleep." Iris looked distraught, and then she smiled again, hugging Molly to her. Looking at me, she then looked around me and seemed to be searching again.

"What is it, Mom? Are you looking for Dad?"

"No." She grinned. "Eli?" she asked excitedly. "Your husband, is he with you?" Grayson once again laid his hand on my shoulder. Reaching up, I touched his hand, letting him know I understood.

"No, Mom, Eli isn't with me."

"Will he be coming soon? I so want to see him."

"I'm sorry. He had to leave because of his job." My throat tightened as I held back the tears. She had no idea he was gone. It was like it had never happened.

"Well, tell him that Mommy wants to see him soon. Daddy and I have a surprise for him." Smiling down at her, I assured Iris I would tell him. Reaching out, she placed her hand against my stomach and rubbed it gently. As she did, the baby kicked, and she laughed heartily. "Oh!" Tears slid down her cheeks. "Eli, I bet he's happy. Do you know yet if it's a boy or a girl?" She beamed as she ran her delicate hand over my stomach. "He loves children."

The evening had shattered me with what I saw of Iris. The once-elegant and vibrant woman had left a devastated and gaunt lady. Her hands looked so thin and fragile that I was reluctant to hold them in fear I would shear her skin. My heart broke at the sight of her. She was literally grieving herself to death.

After Molly had gone to bed, I went to the living area of the masterful home and sat down on the leather couch. The coolness hit my skin as I sat where I picked up the book that lay on the table beside me. Opening it, I found scattered pictures of the Blake family. The first picture was of a very young shaggy-haired boy. His hair fell slightly over his downcast eyes. His frame was small, and his shoulders were slumped like an animal that had been beaten by its master. His clothes hung on his small frame, and he stood holding the hand of a little girl with long, dark, tousled hair. Her darker olive skin gave her away. She stood almost hiding behind him. Her head barely to his shoulder; you could only see half of her as she gripped his arm. Both were dressed well, but the tale of the haunted looks gave away the pain. There was no emotion noticed from either child.

What had my husband been through? He told me that he and Beth had been adopted, but he never told me what happened, other than his parents had been killed. Looking further, I found pictures of Carter and Beth with both Iris and Grayson and one with a couple I didn't recognize. Looking at the gentleman in the picture, there was no doubt that this was Carter and Beth's birth parents. The tall, slender gentleman had the same mesmerizing blue eyes. His skin was olive in color, and his smile was the same as my husband's. His dark hair swept to the side gave him the look of sophistication. He stood by his petite wife who had fairer skin and was a beautiful blonde with dark-brown eyes.

Looking at it, he appeared much happier as to the prior photo. I skipped through the album, coming across pictures that were his life. There were pictures of ball games and dances, and one of him standing next to a very well-kept old Mustang that he apparently was fond of. He stood leaning against the sleek black car that was polished to perfection. His hand rested on the hood as if he was claiming ownership.

Continuing through the book, I found some pictures of him later on where he appeared to be in his late teens and early twenties. His shorter hair had thrown me, looking more like a military cut. The picture struck me as being off as he had sat in his room on the edge of the bed, looking down and away from the photographer. Anger readily apparent, he sat with his hand drawn into a fist. His jaw clenched and his body was tight. I can't understand why anyone would want to keep a picture that depicted so much rage.

"It's an unusual photograph, isn't it?" Grayson's baritone voice broke through the silence as he walked from behind me. I acknowledged him as he sat down; raising his glass into the air, he pointed to the picture and nodded. "That was a difficult time for him. Taking that picture was all I had to show him how badly he needed help."

"What happened to him?"

Looking over at me, Grayson's face grew hard. "He didn't tell you?"

"No, he told me he had been totally different from how I knew him. It was all he had ever told me. He said that had I known him before I wouldn't have liked him."

Grayson sat his glass on the table and bent over his knees. "I shouldn't be telling you this. There was a reason I'm sure he didn't tell you. Carter had a troubled past, and I'm thankful that he came out on the other side. At least he had some peace before he died."

Grayson raised his hand to his eyes and rubbed them and sniffed as if he were going to break down in front of me and then regained control of his feelings. He had been so stable and such a support for everyone else it had left him no time to grieve himself. "He was a good man, Pop. You taught him well."

Sitting up and looking over at me, he smiled. "Not I, daughter. God did." He took my hand in his and gave it a squeeze, then he stood to leave the room. "I better head to bed. Iris wakes early and needs me."

Before Grayson left the room, I called to him, and he turned and looked over his shoulder. "Why does Iris call Carter Eli?" Grayson looked amused.

"Something else he didn't tell you, I take it?" I looked to him for enlightenment. "His mother and I adopted him. His given name was Elijah Anthony Marelli Davis. Marelli was his father's surname. Iris called him Eli a long time after we changed it to Carter. Another long story, I'm afraid. I'll see you in the morning."

I watched as Grayson left the expansive room and headed to the stairs. Sitting there, I looked through the picture book and studied each picture one by one. As I flipped each page, there were new discoveries. Then I stumbled onto a picture of Carter with Andrea and Molly. As many times as I had passed the picture of Andrea at home, I never really looked at it. The resemblance between us was remarkable. The picture was taken soon after Molly's birth. Andrea was thin and looked sickly, but her facial structure and eyes were so close it could have been me.

Andrea, though she was sick, had a spirit about her that shone through the photo of them. Holding Molly close to her chest, her finger pushed a curl away from Molly's face. Carter's expression was that of loss. It was as if he had already lost his wife as he held to her hand that wrapped Molly to them.

160

I traced his face in the picture and thought of what it might have been like had he been here. My heart was heavy and sank to my feet. My throat was tight, as was my chest. Anxiety washed over me. Catching myself before it went out of hand, I slowed my breaths, taking control, praying all the time for God to end it before it became a full-blown attack. Grayson couldn't help me, as he was so busy with Iris he couldn't grieve, Landon was too far away, Quentin was asleep, and the person who had helped the most was gone.

Closing my eyes, I held the book to me and took more deep breaths. The tension started to wane slowly. My eyes grew heavy, and I gave way to the waves of exhaustion, which reminded me of heat rising off pavement.

I could see his face as he looked down on me. The blue of his eyes shone through the dark, and his smile lightened my heart. "Where have you been? I've wanted to see you so badly."

He winked and ran his hand up my arm. I could feel the warmth radiate against my skin. "I've been here, just waiting for you, angel. All you have to do is close your eyes. I told you I'll be here. You need to rest."

I started to reach for him, but my hands couldn't touch him. He looked at me like I had totally devastated him. "What is it, Bella?"

"I can't reach you." Reaching out, I moved my fingers, trying to extend them. Setting his hand before me, he grabbed hold of me, and I soon felt his arms around me. Picking me up, he cradled me from where I had lain, clutching me to his chest. He laid his cheek against my head.

"I'm so glad you're back. I knew you weren't dead. They tried to tell me you were, but I didn't believe them. Please don't ever leave me again." He carried me to my room, and I could feel the sway of his body as he climbed the steps.

He laid me down and covered me with the comforter. "Go to sleep, Isabella. I'll see you tomorrow." I groaned, trying to open my eyes, but it was no use; I was so tired that they felt as though they were glued shut. My hand clasped his, and I begged him to stay. "Please stay." My voice pleaded.

"I'm not going anywhere." He pushed my hair from my face and traced his finger up my cheek and back into my hair, stroking it gently. "Sleep, Isabella."

Turning over, I looked across the room. I was in Carter's room and in his bed. The feather bed encased me as I tried to shake the fog from my head. It took a few minutes before I started to think about how I got there. The last thing I remembered was looking through a picture book. Then what happened? I lay there rubbing my eyes and tried to put my tangled thoughts back together. Unknowingly, I rubbed my stomach. When I did, the baby started to kick, breaking my concentration. It had brought a smile as I looked down, seeing his foot or hand pushing against my stomach. "Well, good morning to you too, Elijah or Sophia, whichever you may be. Now how do you suppose we got here?" I felt satisfied here, and the presence of my husband was around me.

Stretching my arms over my head, I gripped the pillow and blinked. The sun cast a shadow over the wall and across my bed, landing on a picture on the opposite side of the room. The picture was small, and I was unable to see from where I lay. Rising slowly, I sat on the edge of the bed. Running my hands over my arms, I had noticed I was still dressed in the clothes I had come in the day before.

Walking across the floor, I pushed my hair from my face and tucked it behind my ear. The closer I got, the clearer the image became. There, standing on the deck of a large pristine vessel, was my husband. He leaned against his hand that was atop the gold railing. Against a wall of white were the letters that spelled out the grand lady's name in script blue, the *Blue Angel*.

There were so many things that Carter had not talked to me about. The short period we were together, I guess, left him little time to tell me about his home and what a life he led before I came into the picture. I wasn't sure how I felt about the things that he hadn't disclosed to me. I wasn't angry, but I was confused. Why didn't he take the time to tell me about his home and some of the things that he did before he met me? I felt like I was just now getting to know my husband.

Looking at the clock, it was just six thirty in the morning. I didn't normally get up this early, but for some reason, I was reasonably rested, even though the night before I felt like I would never awaken.

Sitting back down, taking the picture with me, I started to go over the events of the night before. The blue of his eyes come back to me in flashes. It couldn't be possible that he was here. It had to be a dream. I had done this the night before, and it had sent hope through me and I wasn't going to let it do that to me again. Lying back on the bed once more, I closed my eyes, and the memory

163

stirred. I had been held by him. I had felt him next to me. I had heard his heart beating and felt the warmth of his body.

His voice, I had heard him speak to me. What had he said? Turning back to my side, I closed my eyes again. "Go to sleep, Isabella. I'll see you tomorrow." That startled me enough that I opened my eyes wide and looked around the room. I walked across the room for any sign of him I could find and saw none.

Opening the door to the hallway, I looked into some of the empty rooms and walked past Iris's room as I did. I looked in to see Grayson standing at the foot of her bed, with Quentin sitting in the chair facing away from the door. Opening the door to the room across the hall, I looked in. The room looked cold and unforgiving, the furniture was sparse, and I felt it a little strange. It didn't match the rest of the house at all. It was decorated in what looked like an old English style. There was a bentwood rocker with a velvet cushion in dark blue in the corner next to a small hanging bassinet of white wicker. White sheer curtains and streamers run from the ceiling to the floor, making it look like it came from an earlier time. The blanket of what looked to have been once lightly used was hanging over the side, waiting for an owner. There was a single floral rug in the center that pulled it together. In the corners were boxes stacked on boxes of unknown items. I sat down in the rocker gently, not knowing if it would hold me up. Through the ivory lace curtain, shadows pass along the bassinet, and I looked down into it, seeing a friend long forgotten. A buff-colored mohair teddy bear sat in his cotton plaid vest against the white and blue adorned bassinet. Picking it up, I looked at it as if it could talk and wondered if this could have been my husband's. He was soft, small, and loveable, the perfect size for small hands. He flopped over to one side as I held it. This wasn't going to be easy. I was going to be raising two children on my own, and I wasn't looking forward to it. Everything felt so unjust, and it pained me to think that Carter wasn't here. He had missed so much already, and the baby hadn't been born yet.

The pain was killing me. The overwhelming grief hit me as I sat there, and I ended up on my knees, not knowing where it came from. I thought this was over. The randomness of the crying jags had left, and now it was back. Why now? Why was I doing this now? Was it because I was here in his house? The halls echoed his voice and life. It was hitting me hard here and was just as bad at home.

Looking down at my wedding rings, I clutched them and held my hand to my heart. I missed him so much. There was no denying what I felt. The rage was there; I was angry and wanted to know why he was taken from me. Laying my hand back on the floor, I knocked over a small antiqued music box, and it began to play a sweet melody that had startled me. The melody was familiar; pictures flooded my mind as I sat listening to the loving air. The tears instantly stopped flowing as I watched the memories unfold before me.

I could hear his voice in a smooth, calming manner call me Cindy as he took my hand and walked me into the large solarium. The tile clicked under his feet as he led me and asked me to dance. His smile warmed me. Instantly, I knew him. He had taken me in his arms and held me next to him as he waltzed me around the room to the tune playing. It was the first and only time I had felt safe and complete from the time I had been abused.

Taking me by the hand, he had held it against his heart. The soft beating of his heart against my hand soothed me. The blue of his eyes was that of my husband, and I saw him for who he was. He had been Eli from South Shore Rehabilitation. I met my husband and fell in love with him only to find him years later and have lost him again.

His loving gesture of reading to me had brought me from the dark and desolate place I had been in. I hadn't spoken or acknowledged anyone for weeks. My counselor had given up on me ever participating in group and had allowed me to sit in the chair, curled up, and listen; only I hadn't. I wanted to be shut off from everything, for as long as I was, nothing could hurt me. My heart and mind was so scattered that I couldn't put two words together if I had tried. Carter's affection and patience had brought me back to the living, and I loved him for it.

He had been there, but for what? He had to have been a patient or he wouldn't have been there. South Shore didn't allow for many visitors. We only had visitors on the weekends because of the therapy groups we were to participate in. His hair was short and cut more like how he looked in the picture I looked at last night. It must have been then it was taken. When I had seen him, though, he hadn't appeared to be filled with so much anger and rage that was reflected in that single picture.

I can remember it being one of the happiest times in my life, after he broke past the pain and guilt I had buried. It was also the darkest part of my life. Carter managed to come see me after his dismissal from the center. I had looked forward to his visits and was often the highlight of my week. Remembering this was a shock. I had met him years prior to our meeting at the hospital, and I wondered if he realized this. If he had, I would have thought he would have spoken of it.

I had fallen for him then. No wonder I felt connected to him when I had taken care of him, even though I hadn't remembered there was a connection. Dear god, he had been my lifeline from the living nightmare I had been in. What was his story? I would have to find out now that I knew he was there and that he was the young man that had loved me through a hideous and dark time when no one else could reach me. The revelation had only made me love him more.

Carter had returned to the mountains for hiding until he knew that Ryan Bentley and his family were safe. They now had 24/7 guard. If it came down to it, he would have to put them in a witness protection program until they could get to Arnell. All he could do was hurry up and wait.

It was early morning, and Carter had been out for a run. He normally enjoyed his runs in the early-morning hours in the mountains because of the spiritual lift it gave him. Today it had left him drained physically and mentally. The entire time he ran, he thought of his wife and children and how hard it was to be away from them. His time away from his wife had felt like a lifetime. He knew there was a purpose to all of this, but it hadn't helped.

Fire burned in him that he didn't find welcoming. He was angry, anger that he hadn't felt for a very long time. What he had dealt with over the last few months was trying him. Sending him through the fire wasn't what Carter had thought God had intended when he took the assignment. With a new wife, a baby on the way, and a new life, it wasn't what he was prepared for. Most recently, he had now found he could potentially be a father of a child that he never knew, a daughter that he had no connection to, and his wife had lost years ago thinking that she was not only dead but also had belonged to another man. It was the only thought she had. What would she do if she found out it was true? If Jenna was alive, and the Jenna he met was Bella's daughter, what would happen if she turned out to belong to them? How could he make it right after all this time? It wasn't only going to try him, but Bella, who he felt was so fragile it might be enough to push her over the edge.

Not only that, but to find that her husband that was thought dead had been alive for the last five and half months was going to be a blow to her. It wasn't his idea to do this, but he could have backed out. It had meant him leaving his job, but he could have done it.

Throwing the keys on the couch, he walked over to the refrigerator and took a bottle of water from it. Taking a long drink in an effort to drown the thirst, he thought of her. Her memory lingered there. The cabin, in the woods of Tennessee seemed so empty without her there. He sat there thinking, trying to reason out every possibility as to why God had put him there and what he was supposed to take from the situation. There didn't seem to be a bright spot anywhere in it, at least none that he could get from it. Kicking off his shoes, he looked around the room and listened to the deafening silence. Silence never bothered him before. In fact, it had been welcomed more than once, but this time, it was gnawing at him.

All he had done for months was work and run, and it was starting to get old quickly. He prayed that soon he would get the call from his superior telling him that he was free to go home to his family, that it was over. He was jittery and couldn't seem to find relief. Music! That was it. He had to listen to or play music. It was the only thing that had helped when nothing else could pacify him.

Standing, I walked to the door, wiping the tears from my face with the back of my hand. As I walked into the hallway, I could hear Quentin and Grayson talking in another room away from Iris. I wasn't sure where he was, but I could hear pieces of their conversation. What I heard took me totally by surprise. Quentin was talking to Grayson about me. He had told Grayson that he went downstairs to check on me, finding me on the couch asleep. He had picked me up and carried me to my room and had put me to bed. It hurt me, and I wasn't sure why. I knew Carter hadn't been there, but that was not the only thing that had bothered me. The words that escaped him caused me to sink deep into myself.

169

Now it was clear as to why Quentin had treated me as he had on the way here. He had asked for permission from Grayson to ask me on a casual date, seeing that he was Carter's father. He had told Grayson that he felt he needed to ask because it had been so soon since Carter's death. He wasn't sure that I would be receptive, but Quentin had told Grayson that he had wanted to ask me and Quentin felt that it wasn't appropriate not to. Quentin also told Grayson that he had been married before. The marriage was a happy one and that he had loved his wife.

I hadn't stayed to listen for any further explanation. Returning to Carter's room, I scribbled a note and left it on the desk in his room. I apologized for leaving Molly behind and assured them that I would be back for her or I would send for her. I didn't say where I was going or why. I wasn't sure how I was going to leave without someone seeing me.

Picking up my purse, I started out of the room and down the stairs. The heat of the summer day hit me in the face, and the humidity in the air caused my clothes to stick to me. Walking across the lawn, I looked for the SUV. Not seeing it, I walked down the cobblestone path to a four-car garage and was surprised to see the Mustang that was in the picture with Carter. It was a sleek convertible in an older style and was found perfect when I found the keys in the ignition. Getting in, I closed the door behind me and pulled the seatbelt over me. Turning the key, it roared to life, and the floor rumbled under my feet. Pulling out of the garage, I was hoping no one would hear me as I knew Quentin would follow me if he found I was leaving. I needed time alone. I needed to get away, but where would I go to? If I went to my parents, they would find me there because my parents were sure to call Quentin. If I went to the cabin, I might be alone for a couple of days, and maybe that was all I needed. I wished I had known where the *Blue Angel* was. Taking time to track her would cost me precious time, so I just drove. Where I ended up, that's where I would be.

CHAPTER EIGHT

Carter stood stiff as he listened to the shaken voice of Landon. Taking a deep breath, he counted to ten in his head before he uttered a word. Things were falling apart quickly, like a house of cards falling in. "What do you mean she is gone? How do you lose a grown woman?"

Landon's strong, unmovable demeanor was mildly shaken. He knew it was serious with her almost six months pregnant, not to mention the medical issues. Arnell was still on the loose. "Quentin assures me everything is going to be fine. There is a tracker on her cell phone, and he is following her. He isn't sure how far ahead of him she is or where she is going."

Running his hand through his hair in frustration, he wasn't sure what to do next. If he stayed here, he wasn't helping much, but without knowing where Bella was headed, he had no way of knowing which direction to take. He also knew if she did not want to be found, she would find a way to hide in broad daylight. "Landon, just keep me updated. I'll think of something. I'm not sure what to do next. Has he tried to call her?"

"Yes, but you know if she thinks it's him or me. She isn't going to answer."

"She's been so stubborn. Whatever she is doing, she is not going to stop until she takes care of it."

"Carter, it's going to be okay. I'm headed that way. One of us is bound to find her. Don't worry. I am sure she is fine."

Carter never said a word as he returned his cell phone to the table. What would have caused her to leave, to just pack up and leave without telling anyone? The helpless feeling he had known was worse. He hated the lack of control over the situation. Being reminded of his childhood or the lack of it made him cringe.

He had to wait for some clue to where she might be. Going out and driving off somewhere seemed pointless. How did his life get so screwed up? Walking out onto the deck, he closed the door behind him and looked out onto the mountain. All he could do was to pray for his wife and children. It was all he had left, praying for peace in the situation they were in and for this rat race to end.

I had been driving around for an hour when I looked down at the gas gauge. It was time to fill up. Obviously, the car had not been driven often. The miles on the odometer were low and so was the tank. Stopping, I quickly filled the tank and walked to the counter to pay when I heard two men talking about Luna-Joy Marina and taking out their boats for the weekend. I surprised myself by asking them if they knew of the *Blue Angel*.

The tall lanky gentleman, whom I guessed to be in his midforties, looked at me with an astounded look on his face as if I had asked him to jump off a cliff. His appearance was of one who looked like he was one of the elite and shouldn't even be at the little roadside store. He stood a little straighter like I was royalty. The other gentleman stood there and straightened his polo as he stood from his slumped pose.

"I'm sorry. What did I say?" Not sure why they were so closed mouthed, I took a step closer to pay the cashier who was also so awed that he didn't reach for the debit card I held in my hand. I placed it down on the counter in front of him.

The tall gentleman cleared his throat and started to speak. "Everyone knows the *Blue Angel* around here. That's Mr. Blake's yacht. Why do you ask?"

I put on a slight smile and looked up from under my lashes, wondering what was coming next. "Mr. Blake said that I could spend some time on her, and I wanted to know where she was docked. Would you happen to know which marina she might be in?"

He placed his keys on the counter and took a step forward, looking at me like he was searching me for the truth. "Mr. Blake doesn't allow anyone on her much anymore. Besides, the owner died a few months back." I choked back and looked up at him like I could have strangled him for reminding me that Carter was no longer with me. "Why are you so interested? Do you want to dig up old stories of Carter? Because if you do, I'm warning you if you get into that, it will turn out badly. He spent a year of his life on that boat. No one thought he would ever come back."

I waved my hand in front of him to dismiss what he was saying. "I assure you I'm not here to dig up anything, sir. I'm looking to make an escape of sorts myself." I held out my hand to him, and it stunned him more when I introduced myself to him. "I'm Isabella Blake. Carter was my husband. Grayson is my father-in-law. I haven't been able to reach him and just wanted to know where I could find her."

He shook my hand reluctantly and continued to tell me that I would find her at the Luna-Joy. "It's about forty-five minutes down the road. Just follow the signs. She's at the pier. Ask the master at the entrance. He can direct you to her."

Taking the debit card from the clerk, I thanked the gentleman and walked to the car and started it with a roar. It wouldn't be long before I finally had a taste of freedom and a chance to think about what I would do next. There had to be a way of finding this monster. If nothing else, I would let him come to me. Rolling down the two-lane highway, I let the wind blow my hair and took in the scent of the ocean. It was close. It had to be. The music played over the wind that swept over me and pounded through the air. The radio was set to an oldies station that I assumed was something that Carter had listened to. It played some of the best music I had heard for a long time. Most of the music was from the sixties and early seventies, but they did play some more modern choices at times. I did fine until I heard the song that played the night Carter had taken me out on our first date and had danced with me on the deck of the lighthouse.

Memories flooded me from that night and how he looked. I wish it had been different for us, that it hadn't taken me so long to trust him. The pain and horror of my past had been so great that I couldn't let anyone in, not even him. Knowing that, it felt like someone had stabbed me through the heart. I pulled off the road and sat for a while as I remembered his face, the touch of his hands on my skin, the way he could calm me like no one else could.

Tears lined my face, and I wiped them away with the back of my hand swiftly, angry that I have gotten to this point yet again. "God, why did you take him? He was all I had. I loved him. I trusted you. I trusted you to make things right. I gave myself to you, and you have left me here alone. I can't feel you. I did everything right, and you took him from me. Where are you? Why did you abandon me?"

Carter paced the living room floor as he waited for a call, anything to say what had happened to her. The phone rang, and he picked up in a rushed movement from the table before him. "Blake."

"Carter, this is Donavan. We think we have a legitimate lead on Andrews. How soon can you get here?"

Carter shook his head in disbelief. He was having trouble trying to protect his wife, and Brooks picks now to call him back home with a lead that may not work out. "I can leave within the hour. Are you sure this one is legitimate?"

"You're questioning a superior officer, Blake. Don't push me." Brooks's voice was hard and stern.

Carter remained unmoved. He didn't get along with Brooks and wasn't expecting it to be changing anytime soon. He stood his ground as he talked to the captain. Brooks could be a real royal pain in the butt. He was fair, most of the time, and knew Carter's work record and ethics. It was the only thing they had that was good between them. He didn't agree with Carter on a lot of things, but he did respect him. "Look, Donavan. I just want to finish up with this whole mess and get back to my wife. I've had enough. Right now my wife is out there somewhere alone because she walked away from her protection. I don't know why or how. She's almost six months pregnant and has been working and going to the academy."

"Whoa, back up. Did you say she is going to the academy?"

Carter clutched the phone harder than he needed. "Yes, I did, and she's going to kill herself doing this or be killed by what she is doing. She could lose our baby. She has had a couple of close calls already. Now if I sound a little testy, guess what? I am. Listen to me, and listen to me very carefully. Whether this works out or not, I'm going to find my wife, and when I do, I am going home to stay. If that means resigning my position, I will do so. I've been married to my job for far too long. My wife and my family come first."

Brooks cleared his throat and then addressed Carter. "Fine. If that's what you want, pull yourself from detail. It shouldn't have taken this long to find him. I know it has caused you a great deal of hardship, and I hate to see you go. You have been an asset to the force. I hate to lose you."

"I'll be there when I can. I have to check on Bella and pack. If something changes, let me know. I want this monster put behind bars." Carter took a steadying breath and shut down the cell phone. Walking into the bedroom, he started to pack the few things he knew he would be taking with him then went to take a shower. Looking in the mirror, he ran his hand over his beard and then started undressing as he readied to get in the hot steamy water that rose clouds over the enclosure.

He removed his shirt and stood looking at his chest in the mirror before him. The rough red-and-white area had left his chest marred. The entrance wound of the stray bullet from the stakeout on the night that was meant for a setup for Carter's preplanned demise by the department had gone terribly wrong. In fact, it very well could have been the real thing. No wonder JC had thought it was his fault. Landon had been with him, but JC was the one that had spotted the assailant. They weren't sure who it was or if they were armed when they had seen the dark figure. JC had hesitated for a split second, and it had cost Carter. Landon had been detained momentarily. Apparently, the owner of the property had seen what he thought had been an attempted break-in. Landon had left just long enough and had seen the figure jump the barrier and head straight for him. Carter didn't have a chance to react until he was right on him. He had managed to pull his gun, and that was as far as it had gotten.

It had only been the grace of God that he was alive. According to the doctor that had taken care of him, if it had been a millimeter closer, he would have died. The bullet would have penetrated his heart, and he would have died instantly. It was difficult to look at knowing he had been that close to death. It wasn't that he was afraid. He knew where he was going if he had died. It was the thought of Isabella and their children being left behind. As it was, it was hard to sit back and watch her grieve for him, knowing himself that he was among the living. It had been all a setup to lure Andrews out of hiding.

Stepping in the shower, his mind was flooded with pictures of her. His heart lay open from the pain of not having her with him. He hated that he was in this profession, something that he had loved and had done for years. Now he didn't care. He could feel her fingers laced in his as he closed his eyes. He thought of the way she had tried to hide from him emotionally and physically through their relationship. He had known what she was going through; he had been there. He wanted to tell her that she wasn't alone. By telling her though, he felt that he was causing more pain than that she was already dealing with. He knew now that it was more than likely the best decision he had made. Now he knew the man that had done such evil things to her was the same man that had done all manner of destructive and demeaning things with him.

A lot of secrets would come out when he was brought in, and none of them were going to be healing. Old wounds would be opened both on his and her part. Jenna would be brought out; he had no doubt in that. He had to find out if Jenna was his. If it were true, he had to try and explain to Bella what had happened both at the warehouse where he bought his supply and how he met her at South Shore. If she hadn't remembered it yet, he had a lot of explaining to do, and it wasn't going to be easy on either of them.

Thinking what they had already been through was hard. The storm was going to get rough before they came out on the other side. Just explaining where and what he had been doing since he had been thought dead was going to be difficult enough without all the compounding elements since then. Maybe she was right. What was eventually going to surface could destroy everything they had.

Standing there as the water beat down on him, he steadied himself against the wall and took in some sharp deep breaths. He had gone through the loss of one wife. He couldn't stand the thought of losing another. He prayed for her constantly. He had prayed for God to protect her and that they would meet in his time. If they never met, if God had no intention of giving him another chance for the love of another woman, he would survive. He had been content with raising Molly and had promised God to help her to learn as much as she could of him and to teach her how to live. He had found out the hard way. When he had changed, it was too late. Andrea had little time left; and even though she hadn't said it, he could see the settled peace on her face, knowing that all was right with him when she took her last breath.

That had been hard to deal with, knowing that he had been married to her and had made it so difficult for her to love him. And yet through everything he had done to his first wife, she had still loved him. He hadn't cherished her or had needed her or loved her the way he should have, and she had never moved from day 1. He hadn't been married to Isabella long, but he had felt they had a strong relationship, but it would be strained when everything started to fall in on them.

Stepping out of the shower, he dried himself off and dressed, preparing to leave for what had been home. Pulling on his shirt, the light blue of the T-shirt he wore reminded him of the button-down that she had worn of his. He couldn't help but smile when he thought of how she looked. He liked that she could put on anything and was still a woman under it all. She made his dress shirt look like it had been made for her and looked feminine in it. The cell phone rang and woke him from his thoughts. "Blake."

"Carter, we know where she is headed."

"Where is she going? Tell me and I'll meet her."

"Carter, you can't."

"Yes, I can and I will. Tell me where she is headed."

"We think she is headed to the marina."

"Why would she go there?"

"I don't know. I can't think of any reason why she would go there."

Carter thought for a minute, then it occurred to him. "The *Blue Angel*. Could she be headed to the *Blue Angel*?"

"I never mentioned it to her. Did you?"

"No, but I can't think of any other reason she would be headed there."

"Obviously, she has heard or has found out something or she wouldn't be headed there."

"You need to stop her before she gets on that boat."

"Don't worry. Quentin is on it, and if I have to, I will call the marina and have it stopped."

Carter sighed and tried to gather his thoughts before he continued. It was hard enough to do his job, but when his wife decided to take a joy ride, it was worse. "Brooks called a little while ago and said he has a lead on Andrews and wants me to come home."

"You need to go then. I'll see to Bella."

"Landon, I'm quitting the force after this. If this works or not, I'm giving up my position. My wife and kids mean more to me than this. She needs me, and I'm not there. I can't stand the thought of betraying her any longer. I'm coming home."

Straightening in the seat, I looked in the mirror of the car and started to drive. The *Blue Angel* would have to wait. I was going home. I needed to see my husband. Stopping at his grave seemed futile, seeing as he couldn't talk to me, but I could talk to him. It would be a long drive, and I wasn't sure that I could make it. From there it was going to be hard to tell where I would end up.

It would take me at least one total day between rest stops and dinner stops by the time I could get home. I couldn't drive it straight through, and I knew that. The problem was that it gave Quentin time to catch up with me. In the back of my mind, it sat there that he was tailing me. I wouldn't get far if he was behind me. Then he didn't know where I was headed or how long I had been gone. He may not have missed me yet, but he would. Pushing my hair back as the wind pushed it forward, I drove on. The air was hot and the humidity rose, and it wouldn't be long before it became unbearable. The only thing that had kept me from putting the top back up on the car was the freedom it gave me. The ocean air was calming, with its salty scent attempting to calm me. It seemed to be working for the longer I drove, the more peaceful I became.

The music blasted through the speakers, taking my mind away from the current situation, and I had no idea of why I needed to go back. Home had drawn me back. For some reason, I needed to go to the cemetery, and from there I would decide what to do next.

Silent prayers were raised from my heart to God as I drove, asking for peace, for the calming and the healing that I had needed for months. My heart ached; my body and soul craved to see my husband just as much as the day he had left me. If it were possible, it was worse. My mind was so cluttered with Molly and taking care of her, the baby, work, and going to school; grieving was the farthest from my mind. I couldn't settle on just sitting down and giving up, but it had felt that way. I had never just sat down and quit anything, and I wasn't about to now. The only satisfaction was going to come from putting this monster away.

It occurred to me that I needed to talk to my mother. She hadn't given me an explanation of what had happened or where Lee was. Essentially, I was back to square 1— plenty of questions and no answers. I needed answers. It was never going to get any better until I knew what happened with me and how I met my husband all those years ago. He was just as much as part of my past as anyone else. That was something I had no answers for. Where and why did I meet him there, and what had happened to him? Why did he stop coming to see me? He could have come to see me after I was sent home, but I never heard from him again. Why had I forgotten about meeting him?

The light turned red on the two-lane road, and I sat watching and waiting impatiently for the light to change. The steering wheel was getting warm under my hands, and I slid them around so that it didn't get so hot I couldn't touch it. The car behind me kept revving his engine impatiently, making me nervous. When the light turned green, I put my foot to the floor and sped on. A truck entered the intersection without warning, and I nearly ran into the side of him before I could stop the car. When I slammed my foot on the brakes, I turned the wheel, making the car turn almost completely around in the other direction.

The car skidded to a stop, and I put it into gear, pulling off the road for a moment. Shifting it into park, my heart was pounding in my chest and my ears. The rapid breathing from the fear made it hard to breathe as I leaned against the steering wheel.

"Are you all right?" A strong masculine voice rang through my ears as I looked up to see a young man standing by my car. His hair was long and swept against his shoulders. His dark eyes looked hollow and searching. If I wasn't already shaken enough, it wasn't any better. The rough exterior from such a young man shook me. He stood holding a helmet, and his unoccupied hand extended to me. "Miss, can I help you? Are you okay?"

I shook my head and turned the key. "I'm fine. Thanks for asking."

"I saw what happened. If you don't mind me saying, I can understand why you would be shaken."

"I'm fine, really."

"You shouldn't be traveling alone in your condition."

"I didn't say I was traveling alone."

He let out a half-hearted laugh. "I don't see anyone in the passenger seat. To me, that would mean you were traveling alone." He held out his hand. "I'm sorry I haven't introduced myself. I'm Truman Walker. Reverend Truman Walker."

Shaking his hand, I don't know what possessed me, but I gave him my real name. It isn't something that I would normally do, seeing that I was alone. I didn't want anyone trying to follow me. "You're Carter's wife."

That was a shock. He knew my husband. "You know my husband?"

"Sure. Carter was one of my best friends. We played ball together in college. I was sorry to hear he passed away. He was a good man. I see he's going to be missing out on something wonderful. I'm sorry."

I run my hand down my stomach. "Yes, I think he would have been very happy."

"Well, I better get going. You sure you're okay?"

"Yes, I'm fine."

"You know God always hears us when we need him. We just have to be willing to meet him. There's a reason for everything, whether we understand it or not. I'll pray for you." He gave me a smile and walked off and mounted his bike and rode away.

Carter had started home then was called and told that the lead turned in was a hoax. He was frustrated and continued toward home. He decided after all this time he was going to meet up with Landon and he was going back to his childhood home to see his family. If Isabella wasn't there, he would go looking for her on his own. He remembered the last time he saw her and how upset she was that he was leaving. He thought he would be home within days, at the least hours. He had seen the tears from her eyes, and his heart broke knowing that he had been the one to put them there. He had walked off that night, thinking he would hold her in his arms within a few hours and their nightmare would be behind bars.

He hadn't wanted any part of this assignment other than to help apprehend the man that had caused so much pain and torture in their lives. He hadn't intended on being the pawn in Brooks's chess game with Andrews. With the position Brooks put him in, that was exactly what he was. All he could do was to stand by and wait for the next shoe to fall, and he hated that position. Picking up his gear, readying himself to leave, the cell phone rang once more. The call went dead as he answered it and left him with cold chills. Even though he knew it was foolish to feel that way, but the lack of conversation made him shake. Calling Landon, he wanted to make sure that hadn't been him calling with Isabella's whereabouts.

"Yeah, Mason."

"Landon, it's me. Did you just call?"

"No, I just talked with Quentin. He thinks she went on past the marina. He's going to stop there first before he goes on. Why?"

186

"I know it sounds strange, but I just got a call from an unknown caller. I think it was Arnell, and if it was, he's going after her."

"Come on, Carter. You can't seriously believe that. It was just a phone call."

"Call it a hunch, whatever you want to call it, but he's going after her." Carter's voice dropped an octave and became very controlled. "We have to find her, now."

"Hang in there, buddy. We'll find her. Quentin's on it. You know he's the best. He'll take care of her. Trust your judgment in him."

Carter ran his hand through his hair and sighed heavily. "We have to find her. Her life is in danger. I have no doubt in it. If we don't find her before he does, I can't imagine what kind of horrors he will put her through."

"Calm down. I'll see to her. Just do what you have to so that you can get back to the business of being her husband and protector."

Carter ended the call without another word. He tried to have the call traced, but he hadn't been on the call long enough to find out anything. Throwing his bag by the door, he placed his cell phone in his jacket pocket and pulled his holster over his shoulder. He still winced at times when he placed it on his shoulder from his earlier wound. It pulled on the scar, making it difficult to move at times. Picking up his bag and jacket, he walked to the door and locked it behind him. Starting the car, he instantly had a feeling of dread. Something was wrong, and he had no idea what it was. Then he thought of the call received from Isabella days ago. If he could find that call, he could make the return call. He would have a hard time convincing her that it was him and that she needed to tell him where she was.

Digging his cell phone out of his pocket, he scrolled over the calls that he had received until he found the number to her cell. The cell phone rang once, and he took in a sharp and ragged breath, trying to control his feelings. The cell rang again and again until it went to her voice mail. "Bella, honey, it's me. It's Carter. I know it's hard to understand, and I will explain later, but you need to go back to Quentin or get to Landon. Call me. I need to know you're safe."

I must have driven in a state of being unaware of time as I had stopped several times but didn't seem to care about what was around me. Looking around as I made my last stop at a local gas station, I had noticed that dusk was setting in. The next stop would be a hotel for the night. I was tired and had felt it for the first time today. Driving into the first hotel I had seen with a vacancy, it looked like something out of an old movie set. It appeared well maintained, and the building had a lot of character and charm. It was large with a white block and bricked front with a revolving door to allow entrance and tall white pillars. That had to be difficult for some people that had a large amount of luggage to carry in. The outside was lit with what looked like old lanterns, but it was modern.

Entering the lobby, I was met with high cathedral ceilings. The windows were graced with ceiling-to-floor draperies in gold. The room was graced with large chandeliers and a gold-and-blue floral tapestry covering the marble floor beneath my feet. I was met by a well-dressed man in a black suit coat, white dress shirt, and gold tie at the main desk. He looked more like he was dressed for a party than as a desk clerk. I already felt out of place. It wasn't something I was used to.

"Good evening, madam. Welcome to the Heritage. May I help you?"

"I would like a room please."

"Occupancy?"

"For one please. It will be an overnight only."

"Yes, madam. I think you will find the suite on the second floor agreeable. We will bring your luggage to your suite. Breakfast will be served in the main dining hall from 6:00 a.m. until 9:00 a.m. Room service is available around the clock. If you should need linens, please dial the desk, and the service will be provided." The gentleman smiled, and his eyes creased as he did. "A physician is always on call should you need assistance. My name is Randall, and I will be your host for this evening. Please call me with request." He handed me the key card and handed me the receipt to the room. "Please enjoy your stay. Your room is 216. You will find it to the right once you exit the elevator."

"Thank you." He nodded in acknowledgment, and I walked to the bank of elevators. When the door opened, I found it to be oversized with a mirror extending from one edge of the back wall to the other. The gold railing trimmed the bottom, and the light above me gave it a romantic glow. This was a five-star hotel; there was no doubt. If I had any doubt, it was changed when I stepped from the elevator. The hallways were long and wide, covered with red walls and ivory trim. The walls were graced with large gold-framed art that took a fourth of the divided walls. The carpeting was a mix of red and gold, and the doorplates were black trimmed in gold. Sliding the card, I made my entrance to a large suite.

Greeted first with a sitting area of red-and-gold arm chairs and a loveseat that looked comfortable enough for anyone to sleep on in great comfort, the area had small antique oak tables with gold globe lamps and lace doilies. I laid my purse on the loveseat and walked on, walking through a small kitchenette with breakfast nook. It looked like something out of an English home in its petite stature. A small round oak table was circled with two oak and wired chairs that matched perfectly. A small, round, short vase held white magnolias, and the scent lifted through the air. The bedroom was large with a king-size bed that covered the back wall. Its mint-green duvet covered it and was accented with red-and-ivory pillows. A small antique oak table sat on either side of the bed, with lamps that were exact to the living area. At the foot of the bed, there was a small dressing bench covered in a red-and-ivory satin fabric that was luxurious in its feel. On the antique oak dresser was a vase of purple irises as well as a large gold-framed mirror. The ceiling-to-floor mint drapes completed the room and made it feel regal. It was one of the most beautiful places I had seen. I lay down on the bed and sank into the duvet and was encircled by it. Thinking that I would only lie there for a short period, I took in the air of the room and its charm.

Looking at the ceiling, I lay there quietly and listened to the silence as it slowly encompassed me. I was exhausted, and lying there felt like heaven. I was lonely, and I missed him. Finding out that I had met him years ago left me with a longing that I had never had. He had literally saved me. I was trapped inside of myself, and Carter had brought me back to life. He had spent months coming to my room. At first he had just had come and sat beside my bed and talked to me. I hadn't said anything to him, for it must have been weeks. Every day he had come to see me and had slowly won my trust in him. He had started reading to me classic books: *Gulliver's Travels*, *Alice's Adventures in Wonderland*, and his favorite, *For Whom the Bell Tolls*; but one that he had read that had caught my attention was *Cinderella*. He had spent days reading each one, but when he had read about the prince capturing Cinderella's heart, he had created a stir in me.

Weeks later, he had convinced me to walk down to the solarium. He had given me a handful of daisies that he had the nurse smuggle in and escorted me to the front and center of the room. We had the room to ourselves, and he had arranged to have the room lit with small tea candles and music playing. Slowly he had drawn me to him and had whispered to me, "Bella, I would do anything for you, anything to make you happy." Standing in front of him, he had told me that he would never hurt me. He had removed the braid from my hair and had let it fall down my back. From that time, I had fallen in love with him. It had turned out to be one of the happiest times in my life. I felt loved and protected by him. I hadn't had a worry of the man that had done such heinous acts to me because he had been there to protect me.

I could feel myself slowly drifting off as I thought of him. I welcomed sleep most of the time because I had dreams of being with him. Other times there were nightmares of what Arnell had done to me. I just wanted to find him and end this. I was tired and wanted revenge on the man that had taken everything from me. Curling into a half-ball shape, I lay on my side and tried to push it out of my head.

Carter was drained as he stepped from the car outside the Heritage. He hadn't spoken to Landon for several hours and was slightly on edge, waiting to hear something, anything. Picking up his travel bag and pulling the strap onto his shoulder, he made his way through the revolving doors and stood before the hotel clerk. Laying his keys down on the counter, he rang the bell, and the clerk walked from the corner office. "Ah, monsieur, bonsoir."

"Good evening, Randall. I should need a room for the night."

"Well, of course. We always have your room, Monsieur Blake, always a pleasure."

He handed Carter the key card and smiled. Room 218, the Royal is ready, sir. Please call if you need assistance. Carter had started to walk to the bank of elevators when Randall called for him. "Monsieur, just a moment." Carter turned and looked at him as the clerk put a finger to his lips. "Monsieur, I do not know if this means anything or not, but a young lady checked in about two hours ago. Very, how do you say, ah, beautiful, dark hair and with child. Madam signed in as Blake."

"Did you say Blake?" Carter looked at Randall stunned.

"Yes, Madam Blake."

Carter pulled out his wallet and opened it quickly. If Randall had witnessed his wife coming to the hotel, he would know her from the picture. He held the picture up to him and took in a deep breath, hoping for the best. "Is this her, Randall?"

Randall's face lit up quickly as he smiled back at Carter. "Yes, Madam Blake, very beautiful." Carter grinned from ear to ear. He had found her. "Where is she?" Carter could feel the stress release from his body.

"Madam's room is next door to your own, 216, Monsieur. Shall I contact Madam Blake?" Randall stood straight and clasped his hands before his chest and smiled widely. "Perhaps send up some pleasantries for your reunion?"

"No, that's fine. Thank you, Randall. You have been very helpful. Could you give me a key to her room? That would be a great help to me."

"But of course, I have a master key. You can get into any room with it." He handed the key to Carter and bowed slightly. "Just return it to the main desk at the end of your stay. Monsieur, and *bonne nuit*."

"Good night to you, Randall, and thank you."

CHAPTER NINE

"Yeah, don't worry. I found her."

The voice awoke me. The room was dim, as I looked across the room to see a figure standing in the doorway; the light flooded behind him. I couldn't tell who it was or why he was there. Slowly, I reached for my handgun as my heart pounded in my chest and up into my throat.

"Fine," the voice whispered. He dropped what he had in hand to the floor lightly. Barely moving, I cocked the gun and pointed it at him.

"Stop where you are. Don't move, or I will shoot you where you stand." The figure never made a move to come closer, and I reached for the lamp and illuminated the room. I could hear a voice coming from the man's cell phone, not being able to tell what was said. As my eyes focused, I saw my classmate from the academy. This wasn't making any sense at all. Was I dreaming?

"Who are you, and what do you want?"

He removed his glasses and set them on the table. Returning to his stance as before, he looked me up and down. "Bella, it's me. It's Carter."

Shock waves ran through me. The voice sounded like him, but the man that stood before me was lean and had the body of a runner. His hair was cut short in a military cut, and he had a full beard. "You, sir, are not my husband. He died months ago. I suggest that you turn around and get out of here before I either unload this gun on you or call the police. Either way, you will not come any closer."

He started to make a step toward me, and I sat at the side of the bed with my gun remaining on my target. "Bella, it's me. Look at me. It's a long story that I don't really want to go into it at this time of the night." The voice on the other end of the cell continued to call out. "Do you mind if I answer him? Otherwise, he will be the one to send the police. You won't have to worry."

I never moved, and he raised the cell phone slowly to his ear. "Yeah, I'm okay." He looked at me warily. "She doesn't believe me. This isn't any time for jokes." He grimaced. "She thinks I'm an intruder. I know. Can you tell her who I am before she shoots me? Stop laughing, Landon. It isn't funny." He turned on the speaker to his cell phone so I could hear the familiar laugh of Landon. The man stood there shaking his head. "Landon! Tell her who I am."

"I'm sorry. Izzy, it's me. Listen, don't be afraid. Don't shoot him. The man in front of you is your husband. It's Carter, honey. Put the gun down. He will explain everything. Try to enjoy your reunion, and for God's sake, stay with him. You aren't protected anymore since Quentin isn't with you. You need him."

"Landon?"

"Yes, Izzy."

"Are you sure?"

"Yes, honey, I'm sure. Carter, good luck, bro. You're going to need it."

He stood there looking at me, and I placed the safety back on the gun and laid it down on the table. I had to be dreaming; this couldn't be real. I buried my husband months ago. I was there and watched them carry him to

195

his rest. A familiar smirk graced his face, and he took a step closer. "You're just as beautiful as the last time I saw you."

Still wondering if what I was seeing was real, he walked to the bed and sat on the edge next to me. I felt my respirations increase and get heavy. "Don't panic, angel. I assure you it's me. No one would be crazy enough to walk in on an armed woman unless it was the one he loved." He laughed as he looked over his shoulder at me.

I tried to speak, but the words came with great distress. It was as if I were choking on glass as I tried to utter even a syllable. "I don't believe you."

"What do I have to do to convince you?"

I sat looking at him stunned at the thought that this could even be remotely possible. He reached for my hand and squeezed it gently in his, and he smiled chastely. "Come on, I have an idea." Standing, I went reluctantly with him as he led me to the vast bathroom. He sat me down on the wood-framed stool that sat before a double vanity. "Angel, I don't know how else to prove to you that I am your husband. Just humor me for now and sit here long enough for me to get rid of the beard. He took a pair of scissors and clipped away the longer part of his beard and then prepared his face to shave. When he made the first stroke down his face, it started to reveal the man underneath, and I reached up for his arm, stopping him. I didn't have to say a word as I stood up. He turned to look over at me. I motioned to the seat and took the razor from him. Gently, I shaved away the beard and saw the man underneath. With each stroke of the razor, tears started to fall as I watched my husband make his reappearance.

Taking the cloth from the sink, I wiped away what was left of the shaving cream, and it was evident who was sitting in front of me. Taking a sharp breath in, I laid my hand alongside his cheek, and he took my hand to his lips and kissed the palm of it. "I've missed you, angel." I couldn't grasp what I saw before me. He was here; he was solid and breathing. "Say something, honey." Placing his arms around my waist, he steadied me as I stared down at him.

"I don't know whether to hit you or kiss you."

Carter let out a little chuckle. "If I have a choice, I would rather be kissed than hit."

"Carter, how could you do that to me?" My voice raised in anger and pain at the thought that he and Landon had both lied to me. "You lied to me. You let me grieve for months, thinking you were dead. Part of me died when they told me you were gone. And JC, how could you do that to him? He has not had a day of peace since this happened. He's had to go through different treatment programs. He thinks he caused all of this."

"Bella, I'll take care of all of that. First, I want to see you, Molly, and my mother."

"Your mother is very ill. She doesn't look like the woman you left behind almost six months ago."

"What do you mean?"

"Your mother has lost weight, and she isn't as well kept as she used to be. She's different. You would have to see her to understand what I mean."

"Tomorrow we are going back to Rose Point, but for now we are going to bed. It's been a long day, and you need to sleep. You have kept Quentin on his toes today. Why did you leave him? He is to be your protector."

I knew why, but I wasn't going to tell him. There was more than one answer to that, and I didn't want to tell him about the conversation I heard between Grayson and Quentin. "I don't know. I just really wanted to get away long enough to think without someone being right on my heels."

"Angel, Arnell is still out there, and he will stop at nothing at coming after you or Molly, not to mention you are pregnant and have had some complications."

"How did you know that?" I asked him, shocked that he knew. I should have realized that Landon had kept him informed of everything.

"I was there. I was with you at the funeral, at the hospital, and at the academy. I couldn't say anything, but I was with you more than you knew."

"You were there. You were the tech at the hospital who was talking to Landon?"

"I was there. I saw the ultrasound." Bringing his hands down from around my waist, he placed them on each side of my stomach that was now very pregnant. As far as I knew, he hadn't seen me after I started showing. He rubbed my stomach gently and grinned. "How is he?"

I couldn't help but smile at him, and I ran my fingers through his hair. "He or she is doing fine for now."

"You don't know yet what sex the baby is?"

"No, he or she is keeping it a secret."

"Just like one of my kids to hide from me. Have you picked any names out yet?"

"I picked two, but it's not set in stone yet."

198

"What did you pick out?"

"Olivia if it's a girl and Eli if it's a boy."

"Eli."

"Yes, seems fitting since his father met me years ago."

Carter's face went pale. "You remembered?"

"Yes, parts of it anyway. Why didn't you tell me?"

"I didn't know myself until a month or two ago."

"Carter, what happened to you? Why were you at South Shore?"

"It's a long story and one I will tell you about, but I need to get you to bed before you pass out from exhaustion. By the way, how did you get here?"

"Ah, I drove your car."

"My car?"

"Well, I guess it was yours. There were pictures of you with it in the family photo album. You were leaning on it. I just assumed it was yours."

Carter thought for a minute and then it clicked. "You drove the Mustang here?"

"Yeah, she got me here in one piece, and she's fun to drive."

"She, huh, Bella, that car hasn't been driven in over seven years. I'm surprised that it even turned over." Carter smirked. "That's Ice Queen, and she can be the devil to drive."

"Maybe she just needed a woman's touch."

"Come on, Bella, time for bed for all of us." He shut the lights off behind us as we walked back into the bedroom. "You must have been tired. You didn't even change for bed." Looking down, I had forgotten I hadn't changed. I had come in and lay down on the bed and had immediately gone to sleep. "Go ahead and change, honey. At least get out of your clothes so you can sleep better. I changed as he sat down in the chair and took off his shoes and then removed his shoulder holster. I watched him as he had winced removing it. He stood and pulled his shirt over his head, revealing his chest. When he faced me, I saw a red–and-white scar that lay almost middle of his chest. My body shook at the sight of it.

Walking over to him, I stood directly in front of him speechless as he watched me. "What's wrong, angel?"

I could feel the burn behind my eyes as I started to trace the area with my finger. "Oh, what happened to you?"

He cupped my hands in his and drew them to his lips and kissed them. "I'm okay. It happened the night that I left. That's why JC thinks all of this was his fault, but I am fine. It's been months ago, and there is nothing to worry about."

"I could have lost you."

"But you didn't, and I am here with you now." Pulling back the duvet, he motioned for me to get in. "I haven't slept well in months." His blue eyes shone as he looked at me. "It's time I got back into the husband and daddy business." I slid in between the cotton sheets. They feel cool against my skin as I watched him finish undressing and slid in with me. I couldn't remember the last time that I slept well since he had been gone. He laid his arm out for me, and I laid my head against his chest as he wrapped his arm around me. His heartbeat was steady, and I felt the heat from his body. He kissed me softly and pulled me close to him. "Good night, angel. I'll see you in the morning." He traced his fingers along my arm as I sighed heavily. "Just sleep, honey." He tenderly ran his fingers up and down my arm as I lay there in the dark. I didn't want to go to sleep. I was afraid I would wake up and find him gone, that it was all just a dream—a silly, wonderful dream.

I awoke to Carter rubbing my belly and listening to his voice. "You better be good and let your momma sleep. I can see you moving in there. Behave yourself. This is your daddy talking. I'm going to have to rein you in quickly. What's that? You think she's beautiful? I think so too." My eyes fluttered open, listening to him. I grinned as I heard him speak to his child, thinking I was sleeping. "Just because I've been gone for a while doesn't mean you can't listen to me now. You know what? You are going to have the best big sister. She is going to love you just like your mommy and daddy. I love you, baby."

"Good morning, amore." I stretched slightly and smiled at my husband. Thank goodness it wasn't a dream. He was here with me and alive. I didn't dream it.

Leaning in, he kissed me softly. The strange and familiar touch left me breathless. I had missed him so much. "Good morning, angel. Did you sleep well?"

"Yes, I did." It felt strange to be lying next to him, particularly when I thought he had died months ago. It was difficult to think that this was not all a dream. "I haven't slept that well in months." Leaning in, he kissed me on the nose.

"You have the cutest button nose I have ever seen. As a matter of fact, I think you are about the most beautiful thing I have seen this side of heaven." Reaching up to his face, I traced his jaw and cheek and felt my face burn. The corners of Carter's eyes creased as he smiled down on me. "Mrs. Blake, you're blushing. I can't believe you still blush when you're complimented."

"I'm so glad you're here. I missed you so much. Where have you been all this time?"

"Tennessee. I needed to be out of the way for Arnell to be drawn out."

"Do they know where he is?"

"They have had a couple of leads, but nothing solid yet." He looked down at my stomach, and that boyish grin came across his face again, and he laughed. "I can't believe that in a few short months, this little guy is going to be with us."

"It isn't going to be soon enough." I groaned. "I don't think I've had one day since I found out that I haven't been sick at any point of the day."

"I know that all too well."

"What do you mean? You haven't had to carry this little guy and have to go to the bathroom every five minutes or get up in the middle of the night because you were sick at your stomach. That's one thing I'm not going to miss."

"Ah, yeah, about that, I knew every time that you were sick."

I couldn't help but look at him and wonder what he was talking about. He touched the end of my nose and grinned as he looked down again at my stomach. "Believe me, I knew every time. I was sick every day and have been. I've had food cravings and swollen ankles, so I know what you mean. Why do you think I'm so lean? I've been running to keep all the calories off me."

"You are still having my morning sickness? After all this time, you are still sick at your stomach?"

"Just every morning, noon, and night." He ticked them off on his fingers as he turned on his side and put his arm over my stomach, and it sat there like he had laid it on a shelf. "Talk about something to deal with when you travel back and forth. Stopping at a roadside rest isn't the most pleasant experience when the ground is spinning."

"Just paying the price of being a daddy." I grinned at him. "I couldn't let you miss out on all the fun. By the way, I ran into a friend of yours on the way here. He said he played on a college team with you. He was a strange character. Never seen a minister with long hair and looked like he belonged in a motorcycle gang before."

Carter ran is finger along his bottom lip and thought for a moment and looked at me a little strangely as he tried to remember who it might have been. "Did he give you a name? Nothing is coming to mind."

"He said his last name was Walker. I'm sorry I can't remember his first name. He said that you were friends and he had heard of your demise."

"Truman?"

"Yeah, that sounds right. He was riding a motorcycle and said his name was Reverend Walker. If you had seen him, you wouldn't have wondered why I questioned him. He had a very rough-looking exterior and looked more like a drifter than a minister."

203

It didn't take long for Carter to figure it out, then he laughed at himself as it had come to mind. "Truman is a minister? That's something I couldn't have imagined."

I found his humor enlightening as he sat up and run his fingers through his hair and ruffled it. "Truman, you had to know him to appreciate the magnitude of what you are telling me."

"Why? Is it that far out there? Don't tell me the man is a stalker."

"No, Bella, Truman isn't a stalker." He laughed as he turned to me. "Truman was a party animal in every sense of the word. When we were in college, he started the parties and was still there after they shut them down. I think he spent the majority of his senior year stoned. He decided one night at a local party that he was going to impress a girl. She was one of the guys' sisters. We were going to meet up with Marci Griggs. Marci was gorgeous, but she was also known as a man eater. She would date the guys just to chew them up and spit them out.

"Truman couldn't get the nerve to speak to her until he was well lit. She walked in the place in her normal arrogant manner, but he had no idea who she was. His whole idea was that he was going to seduce her instead of the other way around. She had quite the reputation. He had a description of her, and it was all he had to go on. Let's just say he tried to pick up the wrong girl."
I couldn't believe what I was hearing at this time. This was a look not only into Truman's life but also into Carter's. "You're kidding?" I giggled at the thought.

"Wait, it gets better. When Truman went over to this girl, one of the guys tried to get his attention." He laughed to the point he shook the bed. It was as if it was happening now in front of him. "He walked up to the girl and gave her a line, and I could have fallen on the floor when he found out it was Landon's mom. She was there to pick him up. He had to leave for the airport. Landon had a national competition he was to attend. What made it better was before he found out who she was, he had dipped her and kissed her, and I don't mean quickly. That was the funniest thing I have ever seen."

The drive back to Carter's home was long. He stewed in silence of the drive. Thinking of the possibility that he and Bella could be the parents of a now six-year-old, if she didn't remember on her own, he would have to talk to her soon. Before he did, he wanted to have some kind of truth, some kind of evidence to give her. In one aspect, he loved the idea that he could have fathered Jenna, but then the circumstances had been wrong. He didn't know her at the time or had loved her when he had performed the act.

Lord knows it wasn't for pleasure because she was drugged and he was high on narcotics and loaded with alcohol. In fact, he barely remembered the events of the evening. The only thing he had remembered was how beautiful she was, and the fact there had been no protection used, even that had been hazy. He shifted in his seat and glanced over at her. She was sleeping quietly with her face turned toward him. She looked angelic. How could he have done such a thing to her? He had been part of her nightmare, and she wasn't aware. Would she forgive him after she found out?

The wind blew his hair as he ran his fingers through it as he often did out of frustration. Even though he had been forgiven by God years ago, his past came back to haunt him on a regular basis. He would see his mother first, and then he would try to catch up with the rest of his family, making the next connection with his daughter. He had called before he left and had spoken with Landon, having him to arrange to be with the family. Landon and his family along with JC and Lily were to fly in and meet them at Rose Point. Landon was to prepare his father of their arrival. Hopefully, they would all arrive close to the same time. All he could hope for was that they would take it at least as well as Bella had. She really hadn't played up to him much. She hadn't reacted as he expected, but he wasn't sure how he expected her to react. How would you react to a spouse who had suddenly come back from the grave? He had seen a mix of emotions fall over her, from joy and relief to anger. They hadn't had a lot of time for a reunion, and Bella's trip had left her depleted. He hadn't yet spoken to her about leaving his position in the department. He certainly had intentions of talking to her about dropping out of the academy. Since he was home and breathing, maybe she would go back to her own job as a being a nurse. That's where she needed to be anyway. She wasn't wired to be an officer; she was a nurturer. Being in a line of business where you may have taken a life to save another was not something he could see her doing. She was a healer; she had that type of soul.

As he drove, he heard her moan slightly and looked over at her. Her hand lay against her stomach gently, but her face grimaced as if she were in pain. Laying his hand against her stomach as not awaken her, he tried to feel the baby move. He turned his eyes back to the road and back to her for a moment. She silently bobbed her head as her eyes remained closed. The next stop was less than a mile away, and they would be home in a little less than an hour. He wasn't liking how she looked or the grimace she displayed in her sleep.

Picking up his cell phone, he called home. The familiar and welcoming voice of his father answered, "Blake residence."

"Pop?"

A silence followed the voice for a moment, and then he heard a voice crack as the receiver moved the phone. "Pop, it's me. Pop?"

"Son, is that you?"

Carter smiled a lopsided grin and breathed a sigh of relief. He hadn't heard his father's voice for months. "It's me, Pop. Are you and Mom okay?"

He heard his father release a ragged breath before he spoke. "We're fine. Are you coming home?"

"I am on my way. Isabella and I will be there within an hour or so. I need to see Mom and Molly when I get there, and I want you to get hold of Cassidy James. Isabella doesn't look like she is feeling well. She's had a rough couple of days, and I really want someone to look at her. Once I get her home, I really don't want her to move for a day or two."

"What's wrong, boy?"

Carter couldn't hide the distress in his voice as he spoke to his father. He was worried about her and he wasn't good at hiding his feelings. "I think she's okay, but . . ." Carter's voice trailed off as he thought about the right words. He didn't want anyone to panic. There had been enough turmoil in the family to last a lifetime.

"But what, son, is there a problem or not?"

"I am not sure, Pop. I just want to make sure she and the baby are okay. She's asleep now, but she has been moaning and acts like she is hurting."

Grayson let out a little chuckle. "She's fine, boy. Your momma did that with Clayton."

"Pop, Clayton died."

"I know that, son, but it wasn't because of false labor pain. Clay died because he had leukemia. No one could have prevented it."

"I didn't know what happened to him. Mom never talked about it."

"Hurt runs deep, boy. She hasn't spoken about him for years. Clayton would have been twenty this winter, but I wouldn't expect you to know that. You were just a little boy when he died."

"I'm sorry, Pop. I know that must have been hard on you and Mom."

"It's fine. Time heals, boy. Your mom will be so happy to see you. I'll have Cassidy here to see Bella, but I'm sure all is well. Just come home."

"I'll see you soon. Kiss Mom for me, and don't tell Molly. I want to surprise her."

"I wouldn't worry about surprising her. She has told us all along that you weren't dead. Says her mother told her

208

that her daddy was fine and would see her soon. Now that's one for the book, isn't it?"

"She talks to Andrea, Pop. It wouldn't surprise me."

"I don't know what I think of that."

"I'll see you soon, Pop."

Carter turned off the Bluetooth headset and headed home.

It wasn't long that the familiar sight of Rose Point came into view. Carter was weary from worry. His wife still lay asleep by his side. He had put the top up on his last stop to take the sun off her and had bought a towel at the minimart in which he had wet in cool water and wiped her face. She was sensitive to the heat, he knew. The event on the beach Landon had spoken of had left her drained, hot, and dehydrated. She didn't feel like she was hot to touch her, so he was hoping that she was just tired. She had barely flinched when he touched her, and he debated on trying to wake her, but if she was that tired, he didn't want to wake her just to tell her to go back to sleep.

It had been so long since he and Andrea had gone through this, he had forgotten what was normal and what wasn't. But then he hadn't followed Andrea's pregnancy as he had Bella's. He loved Molly, but at the time, he wanted his wife to be alive more than he was worried about if she were going to be able to carry Molly. He was wrong about how he handled it, and he knew it.

Turning through the last gate, he saw the large manor and was glad to see the home. Standing outside, unloading the car, was Landon. His sister had walked out the door as he stopped the car and got out. She ran to him with her arms in the air and almost had knocked him down when she got to him. She cried hysterically as she threw her arms around his neck. He rubbed her back, gently comforting her. "It's okay, Beth. I'm home to stay. I am not leaving. It's all right. I'm fine. You're going to see a lot of me." He hated to put her off, but he needed to get to Bella and get her inside. Stepping back, he wiped the tears away from her face. "You okay?" She nodded and held to his biceps not wanting to let him go. "Good. I need you to do something for me. I need you to open the door for me so I can take Bella in." She shook her head and smiled through her tears and went to the door.

Carter opened the car door and reached over her to unbuckle her belt. "Angel, we're home. I need to get you inside." She moaned slightly when he spoke to her and rattled something off that he couldn't understand. "I am taking you inside to rest. Everything is going to be okay." He picked her up and couldn't believe how incredibly light she felt for being close to six months pregnant. She laid her head against his chest and sighed, and he felt his heart leap as she lifted her hand slightly and tapped his chest. Carter smiled down at her, and she continued to sleep soundly. Landon and Beth had followed him upstairs as he took her to his room and deposited her on his bed. He walked across the room and turned the air up just slightly and tried to make her comfortable.

"How is she?" Landon had taken a step forward as Quentin entered the room. Before Landon had gotten an answer, Quentin had slapped Carter on the back and had asked the same thing.

"I think she's okay, but I am going to have Cassidy look at her to make sure. Where's Molly?"

Landon pushed his hair back away from his eyes and then rested his hands at his waist. "I think she's in the nursery. She was listening to a music box earlier, and I heard her talking earlier. Maybe she's playing house or something."

Carter kissed Isabella's forehead and wiped her face with a cool cloth. "Can you stay with her until I get back? I really want to see my little girl and my mom."

Quentin straightened and took the seat by her. "I'll stay if you want to go see them. I don't have anything else to do right now." Carter acknowledged him with a nod and turned to walk out the door when he heard her stir.

"Carter." She had struggled to say his name it seemed. He watched her as he walked back to the edge of the bed and sat down. Her face remained pale, and her cheeks were flushed. The concern started to rise in him once more as he watched her. Her eyes remained closed, and she moved her hand slightly, and he took it in his.

"I'm right here." He took her hand and opened her palm, kissing the center of it.

"Don't leave me again."

"I am not going anywhere, angel. I was going to see Molly and Mom. I'll be right back."

"Promise?" she whispered.

"I promise."

Quentin looked over at him and nodded, and he stood as Bella drifted off once more. "Don't worry, man. Cassidy is here and will be up soon, and I'll sit with her until you get back."

Carter turned to walk out once more and stopped at the door and looked back at her. Quentin sat in the chair

by her with his hands crossed over his knees and leaning toward her. Carter knew that he had come back at the right time. He could see it written all over Quentin's face. He was in love with his wife; it wasn't hard to see that. Turning, he walked down the runner-lined wood hallway and down to the nursery. Molly lay asleep on the rug curled up with the bear that had belonged to his brother Clay. He had remembered him carrying the bear around by the ear for months. It was a sad time when Clayton had died, and he hadn't understood. He was far too young to understand. Carter stooped down to see his daughter and found that she was sleeping peacefully and kissed her cheek. Standing, he walked across the hall to see his mother. Looking in, he could see the small frail-framed woman lying in bed and his father sitting next to her. His mother lay there with her eyes closed, and his father sang to her softly. The tune being familiar, he listened before he had gone on farther. Then he recognized it as "Where Do I Begin?" His father's baritone was soothing to him as well as it was to his mother. He remembered his father singing little made-up songs to him when he was small and especially when he and his sister had first come here to live. His mother sang to him a lot, but she had sung to him "You Are My Sunshine" many times over, and he had loved her for it.

He leaned against the doorjamb and listened as his father finished his song to the woman he still loved. It had warmed his heart to hear his father singing to his mother. He loved his father as much, if not more, than when he was a child. Walking into the room, his father heard him and looked over his shoulder. When he had seen him, he stood slowly and turned to him. His father looked tired, and the lines in his face had increased dramatically since he had been gone, but he had never been so glad to see anyone. Carter took two steps forward, and his father met him with an embrace. "Oh, son, it's good to have you home. Your mom is going to be so happy to see you. The last few months has taken a toll on her."

His father stepped aside, and Carter made his way to his mother. He sat down on the edge of the bed and took her hand in his and felt the frailty of it. She looked so thin and had appeared to have aged greatly in the last few months. His heart broke as he looked down on her.

Carter swallowed hard and spoke softly as not to startle her. "Mom." Iris lay still as he brought her hand to his lips and kissed the back of it then gently rubbed it. "Momma, I'm home."

Iris slowly opened her eyes and looked upon her son, and he was greeted with a warm and loving smile. She raised her hand weakly to his face and caressed it. "Eli, oh, Eli, where have you been? I've been worried about you. You should have been home from the ball game hours ago." Carter was stunned that his mother's thoughts had turned back to when he was a boy. "You should have been home for supper. Clarice simply made a delightful supper, your favorite, honey. Did you bring Landon with you, and where is Beth? Is Beth home from ballet practice yet?"

He took his mother's hand and assured her that he and Beth were fine all the time, feeling the pain and the burn behind his eyes. What had happened to his mother? "Landon is with me, and Beth is fine. She's here with me."

His mother smiled widely and pulled him gently to her and hugged him and started singing "You Are My Sunshine" and drifted off to sleep. Carter couldn't help himself. He cried in his mother's arms at what he was seeing and clutched her to him. If it weren't bad enough that Bella was not feeling well, his mother was ill or had a breakdown of some sort. Grayson placed a hand on his son's shoulder as to tell him to let her rest. He placed the blanket up against Iris and walked back to the edge of the room. Grayson had followed behind him and started to explain what had happened. Not that he was satisfied, but she was being treated. There was no guarantee that she would be the mother he had known, but they would work with her.

Small feet ran through the door, and small arms wrapped around his legs. With one swoop, Carter picked up Molly, and she had thrown her arms around his neck in an instant. Wiping away the tears quickly, he hugged his daughter without hesitation. Molly kissed him on the cheek with a smack of her lips.

"Daddy, are you home? Mommy say you be home. Me so glad to see you." She hugged him tightly around the neck, and Carter couldn't believe he had spent so much time away from her. She must have grown a foot since he had seen her last. Leaning back, she placed her hands against his face and looked him pointedly. "Daddy, where did you go? I missed you so much. Mommy cried and cried for a long time. Didn't you want to be with us?"

Carter knew it would impact his daughter, but not this way. When he had thought of what she must have been through in the last few months, he couldn't believe he had

214

allowed his job to dictate what he was doing with his life. An ordinary marriage would have fallen apart and could have crippled his family. His decision was going to stand. There was no way that he was going back, especially if it meant that he would be taken away from them again. It didn't matter if it were voluntary or not.

"Tink, it's hard to explain, but no, I never wanted to be away from you or Mommy. I'm so sorry, Tink. Daddy is never going to leave you or Mommy again."

CHAPTER TEN

Carter found himself in a familiar situation as he sat watching her from a chair over his steepled fingers. Cassidy had told him that everything looked fine, but it hadn't stopped the worried thoughts that had run through his mind. She had been under a lot of strain and tension, and that couldn't have been good for his wife. Their marriage sure had taken a beating, and it was still young. Just in the short period of time he had been gone, he could see a change in her. She was much more confident and if he dare could say fearless, but that wasn't what had bothered him the most. She had seemed distant from most people. She hadn't been close to anyone, not even Lily, who was the closest friend that she had, and she had talked to her little since all this had started. Most of her attention had gone to Molly and school, and that was dangerous, as far as he was concerned.

Her determination in getting through the police academy had driven her to the point that her personality was that of revenge and control. He had seen that behavior in himself from years ago, and it had led to no good. He still possessed some of the traits, but it was at least stable compared with what it had been. That continual need to control had driven him into a life of drugs, alcohol, and other activities that he had no desire to remember. It had turned him into a hard and unloving and uncaring man. It had left him with nothing more than a shell, and he was lucky to survive.

That kind of power was destructive, and he knew it all too well. The time he had spent in South Shore had shown him how to manage his need to control, and God had taken over the rest. It had been a long and difficult road to recovery when it came to the substance abuse problem it had left him with. Living through what it could do to a person, he saw the dangers along with the threat of what it could do to the tiny life that she carried.

He looked at her delicate features and remembered how timid she had been as far as an intimate relationship, and he was hoping that it hadn't set their relationship back. She had seen what had happened as a betrayal from what he gathered from their conversation, and he understood how she could. He had all intention on going to work for his father, if that's what it took to mend the relationship he had with her, and to get out of the detective work that had cost them precious time together.

Isabella started to stir, and he thanked God as she started to flutter her eyes open, finding herself in his room. She looked around the room without turning her head completely over to him as if she were wondering how she had gotten there. Leaning into her, he watched her as she started to turn her head.

"Bella, you okay?"

She stretched slightly as she looked over to him and rubbed her stomach gently. She blinked her eyes as if she was lost. "Carter?"

"Yes, angel, I'm here. Are you feeling okay?"

She rubbed her eyes and looked around again and seemed to be shocked at the idea that he was there. It was if she hadn't remembered being at the Heritage with him the night before. "Carter, is that you?"

"Yes, Bella, it's me. Are you okay?" He was starting to get nervous at her reaction, then she started to grin.

"You're here. I didn't dream it."

"No, you didn't dream it." The relief flooded him as he looked down and then run his long deft fingers through his hair.

"What's bothering you?" she questioned him, and he looked at her in surprise.

"Nothing. Why do you ask?"

"Because you always do that when you're frustrated or something is on your mind."

Carter chuckled a little at her and then smiled at her. "You know me better than I thought. There isn't anything wrong. I am just glad that you're here, and we can get back to normal."

"Our life is far from normal."

"Well, that is about to change. It is going to be more normal than you could ever think possible."

Turning on her side, she supported her head with her hand and looked up at him, intently wondering what he had in mind. "What do you mean? I thought we were okay?"

"Not us, Bella. The life we are living is going to change. We have two children to raise now. I don't want to take a chance on something happening to me and leaving you alone to raise our children. I want to be able to grow old with you and see our children bring children into this world of their own. With what I am doing, I have no guarantee of that. The night I left you on assignment, I hated myself for what I put you through. Being away from you and our children was like serving a prison sentence, and I never want to be without you again. I talked to my father and he agrees with me, and I wanted to talk it over with you, but I have another position waiting on me in my father's company if I want to take it. I think it would be the best decision I have ever made. It would mean I could be with you and the kids without risk, and you could practice your nursing if you wanted, or you could be a stay-at-home mom. With my salary, you wouldn't have to work if you didn't want to. You would never have to worry about if I were coming home in one piece. It would be a given."

Bella watched his face as his jaws strained, waiting for her response. "You and I both know you wouldn't be happy doing anything other than what you are doing. It's that simple. It was what you were born to do, and you know that, and so do I."

He couldn't argue with her logic. It was true. He felt it was a calling to do what he did, to be able to give people peace in what had happened to their loved ones when no one else could tell them. Most of the time, the only answer lay with the dead, and they could not verbally tell them what happened. He felt like if he went back though, it meant being away from his family again, and he wasn't ready to part with them, especially when he had missed most of Bella's pregnancy.

Bella pushed her hair back away from her face and sat up in the bed. That was when she realized that she was in bed again and he was looking down on her. He watched her sit up, and then he picked up on what she had in mind.

"Nothing is wrong. You were exhausted from the drive and all the things you have been pushing yourself to do. You need to take it easy. You were put on medical leave to rest and take care of yourself."

"But—"

"No." He pointed to the bed and looked at her sternly but lovingly. "No ifs, ands, or buts about this. You are going to take care of yourself and this baby if I have to sit on you. You are going to do what your doctor tells you, and I want you to quit the academy. There is no way you are cut out to be an officer."

Carter knew he had pushed too many buttons when she threw the covers off her and stood before him. "You listen to me, Mr. Blake. I am a grown woman, and I will do this. I want to do this for a very good reason, one of which is vindication. You're my husband and I love you, but I will get this monster, and then and only then will I consider doing something else. He tried to kill me, you, and did succeed in killing Jenna. And I want to see that man pay for every life he disrupted."

Carter rubbed his hand down his face, trying to think of a way to get her to understand why he thought it was a bad idea. Once again, there was the loss of control that he hated. "Isabella," he gestured, "I just want to make sure that you and this little life you are carrying are protected. You are everything to me, and the thought of you in harm's way scares me to death. I have watched you, and what you are doing is dangerous, I know. Just try to do it my way, at least for now. I know that you want this baby born happy and healthy just as much as I do. Can we just concentrate on that for now?"

Sitting on the veranda of Rose Point, I looked out onto the lake and watched as the sun left the sky and settle into the dusk. The few floodlights illuminated the lake before me, making a soft glow on the water. The cobblestone walk and veranda led into an unbelievably large rose garden that was surrounded with a stone wall laden with weeping willows, oak trees, and Japanese maples. In a distance, a swan and its mate enjoyed the lake and fountain as it floated in grace across it. The sun was about to set in golden hues, pinks, and purples, when I heard Carter's shoes click against the stone. "For a summer night, it seems cool. There must be a storm brewing." I never said a word as he took his place in the oversized armed chair that looked like it should have come from an old English home and ottoman that matched. I was still angry with him, although I knew that I shouldn't be. Getting caught in my anger was what got me in the position that I had been in before. The guilt of being angry with him before he had gone on the assignment had eaten at me for months. I just couldn't get over that he had betrayed me and then he wanted me to drop out of the academy. I was just as good as anyone else in my class. As a matter of fact, I was in the top 2 percent. I may have been slow at getting started because I was pregnant, but I wasn't going to let that stop me. With everything that had happened, it had made me even more determined to finish.

I stared out onto the garden, taking in its breathtaking beauty. I could hear the squeak of the chair as he pulled it against the stone. I could feel his eyes on me, and I knew I wasn't going to win, but then I was going to make him work for it. Through the corner of my eye, I could see him sitting down and cross his forearms over his knees and clasp his hands together. "Isabella, sooner or later, you're going to have to talk to me. I am trying desperately to understand what your point is in this. You know mine. For months, my aim has been to protect you. I never expected to have to be gone so long. I hated that I couldn't tell you what was going on. I had asked Brooks to take me off the assignment, and he denied me. The only other option I had was to walk off the job. I knew what Arnell had done to you, and I wanted him put away so that he could never hurt you again.

"I have spent the last few months sorting out details of what I could do to nail this guy to the wall, and yet we haven't been able to find him. I'm willing to take a job in my father's firm to be home with you. You are the most important thing in my life. It's that reason, and only that reason, that I stayed where I was for so long. I knew everything you did, everywhere you went, and it killed me to be at my own funeral and to see you so devastated. Do you have any idea?" He rubbed his hand down his face and collected himself as I turned to him. "I wanted so badly to tell you who I was and to take you in my arms and tell you it was just a bad dream and it had all been a setup. I wasn't supposed to be there at all. I took the guard's place that was to be there just so I could be. I was worried about you and the baby. I was worried when you had no reaction, and I was even more worried when I did see one. I stood in silence and watched you be driven away, not knowing when I would ever get home. I signed out against medical advice to be there. I had surgery in that time frame. I wasn't to drive for six weeks, but I was there. I ended up in a military hospital after that for four weeks, living on antibiotics and going through rehab.

I just want to know if you still love me. Is there anything left in this marriage to save? Is there anything in you that wants to take me back as your husband?" I could feel the heat rise in me, and my skin prickled at his words. I took some short breaths and tried to control the fear that was starting to rise in me.

"I know about Quentin. It's obvious to me that he is in love with you. Maybe I have stayed away too long. If you're in love with him, I can understand that. I can't say that I accept it, but I can understand it. He has been there for you. I just want you to know that I want to try. If you want to try, I think some alone time is needed. I'll take you wherever you want to go. It doesn't matter to me as long as I get to be there with you."

Thinking about what he had said had thrown me for a loop. Quentin? He thinks I'm in love with Quentin? That's the furthest thing from the truth as he could get. Turning to him, I couldn't contain the emotion in my voice or the pain that had shot through me. I didn't only hurt for me, but for him. Taking his hand from his knee, I looked at him and felt as though I couldn't breathe. I don't think anything could have hit me any harder than what he had said. "How could you think that I could fall in love with anyone else? Do you think I could forget about you so quickly? Quentin is a friend and officer assigned to protect me, and that is all. I could never love anyone like I love you. You crazy, cynical man, look at me. Look at what we have. For months you have tried to explain to me what real love is, what God's idea of love is. Just because you were gone didn't mean that my feelings for you did. I prayed every night for peace, for God to make me feel whole again because such a large piece of me was gone. Having you in my life filled in the brokenness that was left by a hideous monster that had taken every good thing from me. He had taken my daughter and then had taken you, or so I had thought."

Carter traced my cheek and looked at me guarded. "You still love me even after all I have put you through the last few months?"

"Of course, I do. How could you think I didn't? You mean everything to me."

He let out a breath as he reached for me. I found myself in his arms, finally feeling safe for the first time in months. Placing my arms around his neck, I pulled him into me as close as I could get him. If he were closer, he would have been on the other side of me. "I love you, Carter. Nothing will change that." Taking my face in his hands, he drew me in for a kiss when I felt a flutter.

Laughing, I took his hand, and he looked at me mystified. "What is it?"

Taking his hand, I placed it over my stomach where I had felt the baby move. "Nothing. Your son or daughter is letting you know they are there." As if on cue, our child kicked against his hand, and he smiled and laughed as he felt the tiny foot or hand that pushed against him.

And sliding down onto one knee, he placed his hands on my belly and talked to our baby. "You have excellent timing. We are going to have to talk about Mommy and Daddy time." He paused and rubbed my belly and then laughed and leaned in and kissed me. "I love you too, baby."

Standing, he took me to him, and his lips brushed against mine, almost dusting them. His touch was so gentle, I could hardly feel his arms around me, and I giggled.

"What's funny?" He looked down at me and smiled.

"I won't break," I whispered to him. "You can hold me a little tighter. You aren't going to hurt me." He leaned in and started to put his arms around my waist, and it occurred to me maybe he couldn't get any closer. My belly was a good bit larger than it had been he had held me before, and it pained me to think of it, and I almost came to tears. I couldn't have looked all that attractive. He was right. I hadn't been taking care of myself. Over the last month, I took little time fixing my hair or putting on makeup. On top of everything else, I wore mostly my nightclothes at home or some loose and baggy clothing that looked more like men's workout clothes. There had been nothing feminine about it. The only time that I had worn anything that was remotely girly was to my OB-GYN appointments and when I had left on my own before I had met Carter once again.

"Maybe you can't get your arms around me anymore." I sounded more distressed than I had intended. "I don't know how you could find me attractive anymore. My hair is straight and uncared for. I barely take time to dress in

225

anything nice. Most of the time, I'm in my nightclothes or workout pants and T-shirts with no makeup."

Taking my face in his hands, he looked down at me and smiled. "Isabella, I don't know where you get such crazy ideas. I think you are the most beautiful woman on the face of the earth, and it wouldn't matter if you were dressed in a flour sack. You are my wife, and I think I can still manage to get my arms around you without any problem. Besides, I don't think I have seen you look lovelier than you do now carrying our baby. You positively glow."

"Hey, you guys, how's it going?" Landon bounded through the door in his usual upbeat self. "Come on. Your dad has your mom downstairs sitting at the dinner table. He says it's the first time in months she's been out of bed. I think you're going to want to be there for this. Clarice has a huge spread out, and everyone is waiting. Oh, Lily and JC just arrived, and JC is so elated, you would have thought he won the lottery. He hasn't stopped laughing since I told him you were here. Of course, he thought I was telling a bad joke until your dad interceded." Before he had out another word, Beth had got hold of him and pulled him toward the dining room, and Carter escorted me in.

"I can't wait to see Mom out of that room. Come on."

When we entered the room, JC bolted toward Carter and hugged him, ending it with a slap on the shoulder. He couldn't say a word, and Carter assured him that he was fine. Taking their places, Lily hugged me before she sat down beside her husband. "Glad everything is okay." Leaning over, she kissed me on the cheek and then proceeded to kiss Carter on the cheek. "Welcome back. It's good to see you back with Bella."

Carter seated me and then sat beside me, looking across to see his mother sitting next to his father. She looked much brighter, but her skin was still pale, and she had continued to call him Eli. Carter didn't seem to mind. It had brought him comfort just to see her there.

Clarice and a younger girl around the age of twenty, dressed in a classic black uniform with a white apron, had wandered through with the entrées and eyed my husband as she passed. She bent down a little closer to him than I liked and smiled at him. Ms. Perky seemed to be very interested in him. Carter acted as though he never noticed and set to take a drink of what had appeared to be champagne. My eyes watched her as she and Clarice had made their rounds and she followed him as she rounded the table, devouring him. Female hormones are bad enough, but mix them with pregnancy hormones and you end up with a wild cat. I was ready to claw her eyes from her head when I felt his hand clutch mine and squeeze it.

It must have been obvious to him that I was ready to strike, and he had defused me. Leaning in, he whispered so that no one was able to hear him, "Hold on, tiger. I'll tame you later." And he proceeded to wiggle his eyebrows at me. "You don't have to worry. She has nothing on you."

"She's coming on to you. How am I supposed to feel? I already feel like Shamu."

Leaning into me again, he kissed me on the cheek. "More of you to love, angel." How could I be offended with that lopsided grin?

Looking around the table, my family was all here with the exception of my parents and brother. I wasn't sure he was alive at this point. I stood to go to the bathroom, and Carter took my wrist and asked me where I was going.

"I'm just going to the ladies' room. I have the bladder the size of a pea," I whispered to him. "Why?"

"I just don't want you out of my sight for a second."

"I am totally fine. I feel good, and I am much better since you're here. I promise I will be right back."

The fellows all stood as I started to walk away, and I continued on. The bathroom was a short walk, thank goodness. Another couple of feet, and I didn't think I would have made it. Looking into the mirror, I pushed the lone strand of hair that constantly wanted to fall from my high ponytail. I had managed to dress well, for a change. At least I looked more like a woman instead of a girl stuffed in men's clothing. The blue dress that I wore matched the blue in Carter's shirt perfectly. It was knotted at the chest with a high empire waist. At least I didn't feel like I was wearing a tent. I had even managed to find a pair of taupe kitten heels that I didn't have to struggle to get into. These days, I was having a difficult time finding my feet.

I pinched my cheeks slightly, but I wouldn't have had to. He was right. For the first time, I could remember I actually had some color to my face. Maybe I didn't look as bad as I had felt. Walking back into the room, the fellows stood once more, and I watched my husband. He always looked exceptional. His tailored blue pants fit low on his waist, and the button-down he sported was a pale blue pinstripe opened casually at the neck. His wedding ring shone against the lighting in the dining room and reflected off the crystal in front of him. The blue of his eyes was rich and deep, making his dark hair appear even darker than normal. Looking at him never got old.

He laid the napkin he held in his hand on the table and reached his hand out to me and pulled me in and kissed me on the cheek. The warm woodsy cologne he wore was what I had bought him for Christmas, and it mixed with his body chemistry perfectly. A voice broke the silence as we started to sit down. "Oh my goodness." Carter's mother had spoken up, and her voice was strong. "I am going to be a grandma." She had forgotten. In the few hours that I had talked to her about the baby, she had forgotten and it was new to her again. She laughed, and the look of surprise on her face was magical as she realized that she had another grandchild on the way. "Yes, Mom," Carter answered her, but he was concerned. I could see it in his face. "You will be a grandmother in October."

"Oh, Eli, isn't it wonderful? We have Molly and little Gavin, and now this little one." She beamed as she looked at me. "Oh, honey, why didn't you tell me?" she questioned him, and he wasn't sure of how to answer it, then he gave her a little boyish grin. "It was a surprise, Mom."

Iris looked at me, and she clapped her hands. Oh, we must have a party. Andrea, I'm so happy for you both." Carter had taken a drink and had choked on it when he heard her call me Andrea. I took it to be her mental state and looked over it.

"Yes, Mother, we will have a party." I patted Carter on the back, gently trying to aid him from his choking incident. When he finally came to the point he could breathe, I shook my head at him not to correct her.

"Eli, are you okay?" His mother looked at him, worried.

"I am fine, Mom, just fine." He coughed a couple of times, and we all managed to finish dinner. At the end of the meal, I sat and sipped the water from my glass and watched as Gavin sat in the high chair, smacking the tray and laughing as he did. His toothless smile warmed me as I watched him. The silence was broken once again as Lily cleared her throat. My gaze moved from Gavin as she started to speak.

"I don't know if this is the right time to say this, but I wanted to do this when our family was all together. Since my parents are gone, I wanted to share something special with all of you." She turned her chair slightly toward JC, and he had wiped his face with the napkin and laid it by his plate. He looked over at her, and I could tell he had no idea what was going on. "JC, I haven't said anything because I wasn't sure, at least not until yesterday." JC watched her, and his eyes never left her. "I know that we talked about this before and you wanted to delay it, but we don't always get what we have planned. I haven't felt well for about two or three weeks, so I went to see Dr. Border. I had an appointment scheduled anyway." She swallowed and thought about what she was going to say, and I already knew. "When I did see him, he ran some test, and he did tell me that there was a little something wrong with me." JC stiffened as he watched her. "What is it? What's wrong with you?"

Lily took a deep breath and pushed her golden locks behind her ears. "JC," she tried to smile as the words came from her, "you better get started on the extra room you were talking about."

JC looked at her in bewilderment as what did one have to do with the other. "What does that have to do with it? I just bought the lumber yesterday."

Lily placed her hands on his shoulders and looked directly at him. "JC, unless you want this baby to sleep in the garage, we are going to need a nursery."

JC was stunned and never said a word. Carter clapped his hands and laughed out loud. "You're a daddy, JC!" He laughed. "Welcome to the club of midnight feedings and diapers." I couldn't help myself. I had to laugh with him. JC looked at his wife, stunned, and he went sheet white. I wasn't sure he wasn't going to pass out. Lily watched him in concern, placing her hands on his shoulders. "JC, don't zone out on me. You're going to be a father." He remained sitting there without as much as a twitch. "JC? Oh, say something. Don't leave me hanging here." The next sound that came out of him was all-out laughter, and the tears rolled from his cheeks.

"And you thought you had the flu." He continued to laugh, and Lily didn't know how to react to his outburst. Carter held a fist to his mouth, holding in a strangled laugh. "Sounds like someone else I know." I punched his arm, and he continued to laugh under his breath.

When JC had finally come up for air, he ran his hands down her delicate shoulders and looked at her face and down to her stomach. He looked at her again as she tried to judge his reaction. "How did that happen? Never mind, I

231

know that." He continued to laugh in short burst. "Are you sure? The doctor confirmed it?"

Lily started to lighten up and smiled when she realized that he wasn't upset with her. "Yes, you should be a daddy sometime in February. The doctor gave me the due date of February 14, but we all know babies can't tell time." She giggled, and he grabbed her and hugged her tight and let go quickly.

"Oh, sorry."

"What for?" Lily questioned him.

"I don't want to hurt you."

We all laughed. When the laughter settled down, he looked wondering what he had said that was funny. Lily laughed and took his hand in hers and said gently, "Honey, the deed is already done, and you aren't going to hurt me by hugging me." When he found out it was okay to hug her, he stood up and yelled out, "Woohoo!" And he picked up Lily in his arms and danced around the room with her. "I am going to be a daddy."

"JC, put me down." Lily laughed as he swung her around in his arms. "Put me down before I get sick."

"Sorry." He sat her feet back on the floor, gently kissing her cheek.

Grayson walked over to Lily and hugged her. "I'm so happy for the both of you. We all are."

Dinner slowly quieted down, and Carter stood and took my hand assisting me up. Placing my arm through the crook of his, he walked toward the garden. The sun had set, the darkness had settled in like a blanket, and the stars had lit up the sky. The moon was large and bright, causing a shimmer on the water. Following the cobblestone path, the only light was that from some solar lights that had soaked in the sun. I wrapped my arm around his as we walked and leaned my head against him.

"It's good to be home again. I wasn't sure when I would get to do this. I spent a lot of nights at the cabin, wondering what you and Molly were doing. I did finally get to see you later, but it was hard not getting to be with you." Stopping, he turned and looked at me as if he had seen me for the first time. "I don't ever want to feel that way again. The feeling of being alone night after night, not being able to hear your soft breathing beside me, that had to be the worst silence I have ever experienced. I would reach for you in the middle of the night, hoping to find you there." Taking my face in his hands, he looked down at me in wonder. "I don't ever want to be away from you again."

"Carter, you talk too much. I haven't been able to really kiss you for months. Just kiss me."

"Yes, dear." It was the invitation that he needed. His fingers ran through my ponytail and kissed me gently, and gradually his kiss became a little more aggressive, and I could hear his breathing catch as he kissed my cheek and down to the bend in my neck. Wrapping his arm around me, he took me closer to him. I was wrong. He could get his arms around me and had managed to have me so close I could hardly breathe.

Catching his breath, he leaned his forehead against mine. He tried to speak, but he couldn't keep from kissing me long enough to get anything out but one word at a time. "I. Think. We. Should. Go. Upstairs."

I tried to wrap my arms around his neck, but I could barely reach him with my belly in the way. He bent down a

233

little lower than normal, and I kissed him passionately. Taking my arms from around his neck, he held them in front of him and took a breath. "Now would be a good idea."

It hadn't taken long to get upstairs to his childhood bedroom. For the first time since he had come home, I saw my husband. His laugh and carefree nature were something that I had missed and some of the few things that I loved about the man. My heart leaped as he looked down at me and closed the door and locked it behind him.

"Mrs. Blake, it's been a long time." He smiled down at me and traced his finger along my cheek.

"Far too long, Mr. Blake." Reaching behind me, he released my ponytail, leaving my hair to cascade down over my shoulders. "Would you mind unzipping me?"

Flashing that lopsided grin, I turned so that he could reach me. Pushing my hair to the side and over my shoulder, he slowly unzipped my dress and kissed my shoulder. His lips against my bare skin sent chills over me. Turning around, he held me in his arms and kissed my forehead. "I've missed you," he whispered. Stepping back, he looked over me from my feet all the way up as he unclipped his cufflinks. I stood and admired him as he stood there. Before he finished the task, I pushed the shoulders of my dress down and pulled it away from my body, allowing it to fall and pool at my feet.

"Isabella, you certainly know how to unravel a man."

"I aim to please, Mr. Blake."

"There is no doubt that you do."

Taking my hand in his, he led me over to his bed and pulled away the duvet so that I could lie down. "Make yourself comfortable, Mrs. Blake. I'll be back in a few minutes." As soon as my head hit the pillow, I felt the heaviness of my body against the bed. I watched him as he started to unbutton his shirt and walk into the bathroom.

Carter stood at the bathroom mirror and took his shirt off and laid it across the chair at the door. Thinking of how long it had been since he had touched his wife made him edgy. Over the last few months, he had been lonely, and that was putting it mildly. He had missed her touch, her kiss, the way she laid her arm across his chest while she slept. There were nights that he hadn't slept at all. Missing her was only part of it. It was if she had never existed and he had made her up in his mind. There were a lot of times he had lain in bed thinking of the last time he had held her next to him, the last words that he had said to her, and how she had looked when he walked away from her that night. In no way had he ever dreamed he would have found out some of the things he now knew. All he could do was leave it to God when it came down to telling her about the past; and if he had to tell her about Jenna, that she was theirs, it could potentially destroy what they had.

He brushed his teeth and returned his toothbrush and continued to speak to her. His mind was cluttered from what had been going on, but he knew it was time to put it behind him and reunite with his wife. "I don't think I have seen you look any better than you did this evening." He was running his fingers through his hair as he walked out of the bathroom. "Even though you have told me you feel

unattractive, I haven't found you more desirable."
Standing at the foot of the bed, he looked down at her lying there in her lace bra and panties. "Isabella, you're a picture." When she didn't answer, he walked up and sat down on the edge of the bed and looked down on her. Her eyes were closed, and he watched the slow rise and fall of her breaths. He stifled a laugh as he looked down on her. She had fallen asleep in the length of time it had taken him to walk into the bathroom to take off his shirt and brush his teeth. "Isabella, you know how to unravel a man." He covered her and kissed her on the cheek, and she barely moved. What was another night when it had been months? He didn't bother finishing undressing; he just removed his belt and emptied his pockets, placing the contents on the dresser. Crawling in beside her, she turned over as he lay down, and without opening her eyes, she had laid her arm across his chest and her hand splayed on the center over his heart. Wrapping his arm around her, he pulled her in close, smelling her perfume. He was home. It was a welcome and comfortable feeling. She sighed as she snuggled into him. Leaning in, he kissed her forehead and pushed her hair back away from her face. "Good night, Mrs. Blake. Sweet dreams."

CHAPTER ELEVEN

"Eli! Where are you? You little brat, you've embarrassed me for the last time in front of my friends." Carter hid behind the door under the stairs, hoping that his foster father would give up and walk away. The stairwell was hot, and he was sweating as he listened to the roar of his voice.

"When I find you, boy, I'm going to beat you to a bloody pulp." He heard the heavy footsteps walk the floor and the crack of the wood under them. He couldn't let him find him because if he did, he would do exactly as he had said. His breathing was shallow and heavy, hoping that Arnell wouldn't be able to hear his gasps as he had run to hide. It hadn't been anything for him to beat him with a belt to the point it would leave him with buckle marks and bleeding. When he was through most times, he would have him do unspeakable things to him and with him, things that he hadn't understood. And it had happened so often that he had soon become numb to it. He felt as though he had allowed it to happen. He only did the things Arnell had asked to protect his sister. He had no idea of what he had done to her other than she would sound as though she were in pain, and she would cry uncontrollably.

"If you don't come out, I'll go after her." Carter closed his eyes and took deeper breaths. "You know I'll do it." Carter heard his footsteps as they walked away, and he sat down on the floor. He had no tears left for what had happened to him. He had accepted it, but the beating had become one too many. He hadn't done anything, nothing to warrant him hitting him, unless you counted correcting him, and Carter thought he was doing the right thing. It wasn't long before he heard the heavy footsteps again, and this time, he heard the scream of his sister. "Top it," she had said in a muffled cry. "Hurt me."

"All right, boy, this is your last chance. Wherever you are, I want you to come out. I'm going to count to three, and if you aren't out, I'm taking her with me. It's your choice. One . . . two . . ."

Carter stood and run his fingers through his hair and slowly opened the door to the closet under the stairway. When he stepped out, he saw Arnell standing before him, holding on to his sister by the arm roughly. Looking at him, he stood there dressed in a business suit, every bit of the CEO of a large corporation. No one would have ever known the man lived a double life. All Carter could see were those green eyes that tore his body apart every time he looked at him. "So you decided to join the party. Get out here, boy." Carter walked tentatively toward him, not wanting to give him the opportunity to hurt either of them. It was always the same. Arnell got his kicks out of hitting them and making them perform the way he said good boys and girls were to act. Carter had started to accept it as the normal.

"Eli," his sister had cried, "no, no."

Carter had known all too well the man and what his intentions were. He had in the past made his sister watch as he was beaten, and Arnell would have him against the wall, shoving himself at him. He made demands on Carter that no child should ever have to do. He would blame it on him and his sister along with his wife that he never got the attention from, so he would take it out on them. She was no better. She would push them around and tell them all they were was extra money in their pocket each month. She made them work like common house slaves until they dropped. It wasn't that the house was not well kept; it was. Eldora had maids and a housekeeper that came in on a regular basis. It was just so she could do what she wanted with them, control. At times she also had taken turns at Carter, but she was much more cunning than her husband. He was so starved for attention that he accepted her when she would take him and hug him. That for a while felt good to him; it was like having his mother back. He missed her terribly, and the feel of Eldora's arms around him made him feel safe and warm once again. That all changed one evening when she had taken him to her bedroom where she sat on the edge of the bed and rocked him, that evening after Arnell had literally beaten him. She sat on the edge of the bed dressed in a corset, her underclothes, and garters as if she was dressing to go out for the evening. He could still see her, and he had not been afraid, but he should have been. That's when it became worse. He went to her as she held her arms out to him, and the tears burned his face. The cuts on his lips from where Arnell had backhanded him were bleeding, but that wasn't the only marks he had left on him. He had left mental marks on him that was worse. She had sat with him in her lap, rocking him as he had cried. She had stroked his hair and patted him as his mother had when he had a nightmare. She had told him that night for the first

239

time that she loved him, and he had believed her. For the first time since his parents had died, he felt as though he had found someone to love him and someone he could trust.

It had never occurred to him that she would harm him in the way Arnell did. When she started kissing him other than on the cheek, it had started to feel strange to him, but what was worse, his body reacted to it and he had no idea what was happening to him. She had him sit by her while she removed her corset. He sat so still it was if he were paralyzed by what he had seen. His body chilled as he watched her. When she had sat back down, she had him sit down on her lap facing her and proceeded to kiss him, and he hadn't liked it. She instructed him on what to do and placed his hands on her, showing him each move.

He jumped when he heard Arnell's voice yell for him to come closer, and he released Beth and grabbed for him.

Carter woke himself, gasping for air, and sat up in bed. He ran his fingers through his hair that was now damp with sweat and looked over onto his sleeping wife. He hadn't awakened her. Running his hand over his face, he slid out from under the covers and walked down to the veranda. He knew he wasn't going back to sleep anytime soon. He hadn't had a nightmare for some time, but when he did, he knew he wouldn't be going back to sleep. At least he had gotten over the fear of sleeping. For years after he had come to live here, his mother would sleep in a bed on the opposite side of the room, so if he woke up, she would be there. The night terrors had ended around the age of twelve, but the nightmares remained rampant until he was twenty-two.

The nightmares, along with the drug addiction, had driven him into a state of being on the edge of suicide. He had held his father's thirty-eight-caliber revolver to his head and threatened to shoot himself as his father stood there in horror at what he saw. His parents had no idea of what he had endured as a child, only what the people from child welfare knew. He hadn't told a single soul other than his physician, and he hadn't wanted to tell him. It had taken all he had to tell him what they had done.

He sat down in a large Victorian chair on the veranda and looked out onto the water. It was soothing here. The still of the night was still upon the earth as he looked into the sky and watched the stars twinkle against a blanket of velvet. If it had been a few years back, he would have been sitting there with a bottle of whiskey and pills, trying to drown the nightmares. The thought of Eldora's hands on him still made his skin crawl. It had been difficult for him when he and Andrea had first gotten married. He did what he thought he should do as a husband, but most often he would back down. He would see Eldora's face or that of Arnell when it came to anything that was of a sexual nature. The first time Andrea had put her hands on his chest, he panicked. It wasn't a manly thing for him to do, but it had ripped through him. It hadn't been that he hadn't loved his wife. He did, but he couldn't get it out of his head that he had been treated that way by two adults that were to be caregivers. He had been numb for years when it came to a human touch. It was hard to let his adoptive mother touch him, and that was only if she had to. He took care of himself, and his mother had never been allowed in his room when he was changing or bathing when he was tiny. He would lock the door behind him, not allowing her in until he was fully clothed.

The scars he wore were no longer visible, but he did have them. They continued to haunt him, but at least he was able to control his behavior. He had been totally out of control when he was a teen and just before he met Isabella at South Shore. She had no idea of who he was then.

The image of Jenna came to mind while he sat there. What if she was Bella's baby girl and he was the father? Isabella would never forgive him for his part in it. He was doing it because he was asked to, but he had not used his better judgment. For one, he had none at the time. His only concern at the time was getting his fix. He had traveled to that warehouse for six months for his drugs to keep his addictive behavior at bay. His parents finally figured it out when his behavior changed. He had become violent and eerily quiet for no reason. The drugs made his moods easy to manage, and it numbed him to his thoughts, but it also had gotten him kicked out of college. Yale dealt with the honor system, and someone had seen him dealing with another student off campus. He had never found out who it was, but he had managed to keep it from his parents what had gotten him kicked out until that night when he was found with a gun in his hand.

It had almost cost him his life, and it had affected Andrea's almost to the day she died. He still fought the urge, especially on nights like tonight. If he had not any control, a bottle of scotch or whiskey would be sitting with him. In these times, he only had God to talk to. When he had reached rock bottom and thought he was going to die,

God had gotten hold of him and pulled him out. All he had to do was call out to him. It hadn't fixed everything, but it had made it bearable, and he had gone through rehab, rocky, but he had gone through it.

Knowing how he acted the night he had stopped and taken a bottle of whiskey home a few months back, it was a given he could never do it again. He had seen what it had done to him by the evidence left on Isabella. He had left his mark behind, and it had haunted him that he had done that to her. She was the love of his life, and he had purposefully hurt her. Even though he had suspected that she was having an affair, it left him no right to put his hands on her, and if he had stepped back and thought, he would have known better. She still had times when she wasn't sure about herself with him. She still had fear; he could feel it in the way she touched him and how she looked at him. It hadn't been him. Just like him, she still lived with the nightmare of someone else touching her without her consent. She had been older and had blocked it out of her mind for the most part. It had been her defense to protect herself; he knew that. He had tried to forget what had happened to him, but there were days when it was fresh in his mind, as if it had just happened.

The French door creaked open behind him as he sat there. It was too early for anyone to be up and roaming about. He sat there cautiously, but he wasn't going to act until he knew for sure who was behind him. The security to the house was tight; it was unlikely anyone could get past it.

"Having trouble sleeping?" The voice called out from behind him. The tension left him as he heard the footsteps approach as his father sat down in the chair beside him.

Carter rubbed the back of his neck and gave a half-hearted chuckle. "Yeah, I still have problems at times."

Grayson looked over at his son as Carter continued to look out into the night. "You know I am always here to talk to. Just because you're not a little boy anymore doesn't mean I can't listen."

"I know, Dad. It isn't as bad as it used to be. I do much better when Bella is asleep beside me."

Grayson laughed, but it was restrained. "I know the feeling, son. I haven't been doing so well either. Your mom slept in a bed by herself for the last four months. I have been in the room, but the couch isn't anything like sleeping next to your wife." Grayson thought for a moment, then looked at Carter as he continued to stare out into the night.

It was as if Carter could read his father's mind. "No, Dad, everything is fine. She's with me, and she is sound asleep."

Grayson leaned forward with his arms crossed over his knees. "Still having nightmares?"

Carter shook his head in response and then bit his lip as he fisted one hand and covered it with the other. Looking down to the ground, he took a deep breath, trying to release what anxiety remained from his emotional upset.

"Son, you know that God can take away all the pain and destruction that has taken place and put the pieces back where they belong. You're living proof of his power.

Whatever is troubling you can be taken care of through him, and if you need someone to talk to about it, I am always available."

"Dad, it isn't something you can take me for a ride for any more like you did when I was a kid. I wish it were that simple. There have been a lot of things come to the surface in the last few months. I am not sure how things are going to work out."

"Oh, I see." Grayson knew his son well, and if he wasn't willing to talk openly about what was bothering him, he knew it must not be totally him. "Does this . . . include Isabella?"

Carter stood from his chair, took a few steps, and ran his fingers through his hair. Then he rubbed the back of his neck, not saying a word.

"I take it from your silence that I am right."

"It's a long story, Dad, and there's a lot of unanswered questions right now, some that I have indifference about. They could go either way. My past is never going to let me go. It continually haunts me. I am not sure what I will do about it. What I know could cause major damage. What I don't know is worse."

"Then you do have a dilemma." Grayson sat there for a moment quietly as he watched his son try to sort out what was on his mind. "There are some answers to this. You could stew about it a while longer, but that is only going to cause you more grief. You could talk to your doctor or your minister to help you settle this, or you could talk to Isabella. If it involves her, she deserves to know what is going on. If it affects her, you can't leave her out. Honesty is the only thing you have in a relationship. If you break that trust, it is going to be difficult to mend."

"Dad, it's serious." Carter crossed is arms in front of him and remained turned away from his father.

"Son, the only way you are going to solve this is to go to God and then talk to your wife. She might get hurt and she may get angry with you, but if she loves you, she will come around. Whatever it is, you can't keep it from her forever."

"I know. I just don't know the facts, and I hate to say anything until I know for sure. Some of what I know is pretty cut and dry. It is factual, and it is enough to land us in divorce court."

Grayson drew a long breath. "So it's that bad?"

Carter turned around and resumed his position and turned his chair so that he could talk to his father, and they continued talking until dawn had broken. By the end of their conversation, Grayson placed his hand on his son's shoulder and prayed for them both. Their journey could be a long and painful one; he could see it coming. Neither he nor Isabella was ready for this, and it was going to be an uphill battle.

Before Bella had time to get out of bed, Carter had dressed and went for a run. The day, even though it was early, left a heaviness of heat and humidity on him. It was early enough that there was barely any traffic as he ran the streets of Greenwich. The family-oriented area was normally bustling with the excitement of children running and playing and parents working on their yards and admiring their cars. It was normal for weekends for that kind of scene. A run would clear his mind, he kept telling himself, but it didn't seem to be helping him. He just couldn't get the vision of that little girl out of his mind. If she was who he thought, it would be good for Bella to know that her daughter was not dead, but it was going to make it difficult for them.

His run went on for better than an hour, and he stopped at the corner before making his way up the cobblestone path that led to home. Stopping at the first large oak tree, he bent over his knees, briefly taking in a deep breath, and then stretching his hamstrings. Looking at his watch, it was going on nine. He was sure that by now Molly had woken up Isabella, and they would be waiting for him. He had to decide when he would talk to her, and it would have to be soon. With the things that were coming back to her, it wouldn't be long. That was if the drug Cooper had given her hadn't taken immediate effect. She may not remember it at all.

A scream brought him back to reality when he heard a car hit its brakes and the squeal of its tires as the driver tried to stop. Looking across the tree-lined street, he had seen a car in front of a lifeless body of what looked like a woman. A little boy shrieked as he started across the road, and the driver stepped from his car. "Mommy," the little boy cried as Carter and the driver had walked to the front of his car. "I tried to stop. She ran out in front of me. I didn't mean to hit her." The man, obviously shook, pushed his hair back away from his face. When Carter looked down, a plastic ball lay next to the woman on the ground. She ran out to save her little boy.

Carter pulled his cell phone from his pocket and connected to the dispatch, telling them he needed an ambulance and a police crew. As he was on the cell phone, he asked the man to get a blanket if he had one and put it over her to keep her from getting cold. He couldn't tell about injuries; she hadn't moved. She was breathing on her own, and he had checked her pulse. It was there, but faint. He continued to talk to dispatch as he went over to the little boy.

"Hello, little guy. Is this your mommy?" The little fellow nodded his head and continued to cry as he sucked in every breath. "My name is Carter. I am a policeman. I am going to try and help your mommy. Is your daddy home with you?" Again, the little boy hadn't said a word. He just shook his head. "I called for help, okay? Can I look at you and make sure you're not hurt?" The little boy stood still, never saying a word. And Carter looked over him, not seeing the least scratch on him. "Can you tell me your name?"

The little boy shook as he stood there and managed to speak and replied, "Ben." Carter got down on his level, hiding the view of his mother. "Ben, that is a very grown-up name. How old are you?" He was surprised when the strawberry-blond little boy held up three fingers. He was tall for his age. "You are a big boy then. Do you mind if I pick you up and we sit over here? They are getting ready to take care of your mommy." Carter could hear the sirens as they approached, and he studied the little boy. Ben soon lifted his arms to him for Carter to pick him up. The driver of the car sat on the curb, and the police questioned him as the paramedics worked with the boy's mother.

It wasn't long before an officer approached them and spoke to Carter. "Good morning," the officer greeted Carter. "Is he the woman's son?"

"Yes." Carter looked at the badge on the officer's chest and recognized the last name. "Haines, are you Grant's little brother?" The officer tilted his head and looked at Carter and then smiled.

"Yeah, don't tell me you're Carter Blake?"

"Guilty," he stated. "My parents just live up the drive across the road. I can't believe it. The last time I saw you, you were tagging along behind Grant. What happened with him? Did he and Shannon ever get married?"

"A couple of years ago, she finally got him to the altar. How about you and Andrea?"

Carter hesitated. "Andrea died a couple of years ago."

"Oh, I'm sorry. I had no idea."

"It's okay. I did meet another lady last year, and we married, and I haven't been happier. We are expecting our first baby in October, and we have Molly."

"I bet she is getting to be a big girl?"

"Three, going on thirty." He laughed. He looked at the little boy he held in his arms and announced, "This is Ben."

"Hi, Ben." The officer reached out to him, and the little boy curled in tight to Carter, holding on for dear life.

"Ben, this is Darren. He's a really good friend of mine." Again, the little boy clutched to him tightly.

"I think you have found a lifelong friend, Carter."

Carter held the boy and tried to talk to him, attempting to persuade him to go with Darren. "Ben, Darren will take care of you and see that you get back to your daddy, I promise." Ben threw his arms around

249

Carter's neck, his little face wet from tears. Rubbing his back gently, he took a deep breath. He knew what would happen if the boy's mother didn't survive. He would end up with strangers. The horror of that still lived with him; he just couldn't shake it. Not all foster parents were like Arnell and Eldora, but he couldn't deny there may be more than he cared to think about. Ben buried his head in the crook of Carter's neck, unwilling to move. He just couldn't bring himself to send him on.

"Why don't you take him home with you? I'll contact children's services and have it approved. Maybe he can be placed temporarily with you, at least until we know something about him.

Carter wasn't sure what to do, but he agreed that he would take care of him short term, and they were soon at Rose Point.

Walking into the massive home, he was greeted by Isabella. Seeing the shock on her face, he held a finger to his lips and motioned for her to come with him. Ben's cheek rested on Carter's shoulder, and his arms dangled at his sides as he slept.

Placing him on the bed, he removed his shoes before covering him. Carter looked down on him as he lay sleeping as if nothing had happened. He was exhausted from the turmoil, and Carter didn't expect him to awaken soon. His cheeks were flushed from the heat and from lying against his shoulder. His mop of strawberry blond hair was wavy, and a small curl kissed either side of his cheeks. Taking Isabella's hand, he directed her out of the room, looking back before he closed the door.

"Who is that, and where did he come from?"

Carter explained the events of earlier in the day and that the boy clung to him after the incident. "It's just temporary. I am sure his dad will come for him soon."

Bella sat down in the chair outside their bedroom, feeling emotionally drained from the child's story. "Poor baby. He must be so scared."

Carter leaned against the door frame with his hands resting on his waist and looking down at the floor. "I am sure he is." He was remembering his own fear when his parents died. That lost raw feeling raised its head, making him feel like that lost and frightened child he was then.

When she looked up at him, he felt the weight of her stare. He was giving himself away, and he wasn't ready to tell her about it. It was a long and hideous story that he preferred not to remember. The little boy that was left in him wanted to run and hide.

"Carter, what is bothering you? You look so, I don't know"—she shrugged—"hurt. Did I do something?"

When he collected himself, he looked at her and smiled. "No, angel, it isn't you. It's nothing you need to worry your pretty little head about." Crouching before her, he took her hand and kissed the back of it, feeling the silky smooth skin of it beneath his lips. "I am fine. I just want you to rest. Be happy and deliver me a beautiful healthy baby."

"You're trying to change the subject on me." He smirked, knowing that he couldn't get by with much when it came to distracting her. She knew him too well to take it at face value.

"Isabella Blake, you are without a doubt the most insightful and direct woman I know." He gently rubbed her

251

hand and watched her face as she waited for a better answer. "Let it go, angel. It's nothing. We are fine. The kids are healthy, and my mom is slowly getting better." Bending down her, he kissed her cheek and smiled. "Now that we are together, I want to spend every minute with you and my baby girl." Rubbing her belly with the palm of his hand, his smile widened. "And whatever this little one is."

Later that night, after everyone had eaten and had settled in, Carter had gone looking for Ben and Molly. Not being able to find them, he went to Molly's room, then to the bedroom that he and Bella shared. When they weren't found there, Carter started to become uneasy as he looked behind every door as he made his way down the hall until he heard his mother talking. Looking in her room, he couldn't believe what he saw. His mother had cleaned herself up, had dressed, and had fixed her hair. She sat on her bed with a beautiful blue gown and the duvet pulled up on her lap. On either side of her were Molly and Ben sitting contently with his mother's arms wrapped around them as she read *Goodnight Moon*. Carter stood at the door with his arms crossed over his chest and leaned in the doorframe. That little boy had brought her back from the state that she had been in. Molly, her usual self, was snuggled in close to her grandmother with her thumb in her mouth. He was surprised to see that Ben had been that content with a stranger. He had leaned into his mother, and his arm rested against her stomach. It was such a charming picture as his mother's voice rose and fell as she came to the end of the book. She laughed and hugged them into her, kissing them both on the top of the head. Ben smiled and hugged Iris, and she hugged him a little harder. "You're such a good boy," she told him soothingly.

Carter watched them. Ben and Molly sat taking in the attention of his mother, seeing how well they were enjoying being there with her he hated to interrupt them. It was time that his daughter went to bed, and he was sure that Ben needed to be going as well. Bella walked up behind him and wrapped her arms around Carter's waist. "Now that is a beautiful picture."

Carter shook his head in agreement. "What are we going to do with Ben?"

"Put him in with Molly, I guess. They're just babies. I don't see anything wrong with it. There is a lot of room in this house, but I can't see putting him in a room by himself. He's been through enough today without tearing him away from everyone."

Isabella patted her husband's arm, knowing he was right. "You do realize he may end up in bed between us before it's over with," Bella had reminded him.

"Yeah, I kind of expect it. If he does, it's okay. I understand some of what he's feeling. He's just a lost little boy. He doesn't know us, but he has taken to us well. I guess that's good on his part." Bella sighed as she leaned into her husband.

"Hey, you two, it's time for bed," Isabella coaxed them.

"Aw, we want to stay," Molly exclaimed, and Ben's eyes got large, and he nodded his head yes.

"Now, now. You know it's bedtime, princess, and tonight you will be having a visitor with you in your room.

Ben is going to stay in your room, at least for now. It will be like a slumber party."

Molly cocked her head to the side and wrinkled her nose as she looked at Isabella. "What's a sumber party?"

Bella laughed at her daughter's reply.

"Not a sumber party, a slumber party. It's like a little party where you talk and play a game or tell each other stories. Then it's go-to-sleep time."

Molly rocked back and forth as she clapped her hands. "Yay, a party."

Molly kissed her grandmother, and so did Ben. Iris laughed and kissed them each. Molly jumped off the bed and headed to her father and was soon followed by Ben. Surprised to look down and see that Ben was reaching for her, she bent down to receive the little boy. He took her face in his hands and pulled it to face him and then kissed her and patted her. Bella was overwhelmed by the little boy's reaction to her and sucked in a sob and held him tight to her. He wrapped his arms around her neck tightly, not offering to let her go.

Walking down the hallway from their bedroom, Carter watched as Bella tucked the kids into bed and covered them lovingly. He loved how she would take the blankets and push them against their tiny body and shake them as she tucked it in around them. The kids laughed as she did, and it was good to see Ben laugh after what he had witnessed that morning. Molly's laughter rang out along with Ben's as she leaned in and kissed each one of them. He loved watching his wife do the simple things. Something as mundane as putting the kids to bed brought a warmth to him and a softness that he hadn't felt before.

254

Seeing Isabella loving them, he remembered the way his birth mother had been with him as a child. He was seeing some of the same characteristics in his wife. Beth had been too young to remember much of what their parents were like, but from time to time, he would remember flashes of his childhood and what it was like with them. His mother was loving, gentle, and loved to play with them. When she would put them to bed at night, she would sing in such sweet tones, it had always helped for them to drift off into a peaceful slumber. He could see her face and smell her cologne. It smelled like lilacs, subtle and fresh. His thoughts were broken when he heard his wife's voice rise slowly as she sang to the children. The soft and gentle lyric was one he had never heard before. It was rare that he heard her sing, but her voice was angelic, and he fell in love with her more as he watched the sweet tender manner she pushed the hair from Ben's face. As she finished, the kids had already closed their eyes and had gone to sleep.

Carter walked from the room with his hand lying softly against his wife's back. Leaving a crack in the door so that if they woke in the night they would be able to find their way to them, he turned to his wife and wrapped his arms around her as she placed her hands on his arms. "Mrs. Blake, you are an amazing woman." Isabella looked at him, questioning as to what she had done.

The corners of her lips slowly lifted, and she leaned in closer to him. "Well, Mr. Blake, what did I do that was so amazing?"

His lopsided smile made an appearance as he looked down at her. "You are a good woman, a lovely wife, and an amazing mother, and you have a voice of an angel. You gave that little boy exactly what he needed. He needed a mother, and you gave him that."

"Well, he's easy, and Molly helped. She gets along well with him and enjoys having someone with her to play with."

"I like to have someone to play with too." He laughed. "It seems to me that you like to get out in the park and play as much as Molly does."

"I have a good playmate," she teased.

"You see, I can be flexible." He laughed and kissed her on the cheek.

She aimlessly traced his arm as he held her. "Don't you think it's time we said good night, Mr. Blake. It has been a very long day. Besides, it's been a couple of days since I was reunited with you, and well, I would like some time with my husband alone."

"Oh, you would?" He kissed her nose and gathered her up in his arms and played like he couldn't hold her up and grunted as if he hurt himself. "Mrs. Blake, I think you might have to take care of me. I think I strained my back."

Looking at him, she thought he was serious until she saw him smile. "That was not nice." She tapped him lightly then hugged him. Carter carried her to their bedroom and chuckled as he did. It hadn't taken him long to make his way to their room, and he had set her down at the side of the bed. Trying to hide his anxiety, he stood before her and took a couple of deep breaths. He hadn't said a word, and all expression had left her face as she stood there. He could feel the burn that ran through him, hoping that the time he had spent away from her wasn't going to come into play on her side. Taking a step toward her, he cupped her face in his hands and looked into her eyes. The thought of being with her was enough to engulf him. His hands shook, and he could only hope that she was unable to feel them. He hated to admit that he was weak but without her help, without them both helping each other, being together could prove to be difficult. When she reached out to touch his chest, he pulled back his chest away from her hand as if it had burned him.

He thought then it was over, that the time had passed for them to be together tonight. It was then she realized. Removing her hand from his chest, she took it back and rested her fingers against her lips. Watching her, he knew well that she had figured it out. Her lips trembled as she watched him. He wasn't sure that he liked the reaction. He didn't want her to feel sorry for him. It wasn't something he had ever wanted. Empathy was one thing, pity was another. Pity made him feel helpless, hopeless, and out of control.

She looked at him in awe, and he realized that she saw through the shell he had encased himself in. She knew because she had lived through it herself. He took another deep breath, trying to keep his emotions in check. He wasn't going to let his past ruin his time with his wife, not after all the time that they had spent away from each other.

CHAPTER TWELVE

Looking into those blue eyes, I hadn't seen it before. My own grief had shielded what I had known in my own life. The idea that I wasn't alone in the fight was a comfort, but the shattering feeling filled me when I came to the knowledge that my gentle husband had shared the same nightmares, the same haunts, bringing me to my knees.

My knees buckled as he held me by the arms, and we both sank to the floor. He hadn't said a word, but it was evident in his face. My breaths shortened as I sat looking at him; he looked lost and broken. What had happened? Why hadn't I seen it before? I was so in tune with others that had been abused. I could spot a victim most days before they ever spoke a word. It hadn't occurred to me that he too had been in my shoes. He had understood because he had been there. He hadn't told me. For some reason, he hadn't told me.

"I'm okay," he whispered. "I didn't want you to know. You had enough to deal with. It was a long time ago."

I heard his breath catch when I reached to touch him and pulled away. "No, Bella, I want you to touch me. Don't be afraid. Don't be afraid to love me. I'm still me." My heart broke as I watched him. Taking me by the hand, he cupped it tenderly as he placed his hand over mine. Placing my hand on his chest, he took a deep breath. I felt his heart race beneath it.

"It's, okay, Bella. You know now. It isn't a secret any longer. I never wanted you to be burdened with it, not after everything you have been through."

Taking my hand from his chest, I ran my fingers down his jaw, tracing every line. I had no idea what his story could be, but I knew it was haunting him. I felt the presence in the room of someone that had not been invited. I had felt it myself many times, the hands of someone who were not welcome, the breath of a stranger, and the rage of a lion on a hunt. "Chase it away, Bella," he said softly. "Don't let him stay."

He took my hand from his face and kissed my palm gently. Taking it, once again, he placed it over his heart. "Still the thunder in me. The storm is raging from my tormented thoughts of what they did to me. Make it stop, Bella. Help me to breathe."

My heart slammed against my chest as I looked at him. It was there, the hurt, the fragmented and distraught look that I had seen on my own face. Sucking in a breath, trying to take in what I had just discovered, I could barely get enough air. I felt faint, and the anger rose in me at what he must have suffered at his predator's hands. My breaths came in short chains as I traced his face and down to his shoulder. Tears welled behind my eyes for him, and I knew he wasn't looking for sympathy. I knew what it felt like. I had wanted to be treated just like anyone else, but I had been fearful. Not my husband—it couldn't be. The strong man I had always known sat before me, looking at me. I could see the remnant of a child that had been tortured and beaten. I wasn't sure what they had done, but I could see the effects of it. I could see the change in him from the time he had brought Ben back to the house.

"What . . ." I couldn't get the words to come and felt the knot in the back of my throat so tight that I thought it would choke me. "What did they do to you?" Turning his head down and away, I could tell he wasn't ready to talk. He sat with his hands resting on his knees, not touching me. Leaning in, I kissed his cheek softly, feeling the harsh brush of his beard against my lips. Taking his hands into mine, I took a deep breath and felt it shatter as I exhaled. "Amore, look at me." He didn't offer to turn his face. Lifting one hand, I pushed his face back toward me so that I could look at it. I wanted to comfort him. I knew he needed it. I needed to show him nothing had changed. I hurt. Every fiber of my being hurts for him. Lifting his eyes to me in the dim light of our room, I could see he still had a fight within him. "It's okay. We are both going to be okay. Someday you're going to be able to tell me what happened, but just like you told me, it isn't going to change a thing. It isn't going to change how much I love you." Sitting in the room in front of me, he remained on his knees, sitting back on his feet. Cupping his face in my hands, I looked directly into those beautiful blue eyes and tried to reassure him, telling him with each word made clear. "I . . . love . . . you."

He took in a sharp breath, letting go of the tension, the strain leaving his face instantly. The strength in the man I had become accustomed to now had the heart of a child, one that had been left to survive on his own. Reaching for him, I placed my hands on his arms. The arms that had seemed so strong and secure when he held me now needed me to comfort him. "Carter, I'm so sorry I didn't see it. I couldn't see past my own grief. God forgive me for not being there for you. All this time, you knew. You knew because you had been through it yourself." Pulling me into him, it didn't take long for him to grasp me tightly to his chest, and I heard a catch in his breath. It wasn't hard to figure out that he was trying to hold it together.

Taking him into my arms as he wrapped himself around me, I rocked him like a mother would rock a child. I tried to console him, knowing that, with what we had been through, there was no consolation to it. You lived through it; you survive it. And if you're lucky, you gain back a part of yourself. All I could do was hold on to him. I found myself praying for him within my heart, then not recognizing I was speaking it out loud. "Please, God, take him and hold him, fill him with your love, show him that you haven't left him. Heal his broken heart, his tortured mind and soul, from that of the evil that was brought onto an innocent child. He means everything to me. He's my very life. I couldn't imagine what has happened to him. Knowing what happened to me, it hurt me to think someone did this to him. My heart breaks for him because I know what he feels. I know the pain, the emptiness it leaves behind. Only you have been able to help me. You feel the void when no one else can. Hold him in your arms and comfort him. Help me to show him how much I love him and give him the assurance that he is not alone. Thank you, God, that you hear us and you still answer our prayer."

261

My eyes remained closed as I felt the warmth wash over me from my feet to the top of my head, and I knew God had heard my prayer. A calm and ease fell on me. How could I have felt God had left me? He hadn't left me. He hadn't moved. I had.

Feeling his hands cupping my face, I heard him whisper. "Isabella." His voice cracked as I opened my eyes from prayer. "I love you. I thank God every day for you that he brought you into my life. He made you just for me. You complete me." A single tear fell from his eyes, and I sucked in a breath, anticipating what would happen next. I hadn't been alone with my husband for months. It was if it were the first time he had touched me. I wasn't going to let what happened on our wedding night to be repeated. We were both broken. Healing was going to come. It was time.

Standing from his kneeling position, he reached for my hand, assisting me up. Slowly, I reached toward him, placing my hand against his cheek, and took in the sight of my husband. I never tired of looking at him. I watched each move and felt the curve of his jaw as my hand cupped his face. "Mrs. Blake, you are without a doubt the most beautiful woman I have ever seen." He traced my jaw down into my neck where he planted a soft kiss. "It's been a long time since I held you in my arms." His hand slid over my shoulder deftly, as if he were afraid I would break. Leaning in against my ear, his words fell on me. "It's been a long time since we have been together. Tell me now if you aren't ready because I don't think I can resist you much longer." His fingers traced the zipper on my dress that ran from my neck to the small of my back. "Is it okay? I'm not going to hurt you or the baby if we do this? You have had such a difficult time, I don't want to—" My lips feathered against his cheek, and he stopped instantly. Once again, he looked at me, and I placed a finger to his lips as he started to speak. "You aren't going to hurt either of us. We are both doing very well. I want you with me. I want to feel you with your arms wrapped around me. I've missed it. I've missed you." Removing my finger from his lips, he took my hand and led me over to his bed.

His hands trembled as he removed the ribbon from my hair and watched it fall over my shoulders. Running his fingers through it, I felt the unforgettable chills that ran down me as that memorable boyish grin appeared. I looked into his beautiful blue eyes, becoming lost to him as he took his rightful place with me once again. My body shook under his touch. He knew my body so well. All it took was a breath against my skin, a look, one that lit with fire and passion, a look of love deep enough to penetrate my soul. With him standing so close to me, I felt the warmth of his body and smelled his cologne that always seemed so intoxicating. He stole my breath from me just by looking at me. He became my reason for living. There was no denying that we were meant to be with each other.

Cupping my face between his hands, he drew me in to kiss me, and my eyes never left his vibrant blues. Drawing in a breath before he leaned in, his hands trembled against my body. His lips grazed mine before he wrapped me in his arms and kissed me more passionately. Feeling as though I had lost all control of standing, I sank against him, my hands resting against his chest. It gave me so much comfort to be there. His body felt like a warm blanket, comforting. I was sheltered as he cradled me against him. I felt the steady beat of his heart under my hand, soothing me. He soon rid me of my dress as he slipped it across my shoulders and it pooled at my feet. My less-than-perfect body leaned against him. His hands drew the curve of my body as if it was like this all along.

"Honestly, Mr. Blake, I don't know how you could find what you see in front of you so appealing."

His smirk reappeared once again. "Isabella Blake, I have always thought you were the most beautiful, most desirable woman I have ever seen, but now I see more of you to love. You glow, and I haven't ever seen you more beautiful. The thought of you is all it takes, the way you smell, the taste of your kiss, the way you look at me. You look at me like I am the only man that has ever existed. Do you have any idea what a shot to my ego you are? After all each of us has been through, you look at me as if I were perfect. Each time you kiss me, each time you touch me is like it should have been, the way it should have been, before the monsters of our past entered our lives. I anticipate each and every moment I can be with you. I need you like I need my next breath."

"Carter Blake, that has to be the most romantic thing you have ever said to me." Wrapping my arms around his neck, I tugged his dark unruly hair, running it through my fingers in silken strands.

"You enjoy that, don't you?"

Looking at him questioningly, I wasn't sure what he meant. "Enjoy what?" I giggled as he hugged me against him, which wasn't easy. My stomach was quite large, and it didn't allow much giving. I had a ways to go, and I already felt like a blimp. My hormones raged, which I guess was good for him in some respect, then again maybe not. I felt like a different person, possessed, being difficult and brutally honest at times. Never intending on hurting someone else's feelings, but I did whatever it took to get my point across. I was an emotional roller coaster, crying one minute and laughing the next. He hadn't seen it yet, but I was sure he would.

"Running your fingers through my hair?"

"I hadn't realized I was."

"You do it often." He arched his eyebrow as he smirked. "Am I your personal worry stone, Mrs. Blake?"

For a reason unknown to me, I pulled my arms away from him and let them fall to my sides. "No, you aren't." Dread filled me with hurt, and my heart sank to my feet.

"I didn't mean that I wanted you to stop. I love when you touch me, even if it's to hold my hand. Don't take it as though I don't want you." My lips crushed against his before he could speak another word. By the time he had released me, his kiss had left us both breathless. Sucking in a breath, I stood holding on to him and encircled his neck again. "Mr. Blake, you talk way too much. It's time that you took advantage of the idea that I am your wife." Running my fingers down the row of buttons on his white linen shirt, the boyish grin I loved so much took the place of the serious look he once displayed. "You know something, Mrs. Blake," he said, tilting my face to his with his fingertips, "you're right." His breath caught as my fingers slowly unbuttoned his shirt. The thoughts of being with him had consumed my mind as I stood in front of him. Forgetting everything outside our own little world that we had created, I remembered each touch of his hands on my body. The sweetness of his breath against my skin shut out every hurt, every bad dream of the last six months. He was my life, every breath I took. My heart beat for him and only for him. Standing on tiptoes, I kissed his soft cheek as he leaned into me. Picking me up, he cradled me in his arms and placed me on his bed. Being with him was all that mattered. I wanted him, craved him. Carter's arms encircled me, draping over my shoulders. Nervous laughter filled the air as he came closer to kiss me.

"What?" he questioned me, staring down with a grin on his perfectly sculpted face.

"I can't believe you can get that close to me with my belly so big."

"Isabella, nothing is going to keep me from loving you, not even our baby. I suggest that you get used to me being this close because I never intend on letting you out of my sight again."

"I love that you're this close."

"Good. Always glad to make you happy, and it doesn't hurt that it feels good to me either."

The laughter soon died away as he raised and removed his shirt. The gloriousness of him in my mind had never faded, but somehow it was now enhanced. My hormones again were getting the better of me once more. It didn't take long before I clutched him to me and crushed my lips to his. The sweetness of him left me without a breath. My heart raced as he touched me, feeling like I was running a marathon. At least I was running to him and not from him.

266

Pushing my now-damp hair away from my face, he swept his fingers through it and lightly kissed my cheek as I tried to regain a small amount of control. He smiled that lopsided grin that always took me to my knees and started to shake his head. "Isabella, what has happened to you? If this is what pregnancy does to you, I think I will keep you barefoot and pregnant all the time. You are insatiable. I guess I could die trying." He laughed. But I was beyond the laughter. It had been way too long since I had been with my husband. My only passion was to see that he found how much he was missed, that I loved him beyond words.

His touch remained gentle, even though I felt I was devouring him. My touch was anything but delicate. In the back of my mind, the lack of control ate at me, making me feel dirty for what I was feeling and doing. I knew that when it was over, I would not be easily dealt with. I felt animalistic, and I didn't like the feeling at all. Arnell had taught me to give my body away, and the only way I could do it was through channeling something I wasn't. Early on, I would cry uncontrollably until Lee had stood outside the door one night, hearing me cry from the mental torture I had gone through from being used by strangers that had forced their selves on me, thanks to my captor. "Flip the switch, Bella," he would cry out to me. It wasn't until I was able to turn my personality to that of someone that wanted to be used for sex that I was able to survive the nightly events with men of all ages and days of being with him. Trying to put it behind, I wasn't going to let it take from me what I had with my husband. He was back, and I was lucky to have him here. No matter how I had him with me made no difference.

267

Waking, I looked over at the red numbers beaming from the clock beside me. Uh, 3:00 a.m. My bladder rarely lets me sleep. Sliding from under the duvet, I looked over to find Ben between us, lying with his arm laying across Carter's chest and Carter's arm wrapped around his tiny body, holding Ben next to him. A small and gentle sigh escaped him as I looked down at them. Carter was going to get attached to this little guy quickly. I knew it was coming. He had a soft and loving heart.

Looking behind me, he remained still and I continued into the bathroom. It didn't take long, and I rolled my eyes as I sat there, feeling like I was waiting for a bus. As I stood and was looking into the mirror, I felt a tightening in my back as it rounded my stomach. Passing it off as Braxton Hicks contractions, I turned off the light and walked down the hall to check on Molly. As I got to her door, my stomach cramped again, and I laid my hand against it. Rubbing my stomach, I could feel it knot, contract, and release. It had taken me by surprise and had left as quickly as it came. Taking in a breath, the pain was relieved, and I stood for a moment before I entered Molly's room. Walking over to her, I covered her where she had kicked the quilt and sheet from her bed. It was almost frigged in her room. Leaning down, I kissed her and tucked the quilt top around her. Rising from my bent state, it had hit me again. This time, I could barely stand from a bent position. Now I was scared. Clutching my stomach, I remained in a semibent state, making my way down the hall to our bedroom. It wasn't good. I could tell this wasn't good. I was no way near my due date. I had just passed the six-month mark, when normally you would have been out of

268

the danger zone. Trying to take a deep breath, I was unable to do so, and a hiss made its way passed my pursed lips. Walking into the bedroom, I tapped Carter on the shoulder in an attempt to wake him. He mumbled something that I couldn't make out. "Carter, wake up." I drew in a breath as he stirred. "Carter, please wake up." I rubbed my stomach as he rubbed his face and drew his hand down over his face.

Making a grunting sound as he tried to awaken, he pushed his hair back away from his face. "Amore, I need you to wake up."

"Mmm, what is it, angel?"

"Carter, we need to go to the hospital. Something is wrong."

That was all it took. He awoke as if a drunk became completely sober in an instant. He unwrapped Ben from him and covered him and stood in front of me. "Isabella, what is it? What's wrong?"

By this time, I was close to tears but trying to control myself, taking in short breaths as the pain subsided. They came in short bursts, but when they hit, they were hard and painful. "I'm having pain, a lot of pain." I braced myself against him as another one hit me, and he supported me with both hands. He sat me down on the bed and turned the light on low in the room. Getting down on one knee in front of me, he tried to reassure me, but I could see the concern in his face. "Bella, I'm going to take Ben down the hall to Landon and Beth. Don't move from this spot. I will be right back." Standing, he leaned in and carried Ben down the hall quickly.

As soon as he left the room, terror filled me. It was happening again. I wasn't going to be able to have this baby either. My past was back on me again, the destruction I received from the hands of a man that tortured me beyond belief. I could see Arnell standing in front of me, laughing. He was laughing just like he did when he had done something to inflict pain on me, his voice ringing in my ears, "Better you lose this brat now. I can still use you for my own pleasure."

Rocking back and forth on the bed, I held my stomach and prayed. "God, please," was all I could get out in a stretch. My voice trembled as I tried to pray, "Please don't take this one from me." Wrapping my arms around my stomach, I talked to the little one that now was in danger. I felt so helpless to protect him. "Please don't leave us. Stay with us, baby. Don't give up."

Carter walked in the door with a glass in his hand. The amber liquid swished in it as he handed it to me. I looked at him as if he had lost his mind. "Take it, Bella." Shaking my head, I couldn't begin to put together what he wanted me to do. "Isabella." He handed it to me, and I reached for the glass, and he placed his hands on my arms as he bent down in front of me. "Isabella, I wouldn't do anything to hurt you. Drink it," he prompted. "Drink it slow. It should stop the contractions." After taking the first sip, I felt it burn as it ran down my throat, almost choking me. I coughed as I took the first drink from the glass. "Easy. Just take sips at a time. You aren't used to drinking it." Pouring just enough soda into it to take the bite from it, he handed it back. "It should help the taste and not be so harsh." He placed my shoes on my feet and coaxed me to finish the drink.

Landon walked into the room dressed in his jeans and a T-shirt. "You ready to go?" Carter turned and looked over his shoulder as he stood from putting my shoes on my feet. "You don't have to go. I can take care of her."

"Blake," I punched his chest with my finger as I stood, now starting to feel a little buzz, "get dressed and quit arguing with him." I could feel the alcohol hit me as Landon stood in silence. I had stunned him. "Well, Carter, I think you took care of the contractions, but boy she is going to have a beauty of a hangover." Carter never said a word as he grabbed his shirt and pants from the chair. It wasn't long before he came out of the bath fully dressed. Even being woken up at three in the morning hadn't hurt him. He still looked perfect.

Taking my hand, he started to walk from the bedroom with me, and I pulled him in and kissed him hard and let out a sigh. "Mr. Blake, has anyone told you how shmexy you are?"

"Oh yeah, Carter, she's smashed." Landon chuckled and looked at us, but I didn't care. My eyes were on my husband. "No, but I'm sure you're going to tell me." I patted his chest exaggerated and stood on my tiptoes and kissed him again. "Yep, you're shmexy."

"Isabella, let's get you out of here and find out what is going on with you."

"Noooothing. I feel good. No more pain." I flailed my arms out as I gestured.

"Isabella, please, let's go. We need to get you to the hospital."

271

Tracing my hand down his chest, I pulled him to me. "Don't you want to stay here and have some fun? Huh?"

Carter's distressed grin let it known he was worried, but he tried to cover it well. "Bella, we need to go. That's what got us in this to start with."

"Pft, no, no, no. Not what happened, nope. That was what he did to me. He did that to me." Carter held me by the arms, trying to convince me, but I wasn't listening. I could see Arnell standing in front of me after he had thrown me down on the bed. He had done such dreadful things to me. It had never come to me before; only parts played out in front of me. He stood above me after he had backhanded me, and I could still feel the sting of his hand against my face. Looking up, he had started unbuckling his belt, and I knew what was coming. He had hit me repeatedly with the belt, with the buckle tearing and ripping my exposed skin. He had threatened me over and over that he would beat me until I had lost the baby I carried. I didn't even know who the father was. It didn't matter. The baby was mine regardless of who it belonged to.

It hadn't taken him long before he had me pinned to the bed. I hated the room, hated the bed. I knew that bed was a source of torture and a time where I lost myself. I had tried to pull from my chains until it had caused ridges in my wrist, causing them to bleed. Many times I had wished I would have died. My baby was all that had kept me alive. It had kept me going, giving me hope. It wasn't an assurance of him doing anything to me because it didn't matter. He would get his kicks any way he wanted. I could feel his breath on my neck as he bent into me. He would bite me or put cigarettes out on me, telling me that I deserved what I got because I was no better than a prostitute. That was all I would be, and no one would ever want me. "You're just like your mother. She was never satisfied with what she had." His fresh dress shirt draped open as he looked down on me, his green eyes penetrating me like a knife. His sandy-blond hair fell down over his forehead as he growled in a release. "It's time I put an end to this. Either this kid goes or you die. Come to think of it, neither one matters, but if I keep you, I can still take care of my pleasure. Torturing you gives me satisfaction after what your mother did to me, and still it isn't enough payoff. I would love to see the look on your mother and father's faces when they"—he dragged his fingernail down my jaw—"if they ever see you again." Getting up in anger, I could see the determination in his face. Picking up a coat hanger, he came at me, and coldness fell on me as I begged him not to do it. He laughed as if it was funny. The alcohol on his breath was sickening as he bent over me and spoke to me in a tone that was from a man with no conscience, no remorse for what he was doing. I hated him. I felt the sharpness of the hanger as it tore through me. Not being able to feel much of anything after that, I was sure the baby was gone. I could feel the warmth of water or blood that had been left behind. He hit me repeatedly and cursed at me as he did. I lay there lifeless, gasping for breath as he put his hands around my neck and pressed until I soon had seen nothing but darkness. Death was coming, and I welcomed it. Anything was better than what I was experiencing.

273

Feeling a tap on my cheek, I looked up to see my husband in front of me. "Bella, we are wasting time. We need to leave." I stood, barely. I couldn't move. It was if I was in a trance. My mind was no longer functioning, and the room was a haze as it shifted. Rapidly it became narrowed. All I could see was tunneled directly on Carter's face. My body became limp, and his arms grabbed me before I fell. Picking me up, my legs dangled over his forearms. "Good thing you don't drink, Bella. You couldn't handle it." I picked my hand up to pat him on the chest, but it was weighted. The words wouldn't come from my mouth, but I kept telling him I loved him over and over. In my mind, it kept repeating, even though he was unable to hear me.

My eyes closed as I heard his heart and felt his chest rise and fall as he spoke to Landon. The words he spoke were halted when we made a few steps down the hall. The men talked briefly, and the sentences were clipped. Recognizing Grayson's voice, I tried to reach for him, but my arm dropped quickly as I did. Trying to pry my eyes open, I squinted to see his salt-and-pepper hair as he stood by Carter.

"Daddy." Trying to make my words come out plain wasn't happening well. "Pray." It was all I could get out. His hand landed softly against my cheek. He stroked it as if I was his daughter, lovingly. "Ben, Molly."

"Don't worry about them. Mom and I will take care of them. Everything will be all right, honey. Carter is with you, and Cassidy will be waiting when you get there. Just rest." Sighing, I returned to a deep and dark sleep.

The car swayed at times, or maybe it was me. I felt sick. "Amore." My voice sounded weak and tired as I drew out the pet name. I loved him, and the thought of losing our baby killed me.

"Shh, it's going to be okay, Bella. We don't have much farther to go." His long, deft fingers swept against my cheek as he held me close to his chest. I could hear his voice, but it seemed so distant. I felt as though I were falling, and it frightened me.

"I'm falling." I gripped his biceps as hard as I could. "I'm falling. Don't let me fall." My eyes felt like they were swollen shut. "Don't let me fall."

"Angel, you aren't falling. It's the alcohol. I have you. You aren't going to fall." Holding me tightly to him, he tried to rock me enough to let me know he was there and that he was holding me.

Panic rose in me, still having the feeling of falling. "Carter, please don't let go of me. Don't let go. I'm going to fall." Taking me closer to his lips, I could hear his voice against my ear. "Angel, I have you. You aren't falling, and I would never let you fall. You're safe with me. You aren't falling." I started to shake as if I was cold, and he pulled a jacket or a blanket from the back of the car and wrapped it around me. A sinking feeling came over me. The more he talked, the farther away he seemed. My arms went lifeless as I leaned against him. I couldn't hold on to him anymore.

"Angel, stay with me." He continued to rock me, but his arms felt as though they were leaving. "Isabella, don't you dare leave me." His fingers pushed my hair away from my face and tracing my cheek. "Isabella, don't leave me."

275

I could still hear his voice, and I held to it as I sank further. "Landon, go faster." His voice shook as he spoke.

"I have it to the floor now. What's happening back there?"

"I don't know. She's pale, really pale. She feels cold, and she is shaking."

"Keep her warm. I'll be there in five."

Lying against him, the last thing I heard was "Call Cassidy. Tell her to meet us at the door." The darkness that I sank into soon became light, beaming around me, warm and inviting. Love shone out from it, and I walked easily to it. Looking closer, I came to a large green field filled with flowers of every kind and size that were imaginable. The brilliant reds, blues, oranges, and yellows reminded me of a crayon box. Trees reached the sky in dark greens, lush and beautiful, standing in groves by a river that looked like glass as the sun hit it. A voice called to me, and I looked over my shoulder, seeing a young woman. Her long dark hair lay in large layers around her face. She had soft brown eyes, and her smile gleamed at me. She wore a long white dress that covered her from head to foot in lace and white ribbons. Greeting me, she hugged me to her. She started to speak, and I instantly knew her.

"Isabella, it's nice to meet you. I knew he would make the right choice. You must miss him. I know he loves you a great deal. I hear him pray every night for you."

"How do you know me?" My voice appeared without me moving my lips or speaking a word.

"I've known you for a good while. I had to see he was taken care of. I didn't want to leave. I had to. My work was finished, and God called me home."

"I don't understand."

"Tell him that I loved him and I never blamed him."

"Who do I say you are?"

"Congratulations. You must be so happy. You share such beautiful children. Jenna needs you both. Listen to him. He knows where she is. You need to go back now." She turned and took a few steps from me, and the brightness started to disappear.

"You didn't tell me your name."

"You need to go back to him. He loves you. Tell him Andee is happy, and I'll wait for him." She waved goodbye and disappeared. The darkness returned as I started sinking away from the brightness of wherever I was.

"Isabella, come back to me." The hand of my sweet husband held mine. His beard rubbed against the back of it as he kissed it. "Isabella, come back to me, angel. Don't leave me."

My heart felt heavy. Why, I wasn't sure. My eyes slowly opened as I tried to focus on his voice. Looking over to my side, Carter sat with his head down and my hand clutched against it.

"Dear God, please don't take my wife. You gave her to me at one of the lowest points in my life. I can't do this again. I can't live without her. I did everything I thought I was to do. My life is yours. If you have to take someone, take me. She has so much more to live for. Our baby is still going to need its mother, and Molly loves her. I know she would miss me, but I would gladly give my life for hers."

277

"Amore." Opening his eyes, he looked down at me as a tear slipped down his face. "Thank god, Isabella." Kissing my hand, he leaned down and swept a kiss across my lips. "Oh, angel, don't ever leave me. I can't go through that, not again."

"I love you." Closing my eyes, he kissed me on the cheek. "The baby."

"The baby's fine. You're going to be okay. Just rest now. I'll be right here."

"Our baby," I whispered, barely audible to him.

"The baby is fine. Sleep, angel. I'll be here with you."

My eyes closed immediately, knowing he was with me and the baby was still with us. A weight was lifted from me as I melted into the bed. The image of a woman ran through my mind as she stood before me before I awoke. Her hair, her face, and her features looked like my own. What did she tell me? Who did she say she was, and why is it bugging me that I can't put it together? The sounds of the room were exaggerated as I listened to my own breathing and that of Carter's. His hand remained covering mine as I lay there.

My body felt tired and weak, and my head ached as if it were being hit repeatedly with a hammer. The wash of the memory from earlier kept coming back in flashes that wouldn't let me alone. The woman's voice kept repeating, "He knows where she is." Where did this come from? Did I simply dream it? It wouldn't leave me alone. The thought continued through my mind. Carter ran his fingers along my arm in an attempt to soothe me and himself. The noise and the rambling thoughts soon died down, and I drifted off as Carter continued to sit beside me. He sang a soft

278

tune next to my ear that I remember well, the one and only song that I could remember him singing to me. I couldn't have fallen any more in love with him than I was at that moment.

I stood in the middle of a large room that was familiar to me. One that had brought such pain before now was a source of happiness. A young man stood in front of me with his hand held out for me. His short military-style cut was perfect, and his blue eyes gleamed as he flashed a crooked smile at me. "You, Cindy, are the most beautiful young lady I have ever seen. Your fairy tale suits you well. To make that fairy tale complete, I have brought you here to have a dance at your very own ball."

Turning on the music, I heard its sweet, hypnotic rhythm; and he turned to me and ran his finger down my cheek. "You are beautiful." He pulled my braid around over my shoulder and removed the band that secured it as I stood stiffly before him. Running his fingers through the curls that came from having it twisted, it fell tumbling over my shoulders. Placing his hand at the small of my back, he drew me in slowly and danced me around the room. My prince had rescued me from a deep, dark, and unforgiving place. His image soon was replaced by the man I had married, and I was at the New Year's party. His words that had charmed me to relax and dance with him was "Dance with me like we are lovers." As if it wasn't hard to imagine myself with him, I had loved him from the first time I had seen him.

The young man at South Shore had been my husband, and he had brought me out of the living hell that I had kept myself isolated in. The fear of living, the fear of being tortured and beaten had followed me into the treatment center. The last few things that I had remembered before his voice had brought me out were those of "*Ms. Cameron, I am sorry, but your daughter, she was just so small, I wasn't able to save her. Again, I am truly sorry.*" I could remember crying in hysterics, then nothing at all. I had gone silent from then on. I felt abandoned, lost in a world that had shown me nothing but pain over months or maybe years. I hadn't been sure as to how long I had been a prisoner of Arnell. I didn't like what was slowly coming back. I wasn't sure of what was real and what wasn't.

CHAPTER THIRTEEN

Carter sat at her bedside as she slept. It seemed as though it had been days since he had brought her in instead of a few hours. Cassidy had met them when they arrived and had stabilized Isabella before she had left for delivery. She had left Isabella under the watchful eye of her partner, Dr. Maxwell Healy. He was confident and seemed well versed in what was happening with Isabella, but he was much more at ease with Cassidy. She had taken care of Andrea and was one of her closest friends.

Cassidy was intelligent and had grown in her practice by leaps and bounds. She kept up with the changing medical field, and her years of experience assured him that Isabella was under the best care. He trusted her judgment, and she had assured him that once she was finished in delivery that she would return and talk to him about Isabella and their child.

The room was cheerful, painted in muted pastels and pictures of babies and parents kissing their bundle of joy. He only hoped that he and Isabella would get that chance. Cassidy did have to laugh when he told her how he had stopped her contractions. It wasn't dangerous, but she hadn't recommended its use on a regular basis. She was safe, and that was all that mattered to him.

Landon had stayed, hoping to give the family an update and had gone down the hall for coffee. Carter had more things on his mind than just when Cassidy would return or where Landon had gone. Jenna came to mind often. Landon, in recent days, had sent a request for a paternity test to be completed on the little girl in an attempt to give them all closure.

It had been performed, and they were now waiting for results to return. If it didn't turn out in his favor, he didn't see any sense in bringing it up until he knew for sure that Jenna belonged to Isabella. She could be anyone's child, but looking at her, Carter was convinced that she belonged to him. She had his blue eyes and his sister's dark raven hair and Isabella's contagious smile. She favored Beth at that age, but he saw Isabella in her, in her laughter, and in her soft and gentle way.

Then there was Ben. He hadn't heard anything from any of his family. Neither Darren nor Social Services had been able to track down any family. The only thing he knew was the boy's father had been in the military and was part of the engineers. The company he had been with was on a mission in the Middle East and up to this point was unable to be reached. It could be months before they knew anything. His mother was in critical condition, and the medical team still questioned her survival.

On occasion, he would look out the window at the passersby, but he paid little attention to them. It was something to occupy his mind, anything to decrease the anxiety he felt. Again, the loss of control loomed at him. He fought it, but he wanted a drink or a combination of pills and alcohol. He knew better. If he took one, it would just increase the hunger, and the issues would still be there to face. Why now? Why was he having problems now? He had dealt with problems in his past. He had been on scenes of victims, of horrific deaths that many would

282

have found exceedingly difficult to stomach. But this, it was falling in on him, and he felt helpless to stop it.

He stood, releasing Isabella's hand, and paced the floor, rubbing the back of his neck. His nerves were raw, and he was tempted to tell Landon to add alcohol to his coffee as he brought it. He knew it was wrong, but he had gotten to the point to where it felt like his skin was crawling. He hadn't had a craving for either of his crutches from the past, but now all he could do was pray. His cell phone shook at his side, and he opened it. It was a text message from his father. He began to read, and the anxiety he had felt started to shift as each word stood out from it. "I am with you always even unto the end of the world." Carter stood in relief. The words filled him completely. "I am praying for you, son. God's way is always perfect, even if we don't understand it. He promises he will be there with us, and I know he is with you now. Call out to him. He is ready to meet you. Don't worry about Isabella. God has her in good hands, I know. He told me so."

Only his dad would know he was struggling. He always knew, and now was no exception. Carter quickly texted his father back and took on the truth of what God had brought to him. "Thanks, Pop. I needed that. I'll let you know when I find out something. Bella is okay for now. The baby, according to Cassidy, is in no distress. I guess at this time, no news is good news. I thank God for that. I should hear about Jenna's results soon. Please pray for us. I am not sure what to pray for, Pop. She's my life." Carter closed his cell phone and placed it at his side. Sitting down, he found himself reaching to adjust his gun holster that wasn't there. This was one of the few times he hadn't worn a gun, and he felt naked without it. After years of carrying one, he would have to get used to not having it. If he were to leave the force, he would no longer be carrying a gun. He would be carrying a briefcase.

Landon walked into the room, holding a cup of coffee in each hand. Handing one over to him, he gestured toward Bella. "How's Izzy? Anything yet?"

Carter took a sip of the coffee and started to comment, but the taste of the coffee took him by surprise. "What did you do with the coffee?" Landon grinned, knowing it didn't have the typical taste.

"I know. Pretty rough, tastes like battery acid."

"Yeah, you could say that. It's worse than what they make at the station, if that's possible."

Landon raised an eyebrow and his cup as he addressed Carter. "You really aren't going to quit the force, are you? You know you wouldn't be happy doing anything else. It's part of you, and it's in your blood."

"How did you find out? I haven't discussed it with anyone but Isabella, and I know she hasn't said anything.

"Brooks, he said you were talking about resigning from the force. He wasn't happy about it. He told me you were one of his best investigators, and it wasn't going to be easy to find a replacement, with your know-how and reasoning."

Carter didn't much care what Brooks thought of him. They butted heads way too many times. He was a good man and a fine officer, but then they were too much alike. Carter shook his head and took another sip of coffee. "I didn't see it as much of a choice. My wife and family come first. I don't know how large that family may become. With Molly and this little one and a question of what will happen to Ben and then there are other factors we don't know at this time, it may increase quickly. I can't leave Isabella with all that responsibility."

"What does Izzy think? She must have an opinion of what you are considering."

Carter turned the cup singlehandedly, and his other hand was stuffed into his pocket. Looking down into his cup, he didn't want to discuss it. Landon was his best friend and now brother-in-law. He and Beth had married in a small ceremony at Pastor Conley's home. It had been small, in the light of what was going on. Beth didn't seem to mind. She was happy that he was alive, and she was just as married to the love of her life. Cooper had never appeared, and she was granted a divorce on grounds of abandonment. Carter cleared his throat before he spoke and then looked down at his wife. "She doesn't want me to leave. She tells me the same thing, that I wouldn't be happy doing anything else. I can't stand the thought of seeing the pain she lived in while she thought I was dead. Nothing could have hurt me any worse than standing at my own funeral, having to watch her cry and not being able to do anything about it. Being that close to her and not being able—" Carter rubbed the back of his neck and sat the coffee down on the table beside him. "She was helpless, and I had no control of what was going on other than to quit. I just didn't think I wanted to get rid of Arnell. He had made her suffer so much not to mention what he had done to my sister."

"And you." Landon took in the sight of his longtime friend, waiting for the answer he was sure to get.

"How did you know he did anything to me?" Carter crossed his arms over his chest, closing himself off.

"I didn't." Landon's jaw clenched. "You just told me. Why didn't you say something? I would have understood. All this time, the fights and addiction to prescription drugs, the alcohol, you were trying to cover it up." Carter ran his hand over his face, and Landon watched him closely. "Does she know?" Landon again gestured to Isabella.

"Not until last night. I didn't tell her. She guessed. I couldn't tell her after what he had done to her. She had enough to deal with without knowing what happened with me."

Landon drank his last drink and threw away the empty cup. He paced the floor and then ran his finger over his chin, and Carter knew he was putting it together. He hoped he was wrong, but he was almost certain now that he knew why he thought Jenna was his. Landon shook his head in an exaggerated amusement. Carter now was sure he got it.

Walking toward him, he sat down in the chair in front of him. "Of course, why didn't I put this together before? It was you, wasn't it?" Carter never said a word for a moment, taking it in. He sat down and stretched out in the chair and placed his hand over his face.

"It wasn't just being upset over Bella and the baby. You were concerned about what she would do if she found out it was you? You were the one that got her out. So putting two and two together, you knew her from then, didn't you? You knew her back then, and she doesn't remember that. Not only that. She doesn't remember that. She doesn't remember that you fathered that child. It wasn't Bentley at all, was it? That child never belonged to him because there was no possible way. That isn't all though, is it?"

Carter sat up in the chair quickly in an attempt to quiet Landon. Carter raised his hand to silence Landon and looked back to his wife briefly. "Do you want her to hear what you're saying? Keep your voice down. She could wake up and hear everything that you are claiming." He sat on the edge of the chair and tried to collect himself. Anger took hold of him quickly, and he tried desperately to control his temper. His jaw clenched; and he took a deep breath, attempting to release the pain, remembering from that time in his life and what pain he had inflicted on Isabella and his own family. "Look, I don't know for sure all the details. You need to keep it down. She doesn't know yet. I intend on telling her everything when I find out the paternity of Jenna. If it came down to it, I don't need the test. I know she belongs to me. It's evident that she is my daughter. She looks like Beth and has my eyes." Carter's mood lightened slightly as he thought of her. She was a beautiful little girl. She had a dark complexion like her Aunt Beth, and her raven hair tumbled down her back in large waves. Her eyes, there was no denying she had the Blake eyes. They came from his father's side of the family, and her dark hair and olive-colored skin came from his father's Italian lineage.

"You're positive that she is?" Landon looked over at his brother-in-law and watched Carter, but his expression was deadly serious. "Oh, man, that is going to be a tough one to explain. Has she remembered anything?"

"Just bits and pieces so far. This isn't going to be easy, and it isn't the only thing that is missing. Isabella has a brother, and I think I know who he is. I just don't know where he is."

"You're kidding, right? This just gets more tangled as it goes."

"You don't get it. This involves you and Beth. Landon, Isabella's brother—" Carter was now extremely uncomfortable. He ran his fingers through his hair and turned his back to his friend. "Isabella's brother is Cooper."

He heard Landon take in a sharp breath, and silence filled the room. "That can't be true. He never mentioned a sister."

"Yeah, well, there are reasons for that. I'll explain it when I get the details. Right now we need to see that she stays calm. She doesn't need any more upset in her life. The most important thing is to keep Isabella calm, so that she can deliver this baby. If she lost this child, I don't know what it might do to her. The details on what has happened in the past needs to stay there for the moment, at least until I can find out what is true and what isn't. Nothing is going to be the same once this comes out. I don't know how I can expect her to deal with it. I'm having a hard enough time dealing with it myself."

"Have you tried to talk to anyone? Pastor Conley, your dad, or her mother?"

Carter tried to calm himself from all the events that were taking place, but it was difficult. "I have talked to my father. He knows all of it now as far as my ties to her. I thought about going to talk to Anita, but with Isabella having difficulties, I just can't leave her. I don't think it is something that I should discuss over the telephone with her. Isabella hasn't spoken to her mother yet, or she would have put it together by now. In a way, I am surprised that she hasn't figured it out before now. She's sharp, but then she has been exceedingly busy."

"Well, with school and working and taking care of Molly, she has had her hands full. By the way, Bella was doing very well in her classes. She was in the top 2 percent of her class and was getting ready to take a forensics class before she came back to Rose Point to see your parents. She has grit."

Carter drew a soft smile as he knew some of what was going on with his wife, from him following her around on campus and taking classes with her. She was superbly intelligent, especially in her science classes. "She's a strong-willed woman, stubborn, and sometimes so beguiling that I have a hard time imagining she belongs with me."

"You love that she challenges you, and you know it. Andrea did the same thing. I know you and my sister had difficulties, but she loved you. Izzy has changed you, something that Andrea was never able to do."

"I blame myself for that. I never loved her the way I should have. It wasn't until her last few weeks that I found the love for her I should have given her our whole marriage. She deserved so much more. I can't make up for it, and I will remember what I denied her until the day I die. She never asked anything from me other than to be her husband and to love Molly. Her daughter was the most important to her, and she chose to save Molly and lose her own life because Molly was a part of me."

Landon sat and looked at him as if he never knew his best friend, and Carter felt the friction that the situation had already caused between them. He knew he had to tell him the truth of the whole situation, but now was not the place or the time for it.

"You were screwed up." Landon's words hit him hard. "My sister said you had issues, but she never told me." Landon ran his hand over his face. "She never told me why. I'm your best friend. Why didn't you come to me when we were growing up? We have known each other the majority of our lives, and you never told me. I told you everything in my life."

"Because I never told anyone. The only time my parents knew there was something that had really been a problem was when I had attempted suicide." Carter hadn't wanted to talk about it but couldn't see a way out of this. He was going to make time to tell him and his family along with his wife. "I promise I will tell you all about it. I need to tell my family why I have put them through so much pain all my life. I need to tell Isabella. She needs to know first."

Landon sat with his elbows on his knees, holding his head at what he had heard, and Carter knew the rest was going to be hard if he heard the rest of the story. He had been his friend all his life and was now finding out that all the things that he had seen him go through along with his sister started with him as a child. Once he found out if Jenna belonged to him, he knew she belonged to Isabella: game, match, set. Isabella would understand on some level, but getting her pregnant while she was drugged, by her brother no less, wasn't going to sit well. His mother wouldn't take it well if she knew all the twisted things that had been done to him. He wasn't sure if he wanted to tell it, because telling it meant reliving them.

"Landon, tell me you aren't going to hold this against me. I apologized to your sister, and being gracious, she forgave me for how I treated her. It wasn't that I hadn't loved her. I did. I just couldn't love her the way she deserved until I gave my life to God. She is the one that introduced me to God. She led me to God. I can never thank her enough for what she did for me. She gave me a gift, one that she knew would change my life. She saved me through the love of Jesus Christ. I was on the road of destruction, and she knew it. She knew she couldn't leave me until I was with God and our daughter had a stable dad. She knew she wasn't going to get better, and she was my connection. I loved her, Landon."

Landon scrubbed his face as he looked up at him, and he choked when he saw the look on his best friend's face. The pain reflected on his face, and Carter wasn't sure if he had lost his best friend. It felt as if he had lived a lie all these years. The pain he endured in his life had made it unbearable to live at times, and he had preferred to keep it buried.

Landon stood and turned away, and Carter sunk into the chair. It had started already. His friend would never forgive him for what he had done to his sister, for the five or so years that his sister went through everything imaginable with him, and now she was gone. She didn't deserve the way he had treated her. There was never a time that he hadn't loved her, but he had never loved her completely until God had gotten hold of his heart just weeks before she had passed away. He had never been able to forgive himself for that. He had told her as she had taken her last breath in his arms that he was sorry and had held her close to him and had told her that he would always love her, and he did. No one would take the part of his heart she had. The one thing other than giving his life to God she had asked him to do was to find a good woman. She had told him that she wanted him to be happy and that he needed a good and loving woman to love him for who he was and to love and raise Molly as she would have. He had promised her, even though at the time he had never had the thought of looking for anyone.

They would have to fall into his lap and led by God to him. He had no intention of falling in love with anyone, because the idea that he may be put in the situation of losing that love may come to him again. He hadn't been sure he could survive something that devastating again.

Carter looked down at his hands that were now laced together across his knees. This was it. This was the beginning of the end for a lot of his relationships. He felt it coming when he found Jenna. This was going to be so destructive. His past had caught up with him. Landon had shifted, and Carter looked up and saw his friend standing in front of him. Here it was. He braced himself for what was surely going to end his relationship with him, and it was certain to cause problems with his sister. Beth only knew partially what had happened to him as a child and nothing of what he had done when he was older.

"Carter, I don't know what to say, man. I am sorry. I didn't realize it had been that bad for you. I don't know what has happened to you, and I don't know if I want to know, but if my sister forgave you, I can't do anything less."

Carter was surprised by his response. It wasn't what he had expected at all, and he wasn't sure how to react. Forgiveness had come quickly. It had to be God. It was the only way he could explain it. "I am sorry, Landon. I wish your sister would have had a better life with me. I don't know what else to say."

Landon sat down and looked at his best friend and put on a chaste grin. "She loved you, and I know that you loved her in your own way. You have taken the greatest blessing of her life and cared for her and loved her. Molly was a gift from her. She was a mother, and she loved her baby, your baby. She could have terminated that pregnancy. Though she knew it meant that she would die, she wanted her for you. She would have done anything to stay with you if she could have. You weren't the only one she commissioned."

"What do you mean?"

"She was worried about you. She asked me to look after you and Molly. She knew when she was gone you would have a load on you, trying to raise Molly. She was worried that you would spend all your time working and caring for Molly to look for someone to make you happy. She didn't want you to live your life without someone to love you. That was important to her. Imagine my surprise when you met Izzy. I knew from the time you took her hand. You hadn't responded to anyone after the accident,

293

but you did to her. Seeing the way she looked at you. She didn't know it, but she loved you then. I can be pretty dense to things like that. It was evident. You need to make it right with her as soon as you can. She is going to need you. And you, brother, need her."

Carter was soon filled with comfort. God had taken care of one of his battles. Isabella would be the hardest. His parents would be upset that he had gone through what he had, but it was behind him. They would grow closer together. It would hurt his mother knowing that she hadn't known the whole story. The worst experience was the night he held his father's gun to his head. She had gotten over it. Oh, he was sure that it had come to mind from time to time. It would be hard to see your son standing in a room holding a gun to his head, high on drugs and loaded with alcohol. He wasn't sure Isabella was going to be so forgiving. "Thanks for understanding. Soon I will tell you the whole story. I think you at least deserve that."

"Enough said. It isn't necessary to go into it, unless it's healing for you."

"Eventually, it is going to have to get out. All of us need to heal from the life I lived and the pain I have inflicted on my family."

Isabella sighed, and Carter turned to see her rub her cheek. Her eyes remained closed, and she placed her hand against her stomach and rubbed it gently. He smiled down at her. He knew she wasn't awake, fully, but she was loving her child the only way she could at the time. Turning her head toward him, he got up and sat down in the chair beside her and turned the side lamp out of her face. Pulling the sheet up a little more, she sighed once again. The look on her face was peaceful, and then came a sweet smile. Her eyes still closed, she hummed a soft lullaby. His heart melted at the sentiment; his wife had literally turned him into jelly.

Landon spoke low, as not to awaken her. "She has you under her spell. I don't remember ever seeing you like this."

"I have been since the day I met her."

Landon looked down on Isabella and watched her as she slept and then placed a hand on his brother-in-law's shoulder. "Think I'll go home. Beth could probably use some help about now. If you need something, call me. I can come back and pick you up if you want to go home and pick up clothes and get a shower."

"I don't know when I'm going home." He turned to Landon and stood, shaking his hand and then leaning in, and slapped him on the shoulder. "Do me a favor and call Bella's mom and dad. The number should be in the address book in her purse. I don't have it with me, or I would do it. They need to know that she's here. Tell them it isn't serious as far as I know right now, and I will call them when I know something different."

"I'll do that." Landon turned and walked from the room. The silence of the hospital only left the click of his shoes on the floor. Carter sat back down by his sleeping wife and rubbed his face with his hand as it scratched over his unshaven beard. He pinched his fingers over the bridge of his nose and then bent down over his knees. He clasped his hands together and offered a silent prayer for his wife and baby. It was looking like it was going to be a long wait.

Isabella sighed and moved her hand that he had clasped, awakening him. The room was dark, and the sun had set outside. They had been there the entire day, and he still hadn't spoken with Cassidy. The thought had come to him that she had forgotten about them, but as soon as that thought came to mind, she walked in the door. Turning on the lowest light setting, she came closer. Dressed in her blue scrubs, she took off her surgical cap, her blonde hair pushed back with a headband. She smiled and spoke in a soft voice, as not to awaken Isabella. "Can I talk to you outside the room?"

"Is there something wrong?" He started to panic, and she shook her head and smiled. Motioning out of the room, he straightened his jeans and shirt and followed her into the corridor. She turned to face him and showed him to a chair that sat outside, and she took the one beside him. Opening the Mac she held in her hand, she looked over the screen, and the light from it illuminated her face in the low-cast lighting.

"I'm just looking over some of the other tests I ordered to make sure they have all come back." Carter shifted in the seat, uncomfortable at the delay. They had waited all day for news. Now it was here. Isabella had slept all day and essentially hadn't moved. "I wanted Isabella to sleep so we gave her a mild sedative when she came in. That's why she hasn't been awake much today. After the all the emotional upset and in light of the condition she was in when she arrived, I was a little concerned." She sat the Mac down on the small coffee table in front of them. "Isabella's blood pressure was very high when she arrived. Has she complained of having any headaches lately, bad ones?"

"No, she hasn't mentioned any. She had them some when she first found out she was pregnant, but she was told that it was hormonal."

"Any complaints, vision problems, blurriness, not being able to focus, sensitivity to light, dizziness?"

"She has had some dizziness on occasion, but nothing extreme. She gets tired easy, but I just thought it was because she was progressing in her pregnancy and trying to do too much. What is it? What's wrong with her? Is the baby all right?"

"Calm down. It's going to be fine. I just need to know how to treat her. She has some protein in her urine, and with her high blood pressure, it suggests preeclampsia. It can be managed, but we have to watch her closely. I will start her on some medication that will take care of her blood pressure. It should take it down to normal. She will need to rest until she can see her normal physician. It appears to be mild, but she will need to take it easy. I want her to stay here for a couple of days before she is sent home. She will need to be on strict bed rest. There is no exception to this. If she wants to carry this baby to term, it's important."

"Then she is in danger?"

"Not if she listens to me. I will care for her and see that she and the baby are well taken care of. Once you decide to take her home, you will not be able to go by car. If you must take her back to Maine before delivery, you will need to fly her, which I don't recommend right now, but she can be airlifted. I will go into more detail on how to care for her at home when she is ready for release. For now you need to stay calm and keep her calm. If the baby were born now, the chances of survival is around 50 percent. I want to keep the baby where he is at least until he is thirty-three weeks. I would prefer she go full term, but it may not happen. We need to hope for the best. Your little baby is going to need all the love and support you can give him along with Isabella."

"Is she out of danger for now?" Carter knew his voice shook when he asked. He felt as if he were going through the loss of Andrea all over. His heart crushed in his chest as he sat there, hoping to hear something good.

Cassidy placed a reassuring hand on his shoulder and smiled. "I know what you're thinking, but don't go there. I want you to remain calm. I am going to do everything I can to protect them both. It isn't something we have to worry over now. Isabella is strong, and she is in good health. The baby is healthy and on perfect schedule. He's growing and looks good for his gestational age. He's moving and has a good solid heartbeat."

Carter tried to relax at the news she gave him. It was a relief that she was not exactly in immediate danger, but she was where she needed to be if something did happen. Cassidy stood to make her leave, and Carter followed. He pushed his hands down into his pockets and looked down at the floor. "She is going to be fine. I'll be back in to see her tomorrow. She will have Dr. Miles tonight. I have asked her to look in on her frequently. She is good at what she does. She interned with me. She has agreed to contact me if there are any problems. I don't foresee any."

"Thank you, Cassidy. I appreciate what you have done for her and our baby."

"Not a problem. Get some rest. I know better than to tell you to go home so I will have the staff bring in a sleep chair for you."

"Thanks." Cassidy turned and walked away, and he stood at the door for a moment. Isabella, what would he do if he lost her? He had lived through that nightmare before and didn't wish to repeat it. Then there was the baby. He didn't even know if he had a son or a daughter. He couldn't explain the feeling that he had. It was beyond hurt. It was beyond feeling helpless. He felt more like something had drained him of every feeling he had. He wasn't sure if he should be angry, hurt, mourning, or relieved and joyful. His wife was still with him and seemed to be stable. His baby was growing and apparently healthy, but it could change quickly. He couldn't imagine how Isabella would react. He was hoping that he wouldn't be alone when she asked. He was brought from his thoughts when he heard his wife call out a name. Walking into the room, he heard it clearly.

"Andee!" she had called out. As he went to her, he saw she was sitting straight up in the bed. "Andee! Where are you? Come back." Carter sat down on the bed in front of her, showing her she wasn't alone. He turned on the side lamp and tried to soothe her. She kept calling out. Even though she looked like she was wide awake, she appeared as though she was asleep. Her eyes were large as she looked around the room. Carter took her into his arms and held her close to him and whispered in her ear that he loved her.

"Angel, it's all right. I am with you." She shook against him as he rocked her. He smoothed her hair from her face and continued to rock her. He gently stroked her hair and sang to her as he did at South Shore. It had calmed her many times when she was having a bad day then, and he had hoped he could do the same now. He started to sing softly a love song that he had heard as a young boy. His mother sang it to him. It was one of the few things that he remembered of her. She would play the piano and sing and have him with her on the bench. He loved the melody and had vowed he would learn how to play it when he was older. When he had come to live with his adoptive parents, they had offered several activities, but he wanted to learn how to play the piano. Iris had set up lessons, and she herself had also taught him. She helped him perfect the melody, and it had given him pleasure to have something that he and his mother had done. Iris was now his mother, but he hadn't forgotten his birth mother, and Iris didn't want him to forget.

"Please don't let this feeling end," he continued and felt her relax in his arms. She sighed and leaned into his chest as he sang. He had been led to her by God. He didn't think he would ever love again, and now he had Isabella. He couldn't imagine what it would be like never to hold her again. His life had been so meaningless before her. Her hand rested over his heart, and he clasped it to him and kissed the top of her head. Turning her in the bed, he pulled her up against him, and she rested quietly. Her breaths were quiet, and she was again peaceful. As she slept, he prayed and prayed to the point he thought he would run out of words. God heard him, he knew, but he wasn't satisfied until he had prayed to the point he was exhausted. His eyes grew heavy, and he closed them reluctantly. *I'll just close my eyes for a moment*, he told himself and pulled her tightly to him and laid a hand against her stomach where he could feel his child kicking in enthusiasm. His hand splayed against her, and he was thrilled just to know he or she was moving. In a few short months, he hoped he would be a father for the third time. Bella nuzzled into his chest as he cupped her to him and gave her a squeeze. He would worry about everything else tomorrow. Right now holding her in his arms was a perfect feeling, peaceful, and he didn't want to miss a minute of it.

Carter's heart felt heavy as he drifted off and had wished his past had been nothing more than a bad nightmare that he could wake up from. The few years of his early life had really messed up his life as a teen and threatened his present. He had been up with Bella almost twenty-four hours, and his body felt weak as his mind raced, but all he had wanted peace, even if it were short-lived.

Brahms's Lullaby played in the background as one more child entered the world. It had played often today and into the night. He took a deep breath and relaxed as the song hit a note that was in the midst of the children's classic and heard no more. Peace soon captured him, and he felt as though he had been lifted up and was being cradled. What a relief he felt as he slowly drifted off.

CHAPTER FOURTEEN

"I want to go to," Carter had told his mother as she sat at the dressing table. He watched her as she placed the earrings in her ears. He loved them. They sparkled against her skin and lit up in his mind like lights on a Christmas tree. She sprayed a soft scent of lilacs against her skin and smiled into the mirror as she looked into her little boy's deep-blue eyes. "I want to take you out, Mommy. You're my girl." Miriam Davis laughed in delight at her son. "You're so pretty, Mommy. I'm gonna marry you when I grow up."

Miriam gathered her son up and placed him on her lap in front of the antique dressing table. She looked into the mirror at his tiny face. His blue eyes shone, and his dark hair set them off perfectly. He had received his father's handsome good looks and his softness with the fairer sex. "I love the idea, son, but I'm already taken by your father."

"When Daddy is through with you, can I have you?"

His sweet innocent look melted her, and she hugged him to her. "Elijah, you are the love of my life, but don't ever tell your daddy that." She hummed a little song as she held him, and he ran his fingers through her long hair. It lay like strands of gold lying against her black dress, and it was soft and silky lying against his cheek.

"Tell me what?" The tenor voice of Alonzo Moretti Davis floated through the air behind them. "Who's after my girl now?" He chuckled as he waltzed into the room in his black dinner jacket. His crisp white shirt brightly shone from under its cuffs and his chest. The tie he continued to work with as he made his way to his wife and kissed her on the cheek. His father was an awesome presence. He loved his wife with everything he had. It had been nothing to walk into a room and find his parents dancing or his father's arms around his mother's waist, hugging her tightly to him.

"Me, Daddy." He held his small hand in the air, getting his father's attention. "I want to take Mommy out on her 'versary."

"It's 'anniversary,' son, and Mommy has a sweetheart." Picking his son up from his mother, he took him and sat down on the bed across from Miriam. His father's large hands were gentle as he patted his back. Alonzo looked at his son, and a slow grin filled his face. "Elijah, do you know what love is?"

He thought about it a moment and said, "Yep, I watch it on TV all the time."

"Yes, that is what the world sees as love. Real love, Elijah, is one that takes care of people, one that loves people when they don't deserve it. It is reserved for one special person in your life that is worthy of that love. You give your life to them and would give your life for them. Mommy and I have that kind of love, and someday when you are old enough, there will be a young lady that you will fall in love with. That young lady will love you for who you are and what you are. Nothing will be in the way of that love. It will be someone that you feel like you will never be able to live without. You don't understand it yet, but you will.

"Mommy and I will be there for you when you need us, and I want to see that young woman bring love and

303

color into your life. Watch for her, Elijah. God will place her in your path, and you will know from the first meeting." Kissing him on the top of the head, he sat him down on the floor and walked to his wife and clasped her necklace around her neck.

Alonzo bent and kissed her shoulder as he finished his task. Glancing over at his son, he had stood and watched his father as Alonzo straightened. Taking his wife's hand, he assisted her from her seated position. He grinned over at his wife. "When should I have her home, Mr. Davis? I do have your best girl, right?"

Carter's face lit up as his father asked him about his mother. "Thirteen o'clock." He laughed. Alonzo and his wife laughed out loud. Alonzo held out his hand to his son and shook his hand. "Done, sir. Thirteen o'clock it is." Alonzo turned and handed his wife her clutch and started to walk out of the room when his sister bounded in. Her hair bounced from her shoulders. Her red pinafore dress rustled as she ran to his father. There was no doubt that she had him wrapped around his finger. Sometimes it made Carter mad that she had so much power over their father, not that he didn't love his sister. He had loved her from day 1 and would have done anything for her.

His father pulled a red lollipop from his pocket and handed it to her, then put her back down to kiss her cheek. He then pulled one from his pocket and handed it to him. "You're the man of the house while I am gone. I am depending on you." He ruffled Carter's hair.

His mother dropped to her knees and kissed the children and wrapped her arms about them. Smoothing his sister's hair, she kissed her cheek and told her she loved her. His sister trotted off to play as he stood before his mother, still reluctant to let her leave him. Miriam looked at her son and smiled broadly. "You are my best guy," she teased. Hugging him, she ran her hand up and down his back, and he had curled his arms around her neck. "I love you, Mommy. There'll never be a girl like you."

Miriam looked back at her son as a tear slid down her cheek. With his tiny finger, he wiped it away. "I love you, Elijah." Collecting herself, she kept her arms around him. "Now as man of the house, you have to promise me you will look over your sister. She's still little and needs her big strong, handsome brother to protect her. Can you do that for me?" Carter nodded his head yes. He could never say no to her. His mother was the center of his life.

She stood and took his father's hand. Her hand looked so small and fragile against his large, powerful one. Carter hesitated a moment, then wrapped his arms around his father's legs and hugged him. "Love you, Daddy." It was rare for him to hug his father and tell him that he loved him; it just didn't come as easy.

Alonzo bent down and hugged him to him. Carter could smell the warm scent of his father's cologne about his collar, and his hair had the smell of tonic where he had smoothed it back, controlling the natural curl in it. "Be a good boy. Mommy and I will be back soon." He stood and guided Miriam out of the room, and he followed them to the living room where Mrs. Rosen was waiting to tell them goodbye. His sister sat on the floor, playing with blocks with Monte, her teddy bear, which was always at her side.

His mother left instructions for Mrs. Rosen, and his father stood behind her, patiently waiting. "There are oatmeal cookies in the jar. They are Elijah's favorite, and Elizabeth has snacks in the refrigerator for later. Don't let her have strawberry ice cream. The doctor thinks she may be allergic to strawberries. The emergency numbers are listed by the telephone, and we can be reached at the Riverfront Restaurant. Alonzo and I will be home around ten o'clock. Make sure Elizabeth gets to bed around eight and Elijah around eight thirty at the latest."

"Miriam, if we don't leave, we aren't going to get there before the place closes," Alonzo coaxed. "Besides, Mrs. Rosen knows what she is doing."

Miriam flashed a smile at him and then to Mrs. Rosen. "I am sure she does. I am sorry. I haven't been away from the children much." Mrs. Rosen assured her that they would be well taken care of and that there was no need to worry. Carter watched as his father put his mother's coat about her shoulders and grabbed his own. Opening the door, he escorted her out, and the door closed behind them. It would be the last time he would see his parents alive. It wouldn't be long before he would answer the door to a uniformed man that would ask for Mrs. Rosen. Carter shook, knowing what was coming. In his mind, he knew he was asleep and wanted to awaken before he heard the words that as a child he didn't understand but knew all too well as an adult. They still rang in his ears even now when the memory came to him. It led to so many painful memories after the fact.

He had seen so many appalling and disturbing things in the time they had been killed until he was adopted to last him a lifetime. The experience he had carried with him into his young adulthood had nearly destroyed him. He sat at his parents' funeral with his arm around his sister, trying to protect her as he had promised his parents. It was all he had left to do for them. He had protected her the best he knew how, and it had led him literally into the door of hell for him. He had wanted to die many times over, but the only thing that had held him together for so long was the fact that his sister had been entrusted to him. It was bitterly cold on the day of the funeral, and it was snowing. It had blanketed the ground and continued as the minister had read pieces of their lives. It should have been a child's paradise. The snow on the ground was just right for sledding, building snowmen, and snowball fights. Instead of the joy that came with being a child, he sat in a disturbing scene that he didn't fully understand. His grandmother sat beside them and was to take them with her. If it weren't for her, they would have no one. His dad's family all lived away. They had no intention of raising a family, especially for children that young. His mother's sister was unable to take them. Her husband would not allow them there. He hated children and refused to take them.

All had gone well until his grandmother had found she was terminally ill. It was then they were taken and placed into the foster care system. Out of the many families they had stayed with, most were good to the children and tried to love them. Both of them had made it difficult. They had no safety net other than each other, making it problematic for them to learn to trust.

His grandmother had leaned in and kissed him and spoke to him softly, assuring him. Carter tried to awaken, but it wasn't until he heard a sweet voice that brought him from the nightmare, and he was glad to hear it. He opened his eyes to see his wife next to him, running her fingers through his hair. He pulled her into him, holding her like she was his only security, his breath coming back slowly. He couldn't get the image out of his head, of how the snow had lain on the caskets as they lowered his parents into the ground. Isabella hugged him, never saying a word. He was happy she wasn't asking questions. At the moment, he didn't think that he could bring himself to talk about it.

Her smile beamed as she looked at him. Curiosity getting the better of him, he couldn't resist. He rubbed his eyes and saw that she had been awake for a while. She had combed her hair, and her skin was soft and smelled of peppermint, her hair still damp as though she had showered. A slow smirk crossed his face as he watched her. "Mrs. Blake, what are you up to?"

Isabella placed her hand to her chest, and her smile became a little larger. "Who, me?"

"Yes, you. I know you well enough that you are cooking up something. You do not hide things well. So what has you in such a wonderful mood?"

"I know something that you don't," she teased. "And I may make you wait until later to find out." She shrugged her shoulders and quickly batted her eyes. She was having fun with whatever she had in mind.

"Oh, you do. So, Mrs. Blake, whatever they gave you must have been good."

She jabbed him a little and laughed. "That was your concoction, Mr. Blake. I certainly don't remember much of what happened. I do know that our baby is happy and healthy."

Taking her close to him and slipping his arms around her, he kissed her on the cheek. "And how do you know that?"

"I talked to Cassidy this morning. She says the baby is healthy and growing like a weed."

"I didn't hear her come in this morning. Was she here long?"

"No, but she was happy about how my pregnancy is progressing and told me that the baby is healthy."

"Did she tell you that you were going to have to take care of yourself? It sounds like you are going to be on bed rest for a while. Cassidy stressed that you needed to rest if you wanted to carry this baby."

"She told me, and I will be careful. I am a nurse, you know. I know what I can do and what I can't."

Carter drew his finger down her cheek. "See that you listen for once."

"I know something else that you don't. It's a surprise. I don't know if I will tell you now or wait till later. Cassidy is going to be coming in about an hour or so. She had a meeting to go to then she will come back. She is going to do another ultrasound. You, Mr. Blake, are going to see your baby on screen and get to hear its heartbeat for the first time. Then there is one other thing."

"What's that?"

"I know what we're having. Cassidy told me this morning. She wanted to wake you up so you knew, but I wanted to surprise you. Make sure that you have your cell phone because you are going to want to call your parents."

Carter laughed at his wife. "That's sneaky, Bella. What is it? What are we having?"

"I am not telling, not yet. I want you to call Landon or Quentin to come down and take some pictures. I want to capture your expression when you find out."

"It must be good if you want pictures. I had Landon call your parents. They should know by now that you are here. I don't know if they are coming. I haven't spoken to them."

"It's okay. They will know soon enough. You can call them from the cell phone when you see the ultrasound."

An hour had passed and Isabella was getting nervous, and it was hard to keep her still as they waited. Carter could see he had his work cut out for him. Isabella was going to be a handful when they did go home. He was going to be at her side constantly to keep her in bed. She was restless, and waiting and doing nothing was driving her crazy. He was going to have to find something to keep her occupied that would keep her attention and would lower the stress. She was used to going to a high-stress job, taking care of kids, and going to class. Now she had nothing she could do but sit and wait. If she had to do this until delivery, he would have to strap her to a chair or a bed to keep her there.

"Hey, guys, ready to see the little one?" Cassidy came in the room, pulling the machine behind her, and took a seat next to the bed. He was glad that she was here. Maybe Isabella would settle down now. "This is it. Are you

310

excited?" Cassidy was happy and bouncing with pleasure as she spoke to them. She proceeded to listen to the baby and then talked to Isabella for a short time, telling her what she needed to do when she did go home and that bed rest was a must for a while at least. Her blood pressure had come back down to normal, and that was a relief to him. At least it was a step in the right direction. Just as Cassidy was getting ready to do the ultrasound, Grayson, Landon, and Isabella's parents walked into the room. Anita hugged her daughter and soon stood back behind Carter. His father had brought the camera and was ready for action.

Having most of the parents here was a thrill for them both. Anita and Jeb hadn't been able to be at any of her appointments, and it excited Isabella beyond belief that they were there. As they gathered and the room hushed, it wasn't long before Carter heard the whoosh of his baby's heartbeat. Isabella took his hand and squeezed it and smiled up at him. "There it is," Cassidy announced as she waved the wand over her belly. Pointing to the baby's heart, it was evident it was beating as he watched it pulsate. What a remarkable feeling it gave him. He had never experienced this with Andrea. He had missed out on so much because of what was going on in his life. He only had himself to blame for it. Cassidy pointed out fingers and toes. They watched the baby as it had placed its thumb in its mouth and the other hand above his head as if it were trying to hide. It was amazing. Every detail was clear and vivid. Carter knew without a doubt in his mind that he would never forget this for as long as he lived. "Now here comes the fun part. Let's see if we can get the baby to move its legs, then we can see what you are." The baby kicked frantically as the cold wand moved over Isabella's belly. "Look at this, Papa." She pointed out on the screen. Isabella smiled from ear to ear as he watched. "You have a boy in there." Carter was overjoyed at the thought of having a boy. Grayson quickly snapped the picture as it was announced, then Cassidy moved the wand again. She measured and then watched him move for a while. "Have you picked a name yet?"

"Elijah."

"Nice, very nice." She continued to wave the wand around until she looked at Isabella and smiled back at her. "He's healthy." Bella laughed a little as she looked at him, then he had felt her eyes on him. He glanced down at her for a moment then returned his stare to the screen. He felt her eyes on him as he watched the screen and watched as the image changed. "Well, my goodness," Cassidy chimed. "We have a passenger that is really lively." Carter watched as little legs and arms flailed all over the place. Suddenly, it hit him that he was a father again, and it was most assuredly a son. He loved Molly, but the desire of his heart was a son. He hadn't let anyone know that part of him. The thought now shocked him that after all the grief and pain of his past, he had so many wonderful things in his life.

"What do think of that, amore?"

Carter's throat tightened, and he hadn't made a sound. Even if he had tried, he didn't think a sound would have passed his lips. Isabella looked up at him, and her smile soon faded. "Carter, are you okay?" He had looked down at her and wasn't sure what kind of expression he held on his face. He was beyond happy. The feelings he had inside of him was indescribable. Isabella had reached over her body to his face and continued to watch his expression. "Carter, you're frightening me. Amore, say something."

He took a short breath and let it out quickly and leaned down over her and scooped her up to him. All the anxiety that had filled him over the last few hours had left, and he was able to breathe. He hadn't realized how it had affected him. He could have lost them both. It had finally hit home. His wife was okay and so was his little man. She ran her hands down his back as he rocked her in his arms. "Looks like someone is very happy with the results," Grayson announced with a chuckle that sounded like his own. The room was silent except for the simple explanation.

Carter kissed her cheek like he couldn't get enough of her. He could have cared less about who or how many were in the room. "Isabella, you amaze me a little more every day." He cupped her face and kissed her again and started to laugh as he did. "A son, you are giving me a son." He turned to his father and smiled broadly at him "What do you think of that? It's a boy. She's giving me a son."

The room rang with laughter. Carter was so happy he could barely put two words together. At one point, he thought he was dreaming. "Make sure and tell Mom, will you? She is going to be so happy. Tell her that Elijah is on his way."

Isabella corrected him. "Elijah Clayton Blake."

Carter was stunned as he looked down at his wife. He felt the blood run from his head to his feet and thought he would pass out. "Angel, where did you get the idea to make his middle name Clayton?"

"Why not? It's a beautiful name? Besides, I talked with a beautiful woman. I knew her somehow, but I am not sure how. I saw her last night. She told me about a little boy she knew, and his name was Clayton." Isabella smiled as she told him about the little boy and how the lady had told her how much he was loved. "She told me about him, and he sounded precious. She told me he had strawberry-blond hair like Ben and had beautiful big brown eyes. Andee also told me about Jenna, and that you would know where to find her." She clasped Carter's arms and looked at him with pure joy. "Carter, Jenna is alive. She's just waiting for us to come find her." Carter couldn't believe what he was hearing as he listened to her. "Jenna is alive. Andee told me."

"Wait a minute, angel. Where did you see this woman?"

Isabella shrugged as she looked at him. "I don't know, but it was beautiful. I saw the most beautiful flowers I think I have ever seen, and the grass was so green that it looked like the green in a crayon box. My feet felt so good against it. There was a river that flowed along some big huge beautiful trees, and it looked like glass with the sun shining on it."

Carter choked. He knew what she had seen. "Angel, there's no way. You were with me all night. I held you on the way here and after you were put to bed last night. I never left you. If you had been anywhere other than this room, I would have been with you."

Isabella looked a little shaken at what she was hearing. "But I was there. I know I was there. The woman, she talked to me. Carter, she was beautiful. She had long dark brown hair that lay in long curls down her back. She was dressed in a long white dress that was covered in lace and ribbons. Oh, she glowed." He watched his wife. "Andee, she was real. She was as real as you and I are."

Carter thought a minute, and then it came to him. "What did you say her name was?"

"Andee. She told me her name was Andee."

Carter quickly sat back down before he fell down, and he looked to his father as he did. "Isabella, what else did she say?" His wife sat there for a minute, and he could see her run it through her mind. He soon saw the shaken look in Isabella's face as she put it together. "She said she didn't blame you. She said to tell you she loved you, and she would wait for you." He listened to his wife's voice quiver as she told him what she remembered.

"Isabella, Andee could not have been here." Carter rubbed the back of his neck and felt his eyes water. "Angel, Andee is what I called Andrea. She couldn't have been here."

His heart sank at the thought. She had to be so ill for her to see a glimpse of the other side. She had been a breath from leaving him. Isabella remained in the hospital and was watched over closely by Cassidy. Carter never left her side. If he did, it was to shower and change clothes. That really couldn't be considered leaving her because he used her shower and had his parents or Beth and Landon to bring him a change of clothes. After months of being in bed, Iris had accompanied her husband to the hospital. She had begged him to go home, eat, and rest. Isabella's parents were there, and she and Grayson were going to be staying for a few hours. He had refused to leave her.

Carter was relieved when she was finally released to return home, although the thought of her having talked to his wife that had passed away years ago gave him an unsettled feeling. Running the conversation over in his head like a recording, he remembered some of what she had said to him. The conversation was like a groove, stuck in a record. *She's alive. Jenna is alive and waiting for us.* Up to this point, she hadn't questioned him as to how that was possible.

He sat silently in an oversized Victorian chair, looking out on the lake. Moments before, he had checked on her and found her sleeping peacefully. Her breaths were soft, and she had made a little sigh as he touched her cheek. Her hair was spread across her pillow and looked like silk. Her porcelain skin glowed against the white bedding. She still looked a little pale, but Cassidy didn't seem to be that worried.

For hours he had sat by her and watched her as she slept. When she was awake, she tried to be agreeable with not moving excessively, but it was going to be difficult to keep her down for long. The wheels in her head constantly turned and planned things that needed to be done before Elijah made his appearance. He had taken her a laptop and let her shop to her heart's content for baby clothes and furniture, though they weren't sure what was going to happen. He was a little concerned with that. She had already had several close calls, and they had been lucky that she had carried this baby as long as she had. He feared that maybe he was doing the wrong thing, but she had to do something, and if it made her happy to plan for him, so be it.

He sat there staring out onto the water, hoping things would become clearer as he did. His jaw tightened as he thought of everything that had happened over his life. For some reason, the loss of his birth parents had hit him hard over the last few days, and he could see his mother as clearly as he did the last night he had seen her. The family album lay across his legs as he leafed through it. His ankle crossed against his opposite leg and held it in place as he looked at the picture of Beth and himself with both of their parents. He loved Grayson and Iris as much as he did his own parents, but he felt like a child lost when he thought of his birth parents. What would have happened if they had been allowed to grow up with his birth parents? Would his life now been different as his choice of career, his wife, his family? Of course, Grayson and Iris would not have been part of it, and he had learned so much from them.

He had wanted so much to have gotten to know his birth father. He had seen him little, but when he did, they had spent wonderful times together. His father had been an FBI agent, and it had left him little time for his family. His mother understood the racket and had learned to live with it. He guessed his choice of career came from him, even though it took seeing Isabella in the state she was in to take on that role. He had always felt the need to protect her from their first meeting, a stranger, someone he had

317

barely known. He remembered their first meeting and how she had looked. He doubted that she remembered. She had been so closed off, and he had tried to approach her. She had sat in a chair during one of their group sessions with her knees drawn into her chest. Her eyes had been downcast, and she had refused to talk during group sessions. Her shut-off disposition had somehow touched him deeply. He had been so unlike her. He had acted out from his experience, and she was closed off, but that wasn't what had attracted him. Certainly, she was a beauty, but it was her hollowed appearance that had struck him. She appeared as a lost child, and his heart ached for her. He could tell that whatever had happened to her had stolen her soul.

There had been hours that he had spent with her, talking to her without a response. Their counselor had spoken to him about the time he was spending with her and had advised against it. He hadn't forbidden him, but he felt it wasn't beneficial for him to spend so much time with her. It was the only pleasure that he himself had gained in the time he had spent there. He would take books and music in her room or he would read to her. They would listen to music or he would just talk to her, telling her stories of his family and what he was like as a little boy. He had told her about Grayson and Iris and his birth parents, what he remembered of his life before the nightmare he endured.

He had approached her when he first met her and introduced himself. She kept her eyes averted from him, and he looked at her delicate features. She was beyond beautiful, but knowing how young she was or what he supposed her age was, he had told himself he couldn't get attached. Her hair was in a braid and lay over her shoulder, and her porcelain skin was flawless. He had reached to touch her hand, and she had flinched as he did, and his heart broke. It was then he knew what she had been through was as bad, if not worse, as his own experience, and he wanted to protect her. She had become his at that point and his responsibility.

"How's the proud papa to be?" The soft voice of his mother-in-law came from behind him as she walked onto the veranda and took a seat beside him. He grinned as he thought of his beautiful wife and the son that she carried. It filled him like nothing else. Behind her, Molly bounded on the scene, skipping as she did. Her long hair bounced as she came onto the veranda and was followed closely by her newfound friend Ben.

"I am fine. Just a little concerned about Bella, but I guess that's normal."

"Yes, it's very normal." Anita had squeezed his hand in assurance and smiled. "She loves you, and knowing my daughter, this is the biggest thrill for her, to be able to give you a son. She was so excited when I talked to her earlier. I am so glad she found you. I haven't seen her this happy in her life. She dreamed of this when she was just a little girl." Anita chuckled a little as she remembered her daughter growing up. "She must have been around seven years old when I saw her in front of the full-length mirror in our room. She had taken one of my old dresses that, of course, dragged on the floor, and my heels that were gapped by miles. Her small feet swam in them." She wiped a lone tear from her eyes as she spoke. "With one of my old handbags she had thrown over her shoulder, she talked to her baby doll that was carefully placed on the bed with pillows around it. She told him very matter-of-factly, 'We must get ready to meet your daddy. He is waiting for us, you know. Your daddy is going to be so glad to see you.'" She had taken some of my old makeup and put on way too much blush and bright pink lipstick and thought she was just the picture of a wife going to meet her husband. She picked the baby doll up and rocked him in her arms and kissed it, soothing it as if it were crying. Her husband had a name, and so did her baby doll. You won't believe what their names were. When I think of it, it gives me chills."

Carter looked at her in amusement, but he could tell by the look on her face that she was deadly serious. "With Bella, anything is possible. I can't imagine what she came up with. My angel of a wife has an imagination all of her own." Carter chuckled slightly as he glanced over at Anita. "She is one of the most intriguing people I know."

Anita turned her face down slightly and smiled chastely. "Yes, she does, but she also has a quality about her that I can't explain. She has always had the ability of predicting certain things. I never thought much about it until she met and married you. I just pushed it off."

Carter, being a little more serious, had a partial smirk on his face as he addressed her. "What do you mean, like ESP?"

"No, more like premonitions. She would tell us simple things when she was small, of things that were coming. Like someone in particular was going to call, things like that. She would play with her doll for hours at times, and she would play as if she were married. She would take her little play dishes and set them out on her table and place her doll in her toy high chair and carry on a full conversation. It never occurred to me that it was any more than a child with a make-believe friend. When she met you and started dating you, it still hadn't hit me until your wedding. When they used your complete name, the connection finally dawned on me."

"We didn't know each other before South Shore. I am sure you have figured out by now that I was there."

"Not until Isabella was in the hospital the first time around with this baby. She remembered a young man that was there that reminded her of you, but he was a younger version of you now with a military-style haircut. Then is when I put it together. She called you Eli for years and talked about you up until she disappeared. Her pretend husband all those years ago was Eli, and she had named the baby doll she played with as Clayton."

Carter shook when he heard what his mother-in-law had to say. "You are kidding, aren't you?" Carter watched his mother-in-law, and she shook her head slowly as he sat beside her. Over the last few days, he wasn't sure as to why that would surprise him. He then looked away from her and out toward the lake. "Wow, that's hard to believe." Looking down at his wedding band, he twisted it slightly and wondered if there was such a thing as destiny or premonitions. He knew that God placed people where he wanted them and when he wanted them so that their paths would cross, but this was amazing. For years, as a little girl, Isabella talked to an imaginary husband named Eli and a child that she called Clayton.

321

"She loved you before she ever met you." Anita turned in her chair slightly and addressed him once again. "I know there is something that is bothering you and has been. If I can see it, I know my daughter has noticed it. Do you want to talk to me about it?"

Carter cleared his throat and thought for a moment before he spoke. Yes, he did, and he had a lot of questions that his mother-in-law would be the only one that could answer them. He started to speak when Landon walked onto the veranda. His shoes clicked on the cobblestone as he approached them. "Hey, Carter, can I talk to you?" Carter spoke to Anita and told her that he would speak to her momentarily. She agreed that she would wait for him as he followed Landon away from her and into his father's study, closing the door behind him. Landon stood in front of the desk and leaned into it with his legs crossed at the ankle and his hands supporting him. Carter could tell by his expression that it was important, and he wasn't sure what was coming. It could have been any number of things, but he was certain that what he had to say was going to impact Isabella in some way.

Carter stood in the middle of the room with his hands riding on the waist of his faded jeans. "Okay, we're alone now. Spill it."

Landon looked down at the floor momentarily and then looked back at him. "I can tell by your expression what you have to say isn't good."

"Depends on how you look at it. I guess the best way is just to tell you. I got the results back on Jenna today."

Landon had hesitated, and Carter rubbed his neck then held his hand out in midair at him. "And this is it. So tell me what you found out."

"Carter, the test results were positive. Jenna is your daughter. It's 99.9 percent. You can't get a better result than that."

Carter ran his fingers through his hair, turned away from Landon for a moment, then ran both his hands over his face as he processed the information. Shoving his hands in his pockets, he turned and looked at Landon. "I don't know whether to celebrate a daughter or look into the possibility of burying my marriage."

Carter turned and paced the room. What was going to happen now? Isabella and he now had a daughter that they had no idea existed. He had met her, and she was a beauty. She had a loving spirit about her, but now that he knew, what would they do about it? Ryan Bentley was the only father she knew. She had never known a mother, he guessed, other than maybe Gail. If he told Isabella, what would happen? He couldn't just pull that little girl out of the home she only knew.

"What happens now?" Landon prompted as he stood twirling a pencil and placing back into the pencil holder.

Carter turned back to him and rubbed the back of his neck. "I don't know. I don't know what to do about it. Isabella has to be told, and she needs to know all of it. I am just not sure of when to tell her. I don't want to cause her more difficulties."

"She has to know. You can't keep it from her."

"Yeah, I know. Something that should be happy could end up in a disaster for us as a couple. How should I feel about that? Jenna is my daughter too, and I just met her. She has no idea of who I am, and she has never met her mother. We are strangers to her. Not only that, how am I going to explain to Isabella how I came to be Jenna's father?"

CHAPTER FIFTEEN

Looking around the room, I sat up and discovered I was alone. It was the first time since I had come home to Rose Point that I had awakened and Carter hadn't been there. Pushing up with my hands, I leaned against the headboard and listened to the perfect quiet of the room. The silence was deafening, so much so that it frightened me. Picking up the *Parenting* magazine from the table, I leafed through it so fast that I didn't see the pictures. Tossing it aside, I looked around to see what else I could find to entertain me. If I had to do this for the next four months, I would go insane. I had to have something to do, anything.

The TV remote lay beside me, and I started to flip through every channel, finding nothing but movies that I had watched a million times. The last resort was a local station that played advertisements. Joy, that's what I needed, something that would put me in a stupor. Pushing my hair back, I sighed. "Getting bored with your surroundings, Mrs. Blake?" There he stood in the doorway, Mr. Dark and Dangerous at his best. His arms crossed against his chest. He leaned against the doorjamb, dressed in his faded jeans and black T-shirt that stretched against his well-defined body. His blue eyes danced as he watched me from across the room. I could feel the relief flood over me as he flashed that lopsided grin of his.

"Maybe just a little." I couldn't help but smile at him as he glided over the floor to me. That self-assured stride of his gave the feeling of control. That's what he liked, the ability to control a situation. If I hadn't learned anything from him, it was that. The point was that in this world, there was little you could control.

Sitting down on the edge of the bed, he grinned. "I can see you are frustrated. Could you use a change in scenery?"

"I like the scenery now," I teased.

Carter looked around the room as if he didn't know what I was talking about. "Oh, you mean me?"

"I am always glad to see you."

"And I like spending time with my wife." Picking my hand up, he kissed the back of it and lay it back down, rubbing it gently. His face down turned, he watched his fingers trace the back of it.

"What is it, amore? Something is bothering you. I can see it written all over your face."

Even though his smile continued, the feeling he was harboring something that was desperately disturbing him remained. "Angel, there is nothing to be worried about. You always seem to find something when there is nothing. I want you to relax and quit worrying about everything and everybody." Looking down at me in admiration, he pushed my hair back away from my face. "I thought you might want to go downstairs with the rest of us, that is, unless you like this room." He grinned mischievously.

It hadn't taken me long to tell him I wanted out. "Bella, it's time you got back with the rest of the world." He scooped me up like I was a light weight, and I knew better. His arms were strong and powerful as he held me next to him. "You, my sweet angel, are gorgeous."

I couldn't help myself. I knew better. I knew I must have looked like a mess. I hadn't been out of that bed for days. And my clothes, even though I had taken a shower each day and changed, felt wrinkled and in disarray. After being asleep many times over, my hair had to be in a tangled heap. "I bet you say that to all the pregnant women in this house."

He chuckled as he kissed my nose. "Only you could steal my heart." His stride was purposeful as he carried me through the hall and down the stairs of the massive home. Just being out of that room for a little while was like being let out of prison. He sat me down on the large overstuffed couch and placed the ottoman under my feet. As he did, I caught the scent of his cologne as he leaned into me and kissed me on the cheek.

"You don't have to baby me, you know. I am a grown woman."

"Let him take care of you, Isabella. He gets pleasure from it. Besides, you know you need to be careful, and he sees to it that you are well protected and loved."

Iris walked into the room as graceful as ever, even if it were a bit slower than she had before. She was quickly returning to her normal self and looking more like the lady of the manor. She was followed closely behind by Grayson, who was carrying her tea as she took a seat in the chair beside me. "Let him dote on you. Enjoy it while you can. You will be taking care of little ones and him soon enough. He loves you and has your best interest at heart."

Carter smiled as he knew his mother was right. Isabella would have her hands full soon enough. "Okay, I'll be good, for now."

"Good girl. I want you to behave yourself. Don't be getting up and running around like nothing happened." I crossed my fingers over my heart and raised my hand, and he leaned in and kissed the top of my head. "Is there anything I can get you, a magazine, a snack, or something to drink?"

"Amore, I'm not an invalid. I can get that if I need it."

"You promised me you would be good."

"Okay, okay, I'm fine for now. You don't have to babysit me. I know you have things you need to do."

Carter's cell phone rang, and he picked it up from the table. He looked down at it as if he were agitated. "Blake. I am home with my wife . . ." He pinched the bridge of his nose as he listened to the voice on the other side of the conversation. "I don't know. I haven't decided on what I am doing next. Does it matter? You kept me from my wife for months. Brooks, I couldn't get out of what I was in when Isabella was sent to the hospital the first time. She could have lost our baby then, and you wouldn't let me pull out. I don't care what you want." Carter's jaw clenched as he stood there listening to his boss. His voice was cold, sharp, and cutting. I had never heard him react like this or have never seen this side of him. Someone who was thoughtless and uncaring of what the other person felt. He ran his fingers through his hair, and it was apparent that he was angry with him. "I nearly was killed the last time they set this up. If the answer has to be now, it has to be no. You are a real piece of work . . ."

Knowing I wasn't to be getting up, I still stood on my feet and walked to my husband's turned back. Turning, he looked at me. His eyes were large, and his jaw remained

328

clenched. I shook my head no at him and drew my fingers down his face. My attempt to plead with him to reconsider was taken, and he spoke with Brooks with a calmer tone. I knew in my heart, though I didn't want him to take such a dangerous assignment, it was part of him. His job was part of him, and I wasn't going to be the one to step in his way. He would only resent me later. He took a breath and kissed my forehead and drew me into him. "Can I have some time to think about it? I need to talk to my partner before I make that decision. Yes, later this evening if that's agreeable. That will be fine." Carter disconnected the call and placed his cell phone down on the table.

"I thought I told you to stay put." His voice was stern and so unlike him. His words fell on me like rain. The very thought that he could be that harsh with me surprised me; he never had been like that before. "You need to be off your feet, Isabella. Cassidy left very strict orders that you weren't to be up and wandering around unless it was in the bathroom and to sit in the shower. I made an allowance by bringing you down here with us so that you wouldn't be locked in that room like a prisoner." He ran his hand over his face, and I could see his skin turn pale as he did. "Angel, I'm sorry. I didn't mean that." Taking my hand, he led me back to the sofa and sat me back down. Once again, he was pampering me, but his face was still steely.

He had said it all, and I was rendered speechless as I sat there. What had happened to my husband? This wasn't him, and something had certainly happened more than he had told me. I wasn't sure that I wanted to know. He leaned in and took my hand, keeping his head bowed. "I

329

should have never treated you that way. I'm sorry, Isabella. I will not let that happen again." I felt so cold and indifferent toward him. Saying something was just going to make things worse. I opted to keep my mouth shut as he tried to comfort me. Sitting very stiff and still, he had gotten the message from me that it had hurt me beyond what he could have understood.

"Bella, look at me." Not moving, I sat with my hands laced together in my lap. "Isabella, look at me." When I still didn't move, he slowly guided my face to his, and his eyes looked at me with remorse. "Isabella, I am so sorry. It seems that I tell you that quite often. My intent is not to hurt your feelings. I want to protect you." His hand dropped from my cheek and down to my very pregnant belly. He looked down at it as he rubbed it gently, his large hand splayed over it as if he were cradling it. "My family is the most important thing to me. I lost it twice. I won't go through it again." It was then I understood. He had lost both parents, then Andrea. I couldn't stay angry with him. I had thought months ago that he had died and was willing to sell my soul just to have him back for a short time.

"It's all right, amore. I understand," I whispered to him as he gathered me to him. I never wanted him to have to go through another loss, and I wasn't sure if I could. Carter and my children meant everything to me. I wasn't going to be careless with them.

"Kiss her, son. Hold her. It's a hard and emotional time when you're carrying a child. Don't just tell her you love her. Show her." Iris sat her tea down and walked to where he sat in front of me and caressed his shoulder. "Don't ever go to bed angry. You never know when it could be the last time you will see the person that you love." With that, she walked out onto the veranda with Grayson, arm and arm, and left us in the living room alone. She had touched us both. Carter's hand shook as he held me to him.

"Isabella, I'm not sure what is going to happen next, and my nerves are frayed. Your safety and that of my family is my main concern." Swallowing hard, he tipped my chin so that I was looking directly into his eyes and his forehead furrowed. "Brooks is pressuring me to come back. I don't want to go because it could mean me leaving again, and I don't want to leave you, especially now. I don't want you to ever have to go through again what you went through a few months ago. It's dangerous. This guy is smart and ruthless. I'm not afraid of him, and maybe I should be. But I am afraid for you for more than one reason. You don't need the added stress right now."

Taking my fingers and laying them to his lips, he was silenced immediately. "You have to do what you think is best, not what you think will please me. This assignment, when you complete it, means we can go back to our lives. I won't say normal because there is no such thing as normal with a homicide detective."

"I know you worry, and I don't want that for you."

"I worry about you because I love you. I would worry if you drove across town and didn't come back in the allotted time I thought you should return. My point is you can't protect me from life. Things happen that you can't control. I want you here, yes, but I want you here whole, not in part."

"Carter, I'm sorry to interrupt, but I just received a call from the hospital." Landon was soon in my field of vision, and his face was ghostly. Sitting down in the chair where Iris had been, he clutched his cell and tucked it back into his pocket. "It's bad news." Carter's grip stiffened slightly as he held me. "Dr. Cromwell just called about Ben's mother. She died ten minutes ago." Carter squeezed me gently as I gasped at the news. "I did get hold of the military and tried to hunt down Terry Sullivan, the boy's father. He was killed two months ago on a mission. His engineering platoon was under attack. Terry took a fatal wound. Darren and Children's Services will be here in a couple of days to place Ben."

The memory of being taken from his home as a child flooded Carter. He couldn't let that happen to Ben. He had no idea how he would change things, but he didn't want that little boy to suffer what he had in his life. He had no one, not even a sibling to help him, and that made it worse. At least he had Beth when they went through this.

Carter brought a fist to his mouth and clenched so hard that his knuckles turned white. "Where's the boy?" His voice was low and distraught at the idea that this child was going to be leaving, not only from his home but also without a parent. What if the same thing happened to him? He had no salvation in what was happening to him, and he wasn't old enough to understand what was happening.

"Beth had the children with her out by the lake. She wanted to take them to feed the ducks. It's time for Gavin's nap, so they should be coming in soon." He had no sooner had spoken those words than children's laughter and the cry of a very cranky nine-month-old rang through the house. Beth walked into the room and brought the kids to us and smiled as she bent down and kissed Landon on the cheek.

"I've got a very tired little boy here. Do you want to come along and tuck him in?" Landon stood by his wife, and she immediately noticed the look on his face. "What's wrong?"

"I will tell you upstairs," he replied, taking Gavin from Beth. He clung to his father. As Landon stroked his back, Gavin started to calm down. Wrapping his arm around his wife's waist, Landon guided her out of the room, leaving us alone with two boisterous three-year-olds.

"Hi, Daddy." Molly laughed, and her baby teeth shone as she crawled into his lap along with Ben. With a child on each knee, he squeezed them into him and kissed each one of them on the top of the head. "We got to feed the ducks." Ben smiled and shook his head, and as he did, his strawberry blond curls shook at his temples. His cheeks dimpled as he grinned, and my heart broke for him. What kind of chance would he have now? His parents were gone. I saw the pain my husband went through. After all these years, it still haunted him. "Did Aunt Beth take you on a ride in the boat?"

Molly shook her head no. "Auntie Beth was afraid we would fall out."

"Okay, well, maybe Daddy will take you later. Why don't you and Ben go upstairs and play in your room. Dinner will be ready soon. I hear Clarice is fixing your favorite dessert." Molly clasped her hands together and smiled broadly. "Yay, apple pie." She kissed her father on the cheek. As Ben climbed down off Carter's lap, he clasped Molly's hand, and they ran toward her bedroom, giggling.

"Oh, that poor baby."

"It's going to be all right, Bella. He will have a good family." Carter knew in his heart that they were few and far between. He really didn't want to think of the alternative. "I think I will go up and freshen up for dinner. Would you like to join me?" I couldn't hide the smile he had brought to my face from his invitation. It wasn't long before he had carried me away back to our room. I didn't mind it so much when he was there.

Later that night, after dinner and settling the kids in, he sat on the veranda, listening to the night sounds as they echoed through the air at Rose Point. His mood had been unsettled. It was obvious. Clarice had made a wonderful meal, but Carter had hardly touched it. He tried to relax, but he shifted often and his look out onto the lake, and the beauty of the gardens were vacant. He was present, but that was all. His mind was far from where we sat. The troubled look on his face pained me deeply. The look he had carried the entire day had become worse as the time had gone on. I knew he was worried about Ben, but it was more than that. He had barely spoken a word to me all evening. Reaching across the arm of the chair, I placed my hand on his forearm where he sat in deep thought. "Carter." He continued to stare out into space, his opposite hand fisted on the chair arm. "Carter, what's bothering you?"

Finally acknowledging me, he covered my hand with his and smiled. "There is nothing wrong, Bella. I'm just relaxing and taking in the night."

"You do realize that you are talking to your wife. I know you a little better than that. Come on, amore, talk to me." He shifted in his seat uncomfortably. It's evident he was tortured by something I had no knowledge of. He stood for a moment and walked a short distance from me and rubbed his face with one hand as his other rested in his front pocket of his jeans. Raising his hand to his side, he waved it slightly, still turned away. "Isabella, it isn't easy to talk about. It's the past, and it is hard to dig up things that have been buried for decades." Turning, he watched for a reaction that I wasn't sure how to react to. I had no idea of what he was talking about, but it was enough. It was fighting against him sorely.

"You know you can tell me anything. I'll listen."

"I know you would, and I am grateful that you would. This is something that is going to take some time on my part to piece together." Walking back, he sat down on the ottoman in front of me. His eyes and jaw were softer than what they had been a few minutes before. "I want to talk to about it, and I will. It just isn't the right time, not yet. Trust me. I know what I am doing. Don't worry about me. I can handle this."

Carter awoke early and had left Isabella to sleep. The image burned into his mind of her curled on her side like a kitten. He had stood over her and watched the steady rhythm of her breathing and traced his finger along her cheek. His sweet angel had a lot of storms to weather, and it was coming soon.

Sitting in the study, the glow of the computer illuminated the room. Pushing back slightly from the desk, he studied the files on Arnell Andrews. There was little he could do at four in the morning but work. Arnell's record, except for suspected abuse, was impeccably clean.

Carter, however, knew better than anyone that he was far from being a model citizen. The times he had been to the warehouse he had been there. Even though he had never seen him, he recognized the brash voice of Arnell. Once you heard his voice, breathing down on you, it wasn't easily forgotten.

He had been met most of the time with Cooper and a man he knew now as Gage Dawson. Dawson never seemed to fit in the scheme of things, but then, neither did Arnell. He was a businessman, well known and well thought of among his peers. He handled large organizations and tossed them around like toys. He had led takeovers of small business to large corporations, buying them out and tearing them down and rebuilding them into better and more efficient money makers.

He was a hotheaded cutthroat that did everything and anything to sink a company and buy it out for a song. Although the acts appeared shady, he always came out smelling like a rose. Dawson seemed to have been left out of most things. There was little mention of him, but Carter knew there had to be more to it. Dawson seemed to be more of an afterthought. It had been believed that Arnell hired hits in order to keep his hands from getting dirty. He had his flunkies send out warnings like a pizza delivery service. A finger had never been pointed. If it had, they were taken out in what appeared to be everyday common accidents. The witnesses they had were now under protection. Hopefully, it would come to an end and soon before something else happened.

He came across a clipping of Bella's disappearance, one he hadn't seen before. The story had landed on the front page of the *Daily Earth and Sound*. Her picture off to the right of the story reminded him of the young Cinderella he had met at South Shore. Her smile and wide-eyed innocence bounced off the page at him.

Youth Abducted from a Local Business without a Trace

Fifteen-year-old Isabella Cameron, daughter of Jeb and Anita Cameron, disappeared from her father's business three days ago after a gunman walked into his auto body shop Mr. Cameron had opened twenty years prior. Mr. Cameron stated that the man entered his place of business and demanded that he shut his doors, and when he refused, he pulled a gun on him. During the altercation, his daughter had arrived and was taken hostage by the assailant. The man turned the gun on him and shot him twice. He stated that his daughter made an attempt to flee, but the assailant had recaptured her, pushing her into what looked like an early-model VW van. There are no leads at this time as to where Ms. Cameron has been taken, nor has there been any contact.

Carter looked at the date on the paper, and as he did, he noticed that Isabella had been gone for a little over a year before he had met her at South Shore. Looking through the darkness of that time in his life, he remembered so many devastating things that had led up to that time. Iris and Grayson had rescued him physically, but they couldn't save him from himself. As he grew up trying to deal with the guilt and shame Arnell had brought upon them, he had gotten in more fights than he could count from the time he was nine years old. He didn't always have a reason. Maybe someone just looked at him wrong. The first one he was in was when he had knocked one child to the ground when he was in the fourth grade. He had made fun of some other kid, and Carter had laid him out where he was. His fists were bloody by the time they had pulled him from Spencer Crace. Needless to say, he never made fun of anyone else when Carter had been within earshot.

Iris had started then taking him to therapy, but if the psychiatrist can't get you to talk, they can't help you. He and Beth had went together a time or two, then they had separated them, hoping to give each a little more room to discuss what had happened to them. Beth sat curled up against him with her thumb in her mouth, holding on to him. Most often she would cry if she were taken away from him. He was her protector and her only line to normalcy. It took months for her to warm up to Grayson. She did take to Iris a little sooner, but it still took some coaxing on Iris's part. Carter, however, had sat very cold, even when they had hugged him and tried to show him affection. It was two years before he had called Iris and Grayson Mom and Dad. He had been very ill and had spent a week in the hospital after his appendix had ruptured. He nearly died then. He had pain for several days, but he hadn't let his mother know until he was in the emergency room with a febrile seizure. She only knew then when he had doubled over in pain, and it had left immediately prior to his admission in the emergency room. She never left his side, and when she did, Grayson was with him. They had allowed Beth to stay in the bed with him the first few nights. Her attachment was so strong with him they were afraid it would cause her to retreat further from them. He had opened his eyes to see Iris and Grayson sitting at his bedside as he woke from a medicated sleep. They had never left him. His sister was curled up beside him, and Iris had hold of his hand and was smiling down at him.

He looked up at her that night and asked her if he could call her mom, and she had wrapped him in her arms and kissed him. She had told him, "Eli, that would be an honor for me to be called mom by you." She had been so touched by his request that a tear had fallen down her cheek. He had reached and wiped it away. That night, she sang "You Are My Sunshine" to him. It was the first time since his mother had died that he felt he had found a mother, someone to love him like his birth mother had loved him.

He had looked over at the man that had taken care of him for two years and called him Pop. Grayson had been floored, and Carter had hoped that he wouldn't be rejected. Grayson's large hand had covered Carter's as it lay across his. "You're going to be all right, son. We love you. Mom and I will always be here for you and your sister." It was if a large weight had been lifted from him. He was finally part of a family, one that took no pleasure in pain.

His thoughts had turned to many things as he watched the screen in front of him fade in and out. What was going to happen to Ben? He hated to see that precious little boy go through what he did, knowing that you couldn't always trust the system in what was happening. Children were fearful, and it made no difference in what was asked. They would never tell if they were threatened. Carter knew this all too well. He had been threatened by Arnell to do the same heinous things that were being done to him to his baby sister. He had been beaten, physically, mentally, and sexually abused over the entire time that he had been in the Andrews house. No one would have known. The Andrews were well respected, and no one had questioned them. They thought that he and his sister were just well behaved.

He continued on studying the screen, but he wasn't able to concentrate on it. He pushed his glasses down, which he seldom wore, and rubbed his eyes. Nothing was clear. Every page he turned to, this whole mess just muddied the water a little more. The next thing he needed to do was talk to Anita. That wasn't going to be easy. How do you bring up to your mother-in-law the subject of his wife's abduction and the story behind it? What would he find out? That could open up a whole new mess that he may not be able to dig out of. He now knew about Jenna, but how did she get with Ryan Bentley?

Records had been pulled by the court, including arrest and medical records. Ryan had a clean record. He was squeaky clean, not even with one violation. His medical record is what caught Carter's eye. Ryan couldn't have possibly fathered Jenna or another child. It was in black and white before him. How could he have thought that Jenna could have been his? How did he manage to get her? Isabella had thought for years that she was dead. Surely he knew that he was unable to father children.

"What are you doing up so early?"

Landon's voice broke the silence of the room, and Carter pushed his glasses back on the bridge of his nose. "Oh, just looking at some files and trying to make some sense of this whole mess. None of it adds up. The main interest I have is how did Jenna survive, and how did she end up with Ryan Bentley? He had to know that he was unable to father Jenna."

"He was a kid, Carter."

"And that's another thing. He had just turned eighteen when she was born. Most adoptions take years. He said he had her from her birth. Someone had to sign the birth certificate as if he was the father of her. Isabella obviously didn't. She could have told them I guess that she suspected it, but they would have had to prove it somehow. She had unfortunately been with several men."

"You have to remember that she was protected for the most part. She would have known if there had been unprotected relations between her and a gentleman caller."

"If you want to call them that." Carter gritted his teeth.

"You never told me how you were connected with Jenna. When did that happen, and why didn't she remember being with you before?"

Carter stood from where he sat and paced before his friend. Pushing his glasses up slightly to rub his eyes, he readjusted them and pushed them back in place. "It's a long story." Carter walked over and looked out the ceiling-to-floor window and crossed his arms over his chest and stared out into the darkness. "I had a drug problem. I

341

know that you remember that, seeing as you were the one that normally sobered me up. Before I went to South Shore, I spent a lot of time self-medicating. I used whatever I could get hold of, anything that I could use to block out what had happened to me when I was growing up—drugs, alcohol, anything that I could find to numb the pain and escape that time in my life."

Landon sat down in the desk chair and clasped his hands in front of him as he listened to his friend, watching Carter's movements and the pain that still remained from that time. "Arnell did some hideous things to Beth and me. The scars he left will never heal. There have been times in my life where I blamed my parents for dying and leaving us with that monster. It wasn't their fault, but I had to blame someone. When I found out I couldn't blame them, I blamed myself for putting us in the situation we were in. My parents had asked me to watch over my sister before they left that night. I did all I could, but it hadn't been enough. I was just a kid. Grayson and Iris didn't get to us until I was five. At the time, I was months from my sixth birthday and felt like an old man."

Carter struggled as his friend was now finding out some of his dark secrets. Rubbing the back of his neck, he told bits and pieces of his life, but he had told Landon that it was important for him to tell Isabella, that she be the first to know. The only problem was that she now was considered high risk in her pregnancy. Anxiety and emotional upset were only going to make things worse for her and his baby boy. He had no wish to make things miserable, but he wasn't sure how he was going to tell her or if he should tell her until after the birth. He still had unanswered questions, explaining that he still needed to talk with Anita. He was sure that his mother-in-law would be able to answer more of his questions than he had thought previously.

Turning around, he saw Landon sitting still, looking stern, rubbing his bottom lip. "Carter, I don't know what to tell you, man. If you keep this from her and let her find out on her own, it can be just as devastating. If she finds out that you figured it out before she did and you knew, it could create a deeper well than you can ever find your way out of. You're going to have to tell her, and the sooner, the better."

Carter shifted and looked at Landon with a grin. "What are you doing up so early?"

"Gavin decided it was playtime." Landon laughed as he shook his head. "Beth was up with him last night, so I thought I would let her sleep."

Carter chuckled slightly as he his friend rubbed his eyes. "Do you remember when we used to be coming home at this time of the morning?"

"Yeah, now we're lucky if we make it past ten o'clock."

"You know the older you get, you start to turn into your father?"

"Saw him in the mirror the other day. I looked in the mirror and saw my father staring back at me. Now there is a reality check for you."

A scream rang through the house, and Carter knew immediately that it was his wife. He ran through the house, taking the steps two at a time. By the time he had made it to their bedroom door, Quentin had walked within five feet of her.

343

Quentin had tried to approach her slowly, but she sat in the corner of the room with her legs pulled up to her chest, the best that she was capable of. Her hair fell down over her face as she sat there and rocked back and forth. She had thrown a vase at him, and it now lay with shards around the room. Her cell phone lay on the floor against the opposite wall still open with the screen lit. He was trying to talk her down, but he hadn't approached her any farther. His voice was calming. He made an attempt at getting closer to her one step at a time. Carter could see his wife obviously shaking. He wasn't sure if she were awake or if this was one of her night terrors or nightmares that she had in the past. She hadn't had been able to take her medication to help ease them for months because of the baby. Even though she had them before, she had never been violent with them.

Carter was going to go to her, but Quentin continued toward her, seeing something that Carter had not. Quentin kept his eyes on her and placed his hand behind him as he heard the footsteps of Carter and Landon approach her. "Mrs. Blake? Isabella, can you hear me?" He took one more step toward her. "Isabella, it's Quentin. I'm here to help. No one is going to hurt you, I promise." Carter Looked around Quentin's shoulder as he dipped a little closer to her. "Isabella, put it down. It's just us. Your family is here. No one is here that will hurt you." As Quentin made a last step toward her, Carter could see the silver glint of a small-barrel handgun, his agent-issue firearm. It hadn't been loaded unless she had loaded it. He always kept it unloaded and kept the shells in a separate place because of Molly.

Quentin placed his hand over hers and gently talked to her. Her small cries were evident that something had happened that no one had heard. "Give me the gun, Bella. I'll take care of you. I've never let you down before. Carter and Landon are here, and so am I. No one is going to get to you."

Carter stood frozen in place as he watched the love of his life sit in a panic that was unexplained. Quentin had advanced slowly and crouched to the side of her and whispered to her. Carter had no idea of what he was saying to her, but he could see the clenched teeth and jaws that she displayed and the tears that stained her face. The rapid and ragged breaths that she displayed reminded him of a cornered animal. What in God's name had happened from the time he had left her? She was soundly sleeping and serene an hour ago.

Carter clenched his jaw as Quentin leaned into his wife and spoke to her softly and laid his hand underneath the hand she gripped the gun and squeezed it gently. She released it and started to cry like a child whose heart had been broken. She sunk into the floor, leaning to the right with one arm holding her up and the other splayed over her stomach.

Quentin backed off, holding the gun in his hand and checking it to see that it was loaded. He unloaded the clip and placed it back into the holster that lay on the chest of drawers. His calm and cool demeanor remained, reflecting the professional he was. Carter could see the feelings he held for his wife, and it disturbed him greatly. There was time for that. His wife was his main focus, and he had no intention of upsetting her more than she already was.

345

Walking over to her, he crouched before her and offered his hand to assist her to her feet. "Angel, come on. Let's go back to bed. You need to sleep." Her soft sobs nearly destroyed him. She was so fragile, and this was no time for her to be upset. "Come on, honey." Taking her hand, she reluctantly stood, and he wrapped his arm around her waist, supporting her. He picked her up like a baby and laid her on the bed, inspecting her hands and feet for cuts. The shards from the broken vase lay strewn across the room, glistening like twinkle lights. After sitting her down, he picked her feet up to find that there hadn't been any cuts on them, but she did have one on the palm of her hand. He left her with Landon and Quentin briefly in an effort to find something to clean the wound and cover it to keep it from bleeding.

When he returned, he found Landon cleaning up the glass and Quentin holding her cell phone in his hand. He cleaned the wound on her hand and bandaged it. The area was large, but it hadn't appeared to be deep. He assisted her to lie down and covered her with the duvet. Her eyes remained wide and fearful, and she still sobbed softly. He pushed her hair away from her face lovingly and kissed her on the cheek. "It's okay, angel. You're safe."

Quentin stepped over to Landon and spoke to him as Carter tried to calm his wife and soon left, leaving her cell phone with him. Landon had finished collecting the broken glass and swept the floor of the remaining small pieces then stepped toward Carter. "There was a call from an unknown number. There is no way of tracking it, but you can guess who it was from."

"Why is he constantly torturing us? We don't know where he is or why he is causing such chaos."

"I don't know, but it's obvious that one or both of you are his target."

"When I get Isabella calmed down, I need to speak with Anita. I have a feeling she can shed a lot of light on what is happening here. The sooner I find out, the better off Isabella is going to be."

Landon slapped Carter on the shoulder and left the room, shutting the door behind him. Standing at the edge of the bed, Carter stood looking down at his wife as she lay curled in a ball on her side. Her arms drawn to her chest, she whimpered, reminding him of how Beth had been once Arnell had laid his hands on her. Leaving the bathroom light on, he turned out the light in the immediate room and crawled in behind her, spooning her against him. Kissing her temple, he felt her shudder under him as if she was fearful. "It's me, angel. I won't let him hurt you. I promise with every breath in me I will never let him touch you again."

CHAPTER SIXTEEN

"I promise you I will find you, and when I do, you will pay for every sin your mother ever committed against me. Don't think that he can protect you. He is as damaged as you are. I took him along with his sister. I can't say I enjoyed it that much, but then again, they served their purpose. Just so you know, I do know where to find you and the brats you have and the miserable one that you are carrying. I'm biding my time for now. Just think, after all this time, you may get a taste of a real man again."

The voice was cold and chilling as I listened to him. His hard and coarse laughter ran through me like a lightning strike. "One other thing. You need to tell lover boy to back off, or I will come after that brat he calls a daughter. Molly, is it? That's right, I know, and that isn't the only child I know about. That brat of yours, the one you thought was dead? Guess what, princess—that's not true, and I know where to find her. I bet she would be as good and innocent as you were." His laughter rang through my ears as my heart pounded against my ribs, not allowing me to get a breath.

I had thrown my cell phone across the room, watching it bounce from the wall. As I sat on the floor, I had heard footsteps and watched as a figure made their way into the room. Picking up the nearest thing I could reach, which was a crystal vase full of flowers from the gardens, I hurled it toward the figure, and it smashed against the wall

348

behind him. All I could hear was the voice of Arnell as he laughed and made his threats.

Quentin's voice had broken through the evil and terrifying voice of Arnell's that rambled around in my head. He had made his way to me and crouched beside me. His words had soothed me, but my eyes remained in a blank stare. I shook at the thought that it could have been one of the children or my husband. Quentin spoke to me in a soft tone, whispering to me that he would take care of Arnell. He knew how to take care of me and he wouldn't allow him anywhere near me.

I awoke to a soft light of early morning creeping from under the curtain and tracing across the floor. Carter was lying close to me, still fully clothed, and his arm rested over my belly. His soft breaths came in streams against my neck, sending sweet chills over me. Nothing meant more to me than my family.

I had to get up. The bathroom was going to be welcome for more than one reason. Carter's breathing was easy, and he lay quietly with his eyes closed, looking like a child in a dreamless sleep. As I started to get up, he clasped me closer to him. "Where are you going?" he whispered against my ear.

"I thought you were asleep." I lay facing him, and his eyes opened and looked at me.

"I've been awake for an hour, watching you. You okay?"

"Yes, I was just going to the bathroom."

"Put your shoes on at the edge of the bed." His eyes fluttered a little and then looked back at me.

"Why?"

"There could be glass on the floor. I don't want you to get it in your feet."

Looking down, I saw the bandage wrapped around my hand. I hadn't felt that. I thought for a moment, and I knew what he was talking about. I really didn't want to think any more of it. I didn't remember most of it, and I was glad. "Yeah, about that. I'm sorry I broke the vase. I need to talk to Quentin and apologize for throwing it at him."

"That wasn't all you did, angel. Are you sure you're okay?"

"Yes, what else did I do?"

Bits and pieces flew through my head, and I was trying to put them together. Before Carter could sit up and tell me, it had come in clearly, and I had covered my mouth with my hands. "Oh, dear god, I didn't!"

"Bella, it's all right. No one was hurt." Carter sat with his legs stretched out and pulled me back against his chest. "No one was hurt. Quentin got to you first. You wouldn't have hurt anyone, and you know it." He ran his fingers through my hair, trying to soothe me. I felt sick to my stomach.

"What if Molly, or Ben or, or one of you had come in the room? I could have killed one of you."

Wrapping his arms around me tightly, he held me to him and spoke softly against my ear. "But you didn't, Bella, and you're all right."

Shivers of regret ran from the top of my head to the soles of my feet as I thought of the possibilities. I could have shot and killed any of them. My fear at the time had consumed me. Arnell had threatened me and my children.

350

Knowing I could protect myself, it was my children I was worried about. What did he say about my daughter? Was I mistaken that he had mentioned Jenna and that he knew where she was?

Carter kissed my temple and assured me. "Bella, no one is ever going to get close enough to put their hands on you again. As long as I have a breath in me, I swear I will never let him touch you."

Ben and Molly bounded in the room, smiling as they held hands, and were giggling as they came in.

"Mommy, Daddy." She smiled as she and Ben crawled up the bed and bounced up and down on the bed. "We wanna go outside." Molly sat down in my lap, and Ben scooted in between Carter and me. He wrapped Ben up with one arm against him and laughed.

Carter's expression changed, and he laughed as he watched them. "Oh, you do? What would you like to do outside?" Carter grinned and looked like a child than a full-grown man.

"Boat, Daddy, we want to go out on the boat on the lake."

Ben nodded his head in agreement, and his little curls bounced as he laughed. "Okay, we will go boating, but what if we go on a great big boat for the day?"

They clapped and squealed in unison as he made the announcement. "Only one catch: go see if the others want to go. Go tell Uncle Landon, Aunt Beth, and your grandparents and see if Quentin wants to go too."

"Yay!" They laughed and jumped from the bed and squealed.

351

"What about me?" I heard my voice ring out a little hurt as I thought of him leaving me for the day.

"You know I am not going anywhere without you." He cupped my face in his hands and drew me to him. "I will call Cassidy, but I am sure there won't be a problem. If there is, I can send them with the rest. I will stay here with you. Come to think of it, that isn't a bad idea."

I sat on the deck of the *Blue Angel* as the warm summer sun came down on me, sending a warm glow bouncing across my skin. I was here with my family, feeling more secure now than I had in my life. The love of my life was with me along with my parents and friends that I couldn't imagine ever being without. The brim of my large hat flapped in the wind as we headed out to sea. The voices of the men in my life talking in the background chattered away about fishing. The laughter of the children above them was a wonderful thing to hear. My eyes were closed to the scenes around me as I listened to each sound. I hadn't been out of that room for several days, and this was a welcome retreat. The sound of the gulls soothed me. The sound of the waves crashing as we made our way into the ocean calmed me. The breeze on me and the smell of the saltwater were unbelievably welcomed. The last time I remembered feeling this way was the night of my first date with Carter. His voice ran through my head, and the touch of his hand was ingrained in my mind. The smell of his cologne wafted on the air as I opened my eyes to see him sitting in the chair beside me with that adorable smirk on his face. "Enjoying your dream, Mrs. Blake?"

"The object of my dream sits here in front of me. I don't have to dream about you because I married my dream, but it doesn't hurt."

"I don't think I have seen you this relaxed for a while. Feeling okay? No seasickness?"

"No, not a bit."

"Good, because if you're sick, so am I. I am glad that you finally got over your morning sickness."

I couldn't help but giggle at him. "Sorry, I didn't think you would want to miss a minute of this. I just didn't think you would take it so literally."

"It's kind of embarrassing when you have cravings that you have to send the secretary out for."

"You never told me that."

"It isn't something that I broadcast. Landon seemed to get a charge out of it though."

"Yes, I am sure he did. By the way, how's Lily doing? Did she make it back from belowdecks?"

"I think she's all right. Just a little queasy. JC took her below to lie down. He called the doctor for her before the trip. I guess she can take Dramamine. It isn't a cure-all, but it works well enough. The closer to the center of the boat she is, the less she should feel the shake of the ocean waves."

"Good, I know what it feels like."

He grinned and kissed the back of my hand and clasped it in his. "Unfortunately, I do too. Let's hope that I don't experience the labor pains with you, or I will never be able to coach you through delivery."

"You are going into the delivery room with me?"

"Sure, if you want me there. I thought it was a given I would be there."

"I want you there. I just hadn't thought about it before. I can't imagine having anyone else with me."

"Not even your mother?"

"I love my mother, but she doesn't do well with keeping me calm. I love the idea of you being there."

"This should be an experience. I wasn't in the delivery room when Andrea had Molly."

"Why, if you don't mind me asking?"

Looking down at my hand, he held in both of his he shook his head. "Andrea had so many health issues. They just wanted to get in there and get Molly out. They scheduled an induction, and I was there with her until she was ready to deliver. Cassidy was in her internship and was taking care of Andrea, but her primary wanted as few people in delivery as they could get by with because of her poor immune system. She wasn't the only one at risk—so was Molly. I wasn't in much shape to be there either. Let's say I was self-medicated. In no way am I proud of the way I acted then. It was a difficult time for me, but it was worse on Andrea and Molly. Andrea put up with a lot from me, and Molly had an absent father. I don't want that to happen with this little one. I don't want you to have to do this alone."

Turning slightly on my side, I looked up at him, squinting from the sun as I did. His hair more askew than normal from the ocean air only served to make him more attractive than he already was. "You are going to be a wonderful father to this baby. I have no doubt in that. Little Eli and I are fine. You, me, and his big sister are going to welcome him into this little family. I am much happier in my life now than I ever have been. Just so you're here, that's all that matters to me."

"You don't need the glitz? You found out before I could tell you. I am sure that was a shock."

"Yes, you could say that it was a shock, but need it? No, I don't need it. I am happy with what we have and how we were living before."

"I never let anyone know who I was because of this. I wanted people to see me, not the money."

"I hate to tell you, Carter, but I knew about the lifestyle. I just didn't know it was that extravagant."

"And you treated me like anyone else."

"I didn't really believe them."

"Landon told me that you had a culture shock coming here."

"Landon knew, and he—" I couldn't believe everything that I was hearing.

"Angel, Landon told me every move you made. I knew when you were ill, but that was a given. I knew about the speech you made at church. I knew when you went to the doctor, the hospital, when you decided to join the police academy. I knew all of it. You were never alone. Quentin had cameras in the house, and I had a camera connected to my laptop. There wasn't anything sweeter to me than the night you called me."

"I called you?"

"You don't remember, I am sure. I think you were asleep at the time. I watched you rock Jenna. At least that's what you thought you were doing. My things they had given you were on the desk and on the floor where you had looked through them. That was tricky. I have a wife that is too smart for her own good. I had to give them my cell phone and buy a new one, and send them a copy of my keys. You found them missing and started asking questions. The one thing you didn't find was my license missing. I was hoping you would find out it was a scam, but I couldn't make it obvious. You started to come to the cabin, and I thought you would find me there. I couldn't tell you I was there, but I couldn't keep you from coming."

"That was months ago. I could have avoided a lot of this. I should have done what I had originally had planned. I was going to leave the first chance I had and go alone."

Clasping both hands in his, he kissed them. "No, you shouldn't have. Leaving alone would have been a mistake. Landon had plans on bringing you when he could. He couldn't suggest it, but he could let you dictate it. That way, neither of us was disclosing anything."

"You can't believe how much I missed you."

"Not any more than I did you. I threatened to leave and blow the cover on the whole thing. I would have lost my job, but I didn't care. The only thing that kept me from doing it was the safety of the officers in my charge."

"Well, we are together now."

"If it isn't a problem for you, or if Lily doesn't have to go back, I want to stay on the ocean tonight. We are stocked pretty well. The family and kids seem to be comfortable here, and I want to get you away from some of the stress. There are plenty of bedrooms, so I think everyone will be accommodated."

"You don't have to convince me. I am comfortable. Besides, I get you alone on a romantic cruise with a boat full of family."

He threw back his head and laughed heartily. "Yes, it has possibilities. Make sure that you meet me at midnight in my room."

"I am not sure my husband will like that idea. He has been really protective lately."

"Then I guess I will have to sneak you out." Kissing me, he stood up.

"I better check on the kids. Enjoy the sun, but not too long. The heat will get to you quickly before you know it. I'll send up something to drink. No arguments, Mrs. Blake."

"Who am I to argue with you?"

"Good, listen to me. All I want is to keep you safe."

I sat on the deck of the *Blue Angel* and soaked up the sun for some time, for how long, I wasn't sure. With Lily belowdecks and Beth busy with Gavin, I was left alone with my thoughts. I wondered where my mother and Iris could have gone. Neither of them had been around, and I had felt that odd. As much as everyone had been doting on me, no one was around. Tipping up my sunglasses and opening my eyes, Quentin stood before me, looking down, holding a glass of ice water in his hand.

"Sorry, I, ah, didn't mean to startle you. I just thought you might need something to drink."

"You didn't. I'm fine." Taking the glass from his hand and taking a sip, he sat in the chair next to me. "Where is everyone? I haven't seen Carter, the kids, or my mother for an hour at least."

Stretching out in the lounge next to me, he put his hands behind his head and looked toward me. His face was suffering from the heat as a bead of sweat flowed down the side of his face. "Carter is around, and I saw your mother earlier with the kids. Iris is more than likely with Grayson in their cabin. She's getting better, but it doesn't take much to tire her. JC is tending to Lily. She had a pretty good shade of green going earlier, and Beth is feeding Gavin."

"What about my father?"

"Last I saw him, he was talking to the captain and was getting a lesson in sailing."

"Oh, I see. So you got stuck with looking out for me."

"I wouldn't say that I got stuck with you."

"Come on, Quentin. You came to have some fun, not to take care of an overly emotional fat woman."

His lips curled into a sweet curve as he laughed. "You have never been difficult to take care of, and besides, I don't mind. I used to watch over my sister, and believe me, you aren't difficult."

"Thank you for that. I know it hasn't been easy. I put you in a spot, leaving and then throwing a vase at you. I am truly sorry. I never meant to harm you."

"Isabella, let it go. It isn't important. You're safe, and that is what this was all about. I don't blame you for anything that you have done."

"You know, I think that's the first time you have called me Isabella without prompting you."

Shaking his head, he blushed slightly, something I didn't think he was capable of.

"Well, after a while, you learn."

358

"You have done a lot for me over the months. I am grateful. Molly and I couldn't have made it without you."

"It's my job. Think nothing of it." He tapped me on the shoulder and stood to leave. "Don't stay out here much longer. You're starting to get red." He winked and walked off. For the first time, I saw the person Quentin was. Under all that stern, calculated thinking was a caring and loving individual. I guess Molly was a good judge of character.

It wasn't long before I gathered my book and glass and walked to the cabin to rest before dinner. Standing on my feet, I felt the heat but made it to the cabin easily. It was a good thing that I had gone in the air conditioning when I did. I hadn't been aware how much the heat had affected me. Not knowing just sure how to get to where I was going, I went into the first open door I found. Walking in the large open area, the space was filled with two large L-shaped couches in white, with oversized blue pillows with a gold crest emblazed on them. The floor was covered in large white tiles that shone like glass under my feet. It looked like an elaborate living room on water. From the ceiling hung a suspended large flat-screen television and a sound system that reminded me of a movie theater with overhead speakers around the room. Fresh flowers graced the tables in pinks, white, and yellows that were brilliant in their colors. The main walkway led out onto a separate deck in which there was an infinity pool and deck lounges in gold and blues. To the right of the sound system was a spiral stairway that I had my doubts about fitting through. Taking a step onto the landing and holding to the oak railing, I made my way to the lower deck and looked for the master suite. Carter had told me it was marked well earlier in the day, and it would be easily spotted. The master suite had two gulls carved into the door, holding a ribbon. He had told me that he had bought the boat years before. He didn't say much as to why he bought it or when. The gentleman that I had met previously had told me that Carter had spent a year on the boat, so when did he do that? Did he do that before or after Andrea? It didn't matter anyway. It was over and done with before I ever entered the picture. Walking past the oak-covered walls, I took in the beauty of the space. It was peaceful, serene. I hadn't experienced anything like it before. The gentle rock of the boat reminded me of a mother rocking her child, bringing a smile to me. At the end of the hall, I found the door I was looking for and opened it slowly. The natural light flooded the room through the large open window that looked out onto the sea. A king-size bed sat in the corner with squared oak posts that went from the floor to the ceiling of the cabin. Mirrors lined the back of the headboard. The walls were covered in gold-leaf material, and the sun reflected off it onto the highly polished oak floor. The gold duvet looked rich with navy-blue pillows etched with his initials on them. On the table beside the bed were a mix of daisies, roses, and baby's breath. The smell filled the room with a sweet aroma. At the foot of the crystal vase was a note in very familiar handwriting.

Angel,
I hope this little trip will give you the time to rest and have the relaxation that you have lacked over the last few

360

*months. Know that I never went a day without you being
on my mind or in my heart. You have my heart. Take care
of my baby and enjoy the services on this ship. Your
captain is wise and is at your service 24/7. If you need
anything, pick up the in-cabin phone and dial 39, and an
attendant will see that you are well taken care of. I will
meet you soon. By the way, the beauty of the flowers in
the room could never compare with the beauty I married. I
love you.*

   Carter.

Tracing the signature on the note he left, I smiled. It
felt so good to have him back. His laugh rang in my ears.
The image of his smile floated through my memory and
filled me with a warmth I loved.

Placing the note back onto the table, I looked around
the room, seeking out the closet and shower. To the right
of me were two oak doors tooled in Italian leather. The
pure elegance of the room took my breath away. Turning
the gold knob, I found a walk-in closet as large as the suite
leading to the head.

Between the rooms were racks of suits and dresses.
Shoes lay in open oak boxes, there were ties on gold tie
racks, and a navy-blue chaise adorned the room, covered
with matching gold pillows. A line of open oak drawers
with small divided compartments held an array of
cufflinks, watches, and a wide variety of men's rings. Off to
the side of his collection were divided drawers of women's
jewels. The small areas glistened with gemstone rings,
necklaces, chokers, watches, and bracelets in every color
of the rainbow. One box remained covered in blue velvet

strategically placed and wrapped with a gold ribbon. Standing there and looking down on them, it gave me a sadness I couldn't understand. I assumed they were Andrea's. Thinking about what I had walked into made me feel as if I were violating a sacred part of his life and intruding on her. This is what he held dear. After all this time, Andrea remained. I was living with a ghost of a woman that naturally he found perfect.

Her presence was felt around me, and I wasn't sure if I were to welcome it or reject it. Sitting down on the chaise, I looked around me. There were a few evening dresses, but others were casual attire. Simple dresses hung in a straight line with tags that remained on them. *Andrea, if you're here, I hope the feeling I have is one of acceptance of me. I do remember a visit from you, but I am not sure if it were in my head or if you were really there. I don't mean to intrude. I want him to be happy. I know in my heart that you loved him just as I love him. I promise you I'll take care of him. He means everything to me.*

A small breeze came from nowhere and brushed me, and I was convinced that I had spoken to Andrea. A small voice landed on my ear but was indistinguishable. Something had spoken to me and had relieved my anxiety.

Opening the connecting glass door leading to the large bath, I stood in awe. The brown marble covered the floor and the shower. Oak mirrors with hurricane lamps hung above the marble covered counters and gold-colored basins. Blue and white towels with gold trim were rolled and placed in oak open cabinets. The shower was an open rain fountain, and the gold trim set off the brown marble ledge that stepped into a large garden marble spa tub.

What had I walked into? I had no idea. I knew he was well-to-do, but this was intimidating. I hadn't gotten used to Rose Point and now the *Blue Angel*. My husband, what in the world had he done to gain such wealth? This wasn't just money. This was celebrity status. Turning on the lamp over the sink, music started to play in the background in soft tones. It hadn't taken long before I took in the luxury of the large garden tub and filled it with essential oils of eucalyptus. A few drops had filled the room with a woodsy aroma. Sitting down into the well-scented water, I laid my head against the edge and thought of my husband and the child we would soon have. It had been a rocky six months. It would soon be seven months, and I was scared. The time was fast approaching that this little boy would make his appearance. I remembered nothing to very little of Jenna's birth, most of it bad.

I had seen her, but I had never been able to hold her. They hadn't allowed me to hold her after delivery. I had no memory of anything after that. I couldn't remember much of what it had felt like to be in labor. I vaguely remembered them preparing me for an emergency delivery. Ryan's face was one of the things that I remembered most. It had been embedded in my memory. The fear and torture was apparent; even at his age, he had tried to hide it. Needless to say, he wasn't good at it. Sitting beside me in faded green scrubs with his mouth and nose masked, it was still evident. I had panicked for more than one reason. I had been relieved to be away from Arnell, but the fear of what was to happen next and the weak cries of Jenna were something I would never be able to describe to anyone. The sounds of that day started to clutter the calm of the room as I soaked among the scented bath. The crash of the instruments on the floor returned as I sat there. I wasn't dreaming any longer. It was crashing in on me. My chest heaved and felt heavy as that horrifying event played over in my mind. The room felt suddenly cold, and I could hear the doctor calling to his staff. His voice rang with urgency as he spoke. The feeling of doom and dread swept over me as if it were happening again. Seeing Ryan's face as it flashed before me was fear and panic. The nurses scrambled getting equipment and the tiny warmer and incubator that were in the room. The brow furrowed on the anesthetists as he looked down at me over his mask. A weak and tiny cry once again came to my memory as it dragged me along for the ride. "Take her now. She's fragile." The nurse that stood by my side as the doctor had handed Jenna off had spoken in an eerie calm. "Doctor, we have a problem. I need you now." I could barely see her over the drape that shielded my view of my abdomen. The anesthetist stood momentarily to reach his equipment then placed a mask on my face. "No, no, I want to see her." In a short period, the room was full of nurses and doctors running everywhere. I could see her in the nurse's arms, her body limp; her color was dark and ashen. Her muffled cry escaped in what sounded more like a cry of a kitten. "Ms. Cameron, are you okay?" The anesthetist slowly faded as I felt my breath leave me. The room had become dark quickly. Unlike the last time this had occurred to me, I heard one final voice I hadn't heard before, and I was trying to distinguish it. Rolling it around in my head, I tried to make sense of it, but for some reason, it was more like an unfinished puzzle with pieces missing. "Izzy, don't leave me." The voice of Ryan came through. That hadn't happened before. I hadn't remembered that. He was still with me when I had seemingly had taken my last breath.

Sitting up quickly, I took a sharp and exaggerated breath, leaving my hair to fall down over my face and over my shoulders. My skin rolled in goose bumps, running chills down my spine. *Get hold of yourself, Isabella. You can't let this encompass you. You're away from danger. This isn't happening now. Breathe.*

Leaving the bath, I wasn't sure how long I had sat in the water, but my skin had wrinkled from it, looking more like a prune. Shivering as I dressed, I wrapped the cashmere robe around me and looked in the mirror. My eyes looked tired. The eyes that looked back at me were that of exhaustion with large dark circles. I had been so relaxed earlier, why not now? I couldn't have looked this bad earlier, or Carter would never have let me set foot on the boat. Sighing, I blew out a puff of air and blew my bangs away from my face in frustration. If I didn't get any rest, he would be hauling me back to the mainland quicker than I could say my own name.

Shutting off the light, I walked back into the bedroom we would be sharing for the night. The intimacy had not been wasted. I could feel him here, the small touches he made to make sure that I was comfortable. Sitting down on the edge of the raised king-size poster bed, I looked out onto the water. The water shimmered under the summer sun, and the pelicans danced along ripples on the waves, diving in for whatever suited them.

I had to admit the cabin and the bed were inviting. With the extra weight of the baby, it made it difficult to maneuver, and the shortness of my stature didn't help in trying to wiggle up in the large four-poster king-size bed. The softness of the linens and the luxury surrounded me like a cocoon. The glow of the room and the pure clean smell along with the ocean air encompassed me. I felt as though I were lying on a cloud among the large pillows. He had thought of me in more ways that I couldn't count. A body pillow lay wrapped near the head of the bed covered in royal- and navy-blue cotton linen. Lying there for a moment, I pulled it into me, wrapping an arm and a leg around it, with my head on the corner of it. I picked up the scent of lavender, relaxing me instantly. Smiling instantly to myself, I couldn't see the harm in just resting there. The stress of the last seven months had caught up with my body. My life had been an emotional roller coaster since before I had met him, and it had been on the fast track since I had. My sweet husband had been an enigma. Trying to figure him out was turning into a full-time job. His overpowering personality was sometime stifling, and others, it was a comfort, leaving me wanting to run to him.

Thoughts of a little boy with his heavenly blue eyes and smile float through my mind. The soft giggles of his playing with Carter came to life in my imagination, seeing in my mind's eye of Carter giving him a piggyback ride off to bed or running through a meadow playing with him and Molly while they wait for me to set out lunch for them, his little dimpled cheeks prominent as he charmed his father and Molly to do his bidding. Seeing Carter as he holds him for the first time was something I couldn't imagine. He had barely been able to be around me through the pregnancy, so it had been relatively new to him. My eyes felt heavy. As I lay there, my mind allowed me to think of pleasant things. It wasn't often that my thoughts were that of a pleasant nature. At least I was with the love of my life on a boat in the middle of an ocean. There was no way anyone could get to the kids or me. Carter was more than capable of taking care of us, and I was surrounded by a small army of officers.

Between Carter, Landon, and Quentin, I was well watched. I didn't have to worry about the kids because my mother was watching them, and I was sure that Grayson and my dad were spoiling them rotten. As I lay there drifting in and out, I heard what sounded like a small giggle and I opened my eyes and looked around the room, but nothing was seen. Passing it off as a seagull, I lay there attempting to return to my sleepy state as I looked out the window and watched them dip down in the water and rise again. My stomach stretched as Elijah moved. The small flutter movements had become a little harder over the last month or so, but he had slowed down. His movements had slowed down since my time in the hospital, but I had been assured he was fine. Right now he seemed to have turned completely around. Since I was stretched out on the bed, I guess he had decided that he had a little more room to spread out. Rubbing my stomach, I talked to him and sang "Jesus Loves Me" To him He continued to move around and shove his little feet or hands against me.

"Elijah, I would have never thought I would fall in love with another man, especially one with no teeth and hair, but you have captured my heart, and you aren't even here

367

yet. You, little fellow, need to settle down and rest and let your mommy sleep once in a while. You are certainly the little partier. I bet you are going to be a charmer, just like your handsome father." Rubbing my stomach, he started to calm and seemed to have gone to sleep. That was a rare thing. He was usually up when I was trying to sleep, awake at night and asleep all day, of course. He did seem to like for me to get in the bathtub. He would move and kick like he was swimming as I sat in the warmth of the water. Maybe he would be an Olympic swimmer someday. Now that would be something, wouldn't it?

Regardless of what he grew up to be, I drifted in and out of sleep, seeing him, Carter, and Molly as they played and the sound of their laughter. It hadn't entered my mind that Ben would be in the picture, but he had slowly drifted in. Dreams of them playing together like they were glued together at the hip, I could see myself laughing at them as I watched them play on the beach together. It was all good, and I would wake myself on occasion giggling or the feel of a smile that had crossed my face. I could see them all playing in the surf and Carter chasing them looking back at me with that little boyish grin of his. Not a care in the world had filled any of their faces. I could feel the breeze as the wind off the ocean swept through my hair and could smell and taste the salt from it. The sound of the seagulls and other birds filled the air as the sun had warmed my skin. It had been a pleasant scene watching them and running my toes through the sand. That was until I saw a young woman run into the picture. She played and romped alongside them as if she were part of the family. Her long dark hair flowed down her back in large waves. Her skin was flawless and glowed in a soft brown sheen kissed by the sun.

Carter's voice rose above the noise of the crash of the waves as he picked up Elijah and placed him on his shoulders as the other two made circles around his legs. The woman's laugh was crisp and sweet as she smiled up at him. He had called out to her, "Andee, help me out here." At that moment, the woman had made her way to the blanket in which I sat on and looked at me earnestly. "You must take care of him. His life depends on you." I could hear my own voice quiver as I had answered her.

"But I do. What do you mean? What do I need to do?"

"Don't worry. I'll be there. I promise I'll be there."

She had leapt to her feet and had run. "Wait a minute, don't go. What kind of trouble is he in? What do I do?"

She waved and had gone on and disappeared, leaving the kids and him waving goodbye. It hadn't taken me long to jerk up from the bed and look around the room at the changing light. I had been asleep for some time, and the sun was beginning to set or maybe it was rising on a new day. I must have been asleep for hours.

CHAPTER SEVENTEEN

Walking into a small room, Carter had escorted Anita to an out-of-the-way cabin where they could sit down and talk uninterruptedly. It wasn't his intent to upset her, but he needed to know what had happened with Isabella and what part she had in it, if any. The pieces he had put together, he was hoping were just that. He was hoping none of what he had put together was right, but he was afraid that they were. Anita deserved to tell her part of it. Isabella deserved to know the truth after all that she had gone through.

Carter showed her to her seat and sat down across from her and clenched his hands together lightly. He ran his hand through his hair as he often did when he was uncomfortable with a situation. Anita, seeing that he was struggling with what he wanted to say, broke the ice as she watched his uneasy manner. "Carter, come on. Out with it. I know you brought me back here to talk privately, so this is your chance. It's obvious that it is of some importance, or you wouldn't be this uncomfortable with me."

He stood for a moment and walked a couple of steps away as he ran his hand down his face thinking of what he was going to say. He wasn't in an interrogation room, and she wasn't a criminal. She was his mother-in-law. How he approached this would affect how his wife's family thought of him and would affect Isabella. Turning, he looked at her, and his feelings were worn outward for her to pick up on. This wasn't going to be a simple thing for him or her.

"Anita, this isn't easy for me. I hope you know that." He turned and returned to his seat in front of her. "No matter how I approach this, it's going to bring up ill feelings. It will affect you, Isabella, and me. I don't want to make things worse than they already are. I love Isabella and want the best for her. She is my life, and the life she carries is just as precious to me. I will do whatever it takes to protect my family, and that includes you and Jeb."

"I know that you love our daughter. It has never been a question in my mind. You don't have to worry. Whatever this is, I am more than happy to talk with you about it." Anita leaned forward and clasped his fisted hands in front of him. "Carter, when you married Isabella, you became our son. I don't want you to ever feel like you can't talk to us."

Carter shifted and drew in a breath, trying to control his feelings. "Even if it's about Arnell Andrews?"

Anita drew in a breath and stood facing away from him. The cabin was uncomfortably quiet as she stood there as he remained seated in the chair behind her. He had dreaded this day and knew that it was coming. It hadn't made the situation any easier. Carter had never liked not being in control and was far from in control of this situation.

"I knew that eventually that this was coming." Anita remained facing away from him, and he could tell from her movements that she was pushing tears away. "It's a long and painful story, and one that I was hoping to leave buried."

371

"Don't you think that Isabella deserves to know? Whatever has happened in the past has affected her along with you. She's in pain from it, Anita. She still has nightmares and flashes of memory that she doesn't know what to do with."

Turning, Anita sat down in the chair as Carter allowed her to compose herself before they continued talking. "I had never intended for her to be involved in any of this. It just happened. I would have taken a beating to my death if I had known what he was capable of."

She became quiet, and Carter prompted her. "I know she was in a lot of pain, Anita, and I know partially what happened. I met her several years ago. I am not proud of my past, and she doesn't know all of it either. I do plan on telling her. All of it. I think it's only fair that you get to tell her your side of what happened and why you have kept it to yourself all these years. No one is perfect. I am the first to admit that. If it hadn't been for Grayson, I would more than likely be dead by now. I don't know why I feel I need to tell you this. Maybe it's because I haven't discussed it with anyone other than my counselor." Carter took a deep breath, and Anita again wiped her eyes of stray tears. "When I was just a child, about Ben and Molly's age, my parents were killed in a car accident by a drunk driver."

Anita looked at him in surprise. "I had no idea that Grayson and Iris were not your birth parents."

"There's a lot you don't know about me." Carter looked down and away from her. "When my family didn't take us in, my sister and I were put into the foster care system. We were shifted around for a while until we were placed into a family that was well respected in the area,

372

someone that no one would have guessed would have been involved in the abuse and molestation of his foster children along with being involved in a mound of other illegal activities." Carter took a deep breath and collected himself. "What I tell you stays here. Eventually, I will be talking with Isabella, but not now. Her health and my baby are more important to me right now. Her condition is fragile, and she doesn't need to be upset." Clearing his throat, he looked directly at Anita as she sat intently on every word spoken.

"I would never do or say anything to her that might upset her. She's my baby, Carter. I could never intentionally hurt her."

This was it, and there was no turning back to what was about to be revealed between them. "I am not the person I was six years ago. I was at rock bottom then. I had been through enough from the time I was a child to kill me. I am not making excuses for what I have done in the past. I feel like you. I would much rather leave what happened in the past in the past, but Isabella is starting to remember things I would rather she hadn't. Eventually, she is going to remember things that could destroy both of us, things that involved both of us. When I started going through files and looking into what Arnell was tied into, I found out things I wish I hadn't."

"What kind of things are you talking about?"

"Anita, we are both in this up to our necks. The only way to come out, for either of us, with any kind of relationship with her is to tell her the truth. It's the one thing she values. It has given me nightmares for the last couple of months. I wasn't sure if it was connected, but I am almost positive that what I have heard her talk about and what I remember it is all connected." Carter leaned forward, placing his elbows on his knees and clasping his hands together. His forehead was furrowed in stress as he thought of what had happened. "When I got into my late teens and twenties, I was into a lot of different things that for a normal person would have put them in jail. Since my father was wealthy, he had hired lawyers, good ones. Needless to say, I never spent a day there. Charges were dropped. If they hadn't been, I wouldn't have stood a chance in getting into the academy. I started fighting when I was in grade school. I got into drugs in high school and experimented with small-time stuff. By the time I was in college, it earned me a one-way ticket out of law school. I was caught buying, or so they thought. They never were able to prove buying, but because I was in the area of a pusher, I was expelled. That was a mess. The case was thrown out on technicality."

"What does this have to do with Isabella?" Anita couldn't believe what she was hearing from him. She had no idea what was escaping him.

"Isabella was where I went to buy my fix. I knew she was there. I remembered it after she started talking about Arnell. He was the one that supplied me. His supplier was Gage Dawson. Bringing up her brother or a supposed brother, it started falling into place. I am just trying to put this together, and I am hoping I am wrong."

Anita appeared to be shaken. She drew her hand to her mouth, knowing that she had been found out. Her eyes were large and started to water as if she were going to break down where she sat. "Tell me I am wrong, Anita. I wouldn't blame you for anything that has happened, but tell me that she didn't have a brother named Cooper Lee because if she did, I am in for certain destruction."

She never said a word. "Anita, Cooper tried everything he could to get her out of that prison. He risked his life trying to get her away from a man that had intended to use her and her baby for his own pleasure. He arranged for two different men to impregnate her because he was afraid the man was going to kill her. One of them was Ryan Bentley. He had no idea that Ryan was not capable of fathering a child, and I seriously doubt that Ryan knew himself, at least not until he was older." Running his hand through his hair quickly, he licked his bottom lip and continued. "I would have never been there if it hadn't been for what Arnell had done to me and my sister. He forced me as a child to have sexual relations with him. I had no idea of what he was doing or what kind of repercussions it would leave me with. It wasn't only him. His wife also took advantage of my vulnerability of wanting to be protected and loved as my own mother had."

"Carter, I had no idea. I am so sorry."

"Don't be sorry. There isn't anything either of us can do about the past. I need to know. Was Cooper her brother?"

Anita never moved as it sunk in. "Anita, for God's sake, please, tell me. He raped your daughter over and over. He sent other men into her. He sold her. Your innocent daughter was tortured by this monster. I need to know for my own sanity. I was that man. I was the man that Jenna belonged to. She's my daughter."

375

Anita still sat without reply and choked. He took her by the shoulder and slightly shook her. "Anita, I was there. I did what I had to. She had to get out of there. He was starving her because she was withholding from her customers. He threatened her and her unborn baby and is still threatening her. He calls her and haunts her every chance he gets. He forced Cooper and Isabella together at gunpoint. What kind of connection does he have? Is he her father?"

With an almost hysterical cry, Anita answered through sobs. "I would have never married the man if I had known what he was. I was afraid that he was going to hurt them. He would come in and would threaten to beat me in front of Cooper. He had thrown things at me, choked me, and broke more bones in me than I can count. I left him once and had gone back after he had promised that he would never touch Cooper. I was so afraid of him. Cooper was my baby, and he had threatened to kill us both if I didn't go back to him. I didn't know I was pregnant when I went back. I didn't want him to know. When I found out it was a daughter I was carrying, I knew I had to get out." Anita sat there wringing her hands, and Carter sighed heavily, looking down, holding his head in his hands. This couldn't be happening. What in God's name was he going to do? His nightmare had finally started coming to life. Anita sucked in a breath, and her voice cracked as she continued her story. "You have to remember I was young and had a baby to think of. Arnell, if he had known . . . it wasn't. Oh, I hate that this has to come out. Before Isabella was even thought of, Arnell and I had been married for at least six years. Lee was five years old and had witnessed him

376

coming in and hitting me until I fell to the floor. He saw his father throw me against the wall, knocking me out and leaving me on the floor. He hadn't been that man when I met him. He was a good man, a loving man. I had never seen that side of him. After I married him, the man he truly was arrived. It started on our honeymoon. The night when most women look forward to a new and perfect life with the man they fell in love with, Arnell had smacked me across the face because he said that I had been flirting with his best friend. His best friend was the best man at our wedding. His best man had leaned down and assisted me into the car while he had said goodbye to his family. The train on my dress was sitting outside of the car, and he had bent down and picked it up placing it into the car. That was the exchange there was. He shook his brother's hand and had turned around and saw that exchange and thought I was flirting with him. He hit me so hard that it made my teeth rattle. Thinking that it was just because he had too much alcohol at the reception, I had passed it off. He had promised me that it would never happen again, but it did many times over, and each time just got worse.

"Trying to live with him was like walking on eggshells. He was meticulous about how and when he wanted something done. I didn't work. I stayed at home and took care of Lee and the house. He held the cards for everything. I couldn't talk to my family, I couldn't see my friends, and I was guarded constantly. I couldn't go to a doctor's appointment without him or one of his guards. It wasn't for protection. It was so I couldn't leave. He made it very clear if I had left a second time, he would kill us both. One night, in preparation of his coming home, I had made sure that the house was just right. I had made sure that Lee was bathed, fed, and dressed for bed because the interruption of his son would make him angry. I had taken care of him and had put him to bed early and had continued the evening with fixing my hair the way he liked it and had put on one of his favorite dresses and fixed a meal of his most loved dishes. I had tried many times over to make him happy. Despite what he had done, I still loved the man that I had met before we were married.

"When he came home, I greeted him with a kiss and a hug, which he hadn't reciprocated. He tossed his briefcase in the waiting chair by the door and walked past me like I wasn't there. It was nothing for him to stop on the way home at the local watering hole and throw back a few. It was evident that night he had more than a few. He turned and glared at me and clenched his fists, and I knew I was in trouble. He had offered no explanation until I had foolishly asked him what was wrong. That was my first mistake. The next was stepping away from him. He had some insane idea that I had been with some man I had never heard of and proceeded to slam me against the wall. He kicked me and hit me with his fists until I was bleeding. By the time he had finished with me, I had a broken arm, nose, and three broken ribs. Lee had heard the commotion and had come out of his room and downstairs. He screamed and cried when he saw his father deliver the last blow. Lee was just a baby. He didn't need to see that. He was just close enough to be backhanded by his father, and it had knocked him to the floor. I had crawled to him as he lay on the floor."

Carter sat thinking of the time that Arnell had done the very thing to him, and it had been more than once. He had managed not to break any bones, but he had left his mark behind and now this. He was in deep. Jenna was his and Isabella's. If it had been under different circumstances, he would have been thrilled, but in the light that she was conceived under the extreme circumstances that she had been, there was no cause for celebration. If Isabella knew how and why she was conceived and that it was him, she could very well leave him. He and Isabella had missed out on the first years of her life. He had no one to blame but himself for being so reckless, even if he thought he was doing what he thought was right to protect her at the time.

Anita had continued with her story, and as she did, he stopped her in midsentence. Waving his hand, he shook his head. "Say that again?" He had missed part of what she had said, but he wanted to make sure he heard her right.

"I had an affair with Jeb, his brother. Isabella is his daughter, and I knew he would do something to her if he found out. He did find out about the affair, and I assume that he figured out later on that Isabella was not his." Now it was making sense. "Jeb took care of Lee and me when I finally gathered the courage to leave him for good. During the time that I had left the first time, Jeb had been out looking for me, finding us a state and half away. I wanted away from him as far as I could get. Without the resources, I couldn't get far. He had offered to take me away then. I should have gone. Jeb had tried talking me out of marrying him up to the day I walked down the aisle to him. He had fallen in love with me years before, but I had eyes only for Arnell. Isabella wasn't a mistake. She was a blessing for me and for Jeb. Her arrival was the best thing that ever happened to me. I never wanted her to live her life the way I did. You have told me more about what happened to her while she was gone than she ever told me. She trusts you, or she would have never opened up to you."

"The past may have just caught up with me, and I don't know if we will survive it. I love my wife, but when she finds out what happened, she may hate me."

Anita sat in silence for a moment, letting what had been said between them sink in. Carter knew at that point there was no turning back from what had brought forward by either of them. Then it had hit him. She hadn't asked anything about how he knew about Jenna.

Taking in a sharp breath, it occurred to him there was more than what she was telling him. He stood and paced the floor, placing his hands in his pockets. His body started to chill as he thought about what must be coming next. "Anita." He walked so that he was standing looking down at her, and she slowly raised her head to him. "I told you I was Jenna's father, and you never questioned how I knew she ever existed."

As he stood there, a fresh stream of tears appeared on her. "Anita, did you know that Jenna survived? Did you know where she was all this time?" She slowly nodded her head in acknowledgment. Calming his voice and in an attempt to control his temper, he asked, "Did you know that Ryan wasn't able to father a child?"

"I didn't mean any harm to my daughter or to my granddaughter. Isabella wasn't stable and needed time to heal. I just had assumed that Ryan would bring her back when Isabella was able to care for her. When he didn't, I thought it was the best. Isabella had been through so much trauma with what had happened to her, and with what her body and mind had gone through, I didn't think she would ever be the same. She was so fragile. She came so close to dying when she delivered Jenna that when Isabella survived, she was mentally broken. She was in South Shore for months before she ever spoke a word. A young man that was there finally befriended her, and she was brought out slowly and started healing. She never remembered Jenna. She had nightmares for a while about what I assume were attacks she suffered, but she never thought about Jenna. I thought she was better off with Ryan until she was able to care for her, so we allowed Ryan to adopt her. Ryan promised us visitation while Isabella healed, and we accepted. It was better than letting her go to strangers, and we still had access to our granddaughter. We had no idea who she belonged to. It didn't matter. She was part of our daughter, and we loved her."

Carter scrubbed his hand against his face as he closed his eyes. "Do you have any idea of what kind of pain she has been in? She thinks our little girl is dead. I didn't know she existed until a few months ago. She has grown up with a man that is not her father and draws pictures of three men and a woman that she says are her parents. Obviously, she knows she has a mother that is not Ryan's girlfriend and two other men that she claims are her fathers because that's the best way Ryan can describe what has happened to us. I have seen her. I have been

381

close enough to touch her and tell her that I am her father and wasn't able to." Carter ran his fingers through his hair and turned from her and balled his hand in a fist, laying it against the table before him, trying to gain control of his temper. "She sent home pictures with me that I have kept in a place where Isabella could not see them because I had to prove first that she was who I thought she was." He turned toward her once more with tears piercing the back of his eyes as he continued to grieve for a child he barely knew, but it was his child. She was a part of him, and he missed her just like he would had it been Molly who was missing from his life.

Sitting back down, he sat in a well-produced vintage Victorian chair as he tried once again to control his feelings. He felt out of control, and he hated it. He thought he was prepared for this, but he wasn't. Anita cleared her throat and reached across to him and laid her hand on his knee. "We never meant any harm. We just wanted them both to be safe. I will talk to Isabella if you want me to. She can blame me all she wants, but I don't want you two to have problems. This was our doing, not yours."

"You don't understand, Anita. I was asked to get Isabella pregnant by Cooper to protect her. I was high. I was loaded down with alcohol and painkillers. I barely remember what happened. I didn't have a relationship with her. She doesn't remember because she was drugged by Cooper so that she would submit. I took advantage of the situation. It wasn't out of love, and it sure wasn't for pleasure for either of us. We were both under the influence. Even though Jenna is a blessing, a miracle in my eyes, she was not born out of a loving relationship. She was born out of a relationship at the time that had no meaning. Isabella lived in cruelty. Everything that came from that time was tainted in some way. I know that she loved Jenna regardless of how she got there. She has in not so many words told me that. She doesn't know that I was responsible."

He stood to leave the room and make his way to her and was stopped by his mother-in-law. "If I had known, Carter, you could have raised her and she could have at least had her father."

"She wouldn't have been any better off." Carter clenched his jaw as he spoke the bitter truth of what dwelled in his heart and mind. "I told you there's a lot you don't know about me."

Anita reached out for him, and he winced without wanting to. The pain from an earlier time had come to the surface. The time he spent at South Shore and what led to that time came rushing back. The night before he held a gun to his head, he had sat on his bed in his room after coming home from a drinking binge. Landon had brought him home after he had been gone for days with no one knowing where he had been. Landon had been a good friend and a good Christian man. He was the only one in his life that he felt walked the life he preached to him. Even though he had turned his back on Landon many times, he had never given up on him. He had nursed him back from overdoses of painkillers and hangovers along with getting him out of situations that could have landed him in jail.

He remembered coming home that evening after being gone and sitting there with a glass of whiskey that he had hidden in his room. It was one of many that he had hidden around his room and on the property. His father had tried many times to talk to him without success. The longer he went, the more self-destructive he had become. He clenched a glass in his hand and took a couple of long drinks as if it was his life-giving potion. Suicide had run through his mind many times from the time he was twelve years old. The only thing that had kept him alive was Beth. She was well taken care of by Grayson and Iris, and he was out of strength. Arnell's nightmare of abuse had taken its toll on his mind and his heart. He couldn't hold a job. He had been kicked out of college with no offer of being reinstated. What was worse, he needed to be wanted, loved by a woman. He had many girls or some so-called women that was more than willing to offer themselves to him, but he couldn't. Arnell haunted him so that there was no such thing as a relationship with a woman, casual or sexual. Other men his age had questioned his sexual orientation, and he had resented that.

Sitting down at his desk, he had set about the task of writing a suicide note and had written it out in full. He had thought of what and how he would do it. The place was still being contemplated as the thoughts rolled through his head. It had reduced him to tears, making him feel weak, helpless, and out of control. That was a feeling he detested. He had been in the spot many times where he had no control of a situation and his life was spiraling. Grayson and Iris had done everything they could to show him they loved him, and he knew that they did, but the damage that Arnell had caused him had no fix for it. Picking up the glass once more as he continued thinking about what he was going to do and how he would carry it out, he could see Arnell's face and hear his laugh as he had forced himself on him and the shrill cry that had escaped him while he had taken a belt across his back and had assaulted him. Beth had been forced to watch more times than he could count, and that had been worse. He had allowed himself to be used by Arnell to save her, and yet he had subjected her to the scenes that she had no understanding. Picking up the glass, he took another drink as Grayson had entered the room, carrying a camera and trying to talk to him. It fell on deaf ears as he tried to convince him he needed help. He had come off a binge of alcohol and drugs and was starting again. One drink had led to another, and this had been no different. Landon had sobered him up before bringing him home, and he hadn't been home an hour and had already been in the whiskey and pills.

"You're going to have to get some help, boy. I can't do this for you, but if you don't, your mother and I will be visiting you in jail or at the cemetery. You're killing yourself, and I can't just stand around and watch you do it." The rage heightened in him as his father continued with his speech that Carter at the time had felt was more like a sermon. His father took a picture of him sitting on the end of the bed and told him that someday he would thank him. He had given his son an ultimatum: either he got help or the next time he was arrested, he would spend time in jail until he was ready to go to rehab. His mother was dying more each day, watching him self-destruct, and he hated it, but he hated more what Arnell had done to him and could see no clear way out.

When his father shook his head and walked out of the room, Carter had lifted the glass and took the last drink from it and clenched the glass in his hand so tight that it burst in his fist. The glass lay in shards at his feet. He hadn't felt his hand bleeding and could have cared less. If it had slashed his wrist, it wouldn't have bothered him in the least. He was ready to die. He was numb to any emotion at the time. Other than the internal pain, he had nothing to prove he was alive.

The sound of the shattering of the glass in his mind brought him back to where he was with Anita. Neither of them was going to stand up well under this. He was eventually going to tell Isabella what had happened and that he was involved in it somehow. Anita would have to tell her part. God was going to have to work this out for them because it was going to be a mess for her and for them. Her father knew and wasn't sure that would sit well with her either. All he wanted at this point was for all of this to go away. He wished he didn't have to tell her, but they had a daughter that deserved to know them as her parents and one on the way along with Molly. She had a sister that she had never met.

"Carter, I am sure once she knows what happened, it isn't going to matter. I just didn't say anything because I didn't want her to have to relive it."

"You don't understand. This could mean my marriage. She is never going to understand this, Anita. The man that did this to her and had put her in the position of being beaten to the point that she could have died was me. I met her at South Shore. I was the young man that went to see her. I had no idea she was the same person. I was so messed up that I had no idea she was the same woman that I took advantage of when she was drugged. I did her no favors by what I did."

He pushed out an exaggerated breath and ran his hand through his hair frustrated. "I can't believe after all this time it is coming back to haunt me. I fell in love with the woman I basically raped. Sure, it was to get her out, but it wasn't under her consent."

Carter found himself on the deck of the *Blue Angel*, trying to sort out his mind. It literally made him sick to think that he was part of this. When it was originally thought, he had let it enter his mind, but now he knew for sure that indeed it was him and hated himself for that time in his life. He was going to eventually face her with the truth, and even though it was painful to him, it would be worse when she found out that he was Jenna's father. One of them was as much a victim as the other, but his could have been controlled. He didn't have to go into her, but he had, and he couldn't take it back. The one that had suffered the most was Jenna. If they made it through this mess, how would they explain it to her? And would Ryan even allow them around her, to be part of her life?

The wind on the ocean had pushed his hair back away from his face. As he had several years ago, he found some peace here. Prayer wasn't far off, and he didn't have to speak it to know that God knew what weighed heavily on his heart. He had never uttered a word as he stood there with his head bowed and his eyes closed. He entered and sat at the feet of his Savior. He laid each and every thought, each and every painful memory, and each hurtful event. It had to be laid at the feet of Jesus and be given up. If he didn't, he knew where he would end up. The self-destructive behavior that had brought him to this today would be where he would return. It was plain to him that he never wanted to be there ever again. "God, if you have to take her from me to make things right for her, then do it. He hung his head as his heart broke in pieces. If it takes that for her to heal and to put this behind her, then go ahead. I can't say that I understand it. I don't. But if it's the best thing for her, it's what I want. I love her. She's my life. The baby she carries and the one that I never knew about mean everything to me. I know that you understand what it feels like to give up a child. I'm not ready for that, but I am willing to do whatever it takes. Isabella and our children aren't mine. They're only on loan to me. They are entrusted to me, but they aren't mine. Whatever happens from here on out is in your complete control. I have to trust you, to trust that you know best, and that I have no control. The pain from all of those years that I thought I had given up to you is still there and has been brought to the surface. This is my testing of faith. I know that. Help me to be who and what you want me to be. And please, whatever happens with Isabella and me, take care of her. She's fragile. If nothing else, let her know that I love her."

Carter lifted his eyes and looked out onto the ocean as the sun slowly started to set and was pulled from his thoughts when he heard his father's voice behind him. "Amen."

"Pop, how long have you been here?"

"Long enough to know that you're troubled." Walking up beside his son, he placed a hand on his shoulder. "It's going to work out, boy. Don't give it a thought. Isabella is a good woman. She's been through a lot in her life and she's struggling, but she loves you. You can see it every time she looks at you. She was lost without you while you were gone. She's a strong woman. I have seen God in her life, and I have seen him get hold of her heart. Sure, she is going to be upset. She has the right to be, but you were a victim in this too."

"Pop, I violated her. I purposely took her without her consent."

"You were under the influence, Carter. You would have never done such a thing if you had been thinking clearly. Just think, if it hadn't been for that action, she may not have survived at all. I am not telling you what you did back then was right. It wasn't. Isabella survived, and so did you. From that tragedy, you now have a beautiful daughter out there who needs her parents. God is trying to heal you both from the torment you have both gone through. Let him work it out. He knows what you're feeling."

Carter turned to his father and looked at him, never saying a word, and swallowed hard. "I know this is not going to be easy, son, but you have us. We will always be here for you. God will take care of it. Trust him."

Sucking in a breath, he ran his fingers through his hair in frustration and sniffed back a tear. The controlling man that he was was fighting to keep his emotions in check. Isabella has also left him with his feelings exposed, whether she knew it or not. "I better go check on the kids and Bella. I've been away from them too long." Carter's father smiled slightly and slapped him on the back and placed his hands in the pockets of his trousers.

Carter's weakened state had left him feeling ripped to shreds, and it was hard to think. Nothing was going to be the same, he had convinced himself. The first year of marriage was hard enough without added difficulties, and he and Isabella had enough to deal with. He kept repeating to himself, *God, take it. It's yours. I can't do this alone.*

As he approached the cabin, he had looked in on Molly and Ben. Opening the door, he found them curled up together on the large bed, draped in each other's arms. They had become such good friends, and Molly had taken him on as a brother of sorts. It was a sad thought that Ben would be with another family soon, and it wouldn't be easy to explain that either. Molly had grown so attached to him that it would be difficult for her. Walking in, he dimmed the light and covered them. His daughter's cheeks were rosy, and her hair splayed against the pillow, looking like a halo about her. Ben had pulled her into the crook of his arm, and his arm lay softly against her hair. Ben's tiny curls caressed his cheeks, and his pink lips stood out against the paleness of his skin. He hated that he would soon be gone. In the short time he had been part of the family, Ben had become a part of it.

Walking away, he took one more look and cracked the door to the cabin. Now the challenge came. His wife would be his next dilemma. Maybe he should wait for Anita and try to discuss it with her when her mother could be present. Her delicate condition was something else to consider. Standing at the door, he contemplated on walking through it. Was it the time to tell her? His father was right. He couldn't keep it from her forever. The window was slowly closing in on the time. He had to tell her the truth.

He closed his eyes as he reached the railing by the door and rubbed his hand down his face, trying to calm his intense feelings. He had always been able to control them in the past. If he didn't get a grip, he wouldn't be doing either of them any favors.

He found himself turning around and heading back to the upper decks. He knew where he was headed, and he hated himself for it. The thoughts of having to tell her were ripping his mind into pieces. Walking into the main lobby, he made a turn and walked directly to the small bar that was always equipped with multiple mixers, wine, vodka, and whiskey. The area was lit with a Tiffany lamp that reflected off the solid oak table with glasses hanging overhead. He knew where he was going and walked with purpose. Opening the doors to the cabinet, he reached for the first thing he came to. Removing a container of vodka, he poured, watching it hit the glass along with orange juice.

Sitting down on the white overstuffed couch and turning on the surround sound music, he held the mixed drink in his hand and stared at it. He soon sat it down on the table in front of him. He bent down over his knees and held his head in his hands. Music played in the background, not that he was paying attention to it. All he could see was Isabella's face. He could see her beautiful smile the day that she had walked down the aisle to him. That had been the best day of his life. He had promised to love her with his entire being. He had no idea that there were so many things from both their pasts that would come back to haunt him. He thought that he had rid himself of all of it, but it had come back with vengeance. She was his weakness. He could be strong in most everything in his life, but she could bring him to his knees without question. She had no idea what he was going through. If he could have gotten by without telling her he would.

Rising again, he regained his glass and looked at the mixed drink for a time, then took it to his lips, but he couldn't bring himself to drink it. His promise to Isabella had returned. *You will never have to see that man again.* Drinking it would do nothing for him, and he knew that he couldn't stop with one. He sat there quietly and questioned God, *What do I do?* The answer was there instantly. *My grace is sufficient for thee. For my power is made perfect in weakness.* Carter found himself starting to smile, feeling the weight being removed from his shoulders.

CHAPTER EIGHTEEN

As he turned the knob to the cabin door, he drew a breath in an attempt to calm himself. She didn't need to know at this instant, but if it were brought up, he would know it was time, time to let all of the past to come out in the light of day. If it wasn't, it would keep, and God would be there when it came time to talk to his wife. Walking into the dimly lit room, he found his wife sitting at the vanity, brushing her long dark hair with the antique silver brush he had provided her. Even though she was well into her pregnancy, she was still the most beautiful, most desirable woman he had ever seen.

Her hair draped over her shoulder, falling over a white lace-and-silk robe that hugged the form of their child. She was still able to cross her legs at the knees, and that he found amusing. She had little makeup on, but she needed little as far as he was concerned. He remembered his mother sitting at the same vanity years ago, readying herself for a night out with his father. Even though it was the last time he had seen his parents, it still left him with wonderful memories.

"Hello, gorgeous." Isabella lay the brush down on the vanity, turning her head, and looked him up and down with her big brown eyes. He could see a glow she reflected and a stillness that he hadn't seen before. She did look tired, but much more relaxed than she had been since he had met her.

"Mr. Blake, you are a bold man, entering a lady's boudoir." She gave him a seductive grin and turned so that she could get a picture of her husband.

"Mrs. Blake, you are a beautiful woman."

"And you are a hot mess if I ever saw one. Just how many have you seen?" She was toying with him, and it wasn't like her to be seductive.

"One. You." He slowly sauntered over to her and stood behind her, prompting that she turn and look into the mirror. He placed his hands on her shoulders and looked into the mirror at her. "You, Mrs. Blake, have become a temptress. What has happened to my wife?"

Bending his head, he pushed her hair to the side, planting a soft kiss on her delicate skin. Looking into the mirror, he noticed that her eyes closed and she laid her head to the side so that he had gained easy access. He certainly was not used to his wife being so relaxed with any kind of intimacy. Sure, they had spent time together and they had one encounter in which she was completely his, and that had been the evening he was sure that this child had been conceived.

"Isabella, honey." She hummed at him without opening her eyes. "Are you all right? I haven't ever seen you like this."

She straightened and looked into the mirror at him and her smile widened. "Mr. Blake, you worry too much. You worried when I wasn't as receptive, and now you are worried because I am. I just happen to feel completely relaxed and contented here. I have my family, my children, and the man I love here with me. That's all I need, and just what I wanted."

He couldn't help but smile at her. He would have died for her a million deaths to protect her. He had no wish for her to be taken back to her past. If he could only build a wall around her and shelter her from the roaring storm that was sure to come, he would build a fortress and make sure she was never touched by the outside world. She had suffered way too much at the hands of Arnell Andrews, and now he was part of the turmoil.

He grinned, kissing her cheek, and gently ran his fingers through her hair to the ends as he drew it to his lips. Closing his eyes, he took in the aroma that was hers. She never disappointed. She was always all he needed. She completed him. Pregnancy had not made her less attractive to him. If anything, it had heightened his attraction. The earlier worry had left him just being in her presence. She had for the most part put his life back together, whether she knew it or not.

"Mrs. Blake, why don't you slip into one of those beautiful dresses I bought for you and go topside with me for supper?"

He watched her as her eyes became large, and she appeared stunned. "Those dresses, they're mine?"

"Of course, they're yours. Who did you think they belonged to?"

She covered her mouth that was now agape. "But I thought—"

"You thought what, angel?" He dropped to a knee beside her, getting a better view of her. *What had she thought?*

"I thought they were Andrea's."

He had no idea that would occur to her that what was in the closet belonged to Andrea. "Bella." Cupping her face in his hands and turning her to him, he saw the confusion on her lovely face. "I told you Andrea is gone. I have nothing left of her other than Molly. Everything in that closet is yours, the dresses, casual clothing, shoes, all of it. It belongs to you. I bought it and had it put on the yacht a couple of days ago, hoping we would get to go out on her."

She smiled but choked back some tears as she did. She could melt his heart instantly, and it wasn't hard when it came to her. The simplest of things she did gave him great joy: the smiles, laughter, the funny way she wrinkled her nose when she didn't like something, playing with her hair when she didn't want to talk about something, even the tears.

"Go on," he coaxed. Standing, he held his hand out to her, assisting her. He kissed the back of her hand as he did. As she walked off toward the closet, she turned and looked over her shoulder, and he nodded. He watched her as she disappeared. He decided while she dressed that he would change and wait for her. He had already picked his clothes earlier so he showered and returned to the bedroom, finding her sitting at the vanity once again. He sat on the bed and tied his dress shoes and watched her brush long, dark hair over her shoulder and looked through the mirror back at him. Her black dress set off the shoulders and hugged her, fitting her small and very pregnant frame perfectly. The silver pumps with kitten heels he had bought her graced her small feet. They were low heeled, which made it easy for her to walk. They were an easy on and off, saddening him a little that she required no help in putting them on. He finished dressing, tucking his shirt in. He ran his fingers through his damp hair. Standing, he walked back into the closet and soon arrived back into the room, carrying a small velvet bag, and stood behind her.

"I have something special for you." He cleared his throat as he looked at her in amazement. "It's something that means a great deal to me. It belonged to my mother, and I know that she would want you to have them."

Pulling the bag opening apart, he emptied the contents into his hand. Draping them over his hand, he slowly stretched them out in front of her and placed them around her neck. The string of pearls that was once worn by his mother now graced her neck. The well-worn set glistened against her skin. "They say the more you wear them, the more beautiful they become."

She touched them delicately, barely making contact. "They are beautiful, but don't you think you should save them for Molly? They are her grandmother's."

"Yes, they are. My mother would have wanted you to have them to pass down if you chose to. She and my father talked to me about love when I was still a little boy. The last night she wore them, she had me in her lap, and I admired her through the mirror, just as I am doing with you now. You are soon going to be the mother of my son, and I know that she would have given them to you had she still been with us. This would have made her and my father very happy," he said as he rested his hand on her stomach.

He hadn't seen his wife in the light that he had seen her tonight. It was if she was a totally different person, and he wasn't sure if he liked it. He liked that she was confident and appeared strong. She was bold, assured, and that had never been her persona since he had met her. It was if she had gotten to the point to where she literally had no fear, and that was worse. She needed some fear to protect her.

Later that night, as he waited for her to return from the bath to slip into bed, he sat thinking about what could have changed. He had no reason to be concerned; she was still Isabella. He should be glad that she had become a strong woman. For some reason, it left him mystified. He dimmed the light in the room so that the boat lights, what were left on, allowed a glow on the ripples of the waves. He needed to let it go. He had her in a place where she was protected and for other aspects seemed to be healthy. She hadn't had any problems with her pregnancy since she had been on bed rest. She had been taking it easy and listening to him and Cassidy for a change. It was difficult for him to clear his mind from the day's events, and he struggled at wondering if it were time to tell her the truth.

He stripped the red polo that fit firmly to his chest and laid it aside on the waiting chair, picking up his sleep pants that hugged his frame and sat low on his waist. He kicked off his dress shoes and lay by the bed. He rid himself of his socks and stood barefoot in front of the large window that led out onto the cabin's private balcony. The waves had not been felt, and the sea seemed relatively calm. A flash of heat lightning sailed on occasion against a near-cloudless inky sky. There were few stars out, and the moon was large and bright and beamed on the water, streaking it snow white. Taking in the sights always seemed to give him peace. Crossing his arms over his chest, he tried to let the day melt away and think about nothing but Isabella. She was why he was here. He brought her here to enjoy herself and so that they could spend some much-needed time together in a nonthreatening environment, away from the craziness that had become their life.

Warm arms wrapped his waist as soft lips hit his shoulder with a tender touch, the heat from them setting him instantly on fire. He didn't move. He just soaked in the affection of his wife. Taking her time against his exposed back, she squeezed his arms with a gentle strength, slowly landing soft kisses against his skin. She hadn't spoken a word. She just took her time as she made her way around his body, caressing him as she went. His wife had become sultry. He wasn't sure what he would see when she finally made her way around him. He sucked in a breath, and she seemed to enjoy the fact that he was fighting for control.

The lack of control was not something he had been used to around her. He was always the one that pursued, then it was treading lightly at best. "Hormones," she whispered as if she heard an unasked question from him. Then he understood. The heightened hormones had made her bold. He soon relaxed and let her take the lead. He couldn't say he didn't enjoy it. As a matter of fact, he preferred it.

Opening his eyes, he saw her. Her long dark hair lay in waves down her shoulders, shining like black gold. Her dark brown eyes shimmered in the dim light, looking at him with desire. It was true. They hadn't spent much time alone, especially intimately. With what had happened to her in the past and the medical problems she had endured, it left the physical part of their relationship on the back burner.

She bit her lip and smiled through it. She blushed as she watched him for a response. He wasn't about to disappoint her. She needed him, the closeness of him, and he needed to be wanted by his wife. She stroked the side of his face, leaving a trail with her finger down his jaw line then tracing his lips. Taking her hand, he kissed the inside of her cupped hand. She looked at him with a half smirk on her face and gently traced a line down the middle of his chest. He shook under her touch and hoped that she wouldn't notice. His mind was still reeling on earlier events. No matter how hard he tried to push them away along with a change in his wife's demeanor, his mind kept turning it over and over. "What is it? What's bothering you? Suddenly, you're a million miles away."

"I'm fine, just not used to you taking the lead."

"Is there something wrong with that?" She looked wounded, and he had no intent on hurting her feelings.

"No. Actually, I prefer it. It lets me know that you still want me."

Her face became instantly serious and stunned at the thought that he might have some insecurities. "Always, Mr. Blake, always."

"Then there is no need to say another word." Picking up his wife, he cradled her in his arms as she wrapped her arms around his neck and laid her head against his chest.

He could feel her heart beating against his arm that encircled her. Her breath warmed his skin as she sighed and kissed him. Kissing the top of her head, he sat her down on the soft down duvet and pulled it away from her side of the bed. Putting his hands under her body, he pulled her to where she would be comfortable. The lighting in the room was almost completely dark as he knew she liked it. He had chosen well the silk nightgown that she wore. The baby-blue gown skimmed her body, fitting her perfectly. He pushed the spaghetti straps over her shoulders as he leaned in to kiss them. Her body was tight from the contact but relaxed quickly.

His body tensed as he thought of the possibility of causing her more harm. His movements were stiff, and his breathing was noticeably uncontrolled. They were out and away from any help if they should need it. He should have known better than to take her so far away from her doctor, especially since she had already experienced problems with carrying their baby. Opening her eyes, she looked at him and smiled. "You aren't going to hurt me."

He chuckled slightly. "How did you know what I was thinking?"

"You forget. I know you better than anyone. I love you, Carter. I trust you. You have never given me reason not to."

He was silent for a moment. Looking into her eyes, he was lost in her heart. Everything that was him lived in her. She was his other half. Without her, he couldn't exist. Every beat of his heart was driven by her and had been since the moment he met her. In his mind, he saw her as that innocent, wide-eyed teen who was fearful and with

401

the soul ripped from her. He would have died for her that night. Some of what had happened that night, the night that Jenna was conceived, was brought back to him: the smell of her hair, the softness of her skin. She had whispered to him that night. For the life of him, he couldn't remember what she had said. She lay in front of him, unable to move, unable to react. She had breathed softly, relaxed from the medication given her by her own brother. That night, she had clients; he was just one of them. Between the alcohol and pills in his system, he was unable to appreciate her fully. He looked at her as if she was glass, delicate and fragile, hesitating momentarily; and again, she had whispered something to him.

"Carter." Outlining the form of his jaw, she drew his attention. "Amore, what's bothering you?"

He pushed a lone strand of hair away from her face and kissed her hungrily, never answering her question. Holding her close to him, he found the comfort to ease his frayed nerves. His nose settled in the curve of her neck, taking in her scent. She was soft and inviting. Her arms encircled his neck, and she whispered to him, her warm breath next to his ear. "I love you. Forget about it." How did she know? He let the anxiety leave. She was getting to know him well. He had tried to hide that anything was bothering him.

"Let it go, amore," she breathed. "I want you here alone. I don't want anything else in this room but us. Leave it alone." With her kissing his cheek, it didn't take long to convince him. It was the last words spoken between them. He needed this time with her, needed her. Under the cover of the dim light of their room, she held to him tight, closing her eyes. She didn't seem to have the fear as she had before. She waited patiently for him, trembling under his touch, not from fear as before, but from passion. She was comforting him instead of the other way around. Andrea had tried many times over to comfort him in bad times, but as hard as she had tried, he had pushed her away. He had never physically pushed her away, but mentally, emotionally, he had never let her that close to him.

It seemed effortless for Isabella to hold him, to let him sink his emotions into her. That had never happened before. Even though she loved him, and he was sure of it, she had rarely allowed herself to open herself up completely to him. Her fingers ran through his hair, setting off electrical charges that made him drunk. Closing his eyes, he accepted the comfort she offered and in turn showered the love he felt upon on her. Tears had fallen from him or her, he wasn't sure, but it had made her lips salty and soft as any fine silk. No sounds escaped her as she had taken what he had to offer, possessing him. His mind consumed by her, his heart taken captive by the touch of her fingers on his skin. His thoughts of earlier pain and confusion were gone, and they were one for the first time since their marriage, one soul, one being. It was the only way he felt he could describe it. She fell asleep in his arms, and he had rested his hand upon her belly. The small fluttering movements of their son were starting to erupt. He could feel them rise and fall as she lay peacefully wrapped in his arms. His mind was filled with dreams of this child and what it would be like when Little Eli was born, seeing his wife's face as she held his baby boy close to her, cooing and kissing him. It was a perfect picture. He had never before imagined that he could have the life that he had now with her.

Lying there in the dim light of the cabin, he held his life in his arms. She was his, his breath, his every heartbeat. Without her, he wouldn't exist. Listening to her breathe gave him peace, just to know she was there. The slight rocking of the waves was like a lullaby. The storm had settled in his mind, and soon he drifted off to sleep.

"Hello, son. Is your nanny about?" He stood looking at the strange man dressed in uniform, wondering why there was an officer visiting. The night was cold, and the snow was falling. He had been dreaming of going out in it the next day to do all sorts of magical things. The one thing he wanted to do was build a snowman with his father. They always built one together with the first heavy snowfall. When they were finished, his mother would treat them with hot chocolate with the tiny marshmallows and whipped cream. She always made it on the stovetop, and the kitchen would smell sweet of milk chocolate. They would sit in front of the fireplace, and his father would play his guitar. He would start strumming songs he told them their grandmother taught him when he was little.

His father had never failed to intrigue him. There didn't seem to be anything he couldn't do, everything from skinned knees, fixing broken toys, to taking care of his mother. He loved how his father would walk in from work and dance her around the room, singing as he did. She would giggle as he did and pretend that she wanted him to stop. It ended the same every time. He would dip her and kiss her and tell her, "Miriam, honey, I would take you falling into my world anytime." She would kiss him on the cheek for remembering.

"Mrs. Rosen, there's a man here from Daddy's work." Carter eyed the officer who stood in the door in a double-breasted jacket cautiously. The officer had badge in his hand that he had flashed for Carter to see he wasn't a threat. The snow settled on the man's shoulders and hat. The glint of his firearm shone from under his jacket. He was soon joined by another uniformed officer, carrying a black book and a flashlight. "Hello, young man." He had addressed the officer and stepped back as Mrs. Rosen walked in the room, wiping her hands on the apron. A long gray curl hung down over her forehead. Her kind smile soon disappeared as she had asked him what he needed. Her expression had gone cold as she greeted the officers.

He didn't understand the words that escaped the coated gentleman, but he knew it was bad. He had walked away and went to his parents' room and looked for his toy gun and badge that his father had given him for his birthday that year. It looked real. His father had said that when he grew up, he would teach him the things he knew about fighting the bad guys. He was so proud of his father. Alonzo was his hero. What kid needed a superhero when his father was one in real life?

He heard a high-pitched whimper come from Mrs. Rosen. It had been loud enough that he had heard it upstairs. The sound had sent dread upon him, and something had told him that something was terribly wrong. Placing his toy gun and belt on as he had always done, he ran to his sister and grabbed her close to him. She was already crying, even though she had no idea what was going on. She had felt the tension in the room, and that was enough. He had wiped her face and hugged her to him as the officer looked down on them.

"I'm sorry, son," was all he could manage. He tipped his hat to Ms. Rosen, and she had turned and looked at them. Her hand was over her mouth; the other clutched around a well-worn floral hankie she carried. His heart from that time on had been twisted, and it had only grown worse. It had been hard enough when he and his sister had been left to be raised by his grandmother. Oh, it wasn't that he hadn't loved her, but he much more preferred his parents. When it came down to the point when they were negotiated by the rest of the family, it had left him with a bad taste in his mouth. He had become untrusting of most people. The people who had presumably loved him had abandoned him. His parents had left him to take care of his sister that he had felt a firm responsibility for. He blamed them over and over for leaving them, even though as he grew older, he knew it wasn't their fault. When his mother's sister had rejected them after his grandmother's illness, that had hit him hard. He was bitter, angry, and hated everyone, even himself. From an early age, he had just wanted out. He didn't know how, but he wanted out. As he grew into a bitter and angry young man, it hadn't taken long for him to figure out ways to mask the pain. He started fights and soon traded it for liquor from his father Grayson's cabinet. Before they all ended up in counseling, his father kept it under lock and key, but Carter had known how to find it and would sneak it out of the house in a thermos. He soon graduated to drugs, anything that he could get a buzz from so that it would temporarily help him to forget.

In the beginning, Carter started with ecstasy. It felt good on the way up, so good that he felt like he had escaped for the day. He hadn't felt isolated any longer and had left him with a good feeling. From the time it started working, the high lasted for up to ten hours. Everything was beautiful no matter what it was, enhanced and heightened. Once the high had worn off, it was some of the worst depression he had ever experienced. It wasn't long before he had moved on to prescription drugs. He found them readily on campus. He bought them for a week at a time, then it became more often. He had overdosed a couple of times and was taken to the hospital and wasn't found suicidal, dropping him off the radar as no more than a user. That suited him. Grayson had threatened an inpatient hospital treatment rehab more than once, but each time, Carter had convinced his father that he would quit, and he would on a short term.

He drifted deeper into the nightmare his sleep had brought him to. The room was cold, damp, and dark. The smell of cigar smoke hung in the air as he stumbled toward a partially open door. He had stood and watched as men, and women, for that matter, walked away from them, straightening their well-attired bodies. Women fluffed their hair as they walked away from the young men's rooms. In the real world, people would have noticed that the women that were well dressed had spent time with these young men who were barely in their teens and young enough to be their own sons or grandsons.

407

The men would walk out of the girl's rooms, which was all you could make of it. They were hardly the age of knowing who they were, let alone what to do with their bodies. The unfamiliarity of these girls to what was being done to them was shown in their faces. Some had grown to accept their situation and had been allowed to roam the perimeter; others were not so lucky.

If they were favored by the clientele, they were more than likely unwilling agents and would take chances on leaving. Arnell would take it out in favors for himself or starve them until they complied, whichever it took. For a slight few, he would not only sexually but also physically abuse them. He would beat them with belts, whips, his own fists, whatever it took. Sometimes it would take a girl out of commission for a few days. He would let them heal just enough so that the bruising wasn't so apparent. The young men were another story. The young men most likely would have a younger sister that had been taken along for the ride, giving him leverage on them. He would threaten harm on them, thus keeping them in line.

He walked toward the door and opened it, listening to the creaking of the hinges as it slowly swung open. Standing at the door, he held to the frame. He could see her. Her long dark hair sprayed out against a red satin pillow. Her perfect lips were drawn into a small pout, and her skin looked like a porcelain doll, flawless with a small hint of pink to her cheeks. Her small, delicate frame looked fragile, and he swallowed hard as he gazed at her. Walking into the room, he shut the door behind him. Standing at the foot of the bed, his gaze never left her. She was angelic looking, fragile. His heart quickened and clenched as he clutched his chest. Taking a deep breath, he removed his suit jacket and loosened his tie. Frustrated, he ran his fingers through his damp hair. The rain had taken him by surprise. He hadn't felt it from all the prescription drugs left in him. It wasn't until he had removed his jacket he realized that his shirt clung to his chest. His angelic doll was dressed in a red teddy that was provocative with white lace thigh highs. She was young and lovely, dressed beyond her years, glowing. It broke his heart that someone like her could have been deliberately abused and used. She didn't move as he sat down on the edge of the bed. Her eyes were closed. He traced her face, trying to engrave it into his memory. As his finger traced her delicate features, her lips parted, and she whispered to him. He struggled to hear her.

He shook his head, trying to clear his head, and admired her once again. "Can you hear me?" he had said in a soft tone. "If you can, I am not here to hurt you." She had sighed, and her eyes opened to slits only, her soft breaths in rhythm of the rise and fall of her chest. His mouth was dry as he swallowed again. "I want to get you out of here the only way I know how." Reaching up, he unbuttoned his shirt and tossed it to the floor along with his tie. He had paid the man a bundle to be with her so he had all the time he needed. He didn't want her tortured as he had seen her before.

Removing his belt, he saw her flinch, crushing him. "No, angel, it's not to hurt you." He dropped it on the floor and held his hands up for her to see they were empty. "It's just me and nothing else. I promise you, I am not here to hurt you." He touched her like he was touching fine china.

409

A drew-in breath from her left one lone tear down her cheek. Lifting a thumb to it, he pushed it away. "You're mine for now. No one will hurt you."

A few words escaped her as he leaned in to kiss her. "Amore," she whispered. "My amore."

The air in his lungs sucked away from him. She let a small smile cross her lips, and he held her to him. She had tried to wrap her arms around his neck, but they were so heavy from the medication they had dropped to the bed before she could clasp them. "My savior. You're here." Her words were broken and unstrung as she tried to get the words from her mind to her mouth. "I've been waiting for you."

His mind was shattered as he tried to collect himself. His acts were mindless. He had placed her arms back on the bed and went about what he had purposed in his mind to do. She was nothing to him. He didn't know her. She was a stranger, and that was all he knew. He didn't need to know any more than that. His mind and body were numb. He went through the motions and soon covered her with the sheet from the bed.

Since he had paid for the night, he intended on using every bit of his time. He was spent, and so was she. Pulling his boxers and dress pants back on, he left the remnants of the rest on the floor and the chair and crouched beside her. She wasn't going anywhere. Her brother had seen to that. His eyes were heavy as he lay on his side and forced his eyes to remain open. Her beauty was a wonder to him. She was desperately in need of some food and sun, appearing so thin and pale that a small puff of wind could carry her off like a leaf being ripped from the ground.

His eyes shut, but not for long. He heard the voice of Arnell and his feet stomping on the floor. He rose from the bed and took his shirt and put it on, not taking time to button it. Throwing his tie around his neck, he picked up his jacket as he walked to the door. Looking back briefly, his angel was still asleep and unmoving. His job was finished, and he needed to leave before Arnell knew he had a connection. Slowly he turned the knob as he listened to Arnell scream at one of his flunkies.

"I know he's here. Where is he? Just because he's grown doesn't mean a thing. I will get to him and destroy him if it's the last thing I do. Then again, he's on the path to destruction. The way he's going, he will do the job for me." He started out the door and heard Arnell's heavy footsteps behind him as he cursed him. He had threatened to kill him that night, and he had heard shots fired at him.

As the shots rang out in his dream, it awoke him into a pool of sweat and heavy breathing. He sat up, trying to regain a little awareness of where he was and what he was doing there. He cupped his face in his hand and then ran his hands through his hair. Sucking in a deep breath, his breathing started to slow from the shortened rapid breaths. Looking to his side, he saw the still, silent frame of his wife. She was soundly sleeping, hopefully in a pleasant dream. The pain of the dream ripped through him. After all these years, he remembered. Her words cut him like a knife. She had been waiting for him. What had she meant by that? Had she known he was coming? What was worse, she had called him amore then. She had also had seen him as her savior in a horrific time. That was

worse. She had expected him to save her from that pit, and he had only served to make things worse.

As he started to get up, she mumbled something inaudible and placed her hand against his. Lifting it, he kissed it and placed it back down at her side and covering her back as she was before. She was going to hate him when she found out, and he wouldn't blame her. His lifestyle before all this happened was his own doing. He had done what he thought was right at the time, even though it had only served to make it worse. His father was right. What he had done was wrong, but if he hadn't, she may not be here at all. Arnell was a mean, vicious man and would do what he had to so he could keep what he felt was his.

To keep from awakening her, he went to the private deck and sat there. The expanse of the ocean and the moon shimmering on the water made his problems seem a little smaller. He hated it, hated himself for being so tangled up in this. It was past, and God had forgiven him. All he could do now was pray that she would.

The idea that had dawned on him was that he had been just as destructive and abusive as Arnell. He had raped his wife, and that was what kept running through his mind. She did not consent to it. She had not been aware enough to know who he was or what she was allowing. The pain of her stay had haunted her, and now it haunted him. *Dear God, what am I going to tell her? She's my wife. She knows some of what my life was before her but had no idea how bad it was or that I had anything to do with her getting pregnant with Jenna. I don't want to hurt her any more than what I already have. She doesn't deserve any of this. If I had known, I would have never married her. She deserves so much more than what I can give her. So far, it has been nothing but deceit and pain. I love her. Why is this happening? I have tried to do everything I thought you wanted. I know I shouldn't be questioning you, but why would you put me with a woman that is perfect for me and Molly only for her to be taken away? She's getting close to delivery of our son. It should be a happy time. Instead of being joyous, which I am, this is standing in our way. It's my fault, and I don't know how to fix it. I know you have a reason. I just can't see my way out of this.*

Talking to Isabella is coming, and I have to do it soon. Give me the words to say and the strength to do what I have to do to make this right. Eli needs a father. I have to be there for him if nothing else. And Ben, what is going to happen to him? I can't just send him away. He needs two parents to love him. Molly is going to be ripped to shreds. Isabella is the only mother she has ever known.

Turning around, he looked back in on his still sleeping wife, wishing he didn't have to do this. This mess was eating him up inside. Tomorrow, whether they were in port or not, he would pick the right time and would tell her the truth. She deserved that from him. If she chose to stay, that was wonderful, but if she didn't, he loved her enough to let her go. Life was too short. He had learned from the loss of Andrea that to not be honest was a waste of time. He had fretted and dealt over and over with the loss of Andrea. He could have used that time to heal the wounds between them instead of waiting until she had

413

nearly left him. Regret and shame are terrible things to have to live with. It would end soon, good or bad.

CHAPTER NINETEEN

Awakening from a dreamless sleep, I opened my eyes, finding the darkness still lingering. Turning over to place my arm across his chest, I found him absent from his place next to me. Through hazy eyes, I saw him sitting in the lounge outside of the room. The feeling was heavy in the room, but I couldn't understand why. He had been so passionate and loving, it was odd to find him gone.

Slowly I sat up on the side of the bed. These days, if I sat up too quickly, I may find myself on the floor. Either it was from too much weight in the front of my body or my blood pressure would fall when I stood up. Drawing my robe and cinching it, I wasn't sure which concerned me the worse, my husband's behavior or the idea that I was closing in on D-day. I couldn't remember what it felt like to be in labor, and what I did remember was terrifying. What would happen this time? Would it be a repeat of what happened in an earlier time?

The panic got the best of me. Sometimes being able to control it would have been miraculous. Taking a couple of breaths, I walked toward the balcony. Carter hadn't flinched. It was if he was off somewhere, no way near where we were. He had no idea I was standing behind him. As I stood looking down on him, his fingers lay against his lips softly. His breaths were slow and soft as I watched his bare chest rise and fall. His eyes gazed out onto the horizon, his long frame stretched out in front of him, with his legs casually crossed at the ankles.

Not being able to stand it any longer, my hands rested on his shoulders. "Hey, stranger, if you see my sweet, adorable, handsome husband, could you bring him back to earth? I would love to see him come back to me. He's had far too many worries lately, and I would enjoy soothing them away."

His normal reaction of a lovely boyish smirk never surfaced. The tension ran through me, starting at my feet. The warmth of the season seemed bitterly cold as I stood there with my arms wrapped around his neck and I kissed him on the cheek. He patted my arm and took my hand, leading me beside him.

The earlier good feeling I had was now gone, filling it with doom. "What's wrong?"

"Sit down a minute." He swallowed hard. "We need to talk."

Sitting down beside him, he continued to look straight ahead and looked down toward his feet. I continued to hold his hand and searched his face; it was easy to see something was terribly wrong. Sucking in a breath, I thought for a moment and tried to imagine what could be troubling him so badly. "Is it Ben? Are you worried about him? Because if you are, I know a way we can solve it." His expression never changed. "I would be glad to take him as my own."

"No, Bella. I know that you would take him and love him like he was your own. That isn't what's bothering me."

"Then what is it?"

Carter shifted slightly in the seat but never made an effort to look at me. Instead he wore a haunted, unsettled look and remained looking away from me and drew his hand away. He placed his head in his hands momentarily, then looked out over his fingers. Reaching for him, I turned his face toward me. "Don't hide from me, amore. Something has been troubling you for a while now. I've noticed. I just didn't say anything." With a strangled thought, I twisted the idea that bounced around in my mind as they tumbled out. "Do you not love me? Do you not want to be married to me anymore?" The thought killed me, but I couldn't hold it in any longer.

Clasping my face, I felt every feeling that raced in his mind. Fear loomed from him. "No, of course, not. Isabella, I would do anything for you. I love you, I . . . I never want to be away from you. You and my children mean everything to me."

He slowly told the story of a man I never knew, and it had left me in a fog. This couldn't be the same man I married. I knew he had gone through some pretty amazing things, but I had no idea. The child that had been left behind by his parents along with his sister was a story hard enough to take in its own right. When it came to telling me about the drugs and the recklessness of his youth and early adulthood, I shuddered at what he was telling me. No wonder I felt the connection to him. I truly did have one.

"It's time you heard the truth. Jenna, Ryan, and I are all connected." I watched as he ran his fingers through his hair, not understanding any of what he was saying. "I was there, Bella. When you were in the hands of the man that abused you, I was there. Your brother, I knew him. I met him at the warehouse because it was where I got my supply. I saw you there more than once. Lee made a plan

417

for you to get out. He made a deal with me and with Ryan Bentley. He wanted you out. He was afraid that Arnell would starve you or worse kill you with his bare hands." Carter turned to look at me for a moment, and I stared through him. "The only way he knew to do it was to get you pregnant. He knew Ryan was your boyfriend and had made arrangements for it to be him, but he was afraid Ryan would back out. When Ryan didn't show up on the appointed night, he asked me." Sucking in a sharp breath, I couldn't catch a breath. What in God's name was he telling me? "Isabella, Jenna is mine. She's alive and lives with Ryan and his girlfriend. I saw her. I wanted to tell you when I found her, but I wanted to make sure it was her before I did."

"Isabella." He clasped me by the arms and shook me slightly, trying to gain my attention once more as my mind had wandered back, trying to put it all together. Suddenly, things were making sense. "Did you hear me at all?"

Shaking my head, it was hard to accept that the man I fell in love with was also the man that was part of a scheme to impregnate me, one that was cooked up by my brother. My brother was capable of so many things, but it was hard to hear that he was also part of this.

"Isabella, I don't remember much of what happened, but I was myself enough that I remember you being there. I had been there more than once to take care of my fix. I hated myself. Arnell left my life in a wreck along with everyone that he ever touched. Your brother was desperate. He was going to make a deal with whoever he could to get you out. He didn't care what happened to him, but he didn't want you to suffer."

"I can't believe this." Grabbing my head, I felt my heart sink to my feet. I felt betrayed by the only man I had trusted other than my own father. "You actually were there, more than once. You were with me, purposely came into me with the full intention of getting me pregnant?" Shaking my hand in front of me, I squeezed my eyes closed. "Ryan was never in the picture. He was never . . ."

"No, Ryan was there, and he was one of the two people that your brother confronted. He knew Ryan because of you. He knew me because we were friends in school. I had no idea, Isabella, when we fell in love or when we were married. I hadn't put any of this together or knew for sure until a few months ago. You had problems with the baby, and I never brought it up. I didn't want to take a chance. You and our baby mean everything to me. You have to believe me when I say I had no intention of adding to the trauma you had already been through."

"Do you hear what you're saying? You passed this off, doing this to some young girl as okay. Because it was the past, it was to be forgotten. When you found out the girl you were with was me, you suddenly gained a conscience."

"No, it was never that way." He stood from his seated position and paced the deck in front of me as I tried to sort out what he had told me. "When I found out it was you, it crushed me, Bella. I would have gladly taken the torture he put you through to keep you from suffering at his hand. I took it for my own sister. The things he did were unspeakable. It took me years to tell a therapist what he had done to me. You know more now than my family knows. He would strip me and forcefully perform sexual

419

acts on me and made my sister watch. She was a baby. She had no more idea of what he was doing than I did, but she knew enough that it wasn't normal. The nightmares still linger of what he did and what I did to you. Even though I wasn't violent, it affected you, and I hate myself for it."

"So how did I get there? What do you know about that?"

"I can answer that." The voice from behind me stunned us both. Carter had instantly stopped pacing. "I'm sorry. I heard voices."

"Mom? How can you know any of what is going on here?"

She stepped forward, carrying a drink with her as she did. "Anita, no, don't do this." Carter shook his head and watched her.

"She has to be told. If I don't tell her what is going on, it could cost you your marriage."

"Mom, what are you talking about?"

"Just listen to what I have to say. That's all I am asking."

Carter drew in a sharp breath and pushed his dark hair away from his face in pure frustration.

"Carter and I have talked. I think that it's only fair that you know the whole story. Not just his."

My skin started to prickle as I stood there; ice ran through my veins. "I can't believe this. You knew. All this time, you knew and never said a word?"

"I only knew pieces, Isabella. Please sit down with me, and I will tell you. I never wanted to tell you this. I never wanted to shatter what you felt in your mind was a perfect family."

420

"What are you talking about?"

Carter took two steps toward me, and I winced as he touched me as if he had burned me. "Bella, please sit down, and let us tell you what we know. It's time you know."

Sitting on the edge of the bed, I clasped my shoulders, crossing my arms over my chest. Suddenly feeling chilled, I rubbed them. The weather was much too warm to feel so cold. Carter pulled the chair from the nearby vanity and sat down in front of me.

My mother sat beside me, clearing her throat then turning toward me. "Isabella, this starts way before you were born. You never knew, and I never discussed it with anyone. Years before I had you, I was married to another man. He was a handsome and a very charismatic man, someone that most of the young girls wanted, and I was the lucky girl who married him. I was lucky, so I thought. He was perfect. He was the one I had dreamed of all my life. Flowers, candy, romance, he did all the things a young woman wanted in a husband. That all changed quickly. He soon had shown me what he was like. The first night I was with him, he hit me. He thought I was flirting with his best man, which happened to be his brother. He looked at me that night as if he hated the very breath I took, but I was raised to believe that once you were married, you were married to that man for life."

"I don't understand. Daddy, he would have never done anything like that."

"No, he didn't, and he wouldn't. Your father loves you and me. The man I was with beat me for a pastime. He threatened to kill me and Lee, taking all communication

421

away from me to my family. He wouldn't allow me to go anywhere without his henchmen with me. He raped me more times than I can count, and he tried to hurt Lee more than once. When I had the opportunity, I left. In that time, I packed Lee up, leaving most of what we owned behind and moved as far away as I could. I knew if he found us, he would make good on the promise of killing us."

Watching my mother's face in horror, she rubbed my face, her hands pushing my hair behind my ears. "Dear god, why didn't you say anything?"

"I'm telling you now. You deserve to know what happened."

"But what does this have anything to do with me?"

Carter sat with his arms crossed over his knees. He made a break from looking at the floor and looked at me as if his heart was shattered. I could feel the pain rising from them both. My mother smiled slightly and patted my knee.

"While I was gone, my brother-in-law came looking for me. He eventually found me. Determined that my husband would never hurt me again, he offered to help me and Lee leave for good. My brother-in-law would have done anything to protect me. He loved me, and I was too stupid to see it. He was a good man, so different from his brother. While we were together, the short time we were, he tried to persuade me then to leave Arnell, that he would take care of me and Lee. I didn't know when I made the decision to return to Arnell that my decision had been made for me.

"We had been gone for two months. In those two months, over half of it was used to talk me into staying and never going back." My mother looked down at me and rubbed her forehead. My throat became tight and felt dry. "After I had gone back, Arnell was no better. If nothing else, his behavior escalated. I started becoming ill, and I knew then I had made a mistake by going back. I packed up Lee when I found an out and left for good. I met up with my brother-in-law in Ohio, hoping that Arnell wouldn't try to track us. It was there I found out that I was pregnant with my second child."

It didn't take long for horror to fill my face. "Mom, the baby." I choked. "What happened to that baby? Who was the father?"

Carter ran his hand down my arm as my mother turned from me. A repressed sob slipped from her. Looking at my husband, I wasn't sure now where to turn. "Bella, honey, that baby was you."

"No. No, it can't be. Daddy, Daddy isn't my father?"

My mother turned and got down on her knees in front of me. "Of course, he is your father, and he has always been there for you. He is your dad. Arnell would have killed us all if he had known. If I had stayed, he would have used you as a child or worse killed you. I couldn't let him, Isabella. I grew to hate him. Jeb Cameron is your father. Arnell is your uncle. Your grandmother remarried when he was young, and your father and Arnell are half brothers. When he found out that your father and I had an affair, he threatened your father that he would destroy him."

"Wait a minute, I don't understand. What happened to Lee? I haven't seen him since I was small."

"Baby girl, Lee was taken from me in a custody battle when he was seven years old. You were just a little girl.

423

You couldn't understand it. Arnell took him with him. He had no idea that you two would end up going to school together. Lee tried to protect you, and he couldn't. His father threatened he would kill you if he didn't do what he wanted. He worked for Arnell for a few years against his will. When you ended up at Arnell's place of business, Lee tried to get you out the best way he knew. He was afraid that he would starve you to death or beat you. He made arrangements for Ryan to get you out. I didn't know about Carter until a couple of days ago."

"I can't believe this."

"Bella, that's not all. Lee is Cooper Lee. He married my sister."

I had all I could take. I got up and looked at both of them horrified. "You did this to me. Both of you." Turning, I walked away quickly with my hand over my mouth, attempting to hold in the pain and sick feeling I had. I made it to the deck of the *Blue Angel* and ran to the edge of the railing, feeling as if I were going to throw up.

"He told you, didn't he?"

The rich baritone voice of Grayson broke through the darkness and the crash of the waves. Closing my eyes, I had hoped this had all been a nightmare, hoping that I would wake up and this would be gone. My legs felt weak as I stood there holding the railing. My breaths were short and choppy, and my stomach turned feeling more like Eli was doing somersaults one after another. One hand on the rail and the other on my stomach, I opened my eyes as I felt the warmth and comforting arm slide around my shoulder, offering the support that I so desperately needed.

424

"You know, there are a lot of things in this life that we aren't meant to understand. We make choices in our lives. Some are good. Some aren't. I am not making an excuse for him, but you have to remember that he gave that life up a while back. He isn't the same person. He made a choice he thought was right. His judgment was clouded. It took a long time for him to heal from the effects of abuse that was laid out by the hand of Arnell Andrews. Carter made choices in his life that has followed him and haunted him for a long time."

Turning to my father-in-law, I saw the concern on his face. The tears, what few had fallen, now burned my face as they settled down off my cheek and onto my robe. "You knew? You knew this happened and didn't try to talk to me? Didn't you think that this would hurt me?"

"Yes, I knew, only because Carter was trying to find Arnell. He unearthed all of this when he started looking for him. He found out about him, your real father, and Jenna. Honey, you have to take this for what it is. The past is gone, and it's over. Try to live for what it is now. You have a family, a husband that worships the ground you walk on, a daughter that adores you, and a baby that will soon arrive out of the love you shared with my son. Forgiveness has to start somewhere. God knows I have made mistakes in my life. I can't tell you what to do, darling. You have to decide in your own heart. Ask yourself, do you love him? If you do, accept it. He loves you. He has for a long time."

"How could he love me? He chose to violate me."

Grayson looked down at me with a soft smile. His salt and pepper hair shined in the moonlight. "He talked to me years ago about a young woman that was too young to be going through what she had endured, a young woman that he fell in love with that he needed as much as she needed him. She was a lovely girl with big dark eyes and dark hair that had a very closed-off appearance that hurt him to see so tortured. He spent his time with her while she closed herself off to everyone around her. She hummed a lullaby for a child she no longer had and remained closed off until he introduced her to an enchanted prince and princess. That fellow and his young woman fell in love years ago during a dance he never forgot. That young woman changed his life, and she is still changing it for the better. Think about it before you judge so harshly."

It had been several days since our trip, and I had thought of what Grayson had said to me, but I couldn't get it out of my mind that I felt Carter had lied to me. He had betrayed me, and it was all that came through my mind. *You knew this would happen all along. No man will ever love you, not like you thought they would. Carter was guilty as any of them, if not worse.* Sitting there on our bed at Rose Point, I rested my hands over the top of my stomach. Our baby was just a reminder of what a sham our marriage was. I loved this child, but I felt like our whole marriage was a lie. How could I let myself get sucked in? *Stop it. You're feeling sorry for yourself. The only one that is going to take care of you is going to be you. Your own mother even lied to you!* Drawing a breath, I stood and walked to the window and pushed the curtain back and looked out onto the lawn. There in the late evening sun, I watched my husband talking with Marshall and Landon. There couldn't be a worse feeling than the man you loved had never loved you at all. Looking down at my rings, I pulled them off and sat them on the table, but I couldn't stand the thought of leaving them.

Taking a chain I found on his desk, I strung them and placed them around my neck. The chain was just the right length to let them hang just above my heart. They were getting tight from my swollen hands. Looking down, they had left indentations where they once were worn, so it was a way to wear them and decide what my future held. It was the first time they had come off since Carter had placed them on my hand. The sick and sinking feeling found me quickly in the bathroom heaving as I thought of what had happened. I had a few short months ago prayed to have him back even if it were a short time. I had no idea that was going to be the result.

"Isabella, you all right?"

Standing in the door, he looked down and soon crouched down by me. Taking a cloth from the sink, he wiped my face. "You look so pale and tired. You really need to rest."

Taking the cloth from him, I stood, leaving him there, and he soon followed me. "I'm fine. It's just warm today, really." Walking away, I headed to the window again and looked down onto the finely manicured lawn.

"Bella, it's been days. Can't you talk to me? We have hardly spoken two words to each other since we came back."

Turning, I saw him. He stood at the end of the bed, and his hand rested in the pockets of his faded jeans. His dark, unruly hair was slightly askew from where he dragged his fingers through it. The beautiful blue eyes that

I had grown to love appeared dim as he waited for a response.

"Carter, I don't know what to think. I am not sure what I want to do. I am thinking of going back to Maine and getting an apartment or staying at a hotel until I sort out my own feelings. I think it is only fair to us both."

Taking a few steps toward me, his facial expression sank. Removing his hands from his pockets, he quickly ran them through his hair and turned halfway and then turned to me. "You can't be serious. After all we have gone through to be together. Isabella, I know what happened between us was not ideal, but it was a long time ago. We didn't even know each other."

"No, we didn't." Turning to look back through the window, I couldn't face him. It seemed strange that I could no longer face the man I had given my life and body to. The hurt raged through my body as I could hear his breaths being stacked behind me. "I am not sure we ever have." How could I let such things slip through my mouth even if I did seriously think them? I loved him; there was no doubt about it. My life felt like it was falling apart little by little, and there wasn't a thing I could do. What was going to happen to us? Ben, Molly, and this little baby were my life. My husband, the one person that held me together, had knocked every support away.

"Isabella, please don't do this. We can work this out. What about the baby? He needs a father. Molly has come to know you as her mother, and Ben, what about him?"

"Carter, I am sure that you can handle taking care of Molly. You did for years before I was around, and Ben, if you have the desire, you could adopt him on your own if

428

you wanted. I'll make arrangements with you with this baby. I am leaving in the morning. I would prefer to be alone if you don't mind. I need to pack." My voice never wavered or cracked as I stood there. None of what I was saying sounded like me.

Carter's voice was thick as he replied, "What about our parents? What do you want to tell them? You know there are going to be questions."

"Tell them the truth. Tell them we are temporarily separating, at least until we can sort out our issues. If we can't, well . . ."

"Isabella, I refuse to discuss any idea of divorce. If that's what you want, you are going to have to file, but I promise you, I will fight it."

Turning to face him, I took a deep breath. "Do what you like. I don't hate you, Carter. I just don't understand you."

"Why can't you forgive me? The person I was then is no longer in me. That—" He ran his hand down his face and stood with his arm against the bed frame. "That is punishing me for something I did years ago that I barely remember and for a person I was that I no longer am. Don't, please don't do this to us."

"I am sorry. I really am. I wanted this so badly. I finally believed there was a Prince Charming and a happily ever after."

Stepping forward, taking an opportunity, he placed his hands on my shoulders. "Angel, I am the man you fell in love with. I haven't changed just because the past has come out. I still love you. You're my wife. I am remorseful for the life I led so many years ago, but I can't change it.

What happened, happened. If I could change those events, I would, but I can't."

Before a word could escape me, our lips crashed, Carter not being forgiving with his intimacy. His feelings were not held back as he held me toward him; the heat of his body and the beat of his heart were felt strongly. There was no intention of him letting up or letting me make a step out of the door. There certainly was no thought of how I looked, which was ready to deliver and feeling much like a waddling duck. The ache of my low back and feet had left my mind as he held me and kissed me sensually. My husband had always been an amorous lover, but this was a different side of him. He left me breathless at every turn. The pregnancy hormones weren't helping me. I was angry with myself for not being able to control my feelings, for not being able to switch it off. He had taken what power I held and had taken it for himself. He held everything, including my self-defense and my heart. He had held it for months, and now he was upping his game.

"Tell me you'll stay."

I couldn't get my breath. If I hadn't already fallen for him, I would be doing it over and over again.

"Tell me, angel." He gasped, attempting to gain his breath. "Tell me you'll stay. My life revolves around you. Don't do it, Bella. Don't do it. I'm nothing without you."

My heart was telling me to stay, but my head was telling me to go. *You need the time to put the pieces together, Isabella. Don't let him talk you out of it. He's trying to charm you, and you know that he can. He hurt you. Don't let him do it again.* The shattered pieces of my life lay on the floor of my soul. The man that held me had hurt me as much, if not more, than Arnell.

"You can't possibly believe we can get back to where we were, not after this."

"No, I don't." Tracing my cheek, his blue eyes drowned me. "We have to try, Isabella. We have a family, a life together. You can't honestly walk away."

"I can't stay." I gulped, trying to gain my stance.

The evening had become a blur. We sat in silence at the dinner table with our family and friends. The normal playfulness between us was stifled, and it was seen by each and every person that was there. Carter hadn't touched a thing other than a drink or two of some of the wine that had been passed around the table. Looking down at my own plate, I had pushed the food around on it, making it look like I had eaten, but I couldn't touch a bite. It had taken everything I had to stay where I was. At the end of the meal, we had made our way into the family room, and Carter had told his family and friends the story he had shared with me as a child. The minute it had hit his mother, she had burst into tears. I sat there numb, hearing only bits and pieces of what he was saying. I sat thinking of the man I had fallen in love with and tried to make sense out of why this had happened. No matter how I turned and twisted it, there was no reason for the events to make any rational sense. The longer I sat there in thought, my heart raced as I controlled my breathing. The tears wanted to wash over me, but I held them in as the images of my husband on our first night danced in my memory. I was so scared, but I was happy. The smile on his face, the sweet gentleness of his touch, and the feel of his body next to

431

mine swept in like a breeze across my heart. It literally felt
as though I was bleeding. The sharp edge of the truth had
cut me so deep that I felt I was bleeding to death. My
mouth had gone dry, wishing that I was a drinking woman.
It would surely take away the thoughts and the pain that
has been instilled in me. At the end of summer, I should be
sweltering, especially with the extra weight, but instead I
am chilled. Crossing my arms over my chest, I rubbed my
arms as if it were freezing in the late end of August.

Carter's voice broke through my thoughts. "Not that I
want this, nor do I approve of it, but Isabella and I will be
going through a trial separation." Standing in the middle of
the room, his hands rested on his waist. It never surprises
me how he makes me feel just by sweeping his eyes over
me. "Hopefully, we can work this out. I have every
intention of making this work. I don't know for how long,
and I don't know the details. It's something that Isabella
and I will have to work out together. As for Molly and Ben,
Molly will be staying with me part of the time. We will be
sharing time with her. She deserves to have Isabella in her
life. Ben will be staying with us temporarily as a foster
child. If things work out for us, it is my intent on adopting
Ben into our family. I can't stand to see him go into the
foster care system without someone who will be there for
him and love him the way a child should be loved."

Shifting, he took his mother's hand, who was still
weeping from his confession. His sister sat in awe of her
brother, now remembering what had happened to them
as a child, I am sure. My father sat shaking his head as my
mother sat with her head down and her hands crossed in
front of her. The grown men that sat in the room wore an

432

expression on their face of disbelief of what Carter had now disclosed of his past and of what we were now going through. Quentin, who had been smoking, quickly put down the glass he was drinking from and walked out the door without hesitation. I felt as though that I had now become the outcast of this group, even though it wasn't aimed at me. Carter had not uttered one harsh word.

"I want you all to know that Isabella and I"—he hesitated for a moment as he looked at me with his head slightly bent away from the rest of the room—"we both still love each other, and I am going to do everything I have in my power to show her that I am worthy of her trust if she will just allow me. We will work this out. I promise you, angel, we will work this out."

Wiggling my way up to get out of the chair, he offered me his hand. Reluctantly, I took it as he looked at me without a word. His face told me more than anything he could have said. I stood before a broken man. His hand shook as he held to mine, and I couldn't deny the anxiety and pain that it left me. Somehow I felt this whole incident was my own fault, all of it. Dropping my head and letting my hand slip from his, I held back tears that I wanted no one to see. Walking through the immense house, which was more of a castle, I had to get away from them, all of them.

The home was gracious and inviting, but it felt more like a dungeon for me at the time. With so many rooms, there had to be somewhere I could go. I needed time alone to think. Making a step into the first room off the main wing, I found what was presumably the study. The room was filled with shelves of books and leather couches and chairs. A desk of rich and warm color of what to me appeared to be a dark cherry sat in the middle of the room. In the center was a laptop computer that reflected the only light in the room until I found the switch on the Tiffany lamp on the side of the desk. The warm glow of the green, gold, and red of the cut glass shimmered softly. It was all the light that I wanted. It centered only on the desk. I didn't want to draw attention to me being in the room anyway. Getting away from everyone was the idea, and I really wanted that time.

Moving the mouse, the computer instantly sprang to life and settled onto a page that had been viewed last. The words caught me totally by surprise. The clipping was about me and my disappearance. Thinking back for the first time, I saw what had happened. My father lay on the floor, begging me to run after hearing what sounded more like a firecracker exploding. I had come home and wanted to see my father. Bits and pieces of what my life was as a teen at the time flooded me—the desperation of seeing my father, the thought of him losing his life because of the man who had found it so easy to rip me away from my parents.

The screams that I had made had seemed to fall silent as I watched my father fall to the ground as I was taken. I had no idea if he would survive. Fear ran through me like an electric current, the energy that flew from me. I had tried then to knee the man that had me when he had turned me and thrown me in my prison and had missed. He had threatened me. My mind not processing, I continued to kick and scream until he had found a rope in which he had tied my wrist behind me and my feet

434

together to keep me from running. The cold sticky tape he slapped against my mouth kept me from screaming any longer. Blinking, I continued to read the article. As I continued to click through the archives, I found another I hadn't expected.

This couldn't be. My eyes followed the script as it jumped off the page.

Detective Alonzo Moretti Davis, longtime respected official of the Chicago Police Department, and his wife Miriam were involved in a fatal crash. The vehicle in which Davis was driving was struck in the passenger side, causing the vehicle to rest in a ditch. The investigators state that Davis hit a patch of ice, throwing the vehicle into oncoming traffic. The other vehicle, driven by Arnell Andrews, sustained the least damage. Andrews was found to be intoxicated at the time of the accident. Alonzo Davis, according to the county coroner, died on impact. His wife survived briefly but succumbed to her injuries shortly after.

It left me wondering if Carter knew what had happened to his parents, if he had ever looked into it or that Arnell was involved. I sat in the dim light in the leather desk chair, feeling like my body had been wrapped in it. The events that had taken place over the last few days left me feeling numb to my own feelings. I wasn't sure of what or how I felt. I had no feelings at times. Other times I felt like it was cutting me to the quick. Sometimes the thought of what had been disclosed left me cold. I loved him, but I was angry that I did. I was angry with myself for letting myself love him, then I was so upset with him for doing to me what he had.

Then the words come back to me: *Jenna is mine*. I had been so upset that I hadn't heard it. My mind filed it away quickly. Jenna was with Ryan and his girlfriend. Why? After all this time, the daughter I thought had died was alive, presumably well, and no one had told me. Why would she be with him? She should have been with me. I am her mother.

Walking over to the shelves of books, I pulled down a blue leather-bound one, looking it over carefully. Anything would be good, as long as it took my mind off what was happening. I wanted to escape for a while, and a book was the best way for me to do it. Opening the book, I knew it wouldn't be long before I became lost in it. I recognized the book, *Cinderella*, from years ago. He had read each passage to me. Somehow it felt healing to me. I read the first few lines and started to hear his soothing voice, the voice that had brought me from the darkness so long ago. He had become my salvation then. Why not now? He was right. The man he was had been lain to rest a long time ago. It wasn't long before my eyes became heavy as I lay in the chair curled up, with the book on my chest. I drifted off thinking of the young man that had danced me around the room. I felt loved, and for once, I was free and was no longer fearful in his arms.

CHAPTER TWENTY

It was no surprise when I felt masculine arms wrap around me and lift me from the chair. The book that I had been reading was carefully picked up, closed, and lay on the desk. "Time for bed, angel. You should have been in bed hours ago." The scent of him had soothed me. My eyes were unfocused as he had lifted me, and my head lay against his chest. No matter how upset I was with him, I couldn't deny the love I had for this man.

The sway of his body was familiar as he walked the halls of Rose Point to his childhood room. He gently laid me down and covered me as if I were a child. The weight of his body caused the bed to shift, and I knew that he was sitting there looking down on me. Months ago, just the idea of him looking at me was something I hadn't been comfortable with.

I felt his weight lift from the bed, knowing that his eyes were still on me. I found it difficult to open my eyes but did awaken enough to speak briefly. "I do love you." Feeling a finger trace away a stray hair, he bent down and kissed me softly on the cheek.

"I love you, angel. Sleep well."

I heard his footsteps as they cracked and popped the wood floor as he left the room. Being so tired, I couldn't seem to awaken enough to stop him. I had drifted off quickly and was glad when I woke to find the morning without a nightmare. Carter's side of the bed had not been slept in. Why I had a sinking feeling, I wasn't sure. It was my fault. I was the one leaving. Telling Molly wasn't going to pleasant, and neither was it going to be easy to tell Ben after the loss of his parents that he was about to lose another set.

As the bathroom filled with steam, so did my mind with turmoil. The last few months had been such a roller coaster of events. It was difficult to untangle what was our courtship, which was short, and our marriage, which had been interrupted. Now I was the one standing in the way. Grayson's words came back as I let the warm water wash over me. *Ask yourself, do you love him? If you do, accept it. He loves you. He has for a long time.* Oh, I did love him. There had never been a doubt in that at any time. He was everything I had ever wanted. There hadn't been a time that I didn't feel like he was the other half of me.

Stepping out of the shower, I sat down at the vanity. I still had moments when just getting out of the shower and washing my hair made me dizzy or sick. Wrapping the towel around me, which wasn't easy, I began drying my hair. It was going to take a while, I could tell. Lifting my hands above my head had made me dizzy, and I leaned my head against the wall, letting it pass.

"May I?"

Opening my eyes, my husband stood before me, holding out his hand. Handing him the blow dryer, he turned it on and started to dry my hair. "I remember when you didn't want me doing much of anything for you. Goes to show what a little bit of patience and love can do. By the way, I love to do this for you. All you had to do was ask me."

438

His long, deft fingers ran through my hair, leaving it in large, untangled, soft waves. His cologne and his own scent was something I never got tired of. The touch of his hands on me was never unwelcome. Although there was a wall, a wall that I had put there, I loved the man and everything he was and stood for. The pain and the anger still remained from what I had found out. The seesawing of my emotions wasn't helping anything. I could cry at a drop of a hat or laugh at something that really hadn't been all that funny.

"I know I'm not going to be able to talk you out of it, but I really wish you would stay. You're so close to delivery, and Arnell is still out there. I know what happened is still painful. I don't blame you for being upset. You have every right." Turning off the hair dryer, he ran his fingers through my hair and smoothed it. Crouching down in front of me, he took my hands. "Isabella, it wouldn't have mattered who that girl was back then. I carried guilt over it for years. I had no idea if I had had a child out there, and I hadn't stopped at the time to think of the consequences. I saw a beautiful girl, one that I wanted to get out bad enough that I risked getting killed for. If Arnell had known I was there, he would have killed me."

I couldn't say a word, knowing if I did I would have fallen apart. Standing I took two steps away from him, just enough so that I was out of his reach. The longer I let it go, the more it distanced me from him and anyone else in my life. I felt helpless and alone in a room full of people. I had that feeling before, and I had hated it.

"I can understand it if you said you hated me. I have done some pretty horrendous things in my life. The harm I

439

did you was the worst one and one I will never be able to forgive myself for. Isabella, no matter what happens between us from here on out is your call. You have to willing to forgive me, and I have to work on my own feelings."

He moved his way through the bath and walked away without another word. My husband's lack of words or touch had chilled me. Taking my clothes from the chair, I dressed as I looked in the mirror at the woman that I had become. The plain, ordinary girl I was before I had met him was gone. I had grown up in the last few months, looking totally different from the woman he had married. My appearance most assuredly had changed. In a few months, weeks, or days, I would be a mother. I had gone from a young girl to his wife.

From the moment he had come into my life, he had me by the heart. It was so utterly senseless for me to think that I would be able to walk away from him that easy and not be affected. When it came down to it, Carter and I weren't going to be the only ones affected by our separation. I knew that but hadn't really wanted to think about it. I couldn't stay for that reason. I had to stay because I loved him and for no other.

I now wore designer clothes and jewelry that most women dreamed of. The white maternity dress that I now wore slid onto my very pregnant frame and fit like a glove. The jeweled collar had no need for a pearl necklace or any other type of pendant. A silver bangle graced my wrist. I pulled the chain from under my dress that now held my wedding rings, letting them lie against the silk fabric that hit me just above the knee. The simple silver-studded sandals were easy to put on and perfectly matched my dress. I looked overly dressed for more than a trip home. My hair had fallen down my back and was easily pulled up and placed in a knot on my head, leaving small curls at the neck and the border of my jawline. A few simple tucks of bobby pins had held my hair up neatly.

My mind was filled with difficult truths of my past, present, and future, none of which were any good without him. Letting the past guide me and trap me was smothering. Placing my hand on my lower back, I rubbed it slowly as I sat down on the edge of the bed we had shared in his parents' home. *God, what am I going to do? Am I wrong in blaming him for something that happened so many years ago? You wouldn't have put us in each other's path twice if we weren't to be together.*

It had stunned me when I felt immediately the answer was in front of me the entire time, especially when my back had started aching and hurt again. No, it couldn't be. It was just nearing the end of August. Taking a couple of deep breaths, it passed quickly. There, it wasn't what I thought. Standing, I walked toward the door and picked up my purse and proceeded down to the living area where I found Iris sitting, looking through an album. She sat sipping on a very tall glass of iced tea on the overstuffed couch, smiling at what she was looking at. Without lifting her head, she knew I was in the room. "He was such a beautiful little boy, a very precocious little fellow. He was always taking things apart to see how they worked. He was a stern as a child, acting more like a man than a little boy. He was always my protector. I guess that comes with having to grow up so fast." I sat down beside her and

441

looked over her shoulder. "Look," she said as she pointed to a very stern-faced Carter. He looked to be around ten years old. He stood in front of a rail fence, holding to the rein of a black-and-white paint stallion. Even then he looked fully in control as he stood with a hand on the nose of the beauty of a horse. "That's Big Sky. Oh, he loved that stallion. His grandfather gave him to him. He would go and spend time with his grandparents in the summer. He and Elizabeth would go for a week or two and spend time on my father's ranch in Montana. My father bought him from a local breeder. He thought it would be good for Carter to have something to call his own and to look forward to when he visited."

"He must have enjoyed going to see his grandparents."

"Yes, he did. His Grandma Kate would make sure the kids had a summer like I had when I was a child. Chasing what most people called lightning bugs, I called them fireflies. We would catch them and put them in a jar and watch them light up. It fascinated Carter. He had never had a childhood, not really. He spent his time trying to protect everyone, even me. We did everything we could to give him a childhood. He just . . . refused it. He wasn't a child. He was an old soul, a loner. He did love books, all books. They soothed him somehow. It was nothing to find him curled up in a corner somewhere with a book. I guess they gave him an escape. A *Tale of Two Cities* was one of his favorites, along with *Cinderella*, the classics. I don't know how many times he read the *Picture of Dorian Gray*." She chuckled as she reminisced over the photos in the book. "Just think, you will be reading to this little one before long."

"I don't know, Iris. I feel handicapped. Molly was a toddler when I came into Carter's life, and well, I don't know what the next few months are going to hold for any of us. I'm scared. I don't know what is going to happen when I go into labor. I thought I had lost Jenna. I had medical problems because of Arnell, and I am still having problems. I have come so close to losing this baby." I sat rubbing my stomach. "I haven't felt him move much over the past couple of days."

"Relax. Babies slow down when it gets closer to delivery. It's natural to be a little nervous. Every mother goes through the worries of delivery and if they are going to be a good parent. Believe me, honey, you are going to do just fine, and Carter is going to be there."

"I don't know." I squeaked. "I have been pushing him away at every turn."

She smiled, comforting me. "He will be there, believe me. He isn't going to let this go by without him."

I took a couple of deep breaths, noticing that my back was cramping again. It had been for several hours. I wiggled, trying to get relief. Taking a pillow from the couch, I placed it behind my back. The things that I had done before didn't seem to help as much as they had before.

"Isabella, if you are so worried about Carter being there, why don't you go talk to him? I know he will listen to you. He loves you."

I started to wiggle again then stood to put my leg underneath me. Placing the pillow behind my back, I let

443

out a breath. I felt like I had gone white as a ghost. The pain left me with a shiver running down my back. I didn't take long to figure out that Eli was on his way. At the moment, I wanted to deny it. I couldn't, not now. It was too early.

"Isabella, are you all right?"

She had barely gotten those words out as Carter walked in the room. "Mom, Pop is out back, fussing with Marshall again about the rhododendron bushes." Nothing got by him. He knew as soon as he had looked at me something was amiss. In the fear that rose in me, I felt a tear run down my cheek as I fought my own emotions. He stood a few feet from me. I couldn't move. Just like years ago, I felt that veil of protection that came over me. I heard the voice of a man that had whispered in my ear. "I promise you I am going to get you out of here. Someday I promise you that you will never have to fear for your life again. One day you will be out of here and in the safety of a good man's arms. Until then, I will protect you. If it takes the last breath from me, I will protect you."

I heard a choked sob come from my throat. Before I realized it, he was on his knee in front of me. He held on to me as I cried so hard that I couldn't get a breath. His stern look appeared, as it did from the picture in which Iris had studied so intently. The protection of Carter Blake was the best I could ever have. It came from love, not control. I grasped his biceps and felt the strength in them as tears streamed down my cheeks. His dark-blue eyes questioned as he sat and watched every emotion that shone around me.

"Are you all right, Bella? What is it?"

I squirmed in my seat, not being able to say much as I tried to breathe through the pain. Carter's eyes grew large as he realized I was in labor. His eyes never left me as he spoke to his mother calmly. "Mom, get Pop and Landon. Isabella's in labor." Laying down the book, she took off toward the gardens, leaving us alone. "It's all right, angel. Take a couple of breaths, and let it pass." Taking his cell phone from his pocket, he contacted Cassidy and let her know I was in labor. Slipping his cell phone back into the pocket of his shirt, he smiled from ear to ear. "Angel, it's going to be all right. I'll be there. I promise I won't leave you."

Landon's footsteps hit hard and fast on the wood floors. You would have thought it was Beth at the speed he had gotten to me with Quentin and Grayson on his heels. "Izzy okay?"

Carter's eyes remained on me as he answered him. "She's fine. I want you to get her bag from the hall closet and my firearm from the desk."

"Why do we need that?" I asked him as he continued to watch me every second.

"A little protection, Bella, never hurt anything."

Another contraction had hit me, and it had landed in my back so bad, I thought it was going to split me in two. Taking a few breaths, I blew them out hard. "Carter, I can't do this."

"Yes, you can. You can do this. Think of this little guy." He rubbed my belly, his palm splayed against my stomach. As his hand rounded my stomach, he leaned into me, whispering into my ear. "Peace, Isabella, quiet, relax, and

445

think of the most wonderful place you could be in the world. Think of most relaxing places you could be."

Closing my eyes, I let him take my mind away. "Do you have it?" Shaking my head, I let him know that I was listening. "I know that one of your favorite places is in the mountains, but I want you to think of home. Think of being on the beach, just lying there and soaking up the sun. Feel the warmth of the sun as it hits you. The day is calm, and you can hear the seagulls as the pass over. Start at your feet and let your body start to relax. Let it inch up a little at a time. Do you have it?" Once again, I shook my head as I tried to picture being on the beach with the sand squishing between my toes. It was warm enough. I didn't have to imagine the heat. As I sat there, I tried harder to feel the warmth of the sun and sand and listen to the crash of the waves and the screech of the seagulls. Opening my eyes, my husband remained in front of me and smiled. "Take a deep breath, honey. That one is over. How long has your back been hurting?"

"It started last night. I thought it was just the extra weight causing my back to ache."

"Last night?" He drew it out as he said it. "Okay, let's get you going. When last night?"

"I don't know. Around four, I guess."

"It's nine, so that means it's been seventeen hours, Bella. We need to get you to the hospital now. We can't wait any longer. Eli is coming whether we are ready or not." Standing, he held his hand out to me, and I took it. Walking wasn't the easiest thing in the world. "Dad, can we take the sedan? I don't think she can get in the truck."

Grayson handed him the keys as we walked out the door. Reaching the doorframe, another contraction had hit me, doubling me over. With Carter's arm around me, supporting me, he picked me up like a baby and carried me the rest of the way. "Bella, you never cease to amaze me." In three strides, we were at the back of the sedan. Gently sitting me down, he climbed in beside me. "Breathe. You have been to class, use what you were taught."

He was right. Between Landon, Quentin, and him, I had three coaches during my pregnancy. My Lamaze teacher was beginning to think that I had started to gain groupies for this show. During the early part, Quentin and Landon had taken turns going. It had really been interesting when Carter had walked into the room one evening after he had been to the office. By that time, all three men were there. Landon was coaching me, and Quentin had followed and then decided to stay for security. One of them had always seen that I had someone there for class night. When the teacher and the class had been introduced to him, they had watched me and him in awe, wondering how many more fellows were going to show up.

His soft, boyish grin appeared as he looked at me, and I couldn't help but smile at him. There was a childlike way about him. "We're going to be parents, angel." Kissing me on the forehead, he laid his hand again on my stomach. Looking down, he talked to our unborn baby. "What do think, slugger? Ready to greet your daddy?"

I couldn't help but laugh at him. Here was this stern and in-control man now reduced to jelly over the coming of his child. "You are a big softy, you know that? This little guy is going to have you wrapped around his little finger. He hasn't even taken his first breath, and you have been reduced to a marshmallow."

"I've been waiting for this for a long time. A chance to be a father from the time my baby took its first breath. I want to be there for every first he has. I don't want to be an absent dad. I played that role with Molly for a while and all of Jenna's life. I won't let that happen again."

It wasn't long before another contraction hit me, and I held in a scream as it ravaged me. Feeling a gush of warm water, I knew it wasn't going to be long. I felt my face contort in a grimace. I squeezed his bicep, as it abated. I looked at him, and he knew we were in trouble. His bicep was hard as a rock, but my fingers had sunk into him. "How's Izzy?" I heard Landon ask him. His eyes remained on me. "If you can get us there any faster, I think that would be good."

"This baby is being a little impatient. His arrival is more than likely going to be sooner than later."

The concern arose in Landon's voice as I sat with my legs, no over my husband's. "You have got to be kidding. You are kidding, aren't you?"

"Just drive, Landon." Taking in a breath, he pushed my now-sweat-drenched hair back away from my face. "Angel, don't panic, but I may have to deliver him. I know how. I have done this before. Try not to push, not yet." He dragged his fingers through his hair as he always had when he was agitated. It was soothing, I suppose, a way to release the stress. "Pop, do you have a blanket in here?"

"There's one under the driver's seat. It's an emergency box with some first-aid supplies—silver package on the right of the box."

Ripping it open with his teeth, he pulled it out and laid it on me. He had no sooner done that when I was hit with another contraction. I grabbed his arm and bent toward him. "Eli, he's coming now. The contractions are too close together. I can't do this, not here."

"You can do this," he assured. "If we have to do this, we will. I'm here, Bella. I would walk through fire for you. Calm down." Carter was very calm and collected as he sat there next to me. "Breathe, honey. Landon, how much farther? We have to play catcher here?"

"Next exit. Hold on. We're almost there."

"I'm scared, amore."

"You and this little baby are going to be fine. Cassidy is going to meet us at the door. She will make sure that everything will go well. She knows what she is doing."

By the time the car had stopped in front the emergency room, I had grabbed onto him.

"Carter, this baby is coming now. I feel him."

"Bella, it's all right, we're here. Cassidy is going to take care of it."

Grabbing onto his shirt, I pulled him down into my face. "Carter, now." My breathing had gained, heavy like a marathon runner. "He's coming now."

"Landon, go in and tell them we need Cassidy now. She says he's coming now."

Landon quickly leapt from the car and ran for the emergency room doors. Carter looked at me and took off his watch and laid it in the seal of the window. "Okay, honey. Let me see how close Eli is." His calm outside demeanor left little to the quivering of his hands. "If this is where it has to be, it has to be." Pushing the blanket up along with my now-soaked dress, he removed my panties and put them on the floor. His face never changed in expression as he placed his hand against me. "Angel, when the next contraction—"

He hadn't managed to get the words out, and it had hit me again. "Go ahead, honey. I have him. I can see his head." Wanting to scream, I held them in, and he grinned at me with that crooked smile that I loved so much. "If you have to, scream. I know it hurts."

Cassidy soon was standing at the door as Carter had tried to protect what modesty I had left. "Inpatient is he?" She smiled. "Come on, fellows, let's get her inside." After they had assisted me onto a gurney, they hurriedly pushed me on through the emergency room, with Carter holding on to my hand. Once we had arrived to the floor, the others had been told they would have to wait. Getting on the ward, Cassidy had guided the crew through the delivery room doors. "Carter, you'll have to stay here for a moment. The nurse will be out to get you."

"Carter!"

"It's all right. I'll be right behind you. Do what she says." The doors closed silently behind me as his hand had released mine. The cold and the brightness of the room hit me with the fact that I was without my protector and my support. My breaths came in short, chopping spurts, making my chest hurt. Scenes from Jenna's birth came. The rattle of instruments as they quickly set up rang in my ears. The staff was talking, but they seemed so distant.

450

The anesthetist sat on one side of me, and I could see the tiny warmer where Eli would be.

"Mrs. Blake, are you all right?"

I found it difficult putting two words together. "My hus-band . . ." I managed to get out as he sat there. "Need . . . him."

"Take some deep breaths and relax. Everything is fine. It's anxiety, normal for new mommies. Slow down. He will be here soon."

Looking around the room, he was still talking to me. "Mrs. Blake, the doctor is on her way, and the nurse has gone to get your husband." I could feel the nurse placing an IV, and she looked at me over the mask that she wore. "We are going to give you a little fluid. As soon as I tape this down, we will check you."

"Well, shall we get this show on the road?" Cassidy's voice came from nowhere. Following her voice, I saw her as she approached the end of the delivery room. Sitting down, she took her spot for delivering Eli.

"Carter!" I pleaded as I huffed his name out.

"He's coming, Isabella. He wouldn't miss it. Nurse Brady went after him. He should be coming in the door any second. Relax, honey, I need to check you. Very soon you are going to be holding a very precious baby boy."

I tried to calm myself through her assurance, but it wasn't coming easy. The memory of Ryan sitting by me, not being able to do anything, with the thought of Jenna dying came to me. It was falling in on me, and I was unable to get my breath. The accent of the anesthetist had caught me as he placed some oxygen on me. "Just for comfort, Mrs. Blake. Slow down your breathing. Relax."

451

"Carter! Where . . . is . . . he . . . I need . . . him . . . now!"

The silky voice of my husband had broken the chaos of the delivery room. The sound of his footsteps soon gave me the assurance I needed. "I'm here, angel." He took his place at my head and held my outstretched hand. Taking hold of him, I closed my eyes and took a deep breath. He chuckled. "I couldn't miss the first act. Besides, I know the star of the show."

The nurse had strapped a fetal monitor on me, and I could hear the beat of Eli's heart, strong and regular. What a relief. "Listen to that, angel. He's strong and healthy."

"Okay, next contraction, Isabella. I want you to take a deep breath, grab hold of your legs, and push down for as long as you can. Try counting to ten. Take a breath and start again. His head is right there, so it should be quick."

As the contraction hit me, I did as I had been instructed. Carter's arms supported me as I pulled on my legs. "This is it, angel. You never cease to amaze me. Count 1 . . . 2 . . . 3." His voice vanished as I heard the beat of the monitor shift.

"His heartbeat is dropping. Let's get her prepped, now." Carter looked down at me as he had helped me lie back down then back to Cassidy. "What's going on, Cassidy?"

"The baby is having a hard time. We need to get him delivered."

"Carter, we need to do an emergency cesarean. His heart rate is down. You're going to have to leave. I don't know what I am going to be dealing with here."

"Carter," I begged, holding tight to him.

452

"I promised her I wouldn't leave, and I am not going to." Carter's voice was commanding.

"Look, I don't have time to argue with you. I need to sedate her and get him out. Leave now."

Cassidy's voice was very matter-of-fact, as she took charge. Nurse Brady took him by the arm and drew him away. "Carter, please."

"It's all right, angel. I won't be far away. Everything will be fine." It was the last thing I heard as he walked out the door with Nurse Brady leading him.

"Isabella, we're going to make you comfortable and get Eli into this world."

Oh no. This couldn't be happening again. "Let's get going here. Julia, get the section tray for me. We have to move now, no time to waste."

The instruments clanked together as they moved, and I could feel the cold chill in the room. "Mrs. Blake, I'm going to give you something to help to sleep."

"No, please, no."

"Take a few deep breaths. I'm going to give you something to help relax you and place a little more oxygen on you. It will help you and Eli."

I found myself strapped to the bed with my arms held to hard boards and with lines going every place imaginable. A drape was immediately placed in front of me. "Relax, Mrs. Blake. Listen to my voice. Start thinking about somewhere pleasant, a beach, a place you feel safe. Everything will be fine. Mr. Blake is waiting for you outside the door, and your little baby is going to soon join us."

As he talked, I slowly slipped off. "That's right. Just close your eyes. I'll be waking you soon."

I felt as though I was being sucked down into a dark hole. Darkness started to surround me as the one small beam of light stood over my head. It wasn't long before that dissipated. The pain of my labor had left, and I felt like I was floating over my body and looking down. It was pleasant enough, but I wasn't sure that I liked what I was feeling. The darkness started to rush away as I stood there looking at them rushing around the delivery room. My dress was less than formal. I wasn't in uniform. As a matter of fact, I was walking around in my hospital gown. Why?

Curiosity got more of me than trying to figure out my own fashion sense. The cry of a baby rang through the room, and I followed it to the warmer that sat in the corner of the room. Looking down, I saw a very big little boy with healthy lungs. His dark hair highlighted his olive skin. "He's a big boy." I had heard a nearby nurse say. I looked at her as she cooed and made over the little guy. "Well, Eli, you certainly made an entrance, didn't you? You are a looker, gonna break a lot of hearts." The petite Asian nurse held him close to her and swaddled him in blankets. The crinkle of her eyes let me know that under the mask she wore, she was smiling at him. Once she swaddled him and laid him down, he pulled his fist to his mouth and tried to open his eyes.

So you're the little guy that kicked and kept me awake at night. Your daddy is going to be so happy to see you. I reached to touch him, and when I couldn't grasp him, I gasped at the thought that I couldn't touch him and even more when I spoke his name and couldn't hear my own voice. *Eli?*

454

What had happened? Walking over the cot in the room, I could see Cassidy was working frantically while I stood with the anesthetist at my side. "Her blood pressure is dropping, 70/30 heart rate in the thirties."

"Come on, Isabella, hang in there just a bit longer. Get another unit of blood on her and hang some lactated ringers. Where's the dopamine?"

A nurse on the telephone called back at Cassidy as she barked orders. "Pharmacy said they would have it here soon."

"Get on it. We need it now. This is going to be over in less than two minutes. I'm not going to let him lose his wife."

Curious, I looked down at the woman that lay unconscious on the bed beside the anesthetist. After getting a closer look, I couldn't believe it. She was talking to me. The woman there was me. That was me lying there. The color in the room was nothing but white and bright lights. *Go back, Isabella. You need to stay with him. It isn't time to leave.* The voice I had heard before was guiding me once again. When a woman stood before me in a floor-length white dress, I knew her immediately. She smiled readily at me.

Andee?

It isn't time yet. You have so many things left to do here. Go back to him, Isabella. Don't be afraid to love. Go back.

Andee, what's going on? How did you get here?

That's a good question.

She didn't give me an answer. She just stood there and smiled.

455

Go back, Isabella. He needs you.

With that, she walked away, and I sucked in a breath and started coughing. My arms still strapped to the bed, I was unable to move.

I heard a little chuckle and a thick accent from the man that sat at my head. "She's back. Welcome back, Mrs. Blake."

Opening my eyes, I saw a man masked beside me. "He's here, Mrs. Blake. Your little man is here and safe. The pediatrician is checking him out, but he has a fine set of lungs on him." The staff laughed as I listened with relief.

"Isabella, everything is fine. I'm just stitching you. You and that precious little boy should be with Carter very soon. I sent Nurse Brady to update him. I am sure he is relieved. We will be sending you to recovery soon, then you will return to your room.

"Eli?"

"Dr. Bruno will bring him over so that you can see him before they take him on to the nursery." The weight of the last few months had been lifted off me. What a relief! He was here and healthy.

"My husband, where is he?"

"He is waiting impatiently for you, honey. Don't worry. He's fine. I'll get him as soon as we finish here. I am sure you are going to want to be with both fellows."

CHAPTER TWENTY-ONE

Carter had been standing with the family, clad in the normal surgical green scrubs, when an intern who had been working with Cassidy had come to update them on Isabella's condition. His knees had immediately hit the floor when he had told them that she was in very serious condition. When they had started to deliver Eli, she had started to hemorrhage. Effects from an early injury had stretched to its limit and had started bleeding profusely. No doubt to him that it had been caused from the damage that Arnell had inflicted.

After five units of blood and multiple medications, Cassidy had managed to save his wife. Eli had been delivered safely and was sleeping soundly in his arms. He couldn't imagine the love that had overtaken him when he held his son in his arms. He looked perfect. Molly's birth had been clouded from drugs and Lord knew what else. He had to ask God many times over to forgive him for the thoughts and feelings that he had about Arnell Andrews. If he had been there at the time they had told him about his wife, he most assuredly would have killed him with his bare hands.

He had contacted the office and had told Brooks that he wouldn't be in for an extended amount of time because of her condition and had put in for extra leave. He would be working from home only, and that would be limited. He wasn't sure how he and Isabella were going to rebuild their marriage, but he was going to be there for his family regardless. His hunt for Arnell Andrews would never end. He would find the man that had caused so much pain and see that he was put away for a very long time. If he could, he would push for premeditated attempted murder. It had been evident to him that he had meant to kill Isabella, not to mention the abuse of her and many others at his hand.

Looking down at Eli, Carter rocked his son. He could see the image of himself. His baby boy had his olive-colored skin and dark hair. Of course, babies changed over time, but he had seen pictures that were kept by his parents. He favored him and his father. Alonzo would have been so proud of his grandson. He now had three grandchildren that his birth parents would never know. He would have been thrilled that he had considered adopting Ben and introducing him into his family.

Isabella had been through a lot, and he still felt panicked over it. His wife had been just a breath away from leaving him. All he could do was admire her and look down on the precious gift she had given him. Wrapping little Eli a little tighter in his swaddling, he pulled him up closer to his face and kissed him on the cheek. The softness of his face reminded him of Isabella's soft kisses that she had so tenderly had given him. Just the idea that he could have been left alone again had caused him to shudder.

As the night had broken onto dawn, he sat praying for his wife. She had only been awake briefly after the birth of their son, and he had missed it. While Cassidy had explained that it was normal, it had still made him nervous. He had told her over and over while she remained in sleep that he loved her and that he was sorry.

458

"Mr. Blake?"

Carter was brought from his thoughts as the nurse had walked in the room. She stood in a blue scrub dress and a mask draped around her neck, and Carter had studied her.

"Dr. Bruno would like for me to take Little Eli back to the nursery. He has a few more tests he needs to do, just routine. You may come see him in about thirty minutes or so. If Mrs. Blake wakes up, I will be more than glad to bring him to her."

After he had determined that she was no threat, he had handed his son to her. "He is beautiful, isn't he? The nurses have been talking about what a sweetie he is."

Carter couldn't help feel the pride well up in him as he thought of the precious life Isabella had given him. "His mother and I think he is. We are, of course, a little biased."

She giggled a little and placed him in the crib, readying their departure. "Well, all babies are beautiful to me. They are a miracle of God, so they are all precious."

Carter bent over the crib and kissed his son, and the nurse took him away. Pacing before the window, he looked out onto the large garden that was filled with flowering trees and bushes. In the midst of the garden was a patch of wildflowers with a concrete bench that wrapped around them. Daisies, with pink-and-red rose bushes, surrounded a fountain that looked more like a cherub. The basin full of water had made it look as if it were floating. Isabella's favorites were at her feet. She loved roses, but her favorite was a handful of weeds that resembled a flower. He had to laugh to himself when he realized how easily she was pleased. He had called the florist downstairs and had flowers delivered and placed in

459

her room, and it looked more like a garden itself. He had wanted her to see something beautiful when she awakened. The room held the sweet aroma of summer and early fall flowers. Among them were daisies.

The soft rustle of the sheet had caused him to look around. His wife had stretched her arm over her head and wiped away the sleep from her eyes. Looking up at him, she had smiled softly at him. "Amore, green is your color." She then laughed and found it painful and placed her hand over her stomach. "Forgot about that. I must remember to hold it if I am going to laugh."

Sitting down beside her, he took her hand. A tear slid down his cheek, unknown to him until she traced down with her finger. "Isabella, I'm so very sorry." His voice shook as he looked down into her angelic face. "I never would have—" He hesitated for a moment. Her hand lay against his face softly as he had closed his eyes to collect what he had held in for hours in his heart. He hadn't felt the pain and hurt that he had felt since the death of Andrea. The anxiety and fear had been bottled up inside him since his wife had died years ago that it would happen again.

He hadn't loved her fully as he had wanted, and he swore that it wouldn't happen again. When Isabella had come so close to death, it was evident that he had still had held on to what had happened before. It had stopped him from sharing everything he was with her. Never had he wanted her to see just how vulnerable he could be. She knew he wasn't stone and that he could be hurt, but he had never wanted to let her see the fear he still carried. The hard, rough exterior that he held up during his

460

working hours would carry into his family life like a shield. She knew he loved her; that wasn't the issue.

"Things would have been so different if Arnell hadn't been part of my life. I'm not blaming anyone but myself for putting the drugs in my own body. That's my fault, and I accept the responsibility. There hasn't been a day that has gone by that I haven't regretted what I have done in the past. I have wronged and cheated so many people. You have blessed me in so many ways. You have given me love when I hadn't deserved any of it."

Her hand slid from his, and she had laid it against his cheek and smiled up at him. "Amore, you have given me the best of yourself from the day I met you. I will never forget that young man who saved me from Arnell, regardless of the way he did it. I remember some of that night and I know that what you did was not intended for evil. It doesn't matter how I remember or the circumstances of others that had come through the same door you did. I forgave you for it. I'm your wife, and I love you."

"I don't know how things will work for us, but I know I can't do this without you. I know what my life felt like without you. I don't want to do that again, ever."

The days had gone by, and Carter had been able to take his family home. They were about to board for their flight when his cell phone had buzzed in his shirt pocket. He had guided his wife in the private plane and then stepped back from the boarding deck. Looking at the number he wasn't familiar with, he took it and was surprised when he heard a female voice on the other end.

"Mr. Blake?"

461

"Yes, this is Carter Blake."

"Mr. Blake, this is Sharon Gurney at Child Welfare and Protective Services. I just wanted to let you know that Benjamin's hearing has been moved up to next week. Can you and your wife be there? I would really like to wrap up Benjamin's case so that he can have some structure to his life. I want you to know that this was a simple choice for those who were involved. The hearing is just a formality. You and your wife, I am sure, will make wonderful parents to Benjamin."

Carter was stunned by what she was saying. They had applied for foster care, not for adoption. "Ms. Gurney, forgive me, but I didn't send in for an adoption referral, only for foster care placement."

"Oh, I am sorry, but I thought you and your wife had discussed it. She called me two days ago about adopting Benjamin. I assumed it was a set deal. Of course, we can revisit this at a later date, if you like. In the meantime, we will pursue parents for Benjamin. "

Carter couldn't believe what he was hearing. Isabella had known how much he wanted that little boy to have a home with them. She had pursued the adoption without a second thought. He couldn't see his life any different than having a home full of children with his wife. "No, you misunderstood me. I just want to say something to my wife, and I assure you one of us, if not both, will be there. My wife just gave birth to a son, and I am not sure if she is up to making the trip. Can you hold for a minute, please?"

"Of course, Mr. Blake." With that, he had placed her on hold and took the steps into the jet, finding his wife. She had just settled the children and hadn't made her turn into her seat as he gathered her in his arms. She had startled as he turned her to look at her. She let out a shocked breath and had looked at him as if he had lost his mind. "Isabella Blake, you amaze me at every moment of every day."

She giggled slightly as she ran a finger through the side of hair down to his strong, masculine jaw. "If you are going to ask me to marry you, Mr. Blake, you did that almost a year ago. I said yes, remember?" She smiled and sighed softly, but his expression never changed. "What is it, amore?" She looked at him, studying his expression.

"You are an amazing, loving woman."

Cupping her face, he had kissed her softly and steady. The heat had risen within him, covering him. There were few people in the world that could touch him as she did. He watched her acts of love and kindness as she had loved and cared for him and their children.

"Now what have I done that is so fabulous?"

"Do you really want Ben to come stay with us, to be part of family?" He stood silently awaiting her answer, even though he knew what that the answer would be. He had waited for this since he had held that little boy. There was something special about him. He favored his brother Clay. He remembered Clayton and the joy he had brought to the family. When he died, it had devastated him. He couldn't understand why someone so young had died. Clay was intelligent, and he looked up to him as a big brother. Carter had teased him about being a tagalong and a pest, but he loved that Clay wanted to be with him.

"I love that little boy as much as you. Our family wouldn't be complete without him."

"The Family Court of Connecticut was just nearing the end of Benjamin's adoption." Carter had felt a chill come over him, knowing now that he had a new member in his family. The judge had known his family before he became a Blake. He watched as he signed his name to the adoption document. Clearing his voice, he laid his pen down. "Mr. and Mrs. Blake, the court has accepted the request for the adoption of Benjamin Kingston and from this day forward will be known as Benjamin Blake. Congratulations! You are now the parents of a beautiful young man. Very sharp. I spoke to him in my chamber before the proceedings. He loves you both very much and told me that his mother was such a good mother, but he knew she would want him with you. He particularly loves that his Grandma Iris reads to him. Ms. Gurney, show young Benjamin and his sister into the court please. That's all."

The judge stood and departed the court, and the heavy wooden door opened as the twosome held hands and ran toward us. Molly's giggles had filled the room as she came to a stop in front of her father. "Daddy, is it true? Is Ben my brother too, just like E?"

Leave it Molly to shorten a name that had already been shortened. He laughed at the innocence of Molly and the doubt he had seen in the eyes of Ben. He knew the look. He had it on his own face when his parents had adopted him. He had left his suitcase packed for months, thinking that they would soon tire of him and send him back.

Picking Ben up and sitting him on his knee, he looked at the lost boy as Ben looked down at the floor. "Ben, what's wrong, son?"

Ben kept his head down for a moment then looked up at Carter innocently. "What's 'dopted'?"

Carter couldn't hide a smirk on his face as he looked at his newly adopted son. "That means out of all the children we could have had in our life, we chose you. Today, as of right now, you are my little boy. I'm your dad, and Isabella is your mom, and we are going to love you forever. You never have to worry about where you are going to live ever. Grandma Iris is now your grandma just like she's Molly's, and Grandpa Grayson is your grandpa. You have Grandpa Jeb and Grandma Anita. Molly and Eli are your sister and brother now, so you have a big family." He watched as Ben thought and watched as the little boy's lips slowly moved into a curve. "That's all right, isn't it, that you're our little boy?" Without an answer, Ben had thrown his arms around Carter's neck and kissed him.

In the week that had passed since Ben's adoption, he was slowly adjusting to his family. Carter enjoyed watching Molly and Ben play in the gardens of Rose Point. They had delayed their trip home, temporarily letting him get used to them. The courts and children's services had required it only to make sure that he fit in the family. The plan was to take his family home soon, but there was one other place he wanted to go, back to Knoxville to see his daughter. He had been trying to make arrangements with Ryan and Gail for him and Isabella to see Jenna. He had wanted his family to be complete, but Jenna's age and the years they had spent apart may make that difficult. Ryan was her

legal parent. The best they may get would be visitation.
Then there were Jenna's feelings to consider. Ryan was
the only father she had ever known. He had been the one
to see her take her first steps. He was the one who had
taught her how to ride a two-wheeler. He had been the
one to kiss her and hug her when she fell. He had taken
care of her when she was sick, and he had been the one to
give her the love she needed as she had grown.
Regardless, he wanted to see her and to tell her who he
really was and that he would have never abandoned her if
he had known.

He had watched them play for what seemed to be
hours. They had run and jumped and had made up so
many games that he had thought they would have tired
long before now. They had started to slow down, with
them both playing on a swing that had once been his when
he was a boy. His father had hung it in the oak tree closest
to the patio so that he could watch him and Beth from his
study. He had told him that it had given him many hours of
joy watching them play.

"Penny for your thoughts." Warm arms had wrapped
around his neck from behind him. The scent of her
perfume carried on the wind, and he grinned to himself.
Her breath landed against his skin as she spoke. She had
no idea what she did to him in just the slightest touch.
After kissing his cheek, she sat down beside him. Her way
to the lounge was slow, but she had sat back, putting her
feet into the chair, and smiled at him.

"Thinking about what it was like when Beth and I used
to swing there," he said, pointing to their children playing
on the swing under the tree. Ben was now pushing Molly

the best that he could. Their laughter floated over the garden, and Carter had loved it. Seeing them smile and laugh had given him pleasure.

"They're cute together, aren't they? Such a simple thing as a swing to make them happy."

"Life is so uncomplicated for them." Thinking back in his life, his hadn't been. Every turn he had taken had been complicated, and many layers had followed. He shook his head to dismiss the bad memories and concentrate on the good ones. He had a good life now. He had children whom he adored and would give his life for, and it seemed that his family was growing leaps and bounds. He had a wife that loved him, faults and all, and he loved her. That was enough.

He grinned at her and told her it was wonderful to see the kids having fun. Looking over at her, she had relaxed against the overstuffed cushions. The smile hadn't left his face when he had seen that she had closed her eyes and was asleep. Her eyelashes fluttered against the soft beams of sunlight that filtered through the old oak. Sending the kids in to get ready for supper, he had lifted her and took her in and laid her down on the couch. She had been up with Elijah most of the night. He hadn't settled in as quickly as they would have liked. He had been getting up with him on occasion, but she had been breastfeeding, and he had woken her every hour last night. He could supplement him once or twice with what formula they had, but for some reason, he wasn't satisfied.

She had to sleep when he was asleep; otherwise, she got no sleep. If it didn't soon become somewhat normal, he was going to see about a nurse or a nanny for short term. She had to get some sleep at some point. During the day, his mother helped as far as trying to supplement him while Isabella slept. Maybe it wouldn't be much longer before Elijah let them get one good night's sleep.

Walking down the hall to the nursery, he looked in the small room that was once Clayton's. The crib and small frame bed still remained along with his teddy bear. Molly had at times gone in there and played before Ben had come to stay with them. At times he thought he could hear Clay calling his name. His small round face and wavy blond hair had crossed his mind as he saw him in his mind's eyes, standing there with his bear, asking Carter to play.

Walking on down the hall, he peeked in on his baby boy that was sleeping soundly. He heard his soft breaths as his chest rose and fell. Shaking his head, Carter still couldn't believe he was here.

The cell phone buzzed against his side as he had leaned down to kiss Elijah. Looking at the number, he knew it spelled trouble. "Blake. When? You have got to be kidding. All this time, he's been in my backyard? When's it going down? I know what I said . . . Yes . . . Look, I have a stake in this, and Landon can't do it alone. And JC? I see . . . How long has this operation been going on?" Carter scrubbed his face as he turned away from a sleeping Elijah. "Yeah, I'm here. If we do this, it has to go down now. I won't let him walk again."

Slapping his cell phone shut, he quickly holstered his firearm, hating to leave her again. He had to stop him while he could, while he was in reach. The homicide detective now had become a bounty hunter. If he found

468

him, he wasn't sure what he would do to him. He was grown and certainly didn't lack the ability to protect himself from the evil of Arnell Andrews. As he started to walk out the door, he was met by his sister and Landon who had also been contacted by now by Brooks. "Beth." He encased her with both hands as she stood in panic. "Listen to me. We are coming back. I want you to do something for me. Make sure to look out for Isabella while I'm gone. Look in on Elijah for me so she can rest. She hasn't slept for days. Take care of the kids. We'll be back soon."

"Don't you want to tell her goodbye?" Beth's lips trembled as he stood in front of her. He wasn't sure how to make her feel any better. He knew what she was thinking. She stood to lose her husband, her brother, or both.

"She'll just get upset, Beth, and she doesn't need it right now. She's been through way too much. I just want to spare her the grief. If she's awake before I get home, tell her I'll be home soon to hold her. I'm never going to leave her again." Hugging Beth and kissing her on the cheek, Carter stepped back and allowed her to say goodbye to her husband.

He watched his brother-in-law, which had become more like a brother, tell his sister goodbye. He had assured her he was coming home and was going to make sure that he did. "Take care of Gavin. Kiss him for me. I have to, honey. I'll see you soon." He kissed her and finished holstering his firearm against him as they had walked out the door to an uncertain situation.

469

Sliding into the seat and putting the SUV in gear, his brother-in-law looked at him. He could feel the heat on him as he did. Knowing that he had something to say, Carter tried to ignore it. The weight of Landon's stare pounded on him as he tried to concentrate the road.

Taking a deep breath, Landon turned his head and looked out the side window. "You should have woken Isabella and told her we were leaving."

"Since when have you become an expert on relationships?" His voice cutting, it wasn't what he intended. Arnell had been within miles of them, and that bothered him. His family had been surrounded by security. He had made sure that each of them had been protected, and he had the best officers on them along with his father's security team.

"I'm sorry. I shouldn't have snapped at you."

"You know that anything can happen. I just think you should have told your wife goodbye."

The remainder of the ride to the Sea Scape Warehouse was in silence. The sun had hidden from the sky, and it had darkened quickly. The pavement roared below the SUV as they made their way to the pier. He couldn't get out of his head that he had seen Isabella there years before. The operation had been shut down or had run out before and Arnell had now rebuilt his business. He had been guilty of going back there after he had gone through rehab. When he had found it gone, he never pursued the same area again. Why hadn't he thought that the restaurant fronted for the place? The Sea Scape Restaurant catered to the higher-end clientele and was unique in its delivery. They had rooms, it had been said, that had satisfied those with

470

other appetites, private dining areas where gentlemen could be entertained, so to speak. He hadn't thought anything about Arnell being behind it.

On waking, I find myself on the couch and smiled as I knew how I got here. Stretching, I looked around, not seeing the object of my affection or anyone else in the family. With two children under the age of five and an infant, it was unusually still in the massive house. Sitting up, I listened for any noise that may be about but heard nothing. Looking up at the clock above the fireplace, I noticed that I had slept for at least a couple of hours with no awakening of Elijah crying for his dinner. I ran my fingers through my hair, trying to make it behave. I had left it down, which had been a mistake. It now felt like it was in tangles as I gathered it and pushed it behind my neck.

Walking toward the nursery, I finally ran into Beth as she carried Gavin toward the main part of the house. Stopping in the hallway, I could see the surprise on her face. Beth was never good at hiding what she felt or what was going on. "Beth, have you seen Carter?"

"Not for a while, why?" Taking Gavin in a little closer, she changed hips he rested on.

"I haven't heard Eli cry for some time, and he has been getting up about every hour to eat."

"I just checked on Eli about fifteen minutes ago, and Eli was asleep."

471

Clearing my throat and attempting to remove the knot that now sat on it, I knew there was something wrong. "Think I'll I go see about Eli. Oh, have you seen Ben and Molly? They've been really quiet."

"The last time I saw them, they were with Grayson. I think they were going to help with supper. Grayson talked about grilling instead of a big dinner. I'm not sure what they will do now. Looks like it could rain."

"I'll be down soon. I'm just going to check on Eli." She nodded as I walked away. I heard a rustle as I walked into the nursery. My beautiful baby boy was growing leaps and bounds. When he was first born, the nurse's irony of him being a big boy was that he weighed a little over 4 pounds. Being early, they were concerned, but there were no worries of him eating on time and often. He had gained quickly and had a huge appetite, although I think he enjoyed the contact of my body.

He was awake and sucking on his fist. No crying yet; I had caught him first. Picking him up, I held him against me. The soft smack of his lips let me know it was suppertime for him. Gently rocking him back and forth, he gripped my index finger. The sweetness of him sometimes overwhelmed me, and tears would slide down my cheek as I thought of his father. The love that flooded me was sometimes more than I could stand, sweeping me away, with visions of Eli growing and Carter playing with our children.

The soft sounds of Eli sighing as he started to get his fill was the only sound in the room. His eyes slowly closed as he became satisfied. I could sit and rock him for hours just to watch him sleep. I would have never thought months ago that I would be married, let alone have a baby and three other children. Molly had loved and accepted me from day 1, Ben was a lost little boy who needed a family, and then there was Eli, not to mention finding out that Jenna was out there somewhere.

Tucking Eli in, I watched as his small chest rise and fall with each breath. Such a sweet peace, he was here, healthy. It had been one of my biggest worries. The worry of his father of not being there had disappeared. Carter was alive. His children would never be without him.

A cool breeze passed me, and I turned my head to see where it had come from. It was if a window had been left open and the breeze of a summer rain had come through the room. Looking toward the window, I found it closed and the curtains unmoving. Surveying the room, all the windows were closed. An uneasy feeling had come upon me. Bending down to kiss Eli, I had shaken it off. Eli sighed and clenched his fist next to his face as he slept.

A whisper of a voice had hit my ear. Turning, I answered, "Who's there?" I saw no one in the room as I walked to the hallway. The soft whisper of a voice lay in my ear as if there was someone standing beside me. The voice had been louder this time. Looking behind me, my hand covered my mouth as I saw who stood before me.

"It's all right. I'm not here to hurt you. I'm here to warn you."

Standing there before me was a mirror image of myself. Her long dark, hair flowed down her shoulders and back in flawless drapes of waves. Her white lace dress fit close to her and fell to the floor, covering her feet. Her face glowed as she looked at me. "Isabella, you have to go. His life depends on it."

Catching my breath, not believing what I was seeing, I asked, "What do you mean I have to go? Whose life depends on me? And who are you?"

The woman standing in front of me never made a move as she stood looking at me. "You must take care of him. His life depends on you. He's walking into a trap." Turning her head, she looked over at a group of pictures, all of them of my husband.

"Carter? What about him?"

"You're his salvation. Go now."

"I don't know who you are or how you got in here, but you need to leave. I promise you if you don't leave now, I will get security in here, and they will drag you out."

She smiled slightly. "No one can see me, Isabella, no one but you. I'm surprised you don't know me. I'm Andee. Carter was my husband. Warning you is all I can do to keep him alive."

"How do I know you are who you say you are?"

"Come, take my hand, then you will know."

Slowly, I walked toward the woman who looked and sounded so much like me. I had seen Andrea's picture over and over. This woman could have been her double. Reaching out for her hand as she held it out, my hand had clasped hers. Peace fell upon me as scenes passed before me that I had never seen before: Jenna as a baby then as a child, Molly's birth in which I was no part of, Carter as he sat holding her on the night of her death. Carter had held and rocked his wife as he wept over her lifeless body.

Letting go of her hand, I ran to grab my hand gun, loading it. Turning around to ask her where he had gone, she slowly disappeared. "Andee, where is he?"

The light whisper of her voice carried through the room as I watched her slowly fade. "Follow your heart, Isabella, just follow your heart." Turning, I glanced at Eli once more and took off down the hall and toward the main entrance of the house.

"Beth! Beth!" My voice hopefully would be heard by the right person. I didn't want Quentin to follow me or stop me. I couldn't stop. I had to go. "Beth!"

From the kitchen, Beth had carried Gavin in her arms, looking alarmed. "What is it, Bella? What's wrong?" Her fingers twisted tight against Gavin, trying to hold on to the overactive toddler he had become.

"Nothing . . . yet. I need you to watch the kids. I have to go out for a moment. Eli is asleep now. I just fed him. He should be asleep for a couple of hours. I should be home before that."

As I turned to leave, she took my arm. "Where are you going?"

"Wherever Carter is. I know he isn't here. He's in trouble. I know it."

"But you can't go."

"Where is he, Beth? I have to stop this before Arnell gets his hands on him. I know he's going after him."

"I don't know." She shook her head and had choked when she looked at me. "He left with Landon about an hour ago. They left armed."

"Do me a favor, and don't tell Quentin I'm gone. If he knows I left, he will try to stop me. If he does, Carter is

475

good as dead." Leaving her, I ran toward the garage, hoping that at least one of the cars would have a set of keys in them. Turning the corner into the spacious corral of vehicles, the sky darkened and the thunder rolled as a storm made its way in. Spotting Marshall, I stopped dead in my tracks.

"Marshall?"

"Ms. Isabella. Where are you going on this nasty evening?"

"Sorry, I don't have time to explain. I need keys, keys to any of these cars. Do you have them?"

"Of course, there is always a spare set."

"Give me a set to something that moves."

"Ms. Isabella, I don't think it's a good idea. You just come home from major surgery."

"Marshall, I assure you I am fine. The keys, please," I commanded.

Marshall pointed to a sleek black Aston Martin. I looked at him stunned.

"You won't be needing keys, Miss."

I wasted no time as I sat down in the ridiculously priced car. The seat formed to me. The pedals were made for the foot of a woman. As I left the garage, I prayed for direction and caught it quickly. The pier?

The thunder rolled like apples falling from a crate, and the lightning flashed, blinding everything behind it. I fought to keep my head clear as the rain pelted the pavement, making it hard to see. The sky turned angry as I drove on. The only place I could think of on the waterfront that would be big enough for a large business was the Sea Scape Restaurant. The memory of being there at an earlier time came back in flashes, sending chills through me. I would kill him if I had to. If it meant saving Carter, I would. I had been there. That's why my parents had moved so far away. They knew that if we lived there, it would never go away. The place had been an old, abandoned warehouse. Within the last two years, the place had been rebuilt and established into a multimillion-dollar empire. It catered to the rich and those who had exotic tastes other than food. Why hadn't occurred to me before? My hands shook as I grasped the wheel, watching the rain come down in sheets. Clutching and shifting wasn't something I was used to, but I soon got the hang of it, not having much of a choice, if I wanted to see my husband alive again. It had angered me that he would take a chance on it again after Arnell had one of his men take a shot at him before. I had lost him once and thought him dead. I wasn't going to let it happen for real. *Carter Blake, I am so angry with you* was all that kept running through my head. *You have a wife and little babies at home. How could you?*

Pulling into the parking garage at the Sea Scape, I knew all of this was going to go down quickly. Finding where they had gone in and where they were was going to be the next thing, and I was running out of time if I hadn't already.

Leaving the car, I headed on foot to the end of the Sea Scape. The brick was weathered and old as I walked along the edge. My gun rested on the waist of my jeans as I prayed for some sign of where they had ended up. *God, show me the way.* At the rear exit, the security light beamed beneath the door as it stood ajar. My heart slammed into my ribs, and my breathing became short as I neared the entrance.

Taking in a sharp breath, I knew Andrews was in there. I could feel the monster the closer I got. His voice rang in my ears as I took short steps and hid behind each door and surface. Hearing voices as I walked farther into the warehouse, the area lit into a large open area of nothing but room after room of closed doors. A large reception desk sat in prestige as I looked through the dark and into the illumination of the underground business. The place looked like a respectable place of business. The area was edgy and smart with a large reception area, looking more like a high-end CEO's office. The floor was tiled in large slabs of white marble, and the walls were tiled in a cool white. The only color that was centered in the room was from large portraits of muted women and men. They were made to look like larger pieces of art rather than that of actual people. A few scattered green plants were lining the wall to give it a traditional work environment. The music was calm but exotic. I recognized the place, even though it had been rebuilt and covered up. The first room on the left led to the dock. It was where I had been trapped.

The pain that it brought to me had to be shaken away if I wanted to do what I had come here for. The only way I was going to be able to pass by the receptionist was to act as though I was a client. The man that sat behind the desk was broad shouldered and lean, well dressed in a red linen dress shirt and black tie. His blond hair had been neatly trimmed, making him look more like a major businessman than the one that sold people into slavery. Covering my gun with my shirt, I walked up the desk, hoping not to run into Arnell before I found my husband and brother-in-law.

The place was crawling with cameras. I remembered that all too well, not just because of those that were held there, but for their clientele. They made sure to keep tabs on them at all times. The places at the times that had cameras shut down was when there was a client being served, and Arnell had felt it being in bad taste to video the events, the only thing that he actually had a little tact for. Standing at the desk, the man greeted me with a smile and held out his hand.

"Hello. Welcome to Fine Wines. Won't you come in? My name is Maurice. I will be happy to serve you. Have a seat, please." His hand gestured to the seat before him as he sat behind the desk and awakened his computer. "Have you been to Fine Wines before Miss . . ." He prompted.

"Mrs. Moretti. Abigail Moretti."

"Mrs. Moretti, I'm sure that we can take care of your every need."

He rattled on, and it made me sick to think of what he was telling me, going through lists of names of their 'particular products,' he called them. Randomly picking something to get him to leave the room, he escorted me to the waiting area and made his way down the hall. Once out of sight. I stood and started walking back into the warehouse where the lighting had gotten dim. It wasn't long before I came upon voices. Those were familiar enough that it had sent spears of fire through me.

A call from the darkness startled me as I stepped back into the shadows. "Police. Put your hands where I can see them." When that voice echoed through the room, I knew it was Carter's. Finding my way through the dark, I stood behind the man that had pulled a gun and had fired at the boys, hitting the doorframe behind Carter.

Another shot popped as Carter had ducked behind the frame. "Get him out of here before he gets us all killed." The words ran through me as if a piece of glass had pierced my heart. I remembered those very words. He kicked the magazine from his gun and started to reload when Arnell pointed his gun at Carter's chest.

The next thing I felt was a rumble through my arm and the smell of cheap liquor and cigarettes that caused my stomach to churn. It was then I knew that I had fired against Arnell, just missing his head. Carter stood silent and huddled down at the frame of the door. The sound of running feet from behind him headed toward us. "Just so you know, it wasn't an accident. The next shot will be deadly accurate. Put it down, Arnell. I swear I will pull this trigger. So help me, I will kill you."

Arnell stood with his back to me and his firearm still pointed at my husband. "Well, if it isn't the princess of the night." Keeping his eye on Carter, he knew my voice. "Isabella, you know you can still come back to me. I would hate that you would never have the feel of a real man in your life ever again."

Taking a few steps farther toward him, I didn't waver in the idea that I would kill him if I had to. "Bella, don't do it, honey. You're a healer, not a killer." Carter motioned for me to lower the gun. "Let us take him."

"That's right, Isabella. We wouldn't want a weak female to do the job of a weak justice system."

480

"I will kill you, I promise, if you make one move to fire at any of them. Now put the gun down. Last warning."

I felt a soft grip from behind me and around my hand as masculine arms wrapped around me and the gun. "Flip the switch, Bella," he whispered. "Let me have him." The pain left my body as I stood in front of my brother.

"Come. Isabella, are you going to do this, or is it going to take all day?"

"Step aside, sis," he whispered. "I won't let him hurt you or Carter."

Turning, Arnell drew his gun on me, and Cooper shot him point-blank where he stood. Arnell lay on the floor in a pool of his own blood as Cooper wrapped his arms around me. I shook uncontrollably as I watched him struggle for breath. The gun lay on the floor at my feet as Carter and Landon bent over Arnell. Landon radioed for an ambulance, but I knew well that Arnell more than likely would never make it to the hospital.

Carter soon left Arnell to Landon and found me still being held up by my brother. "Isabella, are you all right?"

Still shaking like there was nothing to hold my body up, Cooper supported me. He looked over me like he was inspecting a fine work of art. He sat me down on the bench and motioned for Cooper to sit beside me. "We will need to talk to you, Cooper. You know that. Don't leave this room."

"He's not a criminal, Carter."

"I didn't say he was. He's here with the FBI. Just sit still until I get Arnell out of here, and I'll get you home."

Time crawled along as I sat on the bench with my hands clenched in fists on my lap. Carter could have been

481

dead. They all could have been. As I looked in the doorway where Carter had stood moments earlier, I saw the woman I had seen earlier. A white mist surrounded her. She appeared angelic. Her smile beamed as she turned, walked away, and disappeared quick as she came. My breath caught as I watched her slowly dissolve.

"Isabella? Hey, Isabella?" Carter gently ran his finger down my face as he broke the trance I had fallen into. "Angel, come on, let's go."

"Cooper, I want to see my brother."

He smiled at me and had taken me to him. After a brief reunion, he led me outside. "How did you know where to find me?"

"You wouldn't believe it if I told you. I don't know if I believe it."

He chuckled. "How did you get here? You must have driven."

"The Aston. Marshall pointed out. I asked him for a fast car, and that is what he picked. Don't say anything to him about it. He was innocent in this."

"You drove Dad's Aston? That's Pop's prize. I haven't even driven it."

"Well, I guess you are now. I don't think I can."

"Oh, Isabella, what else are you going to do? You could have been killed. He would have killed you."

"No, he wouldn't. He wanted me back in the business too badly. Besides, I think he had this sick idea that I was his daughter and not Daddy's. Regardless of what he did to me himself, he wouldn't have let someone kill me and he wouldn't have done it himself. All he wanted to do was torture my mind. By the way, did you get Gage?"

Carter nodded his head yes as he took my hand and walked me down the path to the garage. "Yes, Senator Dawson will be locked up along with Andrews if he survives. Cooper had orders to shoot to kill if Dawson attempted to fire at anyone. He may have done it. I'm glad he did. His intent was to kill us. Your uncle has a long list of felonies, including attempted murder to fight. I don't see his empire lasting long. He was a multimillionaire before this. I doubt that being a CEO of an engineering company will help him now. His patrons and board will likely fold."

Opening the door to the Aston, Carter assisted me in and clicked the belt over me. Sitting down in the driver's seat, he started the car and looked over at me. "You know you shouldn't have come here. It was dangerous. You have Molly, Ben, and a little baby at home to take care of and a body that's still recovering." His voice raised slightly, he ran his fingers through his hair. Sighing heavily, he looked down at the wheel and then back at me. Okay, here it comes. I know he's angry. I know I shouldn't have come here, but if I hadn't he would have been dead and maybe Landon too.

"Isabella, I appreciate what you did. If you hadn't, I don't know what might have happened, but do me a favor. Don't do that again. Drop your police academy classes and go back to nursing. Please? It isn't that you aren't capable. I just want to know that my wife will be home when I get there."

Smiling over at him, I leaned in and kissed him. His crooked, boyish smile lifted me, and his blue eyes shone in the dusk of a warm and stormy summer night. "Mrs. Blake, you certainly know how to unravel a man."

BOOK SUMMARY

Isabella has been left to raise her children supported by her brother-in-law and her bodyguard Quentin. Unknown to her, the love of her life is fighting his way back. As she travels through months of pain from the loss of her husband, she decides to take matters into her own hands and join the force, determined to take out the man that cost the life of her husband and tortured her.

Her life takes a turn when Carter finds his wife after months of being undercover on the cusp of the birth of their child. The pain and rage that gripped him from his youth most assuredly will affect their relationship. With the secret yet to be revealed, he is uncertain of what the outcome will be once he discloses to Isabella what happened years prior. Andrews, after years of causing pain and destruction, will pay dearly for the havoc he caused in so many lives.

AUTHOR BIO

T. L. Arrowood is a critical care nurse, wife, and mother and lives in a small rural town. Since her early teenage years, she has dreamed of working in journalism and writing stories the readers would relate to and fall in love with. She has finally gained the courage to pursue a dream left behind and penned her first novel, *Standing in the Eye of the Storm*. She is also the author of *Stilling the Thunder*.

Dear Reader:

If you enjoyed the story of Carter and Isabella, please take the time to rate and leave a review for *Standing in the Eye of the Storm* and *Stilling the Thunder*. It helps me to know what my readers are interested in and helps with getting the books out there. If this book has helped you in any way, I would like to know how it affected your life.

The book's main intent is to raise awareness of abuse and its victims. If you or someone you know is suffering from abuse, there is help available:

The Abuse Victim hotline: http://www.avhotline.org/

The National Abuse hotline: http://www.thehotline.org/

National Child Abuse Hotline: **1-800-4-A-CHILD (1-800-422-4453)**

CPSIA information can be obtained at www.ICGtesting.com
Printed in the USA
BVOW04s1212031014

369356BV00001B/1/P

9 781785 200335